Reliquary for the Universe

Purusha's Urn

Cover concept and design by John Robert Johnson

Purusha's Urn

For information contact:
Creative Book Publishers International
269 S. Beverly Drive, Suite 1442
Beverly Hills, CA 90212.
www.bookpubintl.com

Purusha's Urn

ISBN: 978-0-9818222-0-4

To my beautiful and brilliant Devon.
I love you to infinity.

Acknowledgments

Writing any work of fiction, especially science fiction, requires tremendous dedication, patience, and resourcefulness, in addition to a minor case of insanity. Above all else, it demands the saint-like understanding and encouragement of the writer's loved ones, as well as the unrequited assistance of countless others who are willing to take the time to answer dozens of preposterous, and often bizarre questions.

I have been grateful for the each word of encouragement I've received from writers, such as Gregory Benford, Dan Brown, and Douglas Preston, as well as Jim & John Thomas, and Greg Bonann. Of course, a great deal of credit for this work must go to my editor, Sasha Miller (Ladylord), who taught me how important it is to "get closer" to my characters. Her mastery of the artform, combined with the passion and patience to teach – with a motivating pinch of salt– helped make this book a reality. Couldn't have done it without her.

Finally, I want to thank my family– Jerry, Marty, Jimmy and Janis – for managing to keep straight-faces whenever I shared my outlandish ideas with them. Particular thanks must go to my beautiful wife, Diane Robin, and spectacular daughter, Devon, for their steadfast and genuine enthusiasm for this endeavor, and their tireless willingness to listen to a man lost in his obsession.

—ʍ—

Chapter 1
Purusha's Urn

i

Even though the sun had risen into the Middle Eastern sky only an hour before, the air was already crackling hot. As the small caravan of dust-covered jeeps made its way through the town, Aaron Koppernick, one of the three senior archaeologists aboard the lead vehicle, thought the road looked more like crushed human bones than sun-bleached gravel. Looking older than his 39 years, his lean, angular features were accentuated by his dark tan, and he sat silently in the passenger seat, listening to the now familiar complaints of his two associates, who had to yell to be heard over the din of the vintage World War II vehicle.

"God, I never thought I'd miss the scent of freshly paved asphalt," said Raymond Allen, leaning forward to massage his backside. "These commutes are getting to be major ass-kickers." A stocky six-footer with curly reddish-brown hair, Raymond's pale complexion seemed to be permanently sunburned, refusing to take on the burn-resistant tan that others had acquired from the Arabian sun.

Just as Raymond sat back in his seat, the jeep went over a deep rut, bouncing Marty Yamashita, the youngest member of the threesome, high enough to bash the top of his head on one of the over-head struts.

"Ow! Damnit!" Marty reached up, reflexively searching for a scalp wound under his thick, jet-black hair. "How 'bout a trade? Your sore ass for my skull fracture." He looked down at his fingers, expecting to see blood. "You'd think with all the oil-money starting to pour into this country, they'd be able to afford decent roads. This isn't fit for a goat."

Aaron, the team leader, smiled. For the last two months, not a single spine-jarring commute to the excavation went by that he didn't feel as though fortune had smiled upon him. At the age of eight, he fled with his parents to the United States from Poland only weeks before the Nazi invasion. Now, barely thirty years later, here he was: a Polish-American Jew leading a major scientific expedition to the land of Ishmael.

As they left the outskirts of the small town they had been quartered in for the last two months, Aaron looked out the jeep's scratched, plastic window, watching the locals open their shops and prepare for another day.

"I don't get it." Aaron mused. "Here's this town– more like village– miles from the nearest major city, and the women are walking around with fancy big hair, smoking American cigarettes and showing off their legs."

"Yeah, I noticed that, too. Not many burkhas around here," Marty said, massaging his scalp. "I thought there was supposed to be some big fundamentalist movement going on over here."

"Not really. Al-Bakr is doing everything he can to eliminate all the tribal warfare. Without his secular government in power we would never have been allowed to launch this expedition. Next thing you know they'll be nationalizing the oil companies. Going to be a very westernized culture," Aaron said. "Look at this." He pointed toward a group of teenagers walking alongside the road, wearing t-shirts with UCLA, Penn State and OSU emblazoned across the chest.

"I haven't seen a single goddamn shirt with Harvard printed on it," Raymond said sarcastically. "Maybe, if we had a halfway decent football team—"

"We've got one?" Marty asked with a quizzical look.

"Difficult not to think of the U.S. as the center of the entire Universe, isn't it." Though he had said it, Aaron knew better and shook his head. "This can't last. We're doing the same thing here the British did in Egypt fifty years ago. Sooner or later, the Iraqis are going to catch on and the door's going to slam shut. Our timing was pure—"

"Pure dumb luck," Marty said. "If that custodian hadn't been snooping around in the Semitic last year, we wouldn't have gotten here at all."

The event was still fresh in Aaron's mind. The year before, in early 1969, a large collection of nineteenth century Near Eastern artifacts were found hidden away in Harvard's Semitic Museum basement, reviving interest in the museum. The building had not functioned as a museum since the Navy took it over during World War II, at which time most of the collection was stored in the basement. Its re-opening later that year played a central role in the final approval of the expedition's funding.

It had been more than sixty years since the Semitic participated in the first scientific excavations in the Holy Land. Aaron and other members of the archaeology department felt it only fitting that the Semitic lead this new exploration of the Cradle of Civilization and mankind's most ancient writing.

Of particular interest were the five thousand-year-old Sumerian ziggurats dotting the landscape near the junction of the Tigris and Euphrates rivers. It was in this region the ancient city of Babylon– and, before that, Babel– once flourished. Aaron knew the passages in Genesis 11:1 by heart, which described the greatest of these temples: the infamous Tower of Babel. The builders, led by the warrior-king Nimrod, planned to climb the Tower so they could behold the face of God. For this blasphemy, God turned their speech to babble and, according to scripture, each person in the panic-stricken horde sought out others whom they could understand. This divided the swirling mass into small factions, which eventually grew to become the distinct tribes, chieftains, city-states, and then the nations of the Earth, with their various native languages.

For most of his life, Aaron thought it just an old Bible story, but the more he studied the more he realized the legend might have some basis in fact. Archaeologists mapping the ruins at Babylon had uncovered the foundation of a tremendous ziggurat, which the locals called Zfegi, more than four hundred feet square and at least six hundred feet tall, making it the tallest man-made structure of the Ancient World. Even though he had done no field work in Iraq, Aaron wrote a brilliant thesis on Zfegi, so it surprised no one when he was selected as team leader for the project.

Zfegi was the area's oldest man-made structure, having been built well before 3500 BC, and Aaron was among those who believed it to be the Tower of Babel itself. Its deep network of tunnels and caves were filled with wondrous artifacts which were amassed by the ziggurat priests. One of Zfegi's greatest mysteries was that, despite numerous conquerors, looters and other vandals, the trove beneath it had remained undisturbed over the last fifty centuries. The exterior, however, did not fare so well. Centuries of powerful desert winds and torrential seasonal rains eroded the mighty tower down to a relatively small, nondescript hill.

As the jeeps pulled up to the base camp, Aaron climbed out, stretched his back and surveyed his team. He could see most of the group was just as weary of the heat as he, and thought some of them even looked ill, probably from the local diet. Homesick for the comforts of Western Civilization as well, he also knew all their hardships would be well rewarded. Each of the participants would not only feel the tremendous gratification of helping to write history, but their academic careers would also benefit. It wouldn't hurt his reputation at Harvard, either.

Since it was the last chamber in the system of caves beneath Zfegi to be explored, Aaron joined the group of archaeologists and graduate assistants as they walked to the guarded entrance leading to the excavation sites. They were met there by the Master Digger, Ejan Khafeer, an old man whom they recruited from the nearby village. Ejan, a breadmaker by trade, was only in his late fifties, but the heat of his ovens and the harsh life of the desert had leathered his skin to that of an old man's. Hired for his thorough knowledge of the area and fluency in English, he spoke with a faintly

British accent as he called the diggers to join the procession.

Aaron was the tallest member of the team, and his gaunt features were already glistening with perspiration. Like the ghost of El Lawrence, with a white cotton scarf trailing behind his long-billed desert cap, he led the group in single file through the areas that had been roped off by other teams. The path they walked so many times was baked hard and, despite the early hour, it was already hot enough to warm their feet through the bottoms of their thick-soled boots.

The serpentine path wound through one of the largest excavations since the Tutankhamen dig, a half century before. Aaron's primary responsibility was to supervise the underground survey and mapping of Zfegi, and to thoroughly catalog any finds. A well-financed operation, unlike previous expeditions to the area, they were using the latest geophysical instruments, such as the new, highly sensitive, portable cesium magnetometers. These devices were responsible for the discovery of the network of caves and tunnels beneath the ziggurat which, until then, had gone undetected.

As Ejan led them into the narrow tunnel at Zfegi's base, their laughter echoed down into its darkness. The entrance was more than fifty meters from their final destination, directly beneath the center of the ziggurat. When they got there, a digger was in the process of widening the opening into the cave they were about to enter so they could walk in, rather than crawl on their bellies. Aaron thought there had been enough of that for the past several weeks.

Inspecting the man's work, Ejan double-checked the new

shoring to make sure the opening was stable. When Ejan glanced inside, Aaron again noticed his unusual silence, and wondered if something was wrong. Maybe his friend's behavior was caused by the knowledge the dig would soon be complete and he would miss their constant bickering, not to mention the additional income for his family. But Aaron quickly shrugged off the concern. Even though the tunnel was dank and smelled of damp, oxidized earth, he was now experiencing the same euphoria the rest of the team was feeling that morning.

The Master Digger waved the group forward, indicating the area was secure and ready for their entrance. One of the graduate assistants emerged from the back of the group. It was Anita Lundin, Aaron's most promising grad student and the only woman on the Zfegi team. Before the expedition her blonde hair fell below her waist, but now it was cut quite short. That, and her freckled complexion gave her the look of a fresh-faced teenager. She offered Aaron her flashlight.

"We think you should be first," she said.

Seeing the rest of the group nod in agreement, he took the flashlight from her and stepped through the narrow opening.

The first thing that struck him was the size of the cave. With its inaccessible location, he expected it to be a small cistern or storage area, but this was more like a cella, or ceremonial vault only the High Priests could enter. He carefully surveyed the room, which was completely empty, except for a few ancient wooden beams that looked as though they might turn to dust if he barely brushed against them. The cave's position, deep beneath the ziggurat, gave it some significance in the overall design of the structure, but he and the others were curious why its median-point was a few feet off center. Why the small offset? He walked to the center of the cave, took three carefully measured steps, and paused to do some calculations in his head. Then he took one more step and found himself standing one foot from the cave's far wall. Sweeping the flashlight beam slowly across its surface, he noticed a subtle discoloration in the soil. After a closer look, he leaned out the opening and motioned Ejan inside.

"What's that look like to you, my friend?" he asked.

Ejan stepped forward, taking the flashlight with him. After studying the stained earth for a moment, he turned to Aaron.

"Could be iron," he said. "There is much of it in this soil. It is nothing of importance." As he backed away from the wall, Aaron brushed past him, lifting the small handpick from Ejan's waistband.

"I don't think so." With the pick, Aaron tapped lightly on the crusted surface of the wall. A small hole immediately opened where the point of the pick struck the thin crust.

Ejan looked about the cella nervously, his fists clinching and opening several times. After studying the rotted wooden shoring, he looked up at the dark ceiling above them. Cave-ins were rare, but the soil at this level was porous and unstable. He looked back at the American, who had been in his home and shared bread with his family, then closed his eyes.

Aaron stepped away from the wall, watching dry, reddish dust begin to stream from the small hole he had made with the pick. He realized whatever was behind this thin layer of dried earth was sitting precisely at the locus of the ziggurat–dead center. Everything radiated out from there.

—⁓—

Outside the cave, some members of the group began to grow impatient, but Marty knew that Aaron, as the first in, had the responsibility of assessing the area before too many other people started trampling around inside. Even so, they had all been waiting for some time, and as Marty stood there gently assessing the size of the lump on his head with his fingertips, he couldn't blame those behind him for grumbling.

Several minutes later, Ejan leaned out of the opening. There was something odd about the expression on his face. He motioned to another digger. "Dr. Koppernick wishes to have a blanket brought to him. Quickly. Quickly."

The digger rushed forward and handed him a rolled canvas blanket, one of several they brought into the tunnel with them. A few minutes later, Aaron emerged carrying a large object which he had tightly wrapped in the dirt-crusted canvas.

"Nothing much in there," he said flatly. "Just this. Fertility totem of some kind. I'll take it back to the tent."

Koppernick squeezed past the others in the cramped tunnel. The group crowded into the empty vault, wanting to see for themselves. Then, one by one, they fell in behind Aaron.

Marty offered to help him carry whatever it was he had found, but Aaron politely refused, hugging the blanket tightly to his chest for the entire walk back to the team's encampment.

Then, as Ejan side-stepped past him in the narrow walkway, Marty couldn't help but notice how focused the Master Digger was on Aaron Koppernick and the object he cradled in his arms.

—⁓—

By the time Aaron placed the find on the large work table inside the expansive tent, he was drenched in sweat. One of the crew handed him a canteen and he sat down for a moment, not speaking. As other members of the team who had not been in the tunnel began to gather, waiting for an unveiling, Aaron stalled for time, unsure how he should proceed. At the very least, it was an anomalous find. If he got careless with the way it was handled, something like this could cast doubt on the credibility of the entire expedition. More likely, he thought, it would turn the world of archaeology upside down.

Finally, he asked everybody to leave the tent except Marty and Raymond. When he turned to make sure they were alone, he saw Ejan standing beside the entrance.

"We won't be going back in today, Ejan." Aaron said, nodding his head toward to canvas-flap door. "Please tell the diggers they can go for the day, too. See you in the morning?"

"Yes, sadiqi. As you say." The old man nodded and bowed, slowly backing out of the tent.

Aaron stood and untied the strap holding the canvas in

place, watching Marty and Raymond as he did. When the canvas crumpled to the table, both of their heads jerked back simultaneously. Then both men turned to Koppernick with the same slack-jawed, stunned expression.

"My reaction, exactly," Aaron said.

The other two men took a step backward to get a better view of the astonishing object, still unable to speak. It was a spherical urn, or karura, supported by the raised trunks and tusks of three ebony black elephants, rearing up on their hind legs. The sphere had an elongated neck, covered with a bas relief of white, cumulus clouds. Among the clouds were patches of dark blue, inlaid with tiny white gems. The sphere itself had an unrecognizable landscape carved on its glazed ceramic surface, with aquamarine oceans, snow-capped mountain ranges and verdant green forests.

The elephants were carved in remarkable detail, right down to the fine wrinkles in the hide, and what looked like sapphires for eyes and large pearls on the end of each tusk. The entire piece was nearly four feet tall and barely a square inch did not have some kind of precious gem embedded in it.

On the top of the urn was a circular golden lid about six inches across. Engraved into its surface was a strip of characters running just inside the lid's circumference. At the center sat a small, crown-like handle, with dozens of faceted white stones set into it. Aaron wondered if they were diamonds. No, they couldn't be, he thought. Precise cutting of gems had not been developed until the fifteenth century AD. The lid's handle seemed too delicate for the otherwise robust looking Karura. It was the most beautiful thing any of them had seen, and they were unable to take their eyes off it.

"Looks like it should still have the damn price tag on it," Marty whispered to himself.

"This is not Sumerian," Raymond said, transfixed. "It's globular. Early Sumerians saw the world as a flat disk." His remark carried some weight, since he specialized in ancient Middle Eastern mythology and iconography.

Aaron agreed. "Look at the land masses. See how the continents are contiguous?"

"Pangea?" Raymond muttered. "Pre-flood? Strange. It's a Pre-Sumer vision of the world, but the thing obviously isn't primitive enough for that. Isn't Akkadian or Amorite, either."

"No, no. This isn't even Persian." Marty seemed sure. "Not even the Tell Halaf were capable of something like this." Aaron knew the Tell Halaf, an ancient tribe of northern Mesopotamia, were known for making some of the world's most beautiful pre-historic pottery.

"Wait a minute," Raymond said. "Could it be Zoroastrian?" Aaron and Marty turned to look at him curiously. "A few of the Zoroastrians could have come down here from northern Iran. Maybe they were using the cella as an underground temple. Would have been a good place to hide important religious relics. Then, when the Moslems chased them all out in the sixth century, they high-tailed it to India, and in the panic left this behind. Anyway, that would explain the Vedic quality. Northern Iranian writing of the period looks a lot like Sanskrit. It would also explain why the cella was empty. If they didn't empty it, the Mohammedans sure as hell would have."

Aaron could see how pleased Raymond was with his analysis.

"I agree on one thing," Aaron said. "No question it was 'hidden'. I dug it out of a fired clay receptacle embedded in the wall. Remember the offset we couldn't figure out? I paced it off. This thing was sitting at the median point of ziggurat. The cella was probably left empty to give looters the impression it was a dead end."

He walked around the table. "If it wasn't for a good flashlight and knowing where to look, I would never have noticed the patched wall. When I poked a hole in it, this stuff started pouring out." He reached into his pocket and produced a handful of the fine reddish dust. "One hundred percent oxidation. I thought the whole compartment was filled with this. But when we pulled away the rest of the clay–" Aaron stopped, put his hands on his hips and began to shake his head slowly, knowing what he was about to say would sound crazy. "Gentlemen, I think this thing was put there while the ziggurat was being built. And that was at least three thousand years before Zoroaster."

"Maybe the dust was a preservative of some kind," Marty said. "A moisture barrier. Corrosion would be a big problem down here. Could account for its good condition."

Raymond jumped on the remark. "Good condition? That's the understatement of the millennium. Look! Has any of us ever dug up an artifact from anywhere, much less this excavation, resembling anything remotely like this? Have we seen a single reproduction of it anywhere? The Sumerians always made copies of their important icons. There should be images of this thing all over the place and we haven't seen a single one! There's no provenance at all."

Aaron stepped over to the urn and inspected the lid more carefully. "Marty, what do you make of these characters around the handle? This isn't cuneiform, is it? Raymond's right. Some of it looks like Sanskrit, doesn't it?"

Marty, whose expertise was in early Mesopotamian writing, leaned in closer and raised his eyebrows. "Hmmm. That's weird. Some look like cuneiform– others look like Sanskrit. But they're both a little off. Maybe this is a proto-cuneiform pre-dating both alphabets."

"Or maybe I'm right," Raymond said. "Old Iranian writing is a lot like Vedic Sanskrit. Maybe this is a hybrid."

Aaron wrinkled his forehead, thinking part of what Raymond said made sense. But the earliest Sanskrit writing was more than a thousand years younger than cuneiform, having been dated around 2000 BC, and the two forms, as far as Aaron knew, were never mingled together. Nearly all Sanskrit literature had been found in India, many thousands of miles away, and no indigenous cuneic writings had ever been found further east than Iran. For Raymond's theory to work, there would have to be other evidence indicating a co-mingling of cultures. And, in the entire excavation, there was none. To Aaron, the urn was looking more and more like some kind of stitched-together relic that borrowed freely from various cultures, traditions and eras. An archaeological Frankenstein, he thought.

Marty leaned past Aaron. "Let's get this lid off. Maybe there's more on the edge or underside."

As he reached for the small golden handle, Aaron grabbed his wrist. "No!" he said. "No– Let's not do that until we've got some x-rays. Besides, look. Some kind of wax sealant here. There might be some easily corruptible material inside. We'll wait until we're in a controlled environment." He lowered his glasses and looked even closer. "Looks pretty brittle."

"Another contradiction," Raymond said with a groan. "Why's the seal carbonized like this and the urn so– so pristine? Inconsistent as hell!"

Aaron shook his head and looked at his friends. "A good reason to keep this just between us, until we know what we're dealing with. Whatever we say, right or wrong, we'll get nailed by the Archaeological Society. I don't know about you, but I don't need that. Remember the names of those anthropologists who bought into Piltdown Man?" Raymond and Marty looked at each other for the answer, causing him to laugh. "Right. Nobody else remembers them, either."

Raymond wiped his neck with a dirty towel. "Okay, so what do we do now? How can we keep something like this under wraps? It's not exactly a shard of old pottery."

"Why don't we just crate it up and one of us can take it back to Baghdad?" Marty suggested. "We're almost through here anyway. We can stow in the University locker until we're all back in the city. It'll stay put for a couple of days."

"Good." Aaron said. "Do it as soon as you can. But don't let it out of your sight. Raymond and I will be two or three days behind you. Oh, and before you pack it, take some pictures, just in case it gets damaged in transit. Okay?"

"Uh– Okay, sure thing," Marty said.

"I'm sorry, Marty. I know you don't like the idea of leaving the site early," Aaron said sympathetically. "But it's too important to ship back without one of us there to keep an eye on it. You're the logical guy." He looked back at the urn. "We're the only ones to know about this. Okay? We'll re-wrap it and you can have one of the grad assistants help you crate it up. Just tell him it's a fertility totem."

"Oh, come on, Aaron. A fertility totem? Nobody's going to buy that malarkey." Raymond said, chuckling sarcastically. "You walked out of the damn hole looking like you were carrying a time-bomb."

"Hmmm. Maybe so," Aaron said. "But we can't risk it getting out that we might have a counterfeit here. It'd spread through the camp in minutes. No. Stick with the totem story. Anybody has problems with it, have them to talk to me."

—⚆—

On the long drive to Baghdad, Aaron rode in one of the jeeps with Raymond and they talked about the potential impact the urn could have on the expedition. The late afternoon sun was blazing on the horizon, making it difficult to drive, even with the extra-dark sunglasses they wore. As they shared a canteen of cool water, Raymond was still pushing his theory about the urn's possible origin.

"Okay," he said. "If it's Zoroastrian, let's just say we set it aside because we didn't consider it indigenous to the site– keeping the expedition focused on the relevant finds and all that. Then we turn the damn thing over to the Society and–

Blah, blah, blah– let them deal with the bugger."

Aaron was unpersuaded. "Yes, but what if it's not what you think? What if it is as old as Zfegi? Or older?"

"God, the chaos!" Raymond laughed. "I can see the headlines: 'Discovery Proves Archaeologists Have Shit for Brains.' Christ! It would be like saying we found a T-Rex skeleton with a bullet hole in the skull!" He coughed and took another swig from the canteen.

"How do we explain it?" Aaron's tone became solemn. "The preservation. The faceted gems. The globular shape. All before the time of Abraham. Maybe even Noah. You said Pangea, Raymond! This thing could be pre-Ice Age."

"You know, we could resolve a lot of this with radio-carbon dating," Raymond said. "When it doesn't date with the rest of the site, that ought to prove pretty conclusively it–"

"What part of the urn are you going to chip off so you can perform the test? An elephant leg? Anyway, C-14 isn't foolproof. The slightest contamination and it can be off by thousands of years. A bad test might just make things worse."

Raymond growled his agreement. "Oh hell, maybe Marty's figured it all out and he's waiting for us with a case of cold beer." He forced a dry laugh and punched Aaron on the shoulder.

For the rest of the journey, Raymond's profanity-laced complaints about the terrible condition of the road became a monotonous drone in Aaron's ear, and his thoughts were focused on the abrupt disappearance of the Master Digger. For more than two months Ejan had been on the job without a single absence, even during the ferocious windstorms that raged across the site. Aaron thought, if he hadn't been so preoccupied with the urn, he would have gone into the village and looked for him. But, with their visas expiring soon, things were rushed. They had a limited amount of time to shutdown the camp, prepare their inventories and document everything with the Iraqi authorities. Upset he had been unable to bid Ejan farewell, Aaron managed to scrawl a brief note to him at the last minute, entrusting its delivery to one of the villagers.

When they reached the compound in Baghdad, Marty was waiting for them in the atrium, standing between two beefy Iraqi policemen. The notoriety of the expedition and the value of its discoveries were a great temptation to black market smugglers, so the government provided substantial security around the compound. As Raymond had hoped, Marty handed each of them an ice cold beer when they climbed out of the jeep, stretching their backs and rubbing their numb behinds. He had set up a small lab in one of the storerooms and headed them in that direction.

"A little excitement here a couple of nights ago," he said with a lopsided grin. "The guards caught two guys trying to break into the locker. Took them away before I could even get out of bed. These secret police are scary. Don't know why anybody would risk breaking in, especially when most of the stuff hadn't even come in from the site yet. Anyway, they've doubled up on security, so there's probably nothing to worry about. This morning, I moved the urn out of the locker and into the main hall's storage room, right in the middle of the compound. Nobody would expect anything to be in there.

Then I got one of the assistants to help me roll the portable x-ray–"

"You've already got x-rays? That's fantastic," Aaron said.

"Good," Marty said. "Thought you might be upset I started before you got here. Pain in the ass doing the film. I'm not that up to speed on x-rays, but I got some decent pictures. Doesn't look like anybody hid their car keys inside the thing."

"What about the writing on the lid? Any time to check it out?" Raymond asked.

"Yeah. A partial translation. It's a weird mixture. Made some blowups. Noticed something else, too."

All this made Aaron smile. "You've been busy, Professor. Good work." Marty had been one of his students and Aaron was always impressed by his ability to take the initiative.

Marty opened the door to the hall and led them to the storeroom at the back. He unlocked the door and walked in first, turning on the light as he went. He had positioned the urn in the middle of the room, on a stand beneath the hanging ceiling lamp, and the affect gave it an otherworldly glow. The three men stood silently by the door, waiting for their eyes, and minds, to adapt to what they were seeing.

"Sure is beautiful," Raymond said. "I'll say that for it."

"So, what've you come up with?" Aaron asked.

Marty walked over to the urn and pointed at the elephants supporting the sphere.

"What? The elephants?" Raymond asked impatiently.

"Not elephants," Marty said, shaking his head.

"Huh?" Aaron stepped closer.

"Mammoths." Marty said matter of factly. "The heads are

too elongated, and no elephant ever had tusks like these. And, after I got it here I cleaned it up and got a closer look at the hide. You can see it's not wrinkled skin. It's fur."

Raymond refused to come any closer to the urn, as if to protest Marty's assertion. Then he folded his arms across his chest and began to circle the room slowly.

"Okay. Someone dug up an old skeleton and decided mammoths would look better than ordinary elephants," Raymond said.

Marty's laugh had an edge. "Right. And then, with 40th century BC understanding of biology, they reconstructed in great detail the physiology of an intact animal. Give me a break, Raymond."

Raymond lost his cool. "Come on. You're not suggesting there were living mammoths when this thing was made?"

"I'm not suggesting anything. I'm just telling you what they are. You don't have to be a paleontologist to recognize the characteristics."

"Dr. Yamashita, we're talking about an animal dating back to the Pleistocene Epoch. Maybe twenty thousand years ago. Jesus, that's pre-Ice... Age." The words died in Raymond's throat as he recalled what Aaron had said in the jeep.

Aaron stood erect, then drained his beer. "All right. Let's calm down. We're just archaeologists, remember? Until we get somebody in that field to look at this, they're elephants. Okay? Where's your pictures, Marty?"

Marty went over to a light table he had set up in the corner of the room. He pulled the film from a large folder lying on top of it, then pushed a button on the side of the table. One at a time, he laid the x-rays on the illuminated surface.

"Okay. I took some closeups, in sections. First the mammoths–- the elephants. Then the sphere. And then the neck and lid. Some surprises there."

"Hmmm– Disappointing. I thought for sure... Look here." Aaron pointed to the bottom of the empty sphere. "There's not even a dust layer. Seal was pretty effective." He stopped to rub his eyes and the back of his neck. "Damn headaches! Must be dehydration. I shouldn't have had the beer. Got any water handy, Marty?"

As Marty left to get them water from the commissary, Raymond held up the shots of the base. After comparing a couple of the images he said, "Looks like there's a partition there, between the base and the sphere."

Looking over his shoulder, Aaron said, "Yeah, the sphere's a closed area. The elephants are attached, but there's no contiguous internal cavity."

Marty entered the room with three bottles of water in time to catch Aaron's comment, and he pointed to the x-ray Raymond was holding up to the light.

"Check out the sphere and how even the thickness is, all the way around the whole piece," Marty said. "Even the underside of the lid appears to follow the rounded contour of the inner surface. Oh, and another thing about this lid." He took the closeup of the lid and laid it on the light table. Using a large magnifying glass, he pointed to some subtle shadows on the film. "You see these four projections coming out from the side of the lid? At first, I didn't even notice them, but they definitely extend about a centimeter into the ceramic material of the urn. Look like locking pins."

Aaron leaned forward and touched the film on the four points. "Locking pins? Are you sure?" he asked.

Marty stepped back from the table, scratching his head. "Judging from the density of the shadows on the film, these pins are made of the same material as the lid. Must've been some kind of spring mechanisms to pop them into place when the lid was closed. Just a guess, though. Nothing like that shows on the x-rays. What's got me really confused is the composition of the lid. This metal looks and feels like heavy ore, but the shadows are extremely subtle, like it's made out of something more like wood. Not only that, if you look closely at the points where the pins extend past the side of lid, you'll see transverse hairline fractures on all four of them."

Raymond leaned forward, picking up the magnifying glass to look at what Marty was describing. "Damn, you're right. Must be crudely forged. Cracked right where the surfaces meet."

"Not so crude," Marty said. "Look at how precise the tooling is. I figure less than a micron of tolerance. Whoever made this thing was really good. Doesn't make sense they wouldn't know how to forge stronger materials. And how do you explain the sphere shape? It's geometrically perfect."

"Maybe its interior was blown," Raymond said. "You know, by a glassblower." He puffed out his cheeks. "Crude glassblowing techniques go back to the early Egyptians."

Marty was shaking his head. "The interior, maybe, but what about the exterior? It would take high pressure injection moulding to get this kind of three dimensional surface detail. I thought maybe the outer-layer had been sculpted over the interior and then glazed. The heat would have expanded the air inside and that would explain the cracked locking pins. But it also would have caused compression fractures in the ceramic around each pin and there aren't any. And, if they'd poured the molten glass into the pre-fired ceramic, it just would have conformed to its imperfections. Either way–"

"Can't be," Aaron said. "If the inner surface is glass, it would have to be from limestone. And limeglass imperfections show up in x-rays. This is clear."

"Any more good news?" Raymond said.

"'Fraid so. Your theory about the writing on the lid is in trouble." Marty reached for the closeup of the lid. "It's definitely a mixture of cuneiform and Sanskrit. But there's no mention of any Zoroastrian deities." He picked up a piece of rolled-up photographic paper and stretched it across the table. It was a shot looking directly down onto the lid. "I picked up a few key words. Here. Elohim, Enlil and, here Ki. Over here I got Ani, Kaun and Purusha."

Aaron looked a little surprised. "Purusha? The Hindu supreme being?"

"Positive," Marty answered. "The Hindu cosmic giant that makes up all the gods and all the matter in the Universe. Purusha's the equivalent of the Brahmanic Supreme Being. According to the writing on the lid, this is Purusha's Urn. So much for Zoroaster. Pre-dates him by a couple of thousand years. Sorry, Raymond."

"Wait a minute." Raymond had a perplexed look on his

face and was scratching the bald spot on the top of his head. "Elohim, Enlil, Ki, Ani and the Kaun all along side Purusha?"

Aaron responded, without realizing what he was saying. "Yeah, I thought this thing looked Hindu. Only thing missing is the giant tortoise beneath the elephants."

"There's one little problem. Enlil is the supreme Sumerian god. And Ki is the Sumerian Earth goddess. They're all part of that Anunnaki mythos,' Raymond said, rolling his eyes.

"Oh god. Not that crap about the ancient deities actually being alien astronauts? Marty asked, chuckling.

"Just the Sumerians," Raymond answered. "And this Elohim– well, that's the name for the first post-flood deity. You should know this, Aaron. Elohim was Shem's God, the first singular deity that wasn't part of a paganistic pantheon– the one true God of the Universe– the Kaun. So, you've got the earliest name for the Hebrew God mentioned in the same breath with the first Sumerian gods on an urn apparently belonging to this Hindu creator of the Universe. Talk about a nice fruit salad."

Aaron scratched his bearded chin. "If I remember my Near Eastern history, wouldn't Purusha have been a contemporary of early Sumerian culture? Around 3500 BC?" Raymond nodded. "Maybe this is an incursion. Maybe the urn represents an historical event. Hindu culture making contact with Sumerian culture. It could have been a gift to the priests of the temple. Or the Sumerians took it from them, as a spoil of war. The Anunnaki legends go back as far as the Gilgamesh epic, so that influence could have found its way into either culture."

Raymond and Marty were both rubbing their stubbled cheeks and frowning. Aaron smiled weakly and said, "Hey, it's only a theory."

"Interesting," Marty said. "But the inscription also says something about Purusha causing the end of all things. It's inconsistent with what we know about this deity. Why would the Hindu change their god of creation into such an asshole? They've already got Shiva for that. And even if they did, why wouldn't they just do it in Sanskrit? If this is a Hindu god's relic, why refer to other deities in cuneiform? That alphabet had been obsolete for thousands of years."

"So, we're right back where we started from," Aaron said. Despite himself, he was giving in to fatigue. "Okay. For now, this is the story we'll stick with. We catalog and inventory it as an intra-cultural relic, crate it up and ship it back to Cambridge." He paused a moment and thought better of the idea. "No, better make it directly to my home. And mark the crate so it looks like personal effects."

Marty shrugged. "That's going to be tough. If the police around here are any indication, the customs boys at the airport will be going through our inventory logs with a fine-tooth comb. If they do a random check and open up the wrong crate, we might not be getting out of Iraq for a long time. Especially if this new Baathist creep, Hussein, takes an interest in what we're doing."

Aaron rolled his head back and rubbed his aching forehead. "Oy. You're right. We have to play it straight and hope we get lucky. Log it as an undated, anomalous find. Just call it an urn. That's all true, so, if we get nailed, the Iraqis can't say we were trying to fool anybody. We'll send it with the first big shipment, so there's less chance of it being the one to get popped open. Make sure my name's on the packing slip and export certificate, so if there's a problem, they come to me."

Raymond raised an eyebrow. "Are you sure you want to do that? Risky as hell."

"Got any better ideas?" Aaron turned to them, his voice growing louder as he spoke. "What else can we do? Are you going to leave it here? If we do, it'll just end up in al-Bakr's presidential palace as a conversation piece. Either that, or it'll go up for auction on the black market. I don't want some former SS Nazi bastard with a fat Swiss bank account adding this to his private collection." Realizing he raised his voice, Aaron took a long, deep breath and turned back to the urn. "No, we don't have a choice. We have to get it out of Iraq."

Marty and Raymond stood quietly for a moment. Finally, Marty spoke up. "You're right, Aaron. But shipping it to your home? Anything marked 'personal' is gonna get opened for sure."

"Just ship it to my home, care of Harvard University Archaeology. The city's the same. With any luck, no one will notice the different street address. If we ship it to the Science Center, it could end up on display in Harvard Yard before we get home. Pack your pictures with it, too, Marty. As soon as it's in the air I'll phone ahead and tell Desta to expect it."

Marty nodded and began gathering up his x-rays and photos.

"Christ, my bladder's about to burst," Raymond said,

heading for the door.

"One more thing," Aaron said. He was standing with his arms folded, staring intently at the urn. "Until it's airborne, I want one of us with it all the time. I don't like the break-in you had, Marty. Whatever this is, it would be worth plenty. Let's get it packed and stuck in with everything else as soon as we can. We'll take a better look at it when we get home. A more complete translation, too."

"Whatever you say, Boss," Marty said, yawning through the words. "I'll crate it myself and pack it with sawdust to make sure it's protected."

Raymond crossed his legs and grabbed his crotch comically. "May I go to the little boy's room, teacher– before I piss my damn pants?"

Aaron laughed, even though he was exhausted as well. He wanted some decent food, a good night's sleep and needed to be at home with his wife and child. Until then, he would not be able to think clearly about things. The bottled water hadn't helped. Lately, he had been afflicted with the headaches on a regular basis, some driving him to the point of nausea. He assumed they were caused by the tension of the expedition's schedule, not drinking enough fluids and the inevitable maladies brought on by a prolonged stay in the Third World.

ii

Three days later, a flatbed truck pulled up on the tarmac at Baghdad International Airport, loaded down with wooden shipping crates of all sizes. Martin Yamashita, two graduate students and an interpreter from the University extension in Baghdad followed closely behind on foot, having left their jeep at the terminal entrance. They were met at the rear of the truck by three scowling customs officials who clearly did not like the idea of their national treasures being purloined by the West.

Marty handed the senior officer a clipboard with the manifest and several pages of logged descriptions of what was being shipped and to where. Attached to that was a manila envelope filled with the export certificates which had been secured by the University with the help of the United States Embassy. These certificates meant the government of Iraq now held a comprehensive file on the contents of each crate. In effect, it was a bonding agreement attributing real value to the artifact being shipped with the explicit promise to compensate the government of Iraq if the artifact was not returned undamaged within a specified period of time.

The three meticulously groomed yet thuggish looking uniformed men were in no hurry. Each packing slip attached to every crate on the truck was cross-checked with its log entry and certificate. Marty tried to watch the process with as much indifference as he could fake, but when one of the officers came to the five-foot-tall crate marked for delivery to a street address which he knew did not match the other destinations, he felt like running for his life.

After comparing the entries, the officer slowly turned to Marty with an odd, stoic expression, then waved over another man who had been standing in the shade of the aircraft. This new man, who wore civilian clothing, was carrying an unusual looking hammer with a long handle and equally exaggerated claws on its business end. Frozen by fear, Marty pictured himself chained to a wall inside some remote medieval prison, and his mouth suddenly felt like he had been licking the hardened dirt path they walked so often over the last few months.

It was nearly impossible to conceal his infinite relief when the senior official stepped forward and inexplicably pointed to the crate sitting next to the one his subordinate had just been scrutinizing so carefully. Twenty minutes later, the conveyor belt was being positioned next to the truck and the handlers emerged from the shadows to help stow the crates in the 707's cargo hold.

When the jet finally roll down the runway and he watched the front wheel rotate off the ground, Dr. Martin Yamashita felt as though the weight of the airliner had just been lifted off his own perspiration-soaked back. He found a telephone inside the terminal and called Aaron with the news.

—ww—

"Thought for sure I was camel shit, Aaron. The head customs agent looked at the crate, then gave me this look like he wanted to eat my liver. The next thing I know, he's opening the crate right next to the urn. Could've knocked me over with a feather."

"Okay, Marty. Well done. Come on back and I'll buy you a beer." Aaron held the receiver down for a couple of seconds before placing the overseas call to Desta.

"Hello, Desta? Can you hear me? It's Aaron." The phone

system in the Middle East was easily twenty years behind the West's and the line was alive with the crackles and hisses of the Transatlantic Cable.

"Yes, I hear you, Aaron. Is everything all right?" It was an hour before sunrise in Boston and Aaron could hear the alarm in her voice.

"Everything's fine. No problems. Sorry about the late call. I wanted to let you know I'll be home next week. I'll telegram my itinerary so you can meet me at the airport. How's things at home? Nikki okay? Hope the phone didn't wake him."

"We're fine. You could drop bombs by that boy's ears and he wouldn't wake up. I should be sleeping so sound without you here. But I guess everybody in the Wailing Wall seems to be having the same problem." She laughed.

"Wailing wall? What are you talking about?"

"Oh, just a little club the faculty wives put together so we could complain about our husbands being away for so long. We meet once a week at Rico's. It's really quite–"

"Listen, I can't stay on much longer. I wanted to let you know I'm having something shipped to the house. A wooden crate. Should get there by tomorrow night, or the following morning at the latest. I want you to have them put it down in my workshop, in the basement. Okay? Don't open it and please don't talk to anyone about it. Especially your Wailing Wall friends. And tell Nikki it's a secret he has to keep for me. All right?"

"What's going on, Aaron? You're not doing anything foolish?"

"It's no big deal. Just something we found at the site I want to study at home for a while before I have to turn it over to the Semitic. I'll explain it all when I get home. Just please do as I ask, okay?"

"Yes, dear. I understand. I'll talk to Nikki about it, too. Don't worry. Just have a safe trip."

"Sounds good to me. Thanks, sweetheart. I love you. And tell Nikki I said hello. I'll see you both in a week." He hung up the phone and rubbed the back of his neck in a futile attempt to lessen the pain of another thunderous headache.

iii

Late that evening, everybody in the old man's village was asleep, except for a group which had gathered in the basement of one of the oldest dwellings. Owned by the same family for generations, nobody in the village could remember when it had not been there. Made of archaic clay and straw bricks, its windows were crudely framed glass, pitted from sandstorms and offering little visibility. Just inside the entry, a spiraling stairway led down to the basement. It was so narrow many of the men had to edge their way down the dim passage, and the sharp curve prevented them from seeing the basement until the last couple of steps.

The stairway opened onto a surprisingly spacious room that was essentially unfurnished. Lit only by candles, it was large enough to hold the more than two dozen men who were now seated on the floor. Every few feet there were small recessed areas in the walls, where ancient reliquaries were displayed. As the candlelight flickered on the ornate glazed surfaces, the men knew each of the relics surrounding them was more valuable than any taken by the Americans. Except for one.

Ejan also sat on the floor, facing the group, silent and rigid. He was the oldest, except for the man behind him who occupied the only chair in the room. The Jeda, Ejan's grandfather, was nearly one hundred years old. He sat facing the group, hunched over, and only able to hear the voices nearest to him. But even with the infirmities of extreme age, it was he who had summoned them all together, from around the world. The Patriarch, every man in the room was of his blood. His children, his children's children, and so on. This was the Oosra Cadima, the Ancient Family.

Had he not been killed during the second World War, Ejan's father would have been the next Jeda. Since that day, Ejan was looked upon as the next in the line of succession, but that ascendancy was now in doubt. His fate would be decided by the Jeda and whatever the Cadima's ancient code of sacrifice and loyalty proscribed.

The women, even if they had been awake at this late hour, would not have joined the gathering. This was a rare and hastily planned meeting of the Cadima, and some of the men still wore their expensive, hand-tailored European suits. Others wore the simple clothes of the local peasantry, while a few of the younger men were dressed casually, in American jeans and French-made sneakers. Some had traveled for the last twenty hours to attend. In response to the Jeda's call, they abruptly stopped whatever they had been doing, no matter how important to their families or their personal fortunes, and immediately arranged for the journey to their ancestral village. They were not a Islamic sect, or part of some secret fraternal order. Despite the odd mix of cultural trappings, the physical resemblance they had to one another was unmistakable. They were a family. After a moment of silent meditation, Ejan rose and stood next to his grandfather, facing the somber group.

"Fashaltu," Ejan said. With the word, a tear trickled down the deep creases in his grandfather's withered cheek. Then Ejan spoke in English. "I have failed. The Karura Lehifthi Kaun has been taken by the Americans. I would willingly have sacrificed my life to prevent it, but I could not take the life of Sadiqi. May God forgive me." Several men in the room nodded, as if they understood the dilemma Ejan had faced, and knew they could forgive his error. But each man also knew his punishment might be more severe than a death sentence. He could be shunned by the family for the remainder of his life. Ejan's fate rested with the Jeda.

He stood motionless for a moment, his head bowed in despair. Then he looked up, searching the faces until he saw his nephew, still dressed in his government uniform. The senior customs officer nodded sympathetically to his uncle, then Ejan continued on around the room, looking every man in the eye.

"Two of our number were taken by the secret police in Baghdad five days ago. Their fates are still unknown to us. We were able to prevent the discovery of the Karura by government agents and it is now on its way to America. Better that than being put on display in the Presidential Palace. So, for now, we will follow. We will be patient. And, with God's guidance, the Oosra Cadima will fulfill its destiny."

Ejan bowed and the group rose quietly to its feet. Then he felt something touch his hand. He turned to see the Jeda looking up at him, a faint and ancient smile on his lips.

iv

Flying in a Boeing 707 from the Middle East to the United States was a grueling trip for even the sturdiest traveler, which Aaron was not. The international flights from Baghdad to the U.S. had two lay-overs. His first was in Athens, Greece, and the second in Frankfurt, Germany. He couldn't contemplate getting any rest until the long, third leg of the journey, to JFK, a brutal fourteen hour flight which Raymond had dubbed the "Ass-Kicker". However, his efforts to sleep were thwarted by another of his persistent headaches, which aspirin had, as usual, not helped. That, and the colicky infant of an American oil worker sitting in the seat directly behind him. Mercifully, he had to change planes in New York and, for the short hop to Boston, flew in one of the new, but smaller, 727 commuter jets.

As his plane coasted to a stop at the Logan International Airport terminal in Boston, he stood up to stretch, and bumped his head against the fuselage ceiling. After experiencing a brief dizzy spell, he stepped into the crowded aisleway, waiting for the tediously slow ritual of opening the plane's door. Being an archaeologist, he wasn't claustrophobic, but he didn't enjoy the occasional elbow in the side or the inevitable hard-soled shoe coming down on his soft-topped sneakers. The worst of it was the astonishing collection of odors congregating along the top of the plane's cabin, not the least of which was the stench of acrid cigarette smoke. Maybe that had caused his episode. He always loathed the scramble to be first off an aircraft, but this time he had been away too long to be the last.

As he came up the new, enclosed walkway, he could see Desta and their eleven-year-old son Niklas in the distance, waiting at the gate. When they were courting, she was a small, petite girl, almost bird-like, with waist-length, dark hair and a pretty face. The birth of their child had rounded off her delicate features and the long tresses had been cut long ago for the sake of convenience. Niklas was small, too, even for his age, but smart as a whip. Aaron didn't know from which side of the family the brains had come, and never assumed they came from his.

Forgetting the physical discomfort brought on by the trip for a moment, he waved to them. Even though they seemed to be looking directly at him, they didn't return his wave or his smile. He felt like rushing forward and taking them both up his arms, but held back, as he always did. Aaron was not a cold man and his feelings ran very deep, but he had difficulty opening up to his emotions. His parents hadn't been demonstrative, and he followed their example. As he drew closer, Desta and Niklas still didn't appear to spot him. It was almost as if he were an invisible ghost, and it wasn't until he was only a few feet away that they finally smiled and ran forward to greet him.

"I didn't recognize you with that silly beard," she said. "How was your flight?"

"Could've been worse. They could've put me in the baggage compartment." He bent down and kissed her quickly on the lips. "How have you two been? I've missed you both."

Desta put her arm around his waist as he turned toward Niklas. "You're too skinny!" she said. "I can feel your bones through this jacket." He smiled at her as he squatted down with both arms held out. The boy ran to him and, after a quick hug, Aaron kissed him on the lips.

"Dad!" He could see Niklas looking around the terminal nervously. "Geez, Dad. Not on the mouth! All I need is for Billy Yamashita to see that."

Aaron laughed. "Don't worry about Billy. Dr. Yamashita isn't coming home till tomorrow." He stood up and motioned them toward the baggage claim area. "Okay, keep your fingers crossed and pray my suitcases aren't on their way to Cincinnati." He wasn't as concerned about his belongings as he was about the few little trinkets he had brought home for Niklas and Desta.

Exhausted from the trip, he let Desta make the drive home. Niklas sat in the middle of the back seat of the sedan, leaning forward with his elbows hanging over the front seat. Aaron listened to Desta's chatter about the latest gossip in the neighborhood as long as he could, then he could wait no longer.

"You haven't mentioned the delivery I mentioned in our phone call. The—"

"Oh, it came last week," she said. "I had them put it down in your workshop, just where you told me. And, no, I haven't told a soul about it."

Then Niklas chimed in, "Yeah, I only told Mrs. Clark." With that, Aaron and Desta both whipped their heads around, their faces frozen in open-mouthed shock. "Just kidding." Niklas giggled.

"Nikki!" his mother said. "I almost drove off the highway." Mrs. Clark, the neighborhood's biggest gossip, had a well-known habit of spending hours watering her front lawn so she could keep track of everybody's activities on her block. According to local legend, she had even been observed doing it one rainy New England afternoon.

"Nikki, that was not funny! If you told Mrs. Clark, by now the whole city would know." Aaron couldn't restrain the grin on his face. The boy possessed the playful sense of humor of someone much older and Aaron liked that, even if it had almost given him a coronary.

As they crossed the Charles River, a few blocks from home, he heard Niklas fall back in the seat and give out a long sigh.

"Everything all right, Nikki?" he asked.

"Yeah— I mean, no. Dad, why do you have to do that stuff? You kiss me like I'm still a little kid. And you always call me Nikki. Can't you call me Niklas, or Nick, or dork-face? Anything but Nikki. I hate that stupid name!"

"You're absolutely right. I can see you're getting much too grown-up for that. From now on, it'll be a firm handshake and 'Hello, dork-face'. But you'll have to be patient. You've been Nikki for so long, it may take time to break the habit. Okay?"

Niklas sat forward, smiling again, and extended his right hand. "Okay, Dad." Taking it with a firm but gentle grip, Aaron shook his son's small hand for the first time.

They pulled into the driveway and Niklas helped carry his father's luggage into the house. Once inside, Aaron's first inclination was to run down to the basement and check the crate. Then he decided it could wait till morning and walked to the dining room. He opened the hutch, took out a bottle of dark red wine and poured two glasses. Leaving the crate and his unpacking for later, Desta and Aaron sat down in the living room to enjoy traditional evening ritual the had both missed for the last three months.

It was a moment of peace and quiet he had been looking forward to for weeks. Niklas was lying on the living room floor, engrossed in a book. Aaron leaned forward and whispered something in his wife's ear. She giggled quietly and Niklas looked up.

"Not until you shave off that silly beard." she said.

—⚌—

Niklas' usual practice was to stay in bed until just minutes before the time to leave for school. As the countdown neared, like an astronaut late for lift-off, he would fly around his room, gathering up his homework and getting dressed. Then he would leap down the stairs and, before he could propel himself out kitchen door, his mother would abort the launch, refusing to let him leave until he drank a large glass of juice and ate the fresh toast she always covered with an ample supply of her delicious, home-made raspberry jam. That was the one thing Niklas didn't mind stopping for. He hated breakfast cereal, often saying "it really is for rabbits," but loved the succulent jam and could eat it right from the jar. As soon as his mother turned her back, he would grab the toast and fly out the kitchen door, which opened onto their driveway, usually slamming it behind him. Then, more often than not, he would come slinking back through the door a few seconds later to pick up his school books, which were still sitting on the kitchen counter. "My absent-minded Professor," his mother would call out as he left a second time.

Today was different. When he flew into the kitchen, she wasn't standing there waiting for him. He stopped dead in his tracks, then heard the water running up in his parents' bathroom. Mom must have been taking a shower or something, he thought. Then he remembered his father was home again and it could have been him. He decided to get his own breakfast, and poured himself a large glass of orange juice. Unlike most kids his age, he didn't mind the pulp. He dropped some bread in the toaster and got out the large jar of raspberry jam. While he was waiting for the toast to pop up, he spooned a mouthful of the delicious red jam into his mouth. As he was savoring its sweet thickness, he noticed the door to the basement was open, so he picked up his glass of juice and walked over to the stairway. He could see the light was on below and, when he heard his father mumbling, went down to investigate.

Even though he always felt welcome there, Niklas didn't go down to the basement much. His father had converted it into a workshop where he studied and photographed things he brought home from the University. Niklas didn't have much interest in his father's "old junk". Since his fifth birthday, when his mother gave him the toy telescope, he only had eyes for the stars. On the verge of being obsessive, he was fascinated with their vast number and constant pattern in the night sky.

He stopped at the bottom of the stairs and saw his father's back as he carried the tall, ugly floodlamp to the far side of the basement. Niklas assumed his father was about to photograph something, since that was what he had always used the light for in the past. As he sipped his juice, Niklas surveyed the book shelves and file cabinets lining the opposite wall. To the left was the long work bench now covered with the small tools, brushes, and solvents his father used to clean the things he was photographing. Amid all the clutter, was a large book he had never seen before. When he looked to the other end of the basement, where his father had set down the floodlamp, he noticed something else. A large, colorful object was sitting on the concrete floor and he realized immediately it wasn't the usual "old junk."

"Nikki? Good morning. I mean– sorry– Niklas," Aaron said, turning around. His tan face, with the exception of a well-trimmed mustache, was now clean-shaven. "What do you think?"

"It makes your face look skinnier." Niklas could see the not so subtle line where the tanned skin met the paler area that had been shaded by the beard.

"No, no. I mean this!" Aaron rubbed his chin with one hand and gestured proudly at the big vase-like object with the other.

"Where'd you buy it, Dad?" Niklas thought his father had

brought home the world's biggest souvenir.

"Nobody bought it. It's from the dig. We found it in the deepest cave in the whole excavation." His father walked toward the object and began staring at its surface.

"It looks like a big lamp with the shade off." Niklas came forward to get a closer look.

"It's an urn. A very, very old urn. Not quite sure just how old. Not yet, anyway. I'll need you to keep it a secret a little longer. Okay, Nik–– Niklas? Don't even talk to Billy about it."

"Sure, Dad. But it looks brand new. Not like your other stuff." Used to seeing old things around the house, Niklas could recognize antiquity when he saw it.

"You can say that again. Maybe you could help me figure out what it is. But I think you're late for school, aren't you? By the way, how's it been going there?" He glanced quickly at Niklas and then turned back to the urn.

Niklas opened his mouth, and then he decided to lie. "Oh, okay, I guess," Niklas said it with a weak smile. "At least the eighth graders are leaving me alone. Now I have just have to worry about the fucking ninth graders."

"Oh, shit," Niklas thought. If he hadn't been paralyzed with anxiety, he would have tried to reach into the air and pull the word back. Unfortunately, he now had his father's full attention, and Niklas watched his face, wondering what painful price he would have to pay for his slip of the tongue. His father walked slowly across the basement floor and stood towering over him, frowning down. The two-toned skin, the new mustache and gaunt face, gave his father an unfamiliar, intimidating visage, and Niklas cringed.

"Is that how you think grown-ups talk, son?" His father's expression seemed more disappointed than angry.

"Sorry, Dad. It just slipped out." Like most kids, Niklas found it necessary to speak in two languages. When he spoke with his friends, he used all the routine obscenities. When he was at home with his parents, he reverted to a more conservative vocabulary. Most of the time, he was shrewd enough to prevent any leakage between those two worlds.

"I don't want to hear words like that in this house again. Do you understand what I'm saying?" Niklas nodded frantically. "You're too smart for it. And, if I ever hear your mother say you've talked like that–" Uh-oh. Here it comes, Niklas thought. Even though his father had never laid a hand on him, he knew there was a first time for everything. "– I'll be very disappointed in you." The words, and the way they had been spoken, struck home. At this point in Niklas' life, his father's approval meant everything to him.

"But I didn't– uh–," he stuttered. "It's just that all the other kids in school talk like–"

"You're not like all the other kids." He rested his hand on Niklas' shoulder. "Just remember, the way you are now is the way you're going to be the rest of your life. You're not going to change– as a person. You may get bigger and know more things, but you'll be the same person inside you are now. The same goes for all the bullies you have to deal with. Someday they'll be grown up and they'll have to live with who they are. And they'll have to look you in the eye."

"Yeah, the one that's not swollen shut." Niklas said it with a sarcastic grin, hoping to erase the frown from his father's face.

The briefest of smiles crossed Aaron's lips. "Okay, Niklas. Get moving! You're going to be late for your daily beating. We'll talk more about this when you get home."

For once, Niklas was relieved to be going off to school. He was angry with himself about the stupid slip down in the basement. "What a moron," he thought. But at least he got the chance to talk about the name thing the night before, so it wasn't a total loss. "Niklas" was a vast improvement over "Nikki". Naturally, he would have preferred "Nick." That had a mature snap, and a symmetry as well. "Nick Koppernick." Yes. He liked that. Most of his friends called him Niklas. Okay, the name Niklas Koppernick didn't exactly roll off their lips, but it was unique and, like his Dad said, he wasn't like the other kids. "Yeah, no shit," he said to himself, as he ran up the basement stairs to the kitchen. In a single move he grabbed a piece of toast, now stone cold, buried it in his mother's raspberry jam and launched himself out the door.

—⁓—

When Aaron heard the kitchen door slamming, he knew his son was off to school and smiled at the normalcy of it. He heard Desta's footsteps overhead, as she walked across the kitchen floor, and her voice in the doorway above.

"Can I make you some breakfast, Aaron?"

"No thanks, dear. I ate something before you got up." He lied. He was too preoccupied to even think about eating.

"Okay. I'm going down to Rico's. The Wailing Wall is having a farewell breakfast. Too bad. Who am I going to kvetch to about my husband's bad behavior?" She laughed. "Be back in a couple of hours." A moment later he heard the kitchen door close again, this time more gently, as she left the house.

For the first time, he was alone with the urn. He stood in front of it, trying to decide what to do first. It was either the most magnificent discovery in the history of archaeology and anthropology, or turn out to be a crushing deception. He moved the floodlamp closer to the urn. The lamp had worked well for his amateur photography, but it was old and gave off too much heat, even smoking at times. He would only be able to use it for a few minutes before he had to turn it off.

Leaning over the urn, he took a small magnifying glass out of his shirt pocket and started to inspect the lid and its odd collection of cuneiform and Sanskrit characters. After studying them for a minute or so, his attention wandered to the black wax seal running along the lid's edge. He imagined a shadowy figure, hovering over the urn eons before, pouring the clear molten wax slowly around the circumference, forever shutting it off from the corruption of air. And then he imagined torch-bearing, robed figures carrying it deep into the tunnels and, finally, the cave, for its entombment. He had never seen or heard of any religious artifact being so carefully concealed and preserved. On the contrary, nearly all had been openly displayed for veneration, bringing authority and respect to those who possessed them.

A few feet away, lying open on his work table, was a recent English edition of the Rig Veda. He had carefully studied the translation of Book X, the Vedic Creation Hymn, and it was there he learned more about Purusha, the Supreme Being of the cosmos, whose sacrifice created "everything that eats and eats not". According to the Veda, the various parts of the cosmic giant's body gave substance to the Universe. From his eye the sun had birth– and– the sky was fashioned from his head. All of the subsequent gods, the gods of old, dwelled in heaven, which was the unmanifest portion of Purusha's body.

But there was a provocative contradiction Aaron never fully understood. According to Book X, Purusha possessed a thousand heads and a thousand eyes, yet there was only one Sun and one sky in the Hindu tradition. Did each eye and head produce its own sun and sky? And did that mean the ancient Hindus knew the Sun was a star? Furthermore, how could what looked like a ancient funereal urn contain the remains of a being who was, essentially, the progenitor of everything?

None of it made sense, but Aaron was convinced the urn's secret could be found in the cryptic inscription on its lid. Maybe Marty had been right. There might be more writing on the thick edge of the lid or its underside revealing why anyone opening the urn would become this Purusha, the cosmic giant.

He took a small pen knife from his back pocket and selected a small area at the base of one of the elephant's feet. A mammoth is a kind of elephant, he thought. He opened the stainless steel blade of the knife and, holding it close to the point, attempted to make a small scratch in the ceramic surface with the broad edge. The steel blade glided smoothly over the shiny material, until its edge caught on a small fold in the elephant's hide. Fur, he wondered? He re-positioned the knife in his hand so the sharpened point barely protruded between his forefinger and thumb, then tried to scratch the same place once again. He repeated this in several different areas of the urn and finally slumped back in puzzlement. A glazed ceramic surface, especially one this old, should have been easily scraped or fractured.

He moved to the metal lid, which looked like heavy, soft gold, and got the same result. When not even the finest shavings came away on the edge of the knife, he wondered if anything could pierce the surface of this increasingly mysterious object. Hadn't Marty described its x-ray as looking as "dense as wood"? Then something about the seal caught his eye.

Under the intense light of the floodlamp he could see a subtle crack in the ancient wax running its entire length. If the angle of the light hadn't been just right, he would never have noticed it. Perhaps the heat of the lamp had expanded the material, widening the hair-thin line enough to make it visible.

He took a small, clear plastic bag from his work table and carefully scraped the material from around the rim of the lid, placing the pieces into the bag for later analysis. After wiping the lid clean of the remaining residue, he grasped the small crown-shaped handle between the thumb and two fingers of his right hand. Steadying the urn with his other hand, he tried to turn the handle, to see if the lid would rotate in place. No luck. It held fast. Bit by bit, he added more torque. Still no movement. Fearing he would break the delicate looking handle, he let go and took his first breath since starting the tedious process. He laid the wiping cloth over the lid, then gently tapped the opposite sides of the rim about a half dozen times with the blunt end of his pen-knife.

The floodlamp's heat caused him to sweat profusely, and he stopped to wipe his forehead and neck. Then another deep breath. He removed the cloth from the lid and, grasping the small handle, gradually increased the pressure.

Just a little more should do it, he hoped. Then, just as he was about to give up for the second time, the lid gave under his fingers. Afraid it would freeze up on him again any second, he continued turning slowly in a clockwise direction for a full revolution before letting go.

Now he used his small magnifying glass to inspect the lid one more time. They never completely translated the circular inscription, other than identifying a few key words, and the admonishment to leave the urn sealed. He hoped Yamashita was right about the possibility of additional symbols or writing being on the underside and edge of the lid, and was intensely curious about the nature of the interior surface, which appeared so perfectly spherical in the x-rays. But what Aaron thought was even more unusual was that they had gone to so much trouble to seal it? Why the complicated pin mechanism? It was the hundredth time he asked himself the question.

The floodlamp directly over his right shoulder was unbearably hot, and he planned to move out of its way as soon as the lid was in his grasp. Reaching for the handle, he noticed a wisp of smoke rising from the lamp's metal shade. Cursing, he vowed to invest in a new light the moment he was finished with the urn. He grasped the handle once more and lifted as slowly as he could. Because it had been tooled with such precision, the surprisingly light-weight lid came up quite smoothly, and the sheered-off contour of a locking pin came into view. The fracture was smooth and perfectly flush to the side of the lid.

He had raised it nearly an inch before he saw the dark, crescent-shaped gap appear along the bottom edge. He took the sides of the lid in both hands and, as if removing the detonator from an unexploded bomb, lifted even more slowly. Bending both of his knees, he looked carefully for any additional markings on the side, but saw nothing.

Tilting his head to avoid blocking the light, he leaned even closer to the opening, trying to peer inside. Even though the skin of his neck was thick and tanned from the Arabian sun, it was still vulnerable to the light's intense heat. The floodlamp was only a foot or so above his head and when he wiped the sweat from the back of his neck, he could feel the small blisters forming there. Despite the stinging discomfort, he was so intent on peering into the urn he paid little heed.

—〰—

Niklas got a couple of blocks from home before he realized something was missing. When he walked past Mrs. Clark a few moments before, she gave him a weird look. But then, Niklas thought, she was always giving him weird looks. As he tried to figure out what was wrong, he stuffed the last of the jam-laden toast into his mouth, licking as much of the sticky residue from his fingers as he could. As he scrubbed his hands on the seat of his trousers, the awful truth came to him.

"Oh, shit! Books!" He spun around and ran. This time, when he passed Mrs. Clark, she was smiling and shaking her head. Weird lady, he thought. He came back through the kitchen door, out of breath, as quietly as he could. He didn't know if his mother was still upstairs, and hadn't noticed if the family car was still parked in front. He assumed his father was still working in the basement because the door was open and the light still on. He grabbed his books from the countertop and, on his way out, paused by the refrigerator. He listened for any movement from above, then decided there was still time for one more quick taste of the jam. He pulled the refrigerator door open and grabbed the jar. With the same spoon he used earlier to smother his toast, he filled his mouth. With the utensil still protruding from his lips and carrying the open jar with him, he tip-toed over to the basement doorway to listen for a moment.

—⁓—

Aaron held the lid as still as his perspiring fingers would allow, and quickly checked to make sure he wasn't casting a shadow. Slowly, his eyes began to accommodate to the darkness inside the urn.

At first, he could only make out a black, spherical object. Unreflective, it seemed to absorb the light from the floodlamp, so he squinted his eyes shut a moment, trying to help them adjust to the darkness inside the urn. When he opened them again he could see the object's surface was alive with swirling wisps of vaguely prismatic colors. The roiling clouds glimmered unevenly, disappearing into the object's depths and then resurfacing. Not much larger than his closed fist, the object was the most fragile, magical thing he had ever seen, and it seemed to grow brighter as he observed it. So mesmerized, Aaron continued to stare into the small opening even while the heat of the lamp hammered at the back of his neck.

Suddenly, a voice emerged from the depths of the black orb. No. Not a voice. There was no sound. It was a thought. A telepathic, alien thought penetrated his brain. Then, an instant later, it was followed by an overwhelming tide of thoughts, too numerous to comprehend. He had trouble sustaining his sense of self-awareness as wave after wave surged upward, through the harsh, burning light of the floodlamp, into his consciousness. In the next instant, their meaning struck him like a sledge-hammer. Prayers, he thought. These are prayers. Countless multitudes, crying out in the common language of thought, begging for deliverance from something terrible. Pleas to God for divine intervention.

Then he heard a voice. Yes, it was a voice this time. Not a disembodied thought, like the others. Loud and close, it seemed to come from behind him and he jerked to his left, expecting to see someone standing right there at his shoulder. But no one. He was sure he had heard it. The tone was controlled and deliberate, without the panic and terror he sensed in the thoughts. And its content was anything but prayerful.

"Close the fucking urn." the voice had said.

—⟋⟍—

Just as Niklas was about to turn from the basement doorway, he thought he heard something below. It sounded like a man's voice, but he couldn't make out any distinct words. He was sure the voice didn't belong to his father. But, after a moment of silence, he shrugged it off, thinking it had probably just been in his head. He was about to tip-toe down the stairs to investigate when a loud popping sound came from below, and then a bright flash of light lit up the narrow stairway. Niklas froze, listening for the stranger's voice again. But the next sound came from above. The ceiling creaked overhead, and he decided it was time to make a getaway before his mom came down and caught him fucking around in the kitchen, late for school again. Slowly, he took two steps backward, licking the spoon one more time before placing it quietly on the counter. Then he spun around and headed out the kitchen door, without giving the voice in his head another thought.

Chapter 2
The Sins of
the Father

i

The obscenity jolted Aaron, and he consciously fought the reflex to step back from the urn. There was something vaguely familiar about the voice. Something in the inflection that struck a nerve. Again, he glanced quickly about the basement, thinking– hoping the chilling words had been delivered by some unseen visitor. But he was alone, wasn't he? Aaron felt as if his heart had stopped, and he couldn't draw air into his lungs.

Then the voice exploded again, this time screaming and filled with rage.

"Close the fucking urn! You're killing everything!"

When the floodlamp popped and burned out in a brilliant flash, Aaron was startled and nearly dropped the lid. The words he had just heard seemed to come from all around him, and the side of his head pounded, as if each of them had struck him there with the force of a bludgeon. Then a revelation knifed through him, temporarily smothering the pain. Had he just heard the angry voice of some vengeful genie, let loose from his encapsulated realm? And what of those spiraling mists that had swirled across the surface of the black orb, glowing like embers above a campfire.

In the next instant, what was happening inside the urn crystallized in Aaron's mind. He had to stop what he was doing. Close the lid. He was igniting an apocalypse. Doing all he could to control his trembling hands, he quickly lowered the lid back into place, hoping it sealed. Then he fell to the floor in a heap, like a marionette whose strings had suddenly been cut, retching and sobbing. His tears mixed with the sweat pouring off his brow, stung his eyes, and the back of his neck twinged from a second degree burn. As he struggled to deny the reality of what had just happened, the clarity of the voice, and the words still echoed in his throbbing head. Had he really caused a holocaust beyond imagination? Was it possible that entire worlds had been swept away in a moment? And for what? To satisfy his pathetic curiosity about something he shouldn't have been tampering with in the first place? A visceral awareness of a monstrous conflagration swept over him like fire in dry grass. Unable to bear the realization of what he seemed to have done, he curled into a fetal position on the stinging cold concrete of his basement floor and wept.

ii

Aaron and Desta's only son had been born in Boston in 1959. For reasons Niklas never understood, they named him after the sixteenth-century Polish astronomer Niklas Koppernick, better known to the world as Copernicus. As far as Niklas could see, there was no familial connection at all, and Copernicus was a Catholic. However, he might as well have been a direct descendant of the famous scientist, because Niklas had been hooked on astronomy since he was five years old.

Mr. Gutter taught his seventh grade science class and Niklas didn't like him. Not one little bit. The teacher rarely called on him and occasionally even made unkind remarks about his diminutive size. Gutter was a graying, thin man, who looked older than Niklas' father, but was actually two years younger. He had a haggard, baleful appearance, with dark circles under his eyes, and Niklas guessed this was because he never got enough sleep and probably used one of those cheap electric shavers, rather than a razor like his father used. Always yawning in front of the class, he also had what Niklas thought was a particularly obnoxious habit of fiddling with his ample nose hairs.

The other thing Niklas noticed about Mr. Gutter was that his hands shook. On one of his solitary visits to the library to do research on the opposite sex, he had gotten the librarian to help him look up the symptom. In one book he found a whole chapter on something called Parkinson's Disease and, based on his classroom observations, Niklas decided this was the most likely diagnosis. He also thought the palsy was more pronounced when Mr. Gutter got upset, which seemed to be every time Niklas raised his hand in class.

On this particular morning, the class was being led out to the school's athletic field. A ninth grade physical education class was running laps around the track as the twenty-four students walked in an orderly fashion to the far end of the grass-covered field and gathered around the yawning instructor.

Mr. Gutter clapped his hands to get the group's attention.

"Okay, today I want to do a little demonstration relating to a couple of subjects we've been learning about in class recently: the Milky Way and our very own solar system. But, first, I need a volunteer."

Niklas knew it was useless, but he raised his hand anyway. He was excited to learn anything he could about the stars and planets and, even if he couldn't participate in the demonstration, he was hungry for whatever it might reveal.

Surprisingly, Mr. Gutter said, "Okay, half-pint." Even the unkind remark hadn't been enough to douse Niklas' enthusiasm. It was all he could do to keep from skipping to the front of the class. Gutter turned Niklas around so he was facing the other pupils and instructed him to reach down and pick up the smallest grain of dirt he could find. Niklas looked up at his teacher with a confused expression, not quite understanding what was being asked of him.

"Were my instructions too complicated for you? Gutter asked in a patronizing tone. "Okay, one more time. I'll speak very slowly so you don't miss a word. I want you to find the smallest grain of dirt you can find and hold it in that little palm of yours." Gutter laughed cruelly at his own remark.

It took all Niklas' will-power to control his anger. He knelt down and did the best he could to find the smallest speck of dirt among the sparse blades of grass. As he pinched at the soil he could hear the snickers of his classmates. Then he stood and held out his palm.

"This one okay, Mr. Gutter?" he asked.

"All right, Nikki," the teacher said with a smirk. "Now I

want you to start walking, and don't stop until you see me wave my arm." Gutter pointed to the distant portion of the athletic field, past the school's softball diamond. Reluctantly, Niklas set off, staring down at the speck in his palm. It was now abundantly clear what Gutter was up to. It wasn't enough to humiliate him in front of his classmates. Now he would be excluded from whatever it was that the asshole was going to demonstrate.

After walking fifty yards, he came to the track and has to wait for a group of wise-cracking ninth graders to jog by before he could continue. Every few yards after that he would turn around, expecting to see Mr. Gutter's wave, but it didn't come. The further he got from the class, the more suspicious he got about the teacher's true intentions. It was not until he was only a few feet from the high, ivy covered chain-link fence running the circumference of the school that the wave finally came. It occurred to Niklas that he should just keep walking, all the way home. But he knew Gutter would try to get him expelled for that, so he turned and faced the class, which was now so far away he could not make out one classmate from another. Only the taller figure of Mr. Gutter, who now appeared to be lecturing the class, was distinguishable.

As he stood there, he visualized the looks he had just seen on the girls' faces and his cheeks reddened. He gritted his teeth and began to walk back toward the class. He stared down at the grain of dirt, comparing it to the size of Gutter's brain, and realized how stupid the shaky old fart had made him look, walking across the huge field covered by billions of grains of dirt, cradling his little speck like it was something special. He angrily brushed it off on his trousers as he neared the class.

Mr. Gutter didn't seem to care Niklas had returned to the group without his permission. He had finished his demonstration and was already leading the group back to the classroom. As Niklas fell in behind his giggling classmates, Billy Yamashita dropped to the back and walked alongside him.

"What an asshole!" Niklas said. "He was gonna let me stand out there all day." He checked to make sure the teacher was far enough away not to hear his remark.

Billy laughed. "Hey, dipshit. What'd you expect? Everybody in class knew what the old prick was up to. I thought you were supposed to be some kind of genus."

'The word is genius, dork!" Niklas did not laugh.

"What's that?" Billy asked.

"A genius?" Niklas snapped.

"No. What you just called me. Dork? I never heard that one before."

"Oh yeah. Dork. Just a word I invented. Sort of a cross between a Do-Do and a jerk." Niklas' frown weakened slightly.

"Oh." Billy's inquisitive expression slowly turned sour. "Wuh... what's a 'Do-Do'?"

Niklas grinned until he caught a glimpse of Gutter leading the class back into their building, and his grimace returned.

"So, what was his stupid demonstration about?" he asked.

"I didn't really get it. Something about the thing you had in your hand being our solar system and, I think, the distance between you and us was the Milky Way. Pretty weird shit."

Niklas understood the comparison that the teacher had drawn, having read about it six months earlier in one of his astronomy books. But this knowledge didn't make the memory of the athletic field insult any easier to take. He had been used to demonstrate the enormous size of the Milky Way galaxy by showing how small the solar system was in comparison to it. If the particle of dust he had selected was the solar system, the distance between Niklas and his classmates, nearly two hundred yards, equaled the diameter of the Milky Way. Niklas also knew that if the comparison had been to the Universe, rather than just the galaxy, he would have had to walk another thousand miles. He bet Gutter didn't know that.

iii

Niklas got home from school at around 3:15 that afternoon. It hadn't been a very pleasant day for him, but he was more concerned his father would still be upset about the obscenity he had let slip that morning. He had all but forgotten the episode on the field, but wouldn't have told his father about it even if he had remembered it.

He dropped his books on the kitchen counter and went directly to the refrigerator, where he selected a large, cold, red apple. He liked them better cold. They were crisper and more refreshing. And he hated having to eat around the soft spots. Before he had closed the refrigerator door, he had already taken a huge bite and a drip of juice was trickling down his chin. He looked around the kitchen, listening for sounds in the house, and didn't see or hear anything indicating anybody was home.

He saw the door to the basement was still open, but when he went over to the stairway, he saw the light had been turned off. He knew his mother liked to keep the door closed, so he pulled the heavy wooden door shut. He went back to the counter, picked up his books and headed for his room. As he made his way up the stairs he glanced into the living room and saw one of the strangest sight he had ever seen.

His mother and father were sitting there, in complete silence. She was sitting on the sofa, still in her coat and clutching her purse in her lap. His father was sitting directly opposite her, in his reading chair, with his face hidden by the hand he held across his eyes. Neither of them was moving or saying anything. For a moment, Niklas thought someone might have died. But who? He walked in quietly, not wanting to startle them. He knew they both were aware he had come into the room, but neither of them looked his way. This really worried him. Something bad must have happened. He sat next to his mother and waited for her to tell him whatever the news was.

After what seemed like several minutes, his mother reached over and put her arm around him. He took this as signal it would be all right to speak.

"What's the matter, Mom? Did somebody die?" Niklas' voice quivered.

His father looked up and Niklas was shocked by what he saw. His father's face seemed gray and the whites of his eyes were reddened, like he had been crying. But Niklas knew that couldn't be. His father was all-powerful. A hero. He never cried.

"Don't worry, son. I just did something..." Then his father's mouth got the crooked, trembling look of someone who was fighting back tears.

Niklas' mother turned to him. "Go upstairs, Nikki, and get cleaned up. Everything's all right. Go on. I'll be up in a minute."

Niklas wanted to defy her. He wanted to run over to his father, to hug and kiss him and make him laugh. He didn't ever want to see his father like this again. It was one of the most upsetting things he had ever seen and he would never forget it. His mother persisted, patting him on the back to get him moving in the direction of the stairway. After deciding that disobeying her would just upset his father more, he got up and went to the stairs, looking back at the scene a couple times, hoping his father would look up and smile. But he didn't.

iv

Aaron had to will himself out of bed the following morning. The first thing he did was call his office at the Science Center and ask two graduate students who were in his doctoral program to come over to the house. Then he went down to the basement. Twenty minutes later he overheard his wife greet two young men at the front door and offer them some coffee, which they politely declined. When she showed them down to the basement, Aaron was pounding the last nails into the wooden crate. The two long-haired grad students were quite scraggly, one of them having a beard that fell half way down his chest.

"Hi– Michael and Benjamin?" Aaron recognized them both but was unsure of their names.

The bearded student stepped forward and shook hands with Aaron. "Hey, Dr. Koppernick, sir. It's Mike. This is my fellow accomplice, Benny. Hope the expedition went well for you."

Aaron didn't feel like chatting with them and he could see his wife's shocked reaction to his unsociable attitude. But he had more important things on his mind.

"I'd like this crate taken over to the campus right away, fellas. I'd take it myself but I'm feeling a little under the weather right now."

"Semitic Museum, right?" Benny asked, as they stepped forward to pick up the large crate.

"No!" Aaron said, raising his voice slightly. 'This doesn't go to the Semitic or the Peabody. Understand?"

Mike stopped and turned around to face Aaron. "But we thought for sure, with the Semitic setting up the expedi--"

"No. This goes directly to the Science Center basement. Okay?" Aaron had said it with uncharacteristic terseness. "Look, it's just some field tools and other stuff that need repairing. I was going to do it here, but changed my mind. Just stick it way in the back where it won't get the way."

"Whatever you say, Doc...uh, I mean, Doctor Koppernick." Mike said.

"Yeah, no problemo, Dr. Koppernick." Benny raised both

eyebrows and shrugged.

The Science Center was located at One Oxford Street, just north of Harvard Yard, beyond the Cambridge Street underpass. It had been designed in the late 1960's by a former dean of the Graduate School of Design, and had cost nearly twenty million dollars to build. Much of the money had come from Edwin Land, the inventor of the Polaroid Camera.

Constructed of pre-cast concrete sections, it was held together by epoxy cement glue. The previous June, when Aaron had watched the work progress, it vaguely reminded him of ancient Egyptian building methods, with the assistance of a few enormous trucks, earthmovers and cranes.

Even though he had seen the architectural renderings, he was very surprised when he finally saw the completed structure. It was nine stories tall, with each succeeding floor having less square footage than the floor below. The stone block components and the vaguely pyramidal shape gave it the look of a modern day ziggurat. The interior waterfall and botanical garden made the Babylonian quality so strong he had been mildly shocked when he learned the architectural similarities had been purely coincidental.

While the 20th century ziggurat was not a temple built to honor some pagan deity, it was designed for the worship of technology. The high priests were astrophysicists, mathematicians, chemists and biologists, and the supplicants were first world governments, high-tech corporations, and some of the world's brightest students. Instead of livestock, grain and precious ores, their offerings were national endowments, foundation grants and the heftiest tuition fees of any educational institution on Earth.

As Aaron watched the crate being carried up the basement stairway and out the kitchen door, he thought about how ironic it was that the urn would soon be interred in such a neo-ziggurat, and wondered how long its new hiding place would remain undisturbed. The Science Center's basement held the Harvard University Collection of Scientific Instruments. The first steam engine, which James Watt had developed around 1850, had been stored there, along with some other rather unheralded developments in the microscope and telescope. It wasn't really a museum, and Aaron knew it rarely got visitors. In fact, several floors of the new building rarely saw any students at all.

While the two graduate students carried the crate out to the van, Aaron paused at the small kitchen table to jot down a note, which he placed in an envelope with another document. He handed the paperwork to Benny, and made one more request.

"Listen, guys. I was sort of stretching University rules by having this stuff at home, so I'd be grateful if you could keep quiet about it. The fewer people who see you bringing it in, the better. Just give the envelop to the clerk. He'll show you where to put it. Okay?"

Mike grinned broadly. "Gotchya', Doctor K. They'll have to pull our fingernails out to–"

"We're cool, Doctor Koppernick." Benny gave Mike a stern look and nodded toward the van.

—ᴡ—

Mike had parked the van in the driveway, just opposite the kitchen door, so they only had to carry the crate a few feet before it was safely tucked into what looked like a mobile opium den. After assuring Dr. Koppernick that the crate, and its unknown contents, would be delivered immediately, they both got into the van and watched Dr. Koppernick disappear into his house. No sooner had Benny slid the sidedoor closed than Mike, who was already sitting behind the wheel, was lighting up another joint. He took one hit and began looking nervously in the rearview mirror.

"Hey, did you see that black Benz go by?" He brushed the trail of ashes off his beard as he stared into the review mirror.

"Nah. What Benz? Come on. Don't bogart, man!" Benny reached for the roach while Mike looked up and down the street.

"I'm tellin' ya, man, it's gone by twice. Just since we got in the vehicle. Some guy with short black hair driving. Looked right at me." He looked at Mike with a quizzical expression. "Do narc's drive Mercedes now, man?"

"Will you cool it!" Benny said, straining to talk without expelling any of the smoke from his lungs. Then he also began looking up and down the street.

"I tell ya, we're being watched, man." Mike said, nodding his head toward an elderly lady who was just a couple of houses up the street, watering her front lawn. She was staring directly at them and made no attempt to conceal her curiosity. After returning the lady's stare, Benny chuckled, but Mike found nothing humorous about the situation.

"Hey, we don't know what's in this crate," Mike said.

"Could be – illegal. Like, you know, contraband, man."

Benny wheezed, again trying his best not to exhale. "Oh man, don't get paranoid on me again. Can we split now? I've got a T.A. gig this afternoon."

They drove slowly out of the neighborhood, sharing the shrinking joint between them. As they passed Mrs. Clark, whose stare followed them like a predatorial hawk, Benny looked out the window, gave her a broad smile and waved good-bye. Mrs. Clark shocked them both when a large smile appeared on her face and she waved back. "Weird old lady," Benny coughed.

—⁓—

Because of the recent construction, the inventory process in the Center's basement was not as meticulous as it could have been. The two grad students carried their cargo to the cataloging desk, which was really just a small cubicle. Mike handed the envelope Dr. Koppernick had given him to the clerk and while the clerk read it and logged in their delivery, he went back outside to move the less-than-inconspicuous-looking van to another location, just in case they had been "tailed". A few minutes later he returned, out of breath. His self-satisfied grin vanished when Benny, noticing the fresh ashes on his beard, gave him a pissed off look.

The clerk provided them with a dollie and the three rolled the crate down a long, partially lit hallway. Although he had acted less than amused by the odor and odd behavior of the two, the clerk had been helpful. Within twenty minutes of their arrival, they were putting the crate into one of the back rooms Dr. Koppernick used to store the archaeology department's materials. Many of the rooms in the basement were used by the faculty to warehouse items they didn't have room for in their own offices. It was also a good place to store the parts of the museum's collection which had been deemed too obscure for display, as if anyone ever came down to look at the old exhibit anyway. It was, after all, 1970, and old things just didn't get the respect they had once received.

As soon as their mission was completed, rather than leaving the building and risking capture, the two future Ph.D's went directly to the Green House Cafe, up on the first floor of the Center. There they ordered their usual herbal teas and began bitching about the war. Coffee was for Republicans.

v

Within days Aaron became seriously ill. His appetite had all but disappeared, his skin color went gray and, at times, he seemed to be having trouble with his equilibrium. At first, Desta wrote these off as symptoms of not eating or sleeping properly, and she blamed the expedition for those problems. But after a month of watching his health deteriorate, she could no longer ignore her husband's physical condition. One evening, after Niklas had gone to bed, she walked into the living room, where Aaron was reading, and confronted him.

"Aaron, you have to go to the doctor. You look terrible!"

"Nonsense. I just have a bug of some kind." He knew something far worse must be going on inside his head.

"Look at yourself." She struggled to keep her voice low, but couldn't manage it. "You're thinner now than when you came home from your trip. Your headaches are worse. You've been complaining about seeing double. Sometimes you even have trouble keeping your balance. Half the time you can't even get up to go to work. Something's wrong. I'm calling the doctor!"

Her tone made it clear nothing he could say would stop her, so he just laid his head back on the chair and closed his eyes in acceptance.

—⁓—

A couple of days later, their family physician, Dr. Max Rosenberg, ordered a series of tests, which Aaron took stoically, as if he knew in advance what they would find. On the way to the hospital to go over the results with his physician, Aaron hadn't spoken a word. Desta felt a tremendous sense of dread, anticipating what the doctor might say. They waited in the examining room for nearly twenty minutes before Rosenberg finally walked in, carrying Aaron's thick file and a large, brownish envelope.

"You have a glioma, a brain tumor, Aaron," Rosenberg said, getting right to the point. "It's right here." He touched the back of Aaron's head, above and behind the right ear.

He opened the envelope and took out a large x-ray of Aaron's skull, hanging it on a back-lit wall panel. "You see this shadow right here? That's it. An astrocytoma. About the size of a golfball. The location of the mass accounts for your double-vision. And it would also likely be the cause of the excruciating headaches you've been having." Rosenberg turned slowly to them with a forlorn expression and folded his arms across his chest.

"Well, you cut it out or something?" Desta asked, standing rigidly next to Aaron, who was slumped in the uncomfortable metal chair. Desta's voice was quivering as she struggled to maintain her composure for Aaron's sake.

Rosenberg turned back to the x-ray and studied it for a moment. "I'm afraid it's too involved with the surrounding neural tissue to operate. That's how it usually goes with these types of tumors because they involve the actual brain tissue and blood vessels. Removing it could kill you outright, Aaron."

"It was the goddamned expedition did this to you!" Desta's outburst did not even phase Aaron, whose deflated posture was in stark contrast to her own.

"Actually, these kinds of primary brain tumors are very slow growing, Desta," Rosenberg said. "This is more than likely a grade 1 tumor, the slowest type. He could have had it inside him for years. It was probably there long before he went to Iraq, Desta."

"Years? Nonsense! He was fine before he left. And then he comes home and falls to pieces." She looked over at Aaron and then back to the doctor.

"We don't know what the trigger mechanisms are for these tumors," Rosenberg said. "Whatever they are, they occur at a molecular level. The cells can lie dormant in the brain for years, sometimes a lifetime, before they become active. I guess it could have been touched off by something during Aaron's trip, but there's no way to know for sure."

"So, what can you do?" Desta sat next to Aaron, who

continued staring at the floor.

"First, I'm going to prescribe a corticosteroid. Might help reduce some of the swelling around the tumor– give him some relief from the headaches. As soon as possible, I want to proceed with an aggressive schedule of cobalt radiation treatments and six weeks of chemotherapy. If you let us take a biopsy, Aaron, we might be able to confirm the cell-type and narrow the scope of the treatment. Without a biopsy, we'll have to go full spectrum. It won't be–"

"No treatments, Max," Aaron said without looking up. His tone of voice was resolute. "No biopsy. No radiation. No chemotherapy."

Rosenberg stepped forward and put his hand on Aaron's shoulder. "But, my friend, you–"

"I've understood everything you've said, but that's how I want it. Don't fight me on this, Max. Please." Aaron let his chin drop back to his chest and breathed deeply.

"It's your decision. But at least take the medication. For the headaches," Rosenberg said.

"He's very tired," Desta said as she gently rubbed the back of Aaron's neck. "We'll pick up your prescription and then we'll go home and talk about the treatments. We'll call you tomorrow, if it's all right. Come, Aaron." Her husband was one of Rosenberg's closest friends and Desta could see he had been struggling to retain his professional demeanor. She stood up and took her husband by the arm.

When Aaron stood, he offered his hand to the doctor.

"Thanks, Max. You've always been very kind to me and my family. You're a good man."

Desta recognized the tone of Aaron's voice. He had made his decision long before this moment, and she knew he planned to let the lethal disease run its course.

—〰—

Late that evening, Desta found Aaron sitting in the kitchen, lost in a large, unusual looking book. He had been making notations and drawing sketches in the margins. As she glimpsed his crude depiction of the urn, he turned to her.

"I don't want Niklas to know. About all this."

Tears filled her eyes. "You have to tell him. He's your son. You can't just let him watch you wither away. It wouldn't be fair to him." She sat down across from him.

"I don't want him to have to deal with this. That's what wouldn't be fair. It's bad enough that you have to know. We'll just tell him I'm sick– that I'll be better. I don't want his hope taken away. I'm afraid what it might do to him. He'll know soon enough how things really are." Aaron grimaced at the thought of his impending mortality.

She stood and looked up, in the direction of Niklas' bedroom. "So you'll lie to him, and that won't hurt him? And you'll leave me to explain your lie? How could you be so cruel? He worships you. And he deserves to know how little time he has left with you!"

"There's something else." He was looking in her direction, but his vision was blurred and he couldn't see her well. "I want to be cremated."

Desta opened her mouth to protest, but he held up his hand. "And I want no service. No Shiva." Judaism interpreted

Genesis 3:19 as an essential part of the body's future resurrection. According to Jewish tradition, by insisting on cremation, Aaron was denying his mortal remains that opportunity. For dust thou art, and unto dust shalt thou return. To him, it seemed fitting.   Aaron rose to his feet and reached for her. They embraced, crying.

"Why won't you fight this? You have so much to live for." She pounded on his shoulder, holding him tight. "Why did this have to happen to you? You are such a good man. Such a good husband. Such a wonderful father. Why?" Desta sunk her face into his shoulder and sobbed.

"Not nearly as good as you might think." He sighed, deeply, reliving the onrush of terrified prayers, and then the voice he had heard so clearly. "Please obey my wishes on these things. Niklas will understand some day. He's a brilliant boy. And he'll be a remarkable man. He takes after you." Desta laughed softly through her tears and they kissed. He knew she would honor his wishes.

vi

Over the following weeks, Niklas watched his father grow pallid and frail. When he asked his mother about it, she would only say his father was not feeling well and that he shouldn't worry. But Niklas knew there was something terrible happening. His father had taken a leave of absence from his position at the University and Niklas knew he would never have done so unless he was very sick. They had visited his office at the Science Center a few times, but never stayed very long. Niklas had often used the opportunity to visit the astronomy department up on the eighth floor. But those visits grew less frequent due to his father's increasing state of exhaustion, unpredictable emotional state, and the strange seizures he was beginning to suffer from.

—⚒—

Aaron noticed Niklas squirming on the small couch in his office, clearly bored. "What are you hanging around here for, Niklas? Why don't you go up to the eighth?" The astronomy department was located on that floor and Aaron knew how much his son liked looking at all the "space stuff" they had up there.

"Is it okay, Dad?" Niklas' eyes lit up. He had been sitting in his Dad's office watching him go through his mail and reading the recent journals.

"Sure. Get going. Just be back here in thirty minutes. You're mother's fixing us a big lunch." He watched Niklas fly out the door of his office and thought about how proud he was that a young boy could take such an intense interest in science. While he had hoped his son would go into his field of study, it wasn't all that important. Aaron knew, whatever Niklas chose to do, his accomplishments would far exceed his father's.

An icicle of pain penetrated the side of his head and he flinched. His vision blurred and he grabbed his neck and squeezed, hoping to choke off the sensation until it subsided. He reached into his pocket and took out the small bottle of steroids, tossing the last tablet into his mouth with the same skill he had acquired with the aspirin.

After the pain faded, he got up and walked out of his office to the elevator, taking it down to the first floor. From there he would have to take the stairway. For some unknown reason, the elevator did not go below the first floor. He walked past the clerk, who, at first, didn't seem to recognize him, but then nodded hello.

"Oh, it's you, Dr. Koppernick," the clerk smiled. "Back again? How are you today?" Aaron had come to the basement several times over the last few months and the clerk had been able to see his declining health. But today, the shocked look on the clerk's face made it even clearer that he could see how sick Aaron was.

"Fine, thank you." He continued down the hallway without stopping, taking out his key-ring and fumbling for the right key. Just as he reached the double doors, he found it. The archaeology storeroom was not meant for the relics and artifacts members of the department collected from around the world. It was intended only as place to keep the more prosaic utensils of their trade. There were excavation tools, audiovisual equipment, old file cabinets and dozens of cardboard mailing tubes filled with the usual collection of site maps and aerial photographs. In the corner stood a brand new floodlamp, used for night excavation and photographic cataloguing. Aaron frowned when he thought about the burned out floodlamp still sitting in the middle of his basement.

He looked around, taking a brief inventory of everything in the room. Boring stuff, Aaron thought. But the more boring the better. He didn't want anything in here that would generate curiosity. The large wooden crate sat at the far end of room. He approached it slowly, almost tip-toeing, as though he didn't want to awaken the monster hiding inside it. When he got close enough to see the nail holes, he stopped. It seemed to be in the same condition it was when it left his home nearly four months before.

"Close the fucking urn," the voice said.

Suddenly, the pain struck again, only this time more intensely than ever before. He staggered backward a step, gritting his teeth, and dropped to one knee. With both hands holding the back of his neck, he looked up at the crate and, through his moans, heard the voice repeat the command over and over again, like an automated beacon sending its warning with undiminishing forcefulness. Was this the same one he had heard months earlier? The four words seemed to have an angrier tone.

Wobbly from the seizure, Aaron raised himself up and frantically looked around the room. He spotted a neatly folded canvas tarp on top of one of the file cabinets. He picked it up and covered the crate, trying to smother the voice still in his head. He pulled the tarp down so anybody walking into the room would only see the canvas. But not being able to see the crate didn't help. He knew what was underneath and inside. He could hear it. Or was it just a symptom of the seizure? Another fiendish trick his disease was playing on his mind; the tentacles of the tumor strangling new neurons and triggering hallucinations. Slowly, he took a single step away from the crate and, in that short distance, the voice faded and disappeared. He didn't care to step forward to check and see if it was still there. He continued to back up until he was against the closed double doors; he stopped and strained to hear the voice, but heard nothing. Thank God, he thought, tipping his back and looking at the ceiling. After standing there for a few moments, he glanced at his watch and left without looking back.

—〰—

When Aaron stepped back into his office he saw Niklas sitting behind his desk. Despite his experience in the basement, the sight put a rare smile on his face.

"Where'd you go, Dad? I thought you left without me."

"How long have you been perched there? I thought I'd have to come up to get you again. They throw you out?" Aaron took a slow, deep breath, smiled and began putting his mail into his briefcase.

"Oh, they're busy setting up some new sky survey or whatever they call it. They're all going over to the observatory, so I came back down. Ready to go?" Niklas got up and walked around the desk. He picked up his father's heavy briefcase and headed for the doorway.

Aaron looked around his office for a moment, not only to make sure he wasn't leaving anything behind, but also to listen. He decided what had just happened in the basement had been an hallucination. Perhaps, it was just part of the dementia brought on by the growing tumor and, in a sense, he was relieved by that possibility.

"Come on, Dad. I'm starving."

Finally, he turned and smiled at Niklas. He wanted to tell

the boy what was happening. About his illness. The urn. Even about the terrible voice. But the look on his son's face squelched the impulse before it could fully form in his head. He locked the door to his office and walked slowly to the elevator with his hand on Niklas' shoulder, believing he would never return.

Chapter 3
Kolaborator

i

On March 30, 1971, two months short of his son's twelfth birthday, Aaron Koppernick died. Despite his steady decline in health, his son had been completely unprepared for the loss. As he stood silently at his father's grave, Niklas was in a state of numbing shock. It was as if his father had been murdered two days earlier, and Niklas found himself dealing with an emotion he hadn't expected to feel: Anger.

Standing with he and his mother during the small service were the Yamashitas, the Allens, Max Rosenberg and his wife, and a few other members of the Harvard faculty who had remained close to Aaron, despite his recent erratic behavior. Niklas recognized most of the people who attended, including Dr. Allen's son, Bob, who had been wounded in Vietnam and now had to walk with the aid of a cane. What Niklas knew of the war was limited to the bloody news footage he saw from time to time on television and the conversations he heard between the teachers at school. He recalled some of them talking about how far away the fighting was, but Niklas felt differently. For the last year he felt as though he had been living in the midst of a battlefield, and the gaping grave in front of him may as well have been caused by the explosion of a mortar shell.

There were also people whom Niklas did not recognize

and he assumed they had been his father's students or had attended the University with him. One was a dark-skinned man who had a lighter-skinned little boy hugging at his leg. Niklas wondered if they could look so different and still be father and son. He didn't know how long they had been there because the two stood a small distance back from the group of mourners, and disappeared before the services were over.

Dr. Allen was very upset. He had been crying so hard that his eyes were badly swollen, and his face was even redder than usual. From a distance, Dr. Yamashita, probably his father's closest friend, looked unmoved and stone-faced. But when Niklas got a closer look he saw a steady stream of tears flowing freely down the man's cheeks. The sight caused Niklas to reach up reflexively to his own cheek. He realized, as the casket was being slowly lowered into the grave, that his face was completely dry. What he was feeling left little room for any other emotion.

In keeping with Jewish tradition, Niklas had recited the Kaddish, an ancient Aramaic poem based upon the Book of Job. He had a vague understanding of the words and how they described the acceptance of God's will. The most difficult part of the poem for him to speak was the testimony of the loving God, even though He had allowed the suffering and death of a loved one.

When the Rabbi had finished saying the Tziduk Hadin, each able-bodied person approached the grave and emptied a shovelful of soil onto the casket. This process continued until no part was left exposed to the sky. A primitive custom, it had grown in popularity during the Middle Ages, and was done to prevent the ghost of the deceased from returning to the body so it could harm any of the living whom it might consider an enemy. The dead are not allowed to take revenge. As Niklas watched the grains of dry earth cascade down onto the box holding his father's remains, he began to understand how small and alone he would be without him.

"I hate this place." He had said it loud enough for his mother to hear and she gripped his shoulder hard, trying to be strong.

"The service will be over soon, Nikki," she said. "Just a few more minutes and we'll be going home."

"No! I hate this place! Everything!" Niklas looked up at the overcast sky and held his arms out to the sides.

Dr. Yamashita and Dr. Allen came up to him after the services. Niklas really didn't feel like talking to anybody and the two men looked quite shocked at his unemotional state.

"I loved your father, Nikki," Dr. Yamashita said. "He was the gentlest, most honorable man I have ever known. And he was so proud of you." Yamashita turned quickly away and Niklas decided it was because he didn't like people seeing him cry. Dr. Allen didn't appear to have the same problem.

"I'm so sorry this happened to your dad, boy. He was such a good man. Christ, I don't think I ever even heard him cuss." A momentary smile came and then disappeared from the puffy-eyed man. "I'll miss him."

That was all Dr. Allen could manage before breaking down again. Even though his son was the one who needed a cane to walk, it was Dr. Allen who required assistance down the hill to their waiting car.

ii

Niklas knew his father had been very sick, but never expected him to die. Nobody had ever given him a warning of that possibility. His mother rarely even talked about his father being ill. Maybe it was something he, Niklas, had done to cause it. And maybe that's why nobody would talk to him about it. He had worshiped his father and everything Niklas ever strove for was measured by how he imagined his father might react to it. He thought his father had hoped he would take an interest in archaeology, because he was always bringing him to his office and sharing his discoveries with him. But from a very early age Niklas felt his destiny was in the sky. The cosmos had seduced him and, in a strange way, it had taken him from his father when he needed him most.

When he was fifteen, Niklas saw his first spiral galaxy, Andromeda, known to astronomers prosaicly as M31. It was magnificent. He had already learned that his own galaxy, the Milky Way, was a pinwheel-shaped collection of over two hundred billion stars more than 150,000 light years across. Andromeda was the Earth's closest major galaxy, and even though it was part of what was called the Local Group, it was more than 2.3 million light years away.

Niklas knew the image he saw on that day had left Andromeda eons before, when pre-humans were scampering across the African veldt. In all likelihood, the shape of the Andromeda he was looking at probably bore little resemblance to what was there at the actual moment in time he was observing it. Even traveling at the speed of light, the image took more than thirty thousand human life times to reach the telescope he was using. Sometimes, Niklas wondered if it was even there anymore. Perhaps, thousands of years in the past, it had been vaporized by some horrible cosmic event. He could be looking at a ghost, the spectral fossil of an extinct behemoth.

—⁓—

He never got the spurt of growth his father had predicted and he remained the victim of taunts right up until he entered college. In spite of those tribulations, his high school years were filled with academic achievement. He was a National Merit Scholar and spent the summer after his junior year at Oxford, attending classes for advanced high school students. He had considered enrolling in the undergraduate program there, but decided there were too many reasons not to turn down the full scholarship his father's alma mater had offered him. His transition to college life at Harvard was seamless and it brought him a joyless succession of Science awards. In three blurry years, he graduated Phi Beta Kappa, Magna Cum Laud.

It was during a summer internship program at Kitt Peak Observatory in Arizona, mid-way through his doctoral program, that he met Anna Berg, a beautiful undergraduate student from UC Berkeley who was interning there. Almost six inches taller than he, Anna was a stunning Swedish blonde, and no bully who had ever assaulted Niklas Koppernick scared him as much as Anna Berg did. Until he met her, he was used to intimidating people, but her beauty and unpretentious intelligence never failed to tie his tongue and plant a lottery-winner grin on his face. He could have done without the grin, but he adored her, and loved making her laugh. What had really put the squeeze on his heart was the way she called him "Nick". It was glorious.

He knew he wasn't the easiest person in the world to get along with and was aware many people had a difficult time dealing with his toxic personality. But from the time he and Anna had first met, the ice block on his shoulder seemed less ponderous. Falling in love with her had had a temporary healing affect on him. After years of living with the nagging questions surrounding his father's death, and having what should have been the most carefree years of his life taken from him, he had finally begun to let go and seek out his own identity.

Anna had fallen in love with his intensely brilliant mind and his biting, if not frequently obscene sense of humor. The physical chemistry between the two bordered on obsessive. By the end of the summer program, they were together constantly, both day and night. The night before they had to leave and return to their respective campuses, they lay in bed together in Niklas' apartment and talked about the future.

"What do you want?" she asked. "In your life, I mean. Tell me how you want your life to be." Anna nestled her head against his shoulder and stroked the patch of hair on his chest.

"Oh, that's easy. Time goes into this inverse feedback loop and we just stay right here for the next fifty billion years, doing it over and over and over and-"

"God, I wouldn't survive the first week." She laughed.

"Yeah, the wear-out factor. Haven't worked that part out yet. Maybe we should do a test week or something. What do you think?" He rolled over on top of her, feigning another round of lovemaking. Anna grabbed him by the hair and wrestled him onto his back. With the weight of her naked body pinning him to bed, he said, "You know, normally I won't put up with people rolling me over like that." He pretended to struggle. "But, in your case, I'll make an exception."

"Okay! Enough lust. Talk to me. Answer the question." She got off his chest and sat cross-legged, facing him on the bed, gathering the sheet in her lap as if to keep his attention on the question.

"What was the question again?" he asked. Anna yanked the thickest portion of his sparse chest hair. "Ow!" he yelled.

"Okay. I give. Let's see. How do I want my life to be? I guess science is my life. I'd like to direct an observatory some day. Maybe get involved in space platform development. I've got some pretty wild ideas about all that. Be nice to have a constellation named after me. Or maybe a quasar." He folded his arms and laid there with an exaggerated look of importance.

"Cut the crap, Nick. You know what I mean."

He could see she wanted to open him up— to find out what made him tick, and he had never allowed anybody to do that. But as he looked at her sitting there, he felt the warmth of his heart push up against the wall of his chest and his sarcastic grin softened. He reached over and took a lock of her long blonde hair in his hand and looked deep into her ice blue eyes.

"I want a home, like I grew up in, I suppose. A family." He turned onto his side and propped his his head up with his hand. "To tell you the honest-to-God truth, I've thought about it ever since my Dad died. I'd like to have a son. I'd name him Aaron. After my father. I'll never lie to him, and he'll always be able to count on me being there for him. He'll get the years I missed. You know, the really good ones, when he learns about girls and how to drive a car. He'll go out on dates, and I'll drink beer with him behind his Mother's back. And every time he does something great, I'll tell him how proud I am."

Anna sat silently for a moment and then asked, "What about your mother? You've never mentioned her. Is she still alive?"

"Oh, yeah." He shook his head, surprised the subject hadn't come up before then. "Boy, has she been through the ringer. She's a great lady, but she grieved for my dad for a long, long time, and she's been sliding in and out of depression ever since his death. She lost nearly all of her family and childhood friends in the Holocaust, and after watching Dad endure the cancer, I think sometimes she has trouble accepting her own survival. You know, the usual survivor guilt syndrome."

Anna closed her eyes and looked down. "Yes, I know about that. Went through it after my folks died. I was supposed to be on the plane with them but had to stay home for a track meet that weekend. Took me a long time to forgive myself for surviving that."

While he had been fairly tight-lipped about his parents, she had told him all about hers and their tragic death in a commercial airline accident just a few years earlier. They had been flying from Chicago to Los Angeles in one of the new DC-10s when it lost an engine and crashed just after take-off, killing all 271 passengers aboard. Niklas could tell how much she had loved them and was always amazed by her cheerful outlook on life despite that wrenching loss.

"Well, I forgive you," he said as his lascivious grin reappeared. "And I'd like to personally thank you for surviving. In fact, just to show you my deep appreciation, I'm going to–"

She chuckled against his lips, and they both continued to laugh as their mouths opened on each other. Then Niklas lost himself in a blur of long legs and swirling blonde hair. Six months later, almost to day, he went to his mother's house, to tell her of their engagement.

iii

Niklas could not have been more shocked and disappointed at his mother's bitter reaction to the news.

"You know what they did and you would still marry one of them? How can you do this?" Niklas had been right. The guilt of being the only remaining survivor of her family had filled his mother's heart with anger, and she needed someone to blame for her abandonment. It was clear to him that Anna provided her with the target she had been waiting to pounce on. She slumped in her chair and put her hand over her eyes.

"Your father would have been so upset."

"That's a lot of crap, Mom, and you know it," Niklas said. "Dad didn't have a hateful bone in his body. Your parents just filled your head with the same xenophobic bullshit that's made Europe a war zone for the last thousand years. Don't get me wrong. I loved 'em, but they were ignorant people who believed whatever gossip they heard."

She lashed back, "Don't use your language with me. Your father never used such words. And how dare you talk about my parents. All of your aunts, your uncles, your cousins– my grandparents– even my little friends– all sent to the camps! To die! And the Swedes? They pretended nothing was happening! Kolaborators! But you don't care. No! Because you never even cared about being a Jew." She had always been angry with him for never bothering to study the Torah and refusing to learn the language of his heritage.

"Mother, just because I didn't get Bar Mitzvah'd doesn't mean I'm anti-semitic." Niklas felt flushed. He had raised his voice more than he meant to and had made her weep, so he decided to back off a little.

He got up and went to a window and tried to open it, but it was painted shut. Several months after his father died, he had convinced her to make some changes inside the house. It would help keep her occupied and eliminate some painful reminders as well, for both of them. She ended up giving a lot of the old furniture away, including his father's personal chair, to some students. But she had done most of the interior painting herself. Now, most of the house's windows were like this one, glued shut by a heavy coat of enamel paint.

He came back over to her and sat down. For the first time in his life he thought his mother looked old. Her crinkled hair had streaks of gray and the skin beneath her cheeks was beginning to sag, hanging from the corners of her mouth and pulling it into a furrowed frown.

"So, you'll marry her anyway, I suppose. No matter what I or your father would think." She sounded despondent.

Niklas rolled his eyes and stood once more. "Mother, for Christ's sake, Anna was born almost twenty years after the goddamn war was over. And her parents were just kids while it was all going on." He went to the front door to leave, but something stopped him. He turned around once more, making the final effort he knew the situation warranted. "Anna and I are going to get married. And I'm not going to wait till I'm finished with my doctoral program to do it. If you can't accept her as my wife, and you decide not to attend the wedding, that's your choice. But it will be a long time before you see me again. Maybe you should think about that concept before you make any decisions you'll end up regretting."

"So what's to think about?" she said softly. "It's your wedding. You're my only son. Of course, I'll come. Just don't expect me to bring any raspberry blintzes."

Niklas didn't know whether to kiss her good-bye or stamp out of her house in frustration. He closed his eyes and shook his head. "Mother, you drive me crazy."

"For you, it's a short trip." She didn't look up.

"I'll give you a call." He turned to walk out.

"I should hold my breath so long," she muttered.

—∿—

Niklas had convinced Anna they shouldn't delay their marriage. He promised he would help out with her graduate studies, and his field research papers had already been submitted. After a brief month-long engagement, they were married in a small ceremony which his mother attended. Even the knowledge Anna was an only child and that both her parents had died when she was sixteen failed to move Desta Koppernick. Her stubborn antagonism over the first few months of the marriage caused Anna many tears and it became a sore subject between the newlyweds.

At first, Anna saw Niklas stand up to his mother. He punished her behavior by staying away, often for months. But, over time, Anna could see his attitude shifting, and he began to show her that blood, indeed, ran thicker than the ink on a marriage certificate. Eventually, he stopped coming to her defense, and, all too predictably, the closer his relationship with his mother became, the more his and Anna's grew apart.

They had tried to have children. Their lack of success in that department had not been for want of an active sex-life. In fact, sex was the most durable part of their relationship. After a few visits to a fertility specialist, it was discovered that her persistent long distance running had effected her ability to ovulate and hold a pregnancy. But she was addicted to her "running high" endorphins, and had refused to give them up. She would let her doctor deal with her ovaries. She could see Niklas was devastated by the fact that he might go through life without having a son. While it bothered her, she had lost so much confidence in the stability of their marriage that she wasn't sure having a child would be the smartest thing to do.

—⁓—

Everyone who knew Niklas Koppernick assumed that the one thing he revered above all other things was the Universe. But, to his way of thinking, the Universe was nothing more than matter feeding on matter. His profession and his own life-experience had taught him that his world, and the universe it drifted in, were capable of the most grotesque violence. The ultimate proof of which had been witnessing his own father's agonizing death. The more he learned about the Universe, the more deeply embedded his feelings of insignificance became. Eventually, he learned to master his despair by acquiring a powerful sense of self and total indifference to everything else. The Universe, benign or not, was no doubt filled with many entertaining possibilities—worm holes, dimensional rifts, even alien civilizations. But he refused to be impressed. The Universe was just a hulking, ravenous beast. To those who suggested this attitude was inconsistent with his obvious passion to learn more about the cosmos, his reply came quickly. "It's just morbid curiosity."

iv

A year after the wedding, Niklas completed his doctorate. Considered by his professors to be the next Carl Sagan, there were many large terrestrial observatories for Niklas to choose from, but KECK, with its two ten-meter telescopes on Mauna Kea, was the most prized of the bunch. Mauna Kea, a dormant volcano, had been determined to be the cleanest place on the planet for an observatory. When Niklas was offered a position there, he jumped at it. Its high altitude provided the least atmospheric distortion and artificial light pollution.

While he had enjoyed working there, Anna wasn't nearly as pleased with the facility. She had delayed her pursuit of an advanced degree in radio-astronomy in order to be with her husband. She hated the humid, tropical climate and the constant headaches that the high altitude gave her, but she tolerated it all for nearly two years. Her physical discomfort was compounded by Niklas' degenerating attitude towards her. One day, things came to a head when he walked into their apartment with a longer face than usual. Anna was lying on the bed, nursing another of her headaches.

"We just got a call from Mike Griffith at Caltech," Niklas said, not really looking to see if Anna was even listening. "It's just what I suspected. The focus of the project is being shifted to surveys. Goddamnit! I didn't come here to do fucking IR surveys!"

"Nikki, don't yell. My head's killing me. What do you want me to do about it? I've hated this place since the day we got off the plane." She growled. "Have you ever looked up 'keck' in the damn dictionary?"

"No. Why would I do that?" The question knocked Niklas off balance, and he asked himself why the name of an observatory would be in a dictionary.

"Check it out. It means 'a heaving of the stomach as in trying to vomit'!" She gave him a quick, patronizing smile, then frowned. "That's how I feel here."

"Well, if they kiss off optical research and IR is the way it's going to be, we're sure as hell not staying!" he said.

"Oh, I see. It's okay if I suffer, but just let somebody fuck with Nikki Koppernick's toy telescope and watch him go supernova."

"What they hell are you talking about?" Niklas asked.

"You know, you are the most self-absorbed, unsympathetic human being I have ever known. If I didn't know you better, I'd add narcissistic to the list."

Niklas came over and sat on the edge of the bed. He gave himself a moment to cool off, then reached over and put his hand on her knee. He didn't make these kinds of conciliatory gestures very frequently and it caused Anna to sit up.

"I know you haven't been happy here," he said. "Maybe it is time for a change. I've been thinking about this for a while. I thought we'd head back to Boston. I've been in touch with Harvard. You could finish up your post-grad at Boston U."

"Boston? Why Boston? What a minute!" She jumped up from the bed, the sudden movement causing her to wince in pain. She clutched the sides of her head and headed toward the kitchen, where she kept her ample supply of aspirin. "Have you been talking to your mother?"

"What if I have? It's not like we talk every day. Christ, I haven't even seen her in six months." He got up and followed her into the kitchenette, where he found her tossing three aspirins into her mouth.

"Yeah, and as far as she's concerned, you should leave me right here. No, make that down in the volcano. Shit. Why is it you can talk to your mother about this, but you don't say bupkis to me until after you've made your decision? Is this some kind of sick Oedipal thing, or something?" Pushing her way past him, she went back into the bedroom and started to change into her sweats.

"Look! This was a good position for me right out of the doctoral program," Niklas said. "Everybody wanted this damn job. I couldn't turn it down just because my wife got altitude sickness, for Christ's sake."

"Yeah, and what about your mother? Did you get her approval?" She pushed past him again on her way into the bathroom, closing the door behind her.

Niklas found himself talking to the door. "All right. Yes. I fucking talked to her. She's my goddamn mother, Anna! I feel bad about not seeing her more of her. If your folks were still alive you'd be talking to them, wouldn't you? She's getting older, and since Dad died she's had trouble with—"

'The Koppernicks and their goddamn guilt-trips!" she said as she burst out of the bathroom and headed for the front door.

"Where the hell are you going?" he asked.

"For a run!" She slammed the door behind her, rattling the thin walls of the apartment.

"Great! Make it a fuckin' marathon!" It was the second time he had spoken to a door in as many minutes.

v

Within two months, Anna and Niklas were making their move to the east coast. It was mid-summer of 1985 and a good time of year to make the move, before the weather turned bad. They had a month or so to get organized for their fall classes. Anna had little trouble settling into her program at Boston University, which had a blossoming astronomy department. Even though he was still quite young, Niklas was offered a full professorship at Harvard, which he accepted on the condition he would be given unrestricted access to the observatory at Oak Ridge, with a guaranteed number of hours per month that he could operate the telescope.

Oak Ridge, which was about thirty-five miles northwest of the University, was operated by the Smithsonian Astrophysical Observatory; twelve years before, it had formed a relationship with the Harvard College Observatory. This joint effort was called the Center for Astrophysics and it was within this organization that Niklas became a key player. His academic reputation and the papers he had written on the likelihood of supermassive black holes being found at the center of the large quasars had cemented his reputation in the field. His arrival at Harvard meant an increased interest in the University's astronomics program and, for Niklas, it meant the freedom to do pure research in optical astronomy.

After completing her doctoral program, Anna accepted a somewhat less illustrious position at Boston U. She was highly regarded in her field, which was in the area of radio-astronomy and microwave radiation. It had been suggested some years before that the seemingly ubiquitous microwave radiation, or "background noise" of the cosmos was a remnant of the Big Bang. While she spent the majority of her time teaching, she managed to do some research on finding ways to separate, or better filter out, the "noise" of the Universe and improve radio signal resolution.

As a side interest, Anna got involved in HRMS, the High Resolution Microwave Survey, which was on the leading edge of the search for extraterrestrial intelligence. When the project was cancelled in 1992, she joined the Phoenix program, a privately funded project scheduled to conclude in 2001. The search for ET hadn't really gained the acceptance of mainstream science or the government's budget committees, so the program relied on corporate grants, volunteerism and donated dish time. Several enormously successful science fiction movies had spurred the public's interest in the SETI program, but the events of September 11th shifted the focus away from the stars. As Niklas has once told her, "Why search the cosmos for monsters when we've got 'em right here in our own backyard?" It would be years before the search for extraterrestrial life regained its stride.

Both Anna and Niklas found their positions extremely exciting and demanding, and they ended up spending little time with each other. Occasionally, they would attend Planetary Society banquets or accompany each other to the department functions of their respective institutions. But all of these activities were performed in a perfunctory manner and, within a couple of years, their relationship fell even further into a state of entropy.

There were moments when the sparks of their early romance would flare up. Niklas often came home from Oak Ridge late in the evening, not wanting to suffer through the late afternoon Boston traffic jams. The aggravating one-hour drive in from the observatory wore on his nerves and he vowed to find a way to make his observations without having to drive there.

Sometimes, on the way home, he would stop by his mother's to chat and this would cause him to be even later. When he finally did get home, he would walk into their brownstone, pour himself a large glass of dark red wine, of which Anna always maintained an ample supply. Niklas had told her about his parent's nightly ritual, and she understood the dark red wine's symbolic significance in his life. After taking a few sips from the glass to lessen the chance of spillage, he would sit down to go through his mail and organize his materials for the following day.

Anna was a morning person. She would take her long runs before the sun was up, six days a week, so she was usually asleep by the time Niklas got home. When he came into the bedroom, he would look down at her and be overwhelmed by her remarkable beauty. Niklas had grown up wearing his "jammies" to bed, but she had what he thought was the peculiar but very acceptable habit of sleeping naked. As she tossed and turned in her sleep, she would sometimes expose a breast, or a long leg. The red wine helped provide Niklas with whatever incentive he might have lacked and he would climb into bed with her, just as naked. And she would always wake for him.

The metronome of this routine went on for several years. It was comfortable, if not fulfilling. But, eventually, Anna became deeply dissatisfied. As the new millennium approached, her career was not on as exhilarating a path as Niklas', and she was thinking more and more about setting out on her own. She was tired of teaching and fed up with snot-nosed graduate students making awkward passes at her. She never thought about meeting anyone else or even casual dating. She was just too preoccupied with her interest in Targeted Searches and Rapid Sky Surveys to think about any of that. One rainy afternoon, some news Niklas came home with helped her make the decision.

"Anna!" Niklas called out as he came through the front door.

"I'm back here. In the office." They had set up a room that functioned as a home office for both of them, with separate computers, faxes and printers for each. Anna used it more than Niklas, because it was where she did most of her correspondence with the Phoenix Project. Niklas walked in, not having taken the time to remove his dripping coat.

"I got the call today. From the NRAO and NASA. They're both on board and we're just working out the details on funding levels. The government has to get in on it now, and that'll close the deal. I can't believe it. After all the bullshit, it's going to happen." He didn't even give Anna a chance to congratulate him. "Hey, you want a glass of vino?"

He left the room before she was able to respond. A minute later, he walked back with two large glasses filled to the top with red wine.

"Here ya' go." Niklas held up his glass. "A toast. Here's to the first mobile observatory on the surface of the goddamn moon and, more importantly, never having to make that fucking drive up to Harvard again." He touched his glass to Anna's and took a long gulp.

"Congratulations. You must be very proud." Her heart wasn't in the compliment.

"Hell, NASA's been so damn politicized, I never thought they'd come across. But, hey, accidents happen." He sipped his wine, keeping his eyes on her.

Anna put her glass down slowly and turned to face him.

"Nick. Can we talk about something before you have any more wine?"

"Sure. What?" His smile started to sag.

"I've made a decision. About us. I'm moving out." She picked up her glass and took her first gulp. Niklas' mouth opened, but he couldn't seem to say anything. "Don't look so shocked. This has been coming for a long time."

"Hey, what is this?" he said. "I come in here with this great news and the first thing you do is drop an anvil on my head. What'd you do, miss your run this morning or something?"

"I never faced up to the way things really are between us. I got comfortable. I think it's great your project is going through. I knew it was only a matter of time. You're going to spend the next thirty years of your life living with it– and for it. There's no room for us in that equation, so, I just think it's a good time to make the break. That's all." She took another long swallow from her glass.

"Christ, I know things have been a little lukewarm around here, but–"

"Lukewarm? Lukewarm means there's at least a temperature. Our marriage doesn't have one. It's not hot, it's not cold, it's not tepid– It's not anything. And it hasn't been for God knows how many years." She drained her glass and went to the living room to pour herself more. Niklas followed.

"I can't change what I am. Or what I'm not. I've crawled over too much fucking broken glass to get here. Okay?"

"I'm not asking you to change. I'm the one who has to do that. So I'm the one who's moving out." She finished pouring and handed the bottle to Niklas. Without noticing it was empty, he tried to pour more for himself and frowned when only a drop fell into his glass.

"Goddamnit." Niklas collapsed on the sofa, dropping the bottle to the floor. "Don't do this. We're smart people. We can find a way to work this out. It's been too long to just walk."

"We're not that smart, Nick. Nobody's that smart. And it hasn't been too long to 'just walk'. It's been long enough." As she sipped her wine, the phone rang. Niklas got up to answer it as if he had been expecting the call.

"Hello.– Oh, hi, Mom.– I did? Sorry, I must have forgot.– I'll come by tomorrow, okay.– Say, Mom, could I call you back in a few minutes.– Yeah.– Thanks,– Bye." He hung up the phone and looked over at Anna, who was staring out the window. "I was supposed to go by there this afternoon, but I got so damn excited about things I couldn't wait to get home to tell you. Should've gone to see her, I suppose.' He laughed weakly. "Good thing I didn't get home late and try to climb into bed with you. You probably would've shot me." He went back and sat on the edge of sofa with his back rigid.

"It wouldn't have made any difference if you had gone to your mother's. We still would have had this conversation tonight. And, yes, I would have shot you." She almost smiled.

"Why don't we go get something to eat. How about that

new Italian place– LaManna's? We can talk more–"

"This is the last time we're talking about it. If we talk about it again, we'll just end up fighting, and I'm too worn out for the battle. I'm going apartment hunting tomorrow. I'll try to find something closer to the campus. Shouldn't take me long."

Niklas looked at her a moment, not really sure how he felt. "Anna– I–" He caught himself. Anna gave him a faint, understanding smile and went back into the office, closing the door behind her. Niklas remained on the couch. It was two in the morning before he finally got up and came to bed. This time, he didn't awaken her.

Chapter 4
The Line

i

As she finished her early morning eight-mile run around the array, Dr. Anna Koppernick tried to convince herself she wasn't the excitable type. Now, well past fifty, she had spent her life cultivating the detached demeanor of a highly disciplined research scientist. Any remnants of her wide-eyed youth, nurtured on the running track and lecture halls at Berkeley and Boston University, where she coasted to a doctorate in astronomy, had been dampened by seven years of unrelenting boredom.

At first, she was exuberant about her appointment to SETI and the High-Resolution Survey headquartered at the Very Large Array near Socorro, New Mexico. But her excitement quickly faded when she realized the person she was replacing had died after eleven years on the job, never once having seen even the briefest Extraterrestrial Intelligent Signal. The numbing reality was, instead of tracking ETIs, most of her time was spent running maintenance checks, reviewing routine data, programming search coordinates, and appearing before semi-literate, semi-interested and semi-sober attendees at various fund-raising events.

But Anna knew this morning could change all of that.

The size of the Array staff had not changed for years. It still required over two hundred astrophysicists, electrical and mechanical engineers, and a small army of air conditioning specialists to keep it fully operational. Of that number, fifty lived full-time at the site. Five years before, living quarters, a small commissary and even an exercise room had been added to handle the full-time personnel. Prior to that, most had lived in the nearby towns of Socorro, Datil or Magdalena. The social life, for those without families, was still relegated to the Capitol Bar on the Plaza in Socorro.

Nothing else about the Array was the same. The discovery of fossilized organisms in the subterranean ice sheets on Mars in 2009 had reinvigorated the nation's interest in making contact, and the number of dishes at the Array had been doubled during a massive 5-year long system upgrade.

Rather than the out-dated Y-shaped configuration, it was now an immense circle of two hundred fifty radio-antennas, each an eighty-one foot diameter parabolic dish. With that, the Array simulated a single interferometric radio-telescope with a fifty-mile diameter, or three times the surface area of Washington DC. On rare occasions, additional tech support was brought in to perform routine computer maintenance and upgrades. That morning, when the ETI had been picked up, a minimum staff had been present at the site, which made it easier to control potential leakage to the press.

Even though she was still recovering from her run, Anna managed to climb the long stairway up to the Signal Evaluation Center, taking three steps at a time. The event early that morning was still being evaluated, and she was pumped up with anticipation.

As she reached the top, the irony of the situation struck her. Here was the very event that had been SETI's raison d'etre and it had all but put them out of business, overnight. Any staffer not present that morning was given an immediate TLA (Temporary Leave of Absence). The rest were under strict orders not to talk about the event with their colleagues or relatives. Nobody was going to be allowed to tell the world, "The telephone works!"

Her first urge had been to call her estranged husband with the news, but some damn technocrat had squelched that. Niklas was the most renowned astronomer on the planet, with a Nobel Prize and his very own remote optical telescope on the dark side of the moon, which he directed from his offices at Harvard University. She really didn't understand why she couldn't discuss it with him. His involvement with NASA had gotten him the highest security clearance. Even higher than hers. Besides, anybody who knew Niklas knew he couldn't care less about what happened at SETI.

She slid her ID cardkey through the door's security module as she toweled the sweat from her neck. When she stepped inside the SEC, she saw three figures huddled quietly around one of the consoles. Dr. Roderick Simms, the Project Director, was the only one to look up and wave her over. The room was refreshingly cool, and dark, except for a small table light, the glow of the monitor and dozens of blinking LED read-outs scattered around the room. She could also see Dr. Carl Marks, the young African-American astronomer who was known affectionately as Commie. Next to him was a tall, slender stranger. His black hair, which was combed straight back, was in stark contrast to his almost anemic complexion. Anna thought there was something oddly familiar about the man, but she wasn't able to put her finger on it. Whatever it was, she had disliked him almost from the moment she saw him.

As the heavy metallic door automatically closed behind her, its sound made their heads turn. Simms stretched to his full height, and she could see he was again taking pride in the fact that he was the only man at the project taller than she.

"Oh, good morning, Dr. Koppernick," Simms said. "This is Mr. Willoughby. He came in on an Air Force transport this morning from Washington. He'll be our liaison with the National Security Agency till we can get a handle on the situation."

Willoughby stepped over to her, extending his cold hand. "Dr. Koppernick. A pleasure to meet you at last. I attended several of your lectures at Boston University a few years back."

She held up her sweaty palms and shook her head, indicating she couldn't shake hands. "I'm afraid it's been more than just a few years." Still out of breath from the long run, she was sucking air between words. "But thank you anyway, Mr. Willoughby. Nice to see you– again." She was tempted to ask him his first name but decided there were more important questions to be answered that morning. She turned back to Simms as she walked over to the console. "What's the verdict? Bogus?"

"You must be kidding." he said. "Whoever did this was totally transparent about it. When you think about the kind of hardware they needed to pull this sort of thing off, ya gotta wonder."

Simms had been handed the job to direct the Array for one reason. Years before, he had publicly criticized the VLA's takeover by SETI, often saying its achievements would only be covered by the tabloids. The NRAO thought his presence would give the project a more credible, mainstream image, which would make fund raising easier as well. In fact, it had. The VLA was integrated into what had once been called the Phoenix Project. It was now part of a massive distributed Array, playing a key role as the central nervous system of the Continental Array.

Several radio-observatories across the country, including the three hundred foot dish at Green Bank and the recently upgraded BETA /Sentinel survey at Cambridge, had been networked into the VLA's powerful central correlator where all incoming signals converged and were evaluated. This, in effect, had transformed the entire country into a single gigantic hearing aid that could concentrate its trillion dollar technology like a high-powered telescopic sight. It was called a Targeted Search Mode and, while scanning Epsilon Eridani in the constellation Eridanus that morning, it had earned its keep.

Commie, who was as adrenalized as Anna by the event, seemed agitated by something Simms had said.

"Hey, just because this isn't what we expected—"

"I never expected anything!" Simms snapped.

"Listen." Commie pushed back from the console. "I agree this looks phony, but just because it wasn't coded and we didn't have to use algorithms to decipher it doesn't automatically make it a hoax. Besides, who's got the technical know-how to target like this? Two hundred fifty individual transmissions, all launched simultaneously."

"What do you mean, 'two hundred fifty individual transmissions', Commie?" Anna had seen the content of the signal on the Secure E-mail Net earlier that morning, but didn't know any of the details about its source.

"The Array was targeting Eradanus. Routine search. Except the signal we got was non-converging," Commie said. "So, either somebody has figured out how to send parallel radiowaves, or each dish in the Array got its own distinct signal."

"Parallel? Impossible," Anna said. "The Array can't even be aligned for something like that. The targeted area would have to be at infinity."

"Yup," Commie said, scratching his head. "But that's the way this looks. The only other possibility is that the transmission source was at the point of reception. Just popped up on the surface of each dish. But that's just as nuts as parallel waves."

"What Dr. Marks is saying is that somebody figured out a way to keep us from tracking their signal to its source," Simms added. "The whole thing looks real flaky."

Anna could see Simms was a little too eager to write the signal off, and this time she agreed with Commie. He had been the one on station when it came in and he obviously didn't like the wet blanket Simms was throwing over the whole thing.

"I've read what the signal said, but I'd like to hear it, too. Mind playing the DAT for me?" It had been automatically recorded on Digital Audio Tape when it spiked the Array at 0130 hours the night before. Simms looked over at Willoughby, who nodded his approval. Commie was already at the DAT machine and he pushed Playback.

"Can you see the line?" the voice said.

Even though she was aware the message they had received was in perfect English, hearing it for the first time still made the hairs on the back of her neck stand up. The voice could not have been more unearthly. She supposed it could have been an electronically-altered human voice, but it just didn't sound electronic. It had tone. Even a subtle inflection of personality. Each word was flawlessly pronounced with a kind of high-speed clicking sound, like a person with a very dry throat. The image of a mantis with incongruous human lips flashed across Anna's mind.

"My granddaddy had throat cancer, and they had to remove his larynx," Commie said. "The only way he could speak was with one of those synthetic larynxes."

Anna shook her head. "I know that sound. It's more electronic than this. This doesn't sound like a device. There's no electronic phasing or metallic twang."

"Maybe," Commie replied. "I don't remember it all that well. It's just the closest thing to this I could think of."

Simms stepped over to the DAT machine and ejected the tape. "Let's get this analyzed. I'm sure it'll turn out to be obvious, whatever it is. Dr. Marks, I want you to check the signal's intensity variation at each dish. Maybe we can get an angle of declination from that. If this thing is what I think it is, a little fundamental geometry should help us figure out its point of origin. Dr. Koppernick, I'd like you to do a comparative analysis of everything we've received during the last twenty-four hours. Use bandwidth and signal strength as your benchmarks. Maybe this clown bounced a rehearsal transmission past us that we can use to fix his PO."

"I'll take the DAT." Willoughby's voice was surprisingly soft, and pleasant, and dripping with self-confidence. If ever a person sounded like he always got what he wanted, Anna thought, this was the guy.

"Let me make you a dub," Commie said. "We should hold onto the origi—"

"Can you go DAT to DAT?" Willoughby asked.

"No. Not right now," Commie said. "The back-up machine is still down. But I can make as many analogs as you want."

"Any competent audio analysis is going to require the original digital recording. Analog won't do."

Anna was unnerved by Willoughby's authoritative tone, even if he was right. He had only been at the VLA for a couple of hours and he was talking as though he was running the show. She didn't like the way he was asserting himself. NSA agents were assigned by no less than the Attorney General and she realized his authority was very real. But, until that morning, the government had kept a comfortably low profile at the project.

"Okay," Commie said. "But at least let me make a couple of dubs for us. Just in case something happens to the DAT. For protection. All right?" Willoughby nodded and watched closely as Commie made the two copies.

Anna had something else on her mind. "Aren't we missing

something here? Isn't the purpose of a hoax to fool you into thinking something is what it isn't?"

"Hey, yeah," Commie said. "I mean, what's the point here?"

Paying no attention to Commie, Simms turned to Anna.

"Sorry. I'm not following you."

"Where's the deception? I don't see it. Even if we don't understand how the signal was sent, it's still highly polarized and in the fifty thousand megahertz range. Looks to me like it's right smack dab in the middle of our parameters for a WOW. So what if it's not encoded. The fact that it's in English is easy enough to explain. Who's been broadcasting the most radio and television signals for the last ninety years?" Anna saw the expressions on Simms' and Willoughby's faces and knew she was about to lose her audience, but she gave it one more try. "Listen, if some lunatic were going to go to this kind of trouble and expense, he'd either be saying, 'This is Jesus Christ calling! Here I come, ready or not!' Or he'd make the message totally indecipherable. Try to sound completely alien. Sounding even remotely human is the last thing he would do! By the way, what part of the network picked this up first?"

"Just us," Commie said. "We were the only ones who heard it. The signal bulls-eyed every dish on the VLA. No spillage. No overlap. I was up here when the incoming signal alert went off. I about soiled my BVD's. It's not like it happens all the time around here, you know."

"Wait a minute!" Anna said. "You mean, our sleepy little corner of New Mexico is the only place that heard this? How's that possible? A signal like this should have cooked the local television reception."

"Great, we pre-empted The Late Show in Albuquerque," Simms said, wryly.

"Must have been shielded somehow," Commie said. "Maybe, instead of a wave, it was a narrow beam or focused microwave, like a maser, with some sort of exterior buffer to prevent spillage. The problem is, there would have to be two hundred fifty precisely targeted transmitters. And I mean perfect. That's the only way nobody else could hear it."

As he and Willoughby turned to leave the SEC, Simms sounded more than a little irritated with his argumentative team. "That's the whole problem," he said. "You both know it's always been VLBA policy for years that at least two arrays have to pick up an ETI for it to be considered legitimate. I've got serious reservations about this thing. In the meantime, you both have a lot of work to do."

Willoughby was expressionless as he and Simms walked out the door. In the silence of the SEC, Anna and Commie could hear the electronic locking mechanism whir as it sealed them inside.

"You know, I love working with that dude. What a supermassive shmuck!" Anna had never seen Commie conceal his opinion of Simms, and now was no exception. "Archimedes' lever couldn't pry his mind open. He's probably a charter member of the Flat Earth Society. And how'd that dick Willoughby get here so fast? Looks like he just beamed in from Zontar."

Anna laughed. The whole confrontation had fired her up. For the first time in years she was excited. Deep inside, she knew they could be on the brink of something important.

ii

Two thousand miles from New Mexico, Dr. Niklas Koppernick walked across the stage of a large Harvard University lecture hall filled with noisy graduate students. He hadn't actually taught any courses in several years, but he occasionally agreed to do what he called "guest-starring roles." The professor of this particular class was one of Niklas' associates, so he had readily agreed to the brief appearance. He put his briefcase on the lectern, opened it to remove his materials and, when he placed the small, colorful bottle of kiddie bubble-blowing soap in plain view, a wave of laughter spread across the auditorium. Niklas had a reputation for coming up with something clever for these rare occasions, which accounted for the larger-than-usual turn-out that afternoon. As he flicked the microphone with his finger, the students quickly stopped their socializing and came to order.

Leaning close to the microphone and speaking in a low, melodramatic voice, Niklas said, "Good afternoon, my name is Copernicus and, yes, I am the center of your Universe." The audience howled with laughter and began clapping as Niklas grinned. No one knew better than he how to get control of an audience of hyper-educated, intellectual over-achievers. "Good. Now that we've gotten the BS out of the way, let's talk about the shape of the Universe."

While the audience's laughter subsided, Niklas reached for the small, brightly colored bottle, which still had the plastic stick with the ring on one end taped to its side. "I'm sure you're wondering about this little toy I've brought today. Most of you are probably too cowardly to admit you used to run around your neighborhoods, screaming like you were on fire, waving these little sticks, and polluting the skies with millions of gooey little bubbles. Well, I'm not afraid to admit it. I did it. Every time I got the chance. And I got pretty good at it, too. Now for one of my better tricks."

Niklas opened the bottle and dipped one of the sticks into the gooey solution. Raising the dripping wand to his lips, he gently blew an enormous bubble, which disconnected itself from the ring and drifted out over the audience.

"There. I just constructed a scale model of the Universe— a Hubble Volume where one inch equals 30 billion light years. The surface of the bubble is a three dimensional representation of the Universe, or space. As the bubble got larger, its expanding radius represented time. So, time and the expansion of space are intimately related. Pretty routine stuff. But here's a new one."

He dipped the stick once more and then produced a second stick, which he also dipped into the bottle. It was a trick he had learned when he was a kid and it never failed to amuse the most jaded gathering. He blew a large bubble with one stick and then, by placing the second ring gently against it, was able to blow a second bubble inside the first. The audience was captivated.

"Okay, nobody sneeze. This is the Universe within the Universe trick— meta-universes to you geeks. The larger bubble, the macrocosm, now contains the micro-Universe.

And the microcosmic Universe, of course, contains its own microcosmic bubble, which I'd be happy to make for you, except I'd have to get inside the big bubble to do it. Inside that bubble is another. And so on, to infinity. Some call this sequencing 'cosmic inflation," where universes are hatched in a 'quantum foam' of energy fluctuations and wormholes. But I prefer to call this cosmic chain of realities the Cosm, and there are some very specific rules about its structure and behavior. Watch." Niklas looked up at the dual bubbles still drifting in front of him and he gently blew in their direction. When the larger bubble moved with the current of his breath, the smaller bubble hesitated and lightly touched the inner side of the larger bubble. Both bubbles immediately burst, showering several students sitting in the front row with a sticky mist.

Niklas nodded to someone at the back of the auditorium and the lights immediately dimmed. He clicked on the small light attached to the lectern and picked up the slide projection system remote. The first picture appearing on the large screen behind him was a striking computer generated graphic of his bubbles within bubbles concept. The bubbles, rather than just being filmy transparencies, had the subtle images of galaxies floating across their surfaces.

The remote clicked again and, in a series of programmed slides, the smaller bubbles began to expand until the images coalesced into a single, giant bubble with an aligned pattern of galaxies covering it.

"My Cosm theory describes a structure of reality more complex than ever imagined, with constituent universes existing within the same state, rather than in parallel, noncommunicating states. And it implies that any Universe existing within the Cosm is identical, right down to the most inconsequential detail, to every other Universe in that Cosm, no matter how vast or small it may be relative to the other Universes."

Using the remote again, Niklas brought up a graphic of two side-by-side bubbles, each the same size but with clearly different galactic patterns on their surfaces.

"Now, visualize, if you will, not only the infinite chain of the Cosm in which we exist, but all the Cosms representing all other potential causal pathways. All of the other possible realities. Infinity fully dimensionalized. This means the Big Bang created countless Universes, each with its own unique sequential evolution of events or realities."

Now the remote brought up a series of images that generated more laughter from the students. The first was the top of a traditional wedding cake, only in this case the small statue of the groom was missing and bride stood alone. "There would be one Cosm where your mother and father never met." Then the picture changed to a postcard shot of Disneyland. "In another, there's no Mickey Mouse." The picture of Disneyland dissolved into a photo of an orange grove. The next slide was of the classic Renaissance painting by Michelangelo titled Temptation of Adam. "In another, maybe Adam passes on taking the bite out of the apple. Jesus, what a dull place that would be. The point is, every possible causal pathway is manifest. And, if that's not complicated enough for you, each of these pathways exists in an infinite crescendo of sizes. So, everything that can happen, does happen, from a microcosmic to a macrocosmic scale. Like I said, bubbles, within bubbles, within bubbles, to infinity. Kinda' makes a DNA helix look like a tinker toy, doesn't it?"

Mesmerized, the audience was totally silent until Niklas said, "You know, it's okay to breathe. It was only a bubble." Niklas used the students' laughter as time to put the lid back onto the bubble bottle. When he set it aside and looked up, it was like a switch being flipped to the off position; the audience immediately quieted. Damn fun, Niklas thought, this sense of power you get when you can control so many people with a simple gesture. "I know it's difficult to imagine a Universe the size of a quark, but current Big Bang cosmology points out our own Universe was once that small. And probably much smaller. The same studies indicate that when the Universe was less than a microsecond old, the physical laws controlling the structure of the Universe were, in fact, the same quantum mechanical laws now dictating the material shape of our subatomic world. Of course, quantum mechanics doesn't influence the behavior of our macrocosmic Universe, meaning the galaxies, solar systems and stars. At least, as far as we know now."

The next image was a pre-programmed series of slides. The screen was completely black except for a small, glowing object that appeared, faded out, and then reappeared in another area of the screen.

"I would never suggest that the Universe ever acted like a quark, even a trillionth of a trillionth of a second after the Big Bang. Otherwise we would be hopping all over the place, obeying Dr. Heisenberg's laws and making all of our futures very uncertain.   But I am saying there are many congruities between cosmic structure and quantum law that are fascinating to consider. And that's how we learn and advance science–" the image of Copernicus on the screen "–by making leaps of logic into new areas of thinking some might call foolish, or even heretical."

As the audience came to its feet and applauded, Niklas gathered up the items he had brought with him and placed them in his briefcase.

"There are cosmologists, such as myself, who believe our Universe may just be a part of an unimaginably vast structure, and what we now see around us is but a needle point in a limitless tapestry. If that's even partially true, we're all even smaller than we thought. Now, any questions?"

When dozens of hands went up, Niklas paused to pour himself a glass of the stale water that had been sitting on the lectern for God knows how long. The first question came from a balding grad student whom Niklas thought looked like the classic egghead.

"Dr. Koppernick, your Cosm theory implies that there are an infinite number of these cosmic chains of universes. If they occupy the same space and time, and don't exist in different dimensions, how would they interact?"

"I would argue with the assumption in the first part of your question. There may well not be an 'infinite' number of Cosms. You saw what happened when my little double bubble moved. The collision of the two membranes caused an explosive event, for both bubbles. This is consistent with aspects of M-theory thinking that attributes different laws of physics to different universes. You have to assume that this sort of catastrophic physical incompatibility was commonplace within the first few milliseconds of the Big Bang. What, in all likelihood, started out as a whopping bubble bath has been in a reductive phase since time began."

Niklas stepped out from behind the lectern. "You look like a guy who enjoys a good bubble bath. They start out great, don't they? But after an hour or so, you're left with a few measly bubbles, and who knows where a couple of them really came from." The group laughed and Niklas stepped forward to the edge of the stage. "If you scoop up a handful of bubbles, you can watch the size of the overall mass shrink. But you don't end up with isolated bubbles, hovering above your hand. As an individual bubble disintegrates, the adjacent bubbles expand, shift and re-connect, maintaining the essence of the aggregate. If the Cosm Theory turns out to be consistent with the bubble bath analogy, we're looking at a system in which you wouldn't be able to tell where one Cosm ended and another began."

"Sounds like this big bubble bath you're describing is sort of a quantum superposition, Doctor," a cocky grad student argued. "Isn't that what you're really talking about here?"

"Oh, I hate that name. How about 'Polycosm' or 'Megacosm'? Maybe we'll have a contest," Niklas grinned. "The winning name gets a year of free lunches at the Greenhouse. Mmmmm." As the students groaned in agreement with what his comment insinuated, Niklas looked around for more raised hands, and nodded to a dark-skinned student standing at the back.

"So, Dr. Koppernick, have you drawn any conclusions about this Cosm Theory? Do you think there is some kind of purpose behind this 'bubble bath' structure?" Some students chuckled at the question, but the one asking it remained serious.

"Ah. You mean, who's playing in the tub?" When Niklas heard the laughter, he looked around the room and frowned. "Isn't that the ultimate cosmological question? The Plan, if there is one, is probably to be the last bubble standing. Maybe that's the point of the whole exercise– to end up with a single surviving Cosm. An immortal version of reality that somehow managed to avoid all the fatal accidents and mistakes of the other realities. Natural selection, on a pan-cosmic scale." He scanned the room, looking for the student who had asked the question, but couldn't find him.

iii

Two hours later, he was sitting alone in his Science Center office, putting the finishing touches on a paper he was about to publish on a globular cluster in the Fornax System. Unlike his very dry research papers, he enjoyed his infrequent speaking engagements more than he used to and found himself actually looking forward to them. They were about as close as he got to a social life and, while he was a brilliant thinker, Niklas had never been a social dynamo. On rare occasions, his friends would invite him to their cocktail parties because they enjoyed his caustic wit, as long as his hosts weren't the object of the conversation.

Niklas was well aware that his becoming the world's foremost optical astronomer had been influenced by many things, including his parents' choice of names for him. But their ignorance of astronomy and the fact that Copernicus was one of history's most mistaken geniuses had caused him some professional embarrassment later in his life. While Copernicus had been the first to state correctly that the Earth revolved around the Sun, he had gone on to claim that the obscure little star was at the precise center of the Universe. Niklas spent the bulk of his adult life atoning for the sins of his namesake– whenever given the chance, he put a good word in for the old boy.

—∿—

For the last couple of years, Niklas was most content when he was working with MOLO. Several generous international grants and the enthusiastic participation of NASA and the U. S. government had won him the greatest astronomy project in history. And, in turn, that project had won him the Nobel Prize. After five years of construction, dozens of excursions to the dark side of the lunar surface, and the tragic loss of three crew members, the Mobile Lunar Observatory was in full operation.

Most astronomers had turned away from the visible universe, to interferometric telescopes measuring the emission and absorption of microwave radiation. Some had chosen to study X-ray and Gamma ray emissions, while others were using inframetrics, Infrared or IR research, to study thermal emissions in a stone cold universe. Both of these methods had been encouraged by the limitations of optical astronomy, such as atmospheric distortion, light pollution and meteorological disturbances. You just couldn't see as far or as well with a "Big Light Bucket."

Even with those earthbound limitations, Niklas had preferred Optical Astronomy and the visible spectrum of light. He did inframetric surveys only on the most distant objects, where the light had shifted into the infrared range. Thanks to Edwin Hubble, science had known since 1929 that the Universe was in an expanding "red shift," and that everything was getting farther away from everything else.

Before Galileo's telescope, astronomers like Brahe, Kepler and Ptolemy had made incredible astronomical observations just using their naked eye. Those were the astronomers he admired most. Even Copernicus had managed to advance the understanding of the stars without the benefit of a telescope. Niklas imagined what minds like theirs could have achieved with even a little help from modern optical technology. They were the true geniuses.

Since its completion, the MOLO project had changed the world of astronomy. For years, KECK had been the gold standard. Then it was supplanted by the Interconnected VLT Observatory on Mount Parnal, in the Chilean desert, which was constructed in the late 1990's. Mt. Parnal was nearly four times the size of KECK, with four 8.2 meter mirrors.

MOLO had made them both obsolete overnight. The darkside location gave it zero atmospheric dust and distortion, zero light pollution and a twenty-four hour per day operational capability that could be matched only by the orbiting Hubble telescope, the HST. The low gravity environment of the moon had enabled the installation of an enormous five-hundred-inch mirror that could be easily re-tasked. It was built on a large, circular rail system enabling a three-hundred-sixty-degree range and, because it was located at the lunar equator, it could observe the entire celestial sphere over a year's time. Two sets of a half dozen fifty-foot solar panels were positioned far enough apart on the lunar surface that one would always be exposed to solar radiation. These stations generated a constant power supply that was delivered to the platform systems via heavily shielded underground cables.

In terms of raw magnifying power, the HST was the only one that could come close, but MOLO dwarfed its 2.5 meter mirror. And, unlike the HST, MOLO's incredibly light sensitive Charge-Coupled Device camera was mounted to a perfectly stable platform. The images reflected by the immense mirror were instantaneously digitized and transmitted by maser, directly to the parabolic dish at the Harvard Smithsonian Observatory. From there, the images were bounced off a satellite, which then relayed them to a dish on the roof of the Science Center. Niklas could review the data in real-time on a high-definition monitor just steps from his office. He didn't even have to make the three quarters of a mile drive up Garden Street to Observatory Hill. Such casual access to mankind's most powerful telescope prompted his colleagues to refer to him as the biggest spoiled brat in the history of astrophysics. Niklas would only have disputed the size reference.

MOLO had recently given him some very interesting information about the Fornax Globular Cluster, and his newest paper included stunning, sharp-focused photographs that astronomers around the world were anxious to see. As he was about to transfer his materials to a disk, his senior assistant, Dirk Anders, barged into his office without knocking. It was common knowledge in the department that this was grounds for summary beheading, but it was also true that the only thing Niklas hated more than being interrupted was having important information kept from him.

"This had better be good, Dr. Anders," Niklas said.

"There seems to be a problem with the transmission signal, Dr. Koppernick." When Dirk got excited about something, subtle remnants of his Danish accent reappeared.

Niklas got up and calmly strode down the hallway to what was fondly referred to as the "Bridge". When he entered the darkened room and sat down in front of the large monitor, he immediately saw what Dirk had been talking about. Running completely across the otherwise beautiful picture of the Fornax System was a pixel-thin line. Pale amber in color and somewhat brighter at the center, it travelled in a slight arc. Without studying the screen carefully, Niklas got up and walked over to one of the control panels. He pushed a few reset buttons and made sure all the external connectors were tight and delivering a full signal. He glanced over at the monitor and, seeing that the anomaly was still there, picked up the phone.

"Hello, this is Koppernick. Could you send someone from TechSup over? We have a video glitch of some kind— If I knew that, I'd fix it myself, for Christ sakes— How soon? Thanks." He hung up and turned to Dirk. "Let me know when the wireheads have it fixed."

—m—

Naturally, Dirk had already checked out all the connectors, the AFT and external cables before he had bothered Dr. Koppernick. He had also spent time studying the screen. Something about the image didn't make sense, so when his boss left the room, he sat back down to look at it more closely.

Except for the anomaly, the transmission was unremarkable. The more distant parts of the Fornax Cluster were visible within the field. The Fornax System was an unusual, spherically-shaped galaxy containing several globular clusters and a particularly interesting white dwarf star. They were the primary reasons Dr. Koppernick had focused his attention there for the last several weeks, and Dirk knew he had no patience for glitches in the system.

Dirk decided it would be smart to eliminate as many of the possible causes of the anomaly as he could before involving his boss again. As Koppernick's senior assistant, he managed the staff and, more important, he had the authority to re-task the telescope. As long as he could get back to the current coordinates, he could move the platform around and see whether or not an adjustment would affect the anomaly.

Figuring out the programs, inputting the altazimuth coordinates, and downloading the pictures would be the fast work. Unfortunately, MOLO itself didn't move very fast. The mobile platform the telescope assemblage sat on was the size of four side-by-side locomotives, and it moved at the same snail's pace that the old Space Shuttles did when they were being trailered to the launching pad. You could walk faster. The good news was he could access the entire system on his laptop, so he could continue working through the weekend from his apartment.

iv

A week had gone by before Willoughby finally checked in from Virginia. Anna was sitting in Simms' office, discussing her comparative analysis, when the phone rang.

"Simms speaking.– 'Morning, Mr. Willoughby." He put him on the speakerphone. "I'm here with Dr. Koppernick. I assume it's all right to put you on the box?"

Willoughby was silent a moment. "Fine, but I'm not all that comfortable talking about this on an unsecured line."

"We understand. What can you tell us?"

"My people spent three days listening to the DAT through every kind of filter you can imagine, at dozens of speeds. We brought in a linguistics expert to identify any accent or regional characteristics. We even had a psychiatrist evaluate the tone and stress level in the, uh– voice, or whatever you want to call it." The NSA agent sounded frustrated to Anna. Poor baby, she thought.

"And you got nothing?" Anna asked.

"The only other thing we could do was try to reverse-engineer it–try to duplicate it. Thought that might tell us how it was made. We sampled animal and insect sounds– musical instruments. We even tried a variation of one of those electronic voice boxes Dr. Marks mentioned. Not even close. It's not electronic. It's not biologic."

Anna suggested, "Can you send it somewhere else—"

"Nobody is better equipped than my team to deal with something like this," Willoughby said in a flat monotone.

Anna fell back in her chair as Simms leaned forward.

"Sounds like you've had as much luck as we have. Dr. Marks has learned that the signal wasn't bounced off—"

"Not over this phone. I'll be there tomorrow morning. Brief me then." Willoughby hung up abruptly without saying good-bye. When Simms and Anna looked up at each other, their eyebrows raised in unison.

Anna couldn't let the opportunity slip by. "So, we seem to have an eccentric billionaire on our hands who's smart enough to fool the NSA. Maybe we should offer him a job." The grin she had on her face was at Simms' expense. She got up to leave. "I'll be over at SEC if you need me."

She stepped outside and looked up at the hot southwestern sun. She could tell from Willoughby's attitude during the call that even the NSA was in way over its head. This was no time to have the lid clamped on so tight. They needed fresh ears on this one and she wasn't surprised when Niklas was the first person she thought of. He was one of the brightest men she knew. And the best connected. She had to contact him, but she suspected her outside calls were being monitored. She didn't want to risk her position at the VLA over what could still turn out to be some kind of billion dollar joke. She would have to be very discreet.

Anna and Niklas had been separated a year before she

took the position at SETI. Some of her colleagues had implied she got the job because of her last name. Others thought her looks had played a role. Fortunately, she was impervious to all the innuendo. She knew she was more than capable of handling the job, and her credentials were not exactly shabby. She was a secure person, and at least Niklas had always appreciated that about her. He had once told her that most people were like him, and used belligerence to mask their fears of inadequacy. She, on the other hand, was more than adequate. When she got the job, Niklas congratulated her but he also made it clear his attitude toward SETI would be the same as it was towards everything else. Anything was possible where the Beast was concerned, so he couldn't be surprised by anything she told him.

"Don't expect me to howl at the ceiling just because you've gotten a message on your billion dollar answering machine from Alpha Centauri," he had said.

—⁂—

Later that afternoon, Anna made the short but tedious drive into Socorro. It was a small college town boasting more Phd's per capita than any other city in the state. She registered at the small hotel where the back-up Techs usually stayed. She had never seen a more revolting place. Maybe the mysterious recording had been made by something resembling the huge spider she encountered in the bathroom sink. After checking the room for other alienesque creatures, she sat down on the edge of the bed and began to stare at the phone.

—⟋⟋⟍—

For the second time in little more than a week, Dirk Anders came flying into Niklas' office. Niklas happened to be engrossed in a very animated phone conversation with someone and would not interrupt it in spite of Dirk's dramatic entrance.

"Let me get this straight, Mother. Anna just called you from a motel room in New Mexico and asked you to call me so you could ask me to call her in her motel room. Have I got that right so far?– Did she sound like she'd been drinking?–Hmmmm– And she wouldn't tell you what's going on?– I see– Christ, what's the number?– Of the motel– Got it.– What about a room number?– At the motel.– Got it– Okay, okay– I won't say who's calling– Thanks, Mother.– Yes, I'll call you when I find out what's going on– Just please calm down. Have a gimlet– Yes– Good-bye, Mother."

As he hung up the phone, he looked up at Dirk with a bland expression, waiting to hear the explanation for the frantic invasion. "Ah. Dr. Anders. Why don't you just move your desk and your computer in here. It would obviously save you a lot of footwork." Niklas got a kick out of delivering lines like that with a totally bland expression. It knocked people off balance and kept them from knowing how he really felt. Dirk, however, had gotten used to this behavior and it didn't rattle him. He had been an extremely bright graduate student and, though he had finished his doctorate and could have taken a staff position at any number prestigious universities, he had asked to remain with the project. While Niklas often treated him like he was a gnat buzzing in his ear, he knew Dirk had an excellent mind and was a thorough researcher.

"You remember the video anomaly we had last week?"

"Yes, I only suffer from short term memory loss. Don't tell me we still have a problem," Niklas said, impatiently.

"Techsup checked out the whole system," Dirk said. "They even ran a test program on the Maser Transmission Circuitry. Everything checked out. So I ran some new tasking coordinates to see if shifting the platform would resolve the problem."

"You shifted the platform? You didn't lose Fornax! If you lost that galaxy, I'll have your Captain Midnight Secret Decoder Ring. And your finger will still be wearing it!"

"No. Everything's saved and backed up on disk."

This was the correct answer and the one Niklas expected to hear. He settled back in his chair.

"Okay. Good– You get to keep the ring. So, you figured out what was causing the problem?"

"Well, yes and no," Dirk said. "I shifted the platform and rotated the telescope to a different declination so it was looking, basically, in the opposite direction. And when I looked at the monitor, no anomaly. A clean picture. But when I moved back to the original coordinates, the anomaly was back again." Niklas nodded, curious. "Then I decided to do the same program again, but this time, with a stepped-rotation back to Fornax, in ten degree increments. I've got the hi-res images on this disk."

Niklas took the disk and slid it into the slot of his computer. Clicking on the disk icon, he selected the entire group of image files and opened them simultaneously. As the images popped up one at a time on his monitor, arranging themselves automatically in the sequence they were taken in, Niklas didn't utter a sound. Each was numbered and slightly overlapping the next. The pictures immediately made it clear the anomaly was a fixed object in space. With each successive move back toward the original Fornax coordinates, the anomaly gradually came into view. Because it was unblurred and slightly luminous rather than backlit by the star field, it was not anywhere near the moon, much less the MOLO platform.

"Quite unusual, wouldn't you say," Dirk said.
Niklas ignored the observation and scratched his beard. He didn't think there really was any such thing as "unusual."

"Okay, let's try something sexy," Niklas said. "I want you to run a spectrographic analysis of this thing so we can compare it to the most distant and nearby objects. Get as many degrees of arc as you can. Let's get as much comparative information as possible in every shot." As Dirk walked out of the room, Niklas leaned toward his monitor to inspect one of the images more closely. Then he abruptly slapped himself on the forehead and reached for the telephone.

—ɯ—

When the phone rang, Anna jumped six inches off the squeaky bed. She had been convinced he would not return her call.

"Nikki?"

"Please, don't call me that. You know it just irritates the shit out of me. What's going on? Mother said you were behaving a little– Swedish. You in trouble with the law?"

"It's a relief to hear your voice. I've been meaning to give you a call."

"Surely you didn't insist on this little subterfuge just to have a friendly chat. What's going on? Did you get canned or something?"

"We got a WOW." She waited for a reaction but got none. "Eight days ago. And it wasn't anything like what we expected." She heard Niklas groan on other end of phone. "God, that must've sounded incredibly stupid,– Saying we expected a message from outer space. But it's true. The problem is, Simms won't take it seriously. He's already decided it's a hoax, and the NSA liaison has the VLA in a headlock."

"His attitude shouldn't be news to you," Niklas chuckled. "He's just an over-paid technocrat. But I don't understand what that has to do with me? You're not going to ask me for money, are you? I'm getting pretty tired of supporting that trendy southwestern lifestyle of yours." She shouldn't have been surprised by his droll reaction to her news, but she was.

"The Array had been targeting Epsilon Eridani, but we're not sure where the signal originated from. We have it on DAT." Enough wise-cracking. She needed him to take her seriously.

"Oh? Eradani?" Niklas had tried to deliver the word flatly, but Anna noticed a subtle shift in his attitude.

"The reason I had to be so careful about calling you is because they've done everything but declare Martial Law at the VLA. The reason I went to all the trouble to reach you is because I think they're probably monitoring everybody's outside calls. Nobody breathes until they say so. They're locking out the whole scientific community. Smells like they're trying to bury this, Nick, and I can't let that happen. I've been here for seven years, waiting for something like this to happen and now— now these government bastards are—I need your help, Nick." Her cool scientific demeanor had left the building.

"Take a run around the block, Anna. Calm down." His impatience was legendary.

"I'm losing it here."

He spoke more calmly. "Go back to the Array. I'll make some calls. I'll get back to you tonight, around ten. Okay?"

"I'll be waiting. Thanks, Nick."

—ᴍ—

As he hung up the phone, Niklas congratulated himself. The Beast had taken its best shot yet, and it had barely fazed him. The news about possible alien contact was not a complete shock to him, but he was somewhat impressed. Although no one witnessed his moment of weakness, he did regret the ever so slight eyebrow twitch, which had occurred when Anna mentioned Eridanus. But it was certainly understandable, considering what he had just been told. Eridani was in the same window as the Fornax Cluster. It was probably just a coincidence that the WOW signal came from the same direction MOLO was looking, and was received at about the same time the strange phenomenon appeared on the far side of the Universe. Even so, if extraterrestrials had finally broken their silence, they must have done it for good reason. But it would probably take SETI months, Niklas thought, for the alien message to be analyzed and deciphered, if that sort of thing was even possible.

He decided to put a call in to his old friend, Karl Mant, who was now the managing director at KECK Observatory. Niklas subtly worked the subject of Eridani into their conversation.

"As a matter of fact, we were surveying in a line-of-sight beyond Fornax a couple of weeks ago. Didn't see anything you can't see a whole lot better. By the way, we're all looking forward to your paper on Fornax. How's it coming?"

"I just finished the formatting today, thanks. Got some shots that'll make you IR wimps cry."

"Hey, I'd be doing optical surveys, too, but what would be the point?" Karl asked. "That moon-monster of yours makes wusses of us all." Niklas appreciated Karl's humor. Many of his other colleagues hadn't taken the development of MOLO quite so well.

"Looks, uh, business-as-usual to you over there, eh?"

"Yeah. Why? You seeing something different?" Niklas' probing had piqued Karl's interest. "You spot a White Hole out there or something? Maybe we should compare notes."

"My, aren't we competitive," Niklas chuckled. "Don't have anything to share with you just yet. But you know you'll be the first. Listen, I gotta run. Do me a favor and give Fornax another look in a couple of days. Let me know if you catch anything unexpected. Okay?

"All right. I'll play your game. Just promise me you'll say hello to that beautiful ex-wife of yours. On second thought, maybe I'll give her a call myself," Karl said.

"Hey, what a great idea. Why don't you? She just loves dirty old geezers."

"Jesus, by the time you kids get back together, you'll be too old to enjoy it." Now Karl sounded more serious. He had met Anna years before, when the couple had first come to Mauna Kea, and he liked her very much. Twenty years their senior, he had developed a fatherly relationship with the couple during their stay at KECK. When Niklas called him to say they were separating, Mant had quietly wept.

"Tell it to Anna," Niklas said. "She's the one who left in the first place."

"Oh, no. I'm staying out of this one. Just tell her I said hello. I'll give you a call in a couple of weeks," he said.

"Thanks, Karl. I'll talk to you then. Bye." Niklas hung up the phone and, for a moment, began to wonder why he and Anna hadn't been able to "shit or get off the pot," as he had been known to put it. But he pushed the indelicate thought from his mind, refusing to let the subject sidetrack him. What was going on beyond Fornax and Eridani was something he was more comfortable dealing with.

He had known for a long time that KECK was configured solely for infrared sensing. If the image MOLO was seeing wasn't active in that range of the spectrum, it would be invisible to KECK. Furthermore, he knew that while KECK and Mt. Parnal were capable of seeing some of the most distant objects in the Universe, they didn't come close to the raw magnifying capability of MOLO. And yet, even with its formidable eyesight, MOLO could barely see the line. With that thought, Niklas remembered something and picked up the phone again. He quickly dialed his mother's number, knowing by this time she would be hysterical and on the verge of calling the FBI.

v

It was still early enough for Niklas to get in contact with Mt. Parnal, the most powerful optical telescope on the planet. He didn't know the director there, but the director knew Niklas by reputation. After the painfully courteous introductions, Niklas learned the VLT had not observed Fornax for many months. However, after implying that they might see something spectacular if they gave it another look, the director said he would try to schedule it in the next forty-eight hours, if the normally thunderous pre-spring weather in the Chilean desert held up and they could get a clear sky for the exposures. They ended the conversation by promising to re-connect.

vi

At ten o'clock that night, Anna was laying on her bed, exhausted but wide awake, when her phone rang. She reached for the receiver in the middle of a painfully wide yawn.

"Nick?"

"Yes. Did I wake you?" He spoke very softly.

"Uh-uh. All the bullshit that's going on has wiped me out, but I couldn't sleep if tried. Listen, be careful what—"

"Yes, I know. Don't worry. I'm just calling to say I've missed you. You never call or write." He was over-acting, so what he was saying might or might not have been a fabrication. She couldn't tell. He just sounded so phony that she could barely stifle her laugh.

"Oh, I've missed you, too, Nikki." This time, calling him by the name had been a slip. She hadn't meant to irritate him and was glad when he didn't call her on it. "Actually, I was thinking about visiting some old friends up in Boston this weekend. Are you available for a little visit?"

"That would be wonderful, dear," Niklas said, really hamming it up. "Oh, Gosh— uh, what's today— the 24th? Wouldn't you know it. I've got a symposium down at NYU all weekend. Maybe you can at least visit with Mother while you're in town."

She bit her lip. "Oh, sure. And I could bring that tape she wanted, too. You know the one. The, ah— the Polka tape."

"Oh, she would really appreciate that, dear. She was very touched by the Polka on Parade CD collection you sent her for Hanukkah last year. Just let me know when your flight is coming in and I'll have a car pick you up at the airport."

"Sorry we'll miss each other. Bye-bye." As she struggled to hang up the phone in the dark room, she rolled her eyes and groaned, "God, do we really have to visit your mother?"

—〰—

After her morning run, Anna was summoned to Simms' office without explanation. She met Commie in the doorway. They were both directed by his secretary, Angela Ryerson, to the main conference room, which was in the building immediately across the parking lot from his office. As they strode across the warming black asphalt, they grumbled about the fact that Simms was the only person on the staff who had his own personal secretary– and whatever else she might be.

"She's not too fond of me," Anna said. "Every time I go in there to talk to Simms, the room temperature drops twenty degrees."

"Gee, I can't understand why. Angie's always been sweet to me." The playful gleam in his eye gave him away. "Come on, Anna. You're competition."

"What! With Simms? Ridiculous."

"Hey, who said Angie's launching the next probe to Venus? Of course, if mammary tissue were brains, she'd have the IQ of Stephen Hawking. But, it ain't and she don't."

Angie was nice to everybody, everybody except her. It was an attitude Anna had run into many times before. She was tall, worked at staying in shape, and she had inherited her mother's high Nordic cheek bones and huge ice blue eyes. Being over fifty but looking under forty didn't help matters, either. As she and Commie stepped through the door, all six men who were standing in the large, chalk white conference room stopped talking and turned to look at her.

When Simms motioned for everybody to be seated, Anna

noticed some unfamiliar faces in the room. Willoughby had come back from Virginia with two "associates". They looked to be in their late twenties and were too well-groomed to be technicians. A few other staff members were also present and Anna nodded good morning to them as Simms called the group to order.

"Okay, folks, you all have met Mr. Willoughby from– uh, Washington. He just returned this morning and has been joined by Mr. Ashton and Mr. Rand from his office. They know who all of you are, so I'd like to just get right to the issue at hand without any more delay." Anna could tell Commie's paranoia had just spiked above the tree-line, and she had a feeling she knew what was coming as well. The two agents were a show of authority.

Simms went on. "As most of you have probably guessed, Mr. Willoughby's office is in Virginia, specifically, Langely. As the National Security Agency advisor to SETI, it is his job to supervise the flow of information between the project and the administration, not to mention the press." Simms cleared his throat before continuing. "He has spent the last week evaluating our recent– event– and has consulted with Washington on what we should do next. I want everybody to give him their complete cooperation. This is obviously an extremely sensitive situation. One mistake and we'll be hearing that Earth is being invaded on the evening news." Nobody smiled.

Simms paused and looked down at some papers on the conference room table for a moment. When he looked back up at the group, Anna saw a change in his demeanor. He looked disgusted.

"I am going to let Mr. Willoughby himself explain what we'll be doing here, and at the other SETI sites, as a result of this signal."

Willoughby, who was sitting next to Simms, stood up and began speaking in his smoothly confident voice.

"Thank you, Dr. Simms. I appreciate your cooperation on this. It is a very sensitive situation which will require the NSA to take temporary direct control of the project. All communication going out of the VLA will be monitored and only the most critical staff will have access to the SEC." This elicited an audible groan from everybody in the room.

Commie went a step further. "You can't do that! This project isn't funded by the government anymore! Especially the NSA– or whoever you work for! The Planetary Society will go ballistic when they find out about this! And what about NASA! You can't cut them out!" The veins in Commie's neck were growing more pronounced, and he seemed ready to come across the table. Willoughby didn't flinch, but Anna noticed the jaw muscles of the agent named Rand tightening. Jesus, a bodyguard, she thought.

"Don't be naive, Dr. Marks. The NSA was designed specifically for this kind of situation. We cannot allow whatever it is that has occurred here to get out until we have a fuller understanding of it. We can't tell people what has happened and then say we just don't know what it is or what the implications are. That would be incredibly irresponsible. The unknown is always more frightening than the known. So, my job– our job is to monitor the situation, and manage the interpretation of the data. We will keep Washington informed of our progress and Washington will decide when and how to release any information to the public. Does everybody in this room understand what I have just said?" Commie slowly sat back down. Nobody appeared eager to question Willoughby's authority, or his description of his mission. "I want to impress upon you all the fact that any failure to obey this directive will result in the most severe repercussions. There is simply too much at stake."

As the meeting was breaking up, Simms called over to Anna and Commie. "Could you folks stick around for a few minutes?" They nodded and sat back down until everybody but Simms and Willoughby had left the conference room.

Willoughby wasted no time. "I want the two dubs you made of the DAT turned over to me immediately. And I want to warn you both that you'll be held personally responsible for any leaks. Dr. Marks, have the tapes in Simms office within the hour." Willoughby left the conference room without waiting for an answer.

"Are you going to sit there and let him do this to the project?" Commie said.

"Look." Simms seemed as upset as Anna and Commie. "I-I,–uh, it's not my fault that the NSA has authority to do what it can do. This wasn't my idea, and there's nothing any of us can do about it. So, live with it, all right! Besides, some nut-case hoax isn't worth getting everybody–"

"Are you serious? Commie snapped. "You still think this is some sort of hi-tech one-liner?"

'That'll be enough, Commie." Anna said it as calmly as she

could. "I think he's is right. It's nothing any of us can change. Let's just hope Willoughby does the right thing." Commie looked stunned by Anna's apparent capitulation. He got up and stamped out of the room without saying another word. Anna turned slowly to Simms. "Listen, Roderick, please forgive him. He's just disappointed things are going the way they are."

Her use of his first name, a familiarity she had rarely taken, put a visible smile on Simms' face. "I understand, Dr. Koppernick– Anna. Just keep an eye on him. The situation isn't worth getting into trouble over. And I mean serious. The NSA's authority here is absolute. I'm glad to see you're being so reasonable about this."

"I think it's more exhaustion than being reasonable. I need to get away for a couple of days. Do you think that would be a problem?" She moved a little closer to him, letting him feel that she trusted him and could take him into her confidence.

"Well, No. I don't think it should be a problem," Simms said. "Do whatever you need to do. I'll fix it with Willoughby. Just don't stay gone for too long. You're too valuable of an asset to the project to lose over something like this."

"Thanks." She smiled warmly and as she walked from the room she passed Angie, who had been standing in the doorway. This time the look of jealousy on Angie's face was less subtle.

—⚬⚬⚬—

When Anna stepped outside, Commie was waiting for her. "What is with you? One minute you're–"

"Nothing's changed. I'm leaving for Boston Friday morning and I don't want anybody else coming along, if you get my drift." Anna sped up her pace, glancing behind them every few steps. "So, I backed off. You should, too. The more noise we make, the closer they're going to watch us."

Commie had to stretch his stride to keep up with her longer legs. "Thank God. I thought you went south on me. What's in Boston? Ah! You're going to see your ex-husband."

"Not quite 'ex', thank you. But, yes. If I can convince Niklas, he'll help us blow this thing wide open. And the recordings of the new signals should be all I need for that. If I can get him pissed off enough, he'll go straight to his friends in Washington– or, even better, the networks."

They rounded the corner of the main building and started up the stairway to SEC with Anna widening her lead. As Commie looked up after her, out of breath, he muttered, "Why do I feel like I should start jogging in the morning?"

They entered the room in a mild sweat, and Anna started pacing back and forth, thinking out loud. A lot was going to be happening over the next few days, and she wanted to cover all the potential bases.

"Here's what we have to do. How many dubs did you make of the original DAT?"

Commie frowned. "Just two. I could make a dub from them, but the loss of another generation would degrade the sound quality quite a bit."

Anna closed her eyes. "Ugh. Only two? You'll have to give them both to Willoughby."

"Shit, Anna! That'll be it for the original message."

Anna sat down and motioned Commie to do the same.

"Go ahead and make another dub of the first tape. Doesn't matter if it's a generation or two away from the DAT. A copy is a copy. I'll take it with me to Boston. It should be enough." Commie nodded. "The next thing we have to do is disconnect the alert system up here. Make sure you check the memory download a few times a day, and check your voice-mail as often as you can. If something comes up, I'll find a way to get a message to you. Okay?" She looked up at Commie and saw him shaking his head.

"To quote Chester A. Riley: 'Man, what a revoltin' development this is.'" When Commie saw the confused look on Anna's face, he couldn't restrain his laughter.

vii

The next couple of days were tense. By Friday morning, Willoughby and his friends were nowhere to be seen, which only served to make Anna more nervous. She didn't like not knowing what they were up to. She tried to be seen with Commie as little as possible. Their best bet was to lull Simms and Willoughby into thinking they had accepted their authority and would obey their directives. Otherwise, who knew what they might be risking.

As Anna rolled her carry-on luggage out to her car, Willoughby appeared from nowhere.

"Dr. Koppernick, good morning. Going to Boston, I hear." He sounded friendly enough.

"Yes, I still have a lot of friends up at Boston U."

"And a husband."

When he didn't say ex-husband, Anna knew he was well-informed and she would have to choose her words carefully.

"Yes, I'm afraid so. Of course, I'd need to book an appointment a month in advance just to talk to him on the phone. He's never had much time for me." Was her phony laugh too obvious?

"A shame. He and I met once, you know. But that was many years ago. I understand he has the MOLO project pretty much to himself." Willoughby had obviously done his homework.

"Oh yes. MOLO. Now that he has plenty of time for. I think they're having an affair." Anna laughed and proceeded to climb into her car, waving good-bye. "See you Monday."

Chapter 5
The Arc

i

Anna didn't like flying. She knew it wasn't a perfected science. Her parent's death was proof enough of that. But this trip was more harrowing than usual. The flight to Boston was one of three direct flights from Albuquerque and, even though there were none of the usual spring thunderheads over New Mexico, the sky was filled with what the pilot had referred to as "clear-air turbulence". It was so terrific that it had kept Anna from ordering anything to eat or drink during the entire three and a half hour flight. The thick-necked businessman who was sitting next to her had made the mistake of ordering a cup of coffee and, in the first unexpected loss of altitude, had spilled it all over himself. The flight attendants did their best to help him clean up and comfort him, and for the rest of the flight he ordered them around like his personal vassals. Anna realized, for some, the skies were not all that friendly.

When she finally got off the plane at Logan International Airport in Boston, she walked slowly down the gangway feeling drained and wobbly. It was several minutes before she felt her stomach settle down and stopped feeling the same sensation of motion she had experienced during the rocky flight. As she stepped inside the terminal, she saw

Niklas standing there, in a crowd of disheveled tourists, holding a small white sign with "Dr. Koppernick" scrawled across it. Dressed like a professional chauffeur, he had even found one of those odd little driver caps with the shiny black brim. In spite of the terrible mood the flight had put her in, his antics got her to laugh. He seemed genuinely happy to see her and insisted on playing out the gag all the way to the parking lot. He threw her carry-on bag on a beat-up metal cart with a fierce look of professional pride and led her out of the terminal at a brisk pace. Then he made her sit in the back seat of the Towncar he had borrowed from an assistant who worked part-time for a limo service. She was laughing hysterically during most of the long drive to her hotel.

"You know, the disguise is a waste of time. I mean, your scruffy beard has been on the cover of Time, for God's sakes. The guy who's following me would recognize you– even with the hat."

His grin disappeared and he looked in all the car's rearview mirrors. "They're following you? Jesus, what are you doing down there, Anna? Counterfeiting thousand dollar bills?"

"It's Willoughby." Her laughter quickly subsided. "The NSA guy. Enjoys his job a little too much. He warned us there would be 'severe repercussions' for letting news of this thing get out. Frankly, the guy scares the hell out of me, but I'm not going to let him bury this in his government bullshit." She had gotten quite angry when she saw Rand board her flight, but then realized it wasn't worth the emotional energy. She would deal with Willoughby when she returned to Socorro.

"Hey, enough shop talk. You're staying at the Wyndham, right?" He looked at her face in the mirror. "Of course, we could have a sleep-over at my place, but– nah! You wouldn't want to stay there. All that Dark Matter all over the place. You know my domestic skills were never what they should have been." She couldn't tell if his invitation was serious or not, but she was relieved when he didn't press it. They hadn't been together in a long time and she had other things on her mind. "Listen, what do you say we get you checked in, then we go to LaManna's and have a nice dinner. Talk a little. Or we could just order room service." Again, he didn't push it any further, so she decided to ignore his sloppy pass. By now, she could tell when he was intentionally grounding the ball.

"Italian sounds great! I'm starving." She remembered the quaint little restaurant quite well and also that she hadn't eaten since early that morning.

A few minutes later he pulled the Towncar into the hotel driveway and rushed around to the side to open the door for her. He refused to let her even carry her purse into the lobby, and followed her to the registration desk. After she registered, instead of going up to her room, she checked her bag with the concierge. She didn't want to leave it unattended in her room, and didn't want it left in the car while they ate dinner, either. To her relief, during the short drive to the restaurant, he allowed her to sit in the front seat.

"You're not going to wear the silly damn hat at dinner, are you? It'll ruin my appetite."

"Hey, what are you talking about?" Niklas said, pretending to be wounded. "This is a great hat. It actually belongs to a honest-to-gosh chauffeur. Besides, I thought you liked men in uniform."

"No way I'm going into a public place with you if you insist on wearing it. Unless you a eat on the other side of the restaurant."

"Oh, all right," Niklas pouted. But when they arrived at the restaurant, Anna still had to yank the thing off his head and toss it into the backseat.

Signore LaManna recognized them both immediately and personally ushered them to a table, ahead of several other couples who had been waiting. Niklas was sort of a semi-celebrity there and he had also been a regular patron for years. They ordered a bottle of Chianti and Anna started eating the stale bread sticks she remembered were always on the tables.

"Boy, you are hungry. And you look great, too. Still staying in shape, I see. Getting up at the crack of dawn and running?" She heard no sarcastic edge to the compliment or the question and was surprised she found it so easy to be with him after so much time.

"Oh, thanks. Yeah, pretty much. I try to make it around the array four days a week." The Chianti arrived and the waiter poured them each a full glass. Anna thought Chianti, with good Italian food, was the only red wine she really liked. In the past, she had gone along with Niklas' preference for dark red cabernet, because of the significance it held for him. But she didn't like what the heavy tannens and histamines in the stuff did to her. She didn't like Chinese food for the same reason. It was usually saturated with MSG, and her body just seemed to be over-sensitive to those kinds of things. "Listen, you have to hear these tapes. Something incredible is going on. We– I need your help!"

He waved her off. "Don't worry about the tapes. We'll get around to them. Why don't we just enjoy a nice dinner and we can deal with the Beast tomorrow. He'll still be there– Or is he a She?" She made an effort to relax and opened the menu as the waiter stepped up to take their order. After they ordered, she held out her empty glass and let him pour her another.

"It's not that easy, when you've been living through it like I have. This is huge, Nick. I'm convinced it's a legitimate WOW. I feel like one of the characters in that old science fiction movie where everybody is looking up with their mouths hanging open, staring at the mothership."

"Oh, that reminds me. Mother sends her love." He smiled, but Anna could see he was watching her reaction closely.

"How's Desta?" she asked.

"Tired most of the time. A little heavier. But a little less cranky. I think she's mellowing. She does all right for someone who's closing in on the big nine-zero."

"Hmmm. We all have our 'zeros' to bear." She shrugged. "I think I was twenty when I met my last friendly one." She gave him an exaggerated frown.

"Oh, bullshit, Anna. I know thirty-year-olds who couldn't carry your running shoes. And I don't think there's anybody who the zero's have been kinder to." His smile was so sincere it unnerved Anna and she caught herself blushing.

"What thirty-year-olds?" Her retort caught him by surprise

and he laughed. Anna watched him and realized they hadn't gotten along like this for more than twenty years. It was nice.

—⟨⟨⟨—

On the other side of the restaurant, Rand sat down and ordered an antipasto and an iced tea. He pulled out a newspaper and tried to look as inconspicuous as possible. He didn't know if they had seen him come in, but it didn't really matter. He would call his supervisor that night from the hotel room and report the two Dr. Koppernicks had spent the evening together. Something he knew Mr. Willoughby wouldn't like.

—⟨⟨⟨—

About an hour later, after a filling meal and catching up each other's careers, Niklas and Anna stood up to leave the restaurant. As Anna was putting on her jacket, she saw Rand sipping a cup of coffee.

"Oh, Christ, this guy has cajones," Anna said. "Look at him! He just comes right in and has dinner with us."

Niklas looked to see who Anna was talking about. "Oh? Is that the guy who's following you? Well, I think I'll go over and introduce myself." Anna tried to stop him, but knew it would be a waste of time. Niklas was wearing that ferocious grin she was all too familiar with. All she could do now was hope Rand had been trained never to over-react.

Niklas walked directly up to Rand and the agent looked up with a shocked expression. Sporting a big, friendly smile, he offered his hand to Rand, who hesitantly reached up to shake it. When Niklas spoke, he did it so everybody in the restaurant could hear him, including Anna.

"Hi, I'm Niklas Koppernick. The beautiful lady over there is my wife, Dr. Anna Koppernick. And may I just say that–" Niklas' smile abruptly vanished and he dropped Rand's hand. "–if I ever see your face again, in this lifetime, I'm going to call the United States Attorney General, whom I happen to know personally, and I'm going to inform him that I recently observed you unzip your fly and wag your pathetic little weenie at a passing school bus of second graders. I won't tell him the kids all got a good laugh out of it, but that's not important. What is important, however, is that you crawl back into your little ant farm and leave my wife and I completely alone for the remainder of your putrid little existence. And you can tell that to your buddy Quilby, or whatever his name is!" Then the smile abruptly reappeared. "Now, have a cannoli. They're excellent here." Niklas sauntered back over to Anna and escorted her from the restaurant.

The people sitting at the tables around Rand who had overheard the colorful soliloquy had a variety of reactions. Some were chuckling, but others appeared quite shocked. An elderly lady sitting nearby spilled her espresso when Niklas had made the "pathetic little weenie" remark. Rand, however, angrily motioned to the waiter for his check. As Anna stepped out the restaurant door with Niklas, she looked back at the agent once more and was met by a disturbing, wolf-like stare. Rand, she feared, had the look of a man who was prone to evening the smallest of scores.

Niklas took her directly back to the hotel. On the way, she started to laugh nervously. "God, I'll never forget the look on Rand's face when you walked up to him. That was great. Stupid, but great. By the way, do you really know the Attorney General of the United States?"

"Artie Sokolsky? Yeah. He used to be a law professor here at Harvard and his kid's an amateur astronomer. They visited the Center when MOLO first went on line. I let the kid look at the monitor and push a few buttons. Guess I made the old man a hero. Anyway, after he got the appointment, we stayed in touch. He's good people. I've been sending his kid a few pictures."

"Autographed, of course."

"Of course," he shot back. "Otherwise he couldn't get very much for them. Right?"

He told her he would pick her up at 8 AM. He had something at his office he wanted her to see, but he wouldn't talk to her about it until then. Whatever it was, he said it could wait until the next morning and that she looked like she needed the sleep. She kissed him on the cheek and said she would see him at eight.

"Jesus, married almost thirty years, and I get a dry one on the cheek," he said, as she was sliding out of the car. Before she could respond, he had put the chauffeur cap back on and was pulling out of the hotel driveway, waving good-bye and smiling.

Anna got her things from the concierge and went directly to the elevator bank. She expected to feel Rand's large hand at any second grab her shoulder, and she mentally prepared herself for the shock. She didn't really relax until the deadbolt had been engaged on her room door. She threw her bags on the bed and went through them, just to make sure the tape was still there. When she pulled it out of the "secret compartment" in her garment bag, a wave of paranoia knifed through her like a cold wind. She imagined the agent had somehow already managed to switch the tape and that, when she put it into the player tomorrow, instead of the alien voice, they would hear Polka's Greatest Hits. God! She took a shower and went to bed. The last time she remembered looking at the clock/radio on the nightstand, it was 2 AM.

ii

As Willoughby listened to Rand's account of what had happened in the restaurant, his grip on the receiver grew tighter and his white face turned a shade of hot pink. He was alone in Simms' office, but knew Ms. Ryerson's ears were alive and well just a few feet away. When Rand finished his story, Willoughby swallowed hard. "Okay. Catch the next plane to Albuquerque. Be back here by tomorrow at 0900."

Before Rand could remind Willoughby it was three hours later in Boston and that he would have to fly all night, Willoughby slammed the phone down in his ear.

Willoughby would have been more angry, but he reminded himself that the young and inexperienced agent had only been following his orders. He also knew the episode in the restaurant had, at worst, been a much needed exercise for Rand's self-control. The agency had threatened to transfer the hot-tempered young man to a foreign office, and Willoughby had intervened on his behalf. But his patience was wearing thin. Any more embarrassing public incidents like the one in Boston and he wouldn't be able to prevent Rand's reassignment to the Kabul station. He pictured the look on the young agent's face as his tormentor humiliated him in front of the other restaurant patrons. "'Ant farm', indeed."

He walked out of Simms' office and saw him whispering something into Ms. Ryerson's ear. At least it looked like Simms was whispering. He cleared his throat and Simms stood up very quickly. The reddish tinge to his cheeks made it clear what had really been going on.

Willoughby was disgusted by the career administrator, but, for the time being, he needed him. "When was the last time you were up in the SEC?"

Trying to sound officious, Simms replied, "Why, uhhh— around three this afternoon. Not much happening up there. No new activity. Pretty much business as usual."

Willoughby continued for the door then turned back to Simms. "What about Dr. Marks? Was he up there?"

"No. Weekends Commie usually goes into Socorro to visit some friends of his over at Tech." Willoughby nodded and left without another word. As he stepped out the door, his peripheral vision caught Simms leaning back to finish doing whatever it was he had been doing in Angie Ryerson's ear.

iii

The next morning, Niklas was half an hour late picking Anna up from the hotel. He knew his tardiness, and the fact that she had probably been unable to go for a long run that morning would contribute to her grumpy disposition. He could always tell when she was running low on endorphins. Whenever she had gotten testy with him, or less tolerant of his behavior, he would say, "For Christ's sake, take a run!" Sometimes the comment helped, but this morning it only made things worse. When he got to the hotel, she was waiting out front.

"Shit, Nick," she said as she climbed into the passenger seat. "If I'd known you were going to be late, I would have at least been able to run around the block a couple of times."

"Good morning, dear. Did you have a nice night?" He had been ready for it all.

"Oh, well. At least you didn't show up wearing the stupid hat." Without saying a word, Niklas reached under the seat and pulled out the hat. Before he could put it on, she grabbed it out of his hand and tossed it out the window. "Not a chance!" Niklas just grinned. It had worked. She laughed and settled back in the seat.

Fortunately, the weekend traffic was light and they got to the campus in about fifteen minutes. All the way there, he kept nervously checking all the rearview mirrors, expecting to see Rand pull up along side of them with his nickel-plated Glock 20 blazing.

When they walked into his office on the eighth floor of the Harvard Science Center, Niklas went straight to the coffee and bagels his assistants always had waiting for him in the morning. She sat down on the small couch while he poured two steaming cups of coffee and sliced a warm bagel in half.

Then he reached into the small refrigerator that was built into his credenza and pulled out a jar of his mother's raspberry jam. He spread a large spoonful onto his half, but left hers plain, the way she liked it.

"Madam?" he said, serving her the banquet.

"Thanks. Now, where's your tape player?" She took the tape out of her purse and put on his desk.

He picked it up and inspected it briefly. Then he said, "Don't worry about the damn tape. I've got something you'll find more interesting. Besides, this is analog tape."

"So?"

"So, this is the Astronomy Department. The Museum of Antiquated Technology is downstairs in the basement." He could see this did not help her attitude.

"This recording is the only reason I came here! Now you're telling me you don't have the proper equipment to listen to it?"

"You know, I really can't understand why you're making such a stink about me listening to this tape. Christ, I'm sure it'll be weeks before you guys get the damn thing decoded and have any idea of—"

"What? You mean I never told you?"

"Told me what?"

"Nick, it wasn't an encrypted signal! It was a voice transmission! In perfect English!"

After a brief look of amazement, Niklas started to chuckle.

"Don't tell me. Let me guess. It was Elvis ordering a pizza. No, no. It must have been Klatu asking for directions to the White House lawn." He collapsed, laughing, into the chair behind his desk, nearly spilling his coffee in the process.

"Nikki!"

"Okay, okay." He held up his hands in surrender. "What did the voice from outerspace say?" This, he thought, was going to be good.

"It said, 'Can you see the line?'. And, somehow, it was targeted at each individual dish, so we had no way of tracking the signal to a source. It was like the words just appeared in two hundred fifty different locations at precisely the same instant."

The patronizing grin could not have disappeared faster from Niklas' lips. He got up and left the room without saying a word. A minute later he re-entered his office carrying an old portable cassette player he had borrowed from one of the staff. He dropped it on his desk.

Along with Elvis, Niklas' sarcastic attitude had left the building. Still saying nothing, he picked up the tape, inserted it into the deck, pushed the PLAY button and stood staring at the machine. As the recording played, he shook his head and his eyebrows pressed together, wrinkling his forehead. He rewound the tape and played it two more times before he went behind his desk and sat down.

Anna removed the tape from the player and, waving it in Niklas' face, said, "It's not electronic or biologic and the NSA couldn't even duplicate it with their most sophisticated audio equipment."

Coming out of his trance-like state, he reached into the drawer of his desk and pulled out a stack of laser prints held together with a thick rubber band.

"Here. Take a look at these," he said.

As he spread the prints out across his desk, she came around to his side of the desk with a confused expression.

"What's all this?" She asked the question before looking at them. Then Niklas watched her as she focused on the pictures toward the end of the series. She gasped. "Oh, my God. What do you have here?" She picked up one of the prints and collapsed onto the couch, staring at it.

"Thought you'd be interested in these. MOLO took them about a week ago. At first we thought it was some kind of video anomaly or system malfunction. Ran all sorts of tests, washed the windows, laid off the hard stuff for a few days, but it wouldn't go away. From the sound of your tape, it seems we're not the only ones who can see this– line thing."

"What the hell is it?" She stared intently at the photo.

"Well, I can tell you what it's not. It's nothing like NGC4565." He wondered if she would know the reference.

"Northern end of Virgo?" she said.

"Very good, Doctor. In Coma Berenices. It's completely unremarkable other than the fact that it looks like a long, thin line– because we're looking at it edge-on. But, uh, obviously, this is nothing like that."

Still staring at the laser print, she muttered, "Yeah, no shit."

"This is much further out than Coma," Niklas said, picking up one of the other photos. "And its dimensions are just too great to be any kind of conventional celestial object." He looked more closely at the photo in his hand. "I mean, this looks like it's billions of light years across." He hammered his finger on the picture, fighting the normal human tendency to be awed. Had to keep the Beast in check.

"Okay, what else isn't it?" she asked.

He leaned back in his chair and frowned. He could only speculate, and he hated having to resort to guessing. But he had no other choice. "I think it's a radiant object, but it doesn't appear to be solid and it doesn't emit any infrared or ultraviolet light. I talked to Karl Mant last week, and KECK can't see anything unusual out there at all. I'm still waiting for a call back from Mt. Parnal. Maybe they'll have better luck than Karl did." This was about as frustrated as Niklas ever got. He sat back and pulled at his beard.

"You said it doesn't look solid. What makes you say so?"

"Well, obviously just another guess. I mean, if you look at it, you can see it's a little brighter at the center and fades as it widens out." His finger traced the path of the thin frown stretching the width of the photograph. "Part of that's probably because the center is closer to us and its light has to pass through a lot less interstellar dust. If MOLO focuses on an area away from the center, that part of the line looks almost translucent. Like you can almost see into it. Other than that, it just doesn't have any of the refractive qualities you'd expect from a solid object. Does that answer your question, Doctor, 'cause I sure don't think it does?"

She had already moved on to the next question. "How do you account for the arc? It looks perfectly geometric."

"Jesus, I haven't speculated this much since the first time I saw you in a bathing suit." He watched her roll her eyes. "Actually, I think the–" The door to Niklas' office opened and Dirk Anders stepped in, looking a little pale. Even so, Niklas wasn't feeling very tolerant that morning. "Dr. Anders– Wait! Don't tell me. You want your office back. By the way, sitting over there, on your couch, my lovely wife, Anna. Anna, this is President Anders. He's my boss."

Dirk seemed preoccupied and didn't act embarrassed at all by Niklas' sarcastic introduction.

"Dr. Koppernick. Pleasure to meet you. I've always had a lot of interest in your work down at Socorro." He nodded to her awkwardly and then turned back to Niklas. "Dr. Koppernick, I think you had better– you should– take a look at the monitor. Right now."

Dirk's almost frightened demeanor got Niklas' attention. He got up and motioned for Anna to follow him.

"What's up?"

Dirk abruptly stopped in the doorway and turned to look at them both and swallowed hard. "It's getting wider."

They looked at each other and then followed him to the Bridge. Several other members of the staff were staring intently at the monitor. When they saw Dirk come in with Dr. Koppernick and the beautiful tall lady, they parted like the Red Sea. Dirk took the middle chair in front of the monitor so he could adjust the feed. Niklas and Anna stood on either side of him and the rest of the group crowded in behind.

"It's hard to tell from just looking at the monitor, but the line is definitely widening," Dirk said. "I'm on full magnification right now, but, as you can see, it's still very thin. The only way to see what I'm talking about is to enlarge a section of an earlier picture and compare it to a more recent enlargement of the same area." He inserted a disk into the computer and brought up two side-by-side photos of the line on a second monitor. "These enlargements are so pixilated that they look pretty much identical. But they're not. This one was taken about six days ago. It's one of the first really good images we got of the thing. You can see the star field is in front of the line for its entire length." He turned to the silent group and appeared to be letting what he had just said sink in for a moment. He turned back to the monitor. "This shot was taken earlier this morning."

Niklas interrupted the demonstration. "How did you figure out there was any change? These blowups are filthy."

"I counted pixels." Dirk looked embarrassed.

"Excuse me. You counted pixels?" Niklas was amused.

"Yes, I counted pixels. I selected a vertical segment from the portion of the line that looked the sharpest on the actual size view and just counted how many pixels thick it was at that exact point on each blowup. Pretty simple." Dirk wasn't so smart that easy solutions eluded him.

"Okay, what if it just appears to be getting wider because it's moving closer?" Niklas said.

"First, there's no blue shift, like you'd expect to see. And, second, the resolution along the top and bottom edges isn't sharpening. If it was moving closer, it would have some measurable improvement in resolution. So far, it's unchanged."

"So, roughly speaking, how much has it widened since last week?" Anna asked, staring at the two blowups.

"Point-zero-zero-four-five degrees. It's gotten about a half percent wider in less than a week. Roughly speaking."

Niklas wasn't totally satisfied with Dirk's conclusions.

"Look, how do you know this is a trend, rather than part of a cycle? Don't you need long term data to make your kind of determination? You've only got two shots here and they're barely a week apart. We need better science here, folks. Assuming your little pixie counting is valid, let's pick the nearest, sharpest point along the line and start doing high resolution exposures every four hours, twenty-four hours a day. That should give us something in–"

Another assistant stepped into the Bridge's doorway and interrupted him, "Dr. Koppernick, Mt. Parnal's on the line."

He took Anna by the arm. "Thanks. In my office." They rushed down the hall to take the call. Niklas jumped behind his desk and picked up the ringing phone. Anna sat down and listened intently, even though she would only be able to listen to one side of what should have been a very interesting conversation.

"Hello, Dr. Keinz? Yes– This is Dr. Koppernick– Yes, I'm fine thank you, how are you." If Niklas had rolled his eyes any further back in his head they would have done a full rotation. "Doctor,– excuse me– did you ever take a look at Fornax?– Yes,– Oh, I see–Really?– I understand, Doctor. " He looked at Anna and shook his head somberly. "Well, let me know if things open up– Yes– Thank you for calling Dr. Keinz. Good-bye." As he hung up the phone he gave Anna a frustrated look. "Shit. Biggest thunderstorms in the history of the Chilean desert. They even had a staffer struck by lightning. No pictures. Not for a while. Aw, what the hell, they're not going to see anything MOLO can't see a thousand times better."

"But it would have been nice to get some outside confirmation." Anna said.

"Yeah, as a wise astronomer once said to me, 'No shit.' " He rubbed his eyes.

"What about the arc?" she asked.

Niklas, without even thinking, lapsed into his customary glibness. "A big boat, filled with lots of animals and this old bearded–"

"Jesus, Nick!" She got up and started to pace the room, waving her arms. "We hear a voice, probably from millions of light years away, describing some kind of unexplainable phenomenon dwarfing everything in the known Universe. And then we find out this phenomenon is probably growing! And, after all that, you're acting like– like yourself!"

Totally unfazed by her verbal assault, he said, "Geez, you really do need to take a run, don't you." He watched her plop onto the couch and bury her face in her hands in apparent frustration, then he said, "All right, okay. What was the question again? Oh, yeah, the arc." He went over to the couch and sat next to her. "I've got a pretty unusual theory about this." Niklas despised the adjective. As he saw it, nothing was "unusual" where the Beast was concerned. So his use of the term now got Anna's attention.

She lowered her hands and looked at him suspiciously.

"What do you mean, unusual?"

"Well, the obvious answer would be that the line is being curved by the pervasive gravitational field of the Universe. Which would mean it's not really an arc, but probably some kind of random tear that's being evened out by the shape of space itself. It's like looking at a human hair." He walked over and took a lock of her blonde hair between his fingers. "Hold a strand of it in your hand and it looks smooth and shiny. But, look at the same strands under a microscope and it looks like mid-winter tree bark. In other words, because of the enormous distance involved, the Universe is sort of rounding the thing off." He let go of her hair and touched the back of her head tenderly. Then he abruptly turned and paced the room, shaking his head.

"But you don't believe that's what's happening here." She leaned forward.

"Nope. Too easy. What we have to remember is the kind of energy we're talking about. The most distant objects we can observe with MOLO look like tiny specks of light. In reality, those things are probably some of the most powerful energy sources in the Universe. Put the biggest Quasar we've got, Virginnis, that far out and it would get lost in the background microwave noise. It would be all but invisible. The capper is that these most distant objects are probably not even half way to the damn line. It's way beyond our Horizon." He came back to the couch and sat next to her. "Let me put it this way. Prevailing wisdom believes the Universe is about fourteen and a half billion years old, but I think this line is over sixteen billion light years away." The Beast was kicking his ass now, but it wasn't playing fair.

"So, what you're saying is that the line is—so far away— we shouldn't be able to see it."

"Give the lady a kewpie doll. This thing is not going by the rulebook. No red shift. No blue shift. No infrared. No ultraviolet. No measurable radiation of any kind, or at least the kind we can identify. But, somehow, we're still seeing it. It's like the tourists have arrived a few billion years ahead of the airplane they're on. God, it has to be putting out energy of an entirely new order of magnitude." He got up and resumed his pacing. "So, to answer your question about the arc, I don't think all the matter, all the black holes and all the hypergiants in the fuckin' universe, lined up end to end, could put a dent in this thing. It is what it is. A goddamn arc." He motioned for her to follow him. "Come on. Let's go see how President Anders is doing."

Anna remained seated for a moment, ignoring Niklas, staring at the photograph of the line. She was stunned by what she had just heard. It wasn't what he had said, so much as how he had said it. Niklas Koppernick was rattled. And that scared the hell out of her.

iii

They spent the rest of the day in the Bridge, watching the monitor and speculating about what it might be. That, and not being able to take her morning run, had given Anna a terrific headache. When they finally went back to his office, she asked Niklas to take her back to the hotel.

"Hey, why not come over to my place? I'll fix you some of my famous Polish sausage and sauerkraut— we'll have a few beers— talk shop— what do you say?" Niklas enjoyed watching her fidget like a little girl.

"Oh, I don't know. It's been a long day and—"

"Come on. It's early! Jesus, don't make me feel like I

cleaned up my place for nothing." That was as hard as he would to try.

"Oh, all right. But not a late one, okay? I'm still recovering from the trip up here."

"Promise. I'll have you all tucked in by nine– ten at the latest." They gathered up their stuff and made the twenty minute drive from the Center to Niklas' home. It was a nice, one story house with a small yard. And it was, even by her standards, amazingly clean. Niklas got Anna a beer and she stretched out on the living room couch and put her feet up. He busied himself in the kitchen broiling up the sausage, chopping peppers and onions. The smell soon filled the house. He dished up their plates and brought them into the living room, setting them on the coffee table in front of the couch. Anna sat up and took a long sniff of the delicious, but totally unhealthy entree.

He could tell she was starving. She ate for about five minutes before stopping to talk. "Mmmm. Your culinary skills have definitely improved. This is quite good." She took a long gulp of the still cold beer and it felt good in her throat.

"Well, I've thought of opening up my own restaurant. I'd call it the Copernicus Cafe. But I hate doing the dishes." It was one of his less effective attempts at humor. Then he lapsed into sentimentality. "Actually, with all the speaking engagements, the paper I've been working on and the trips to DC, I haven't been home very much. Don't spend much time here. Guess you can tell by looking at the place. Hardly looks lived in. Too bad. It's nice here. What about you? How do you like living in 'for God's sake' New Mexico?"

"Oh, it's not so bad. I could do without the damn spiders, though. Big as lobsters down there. I like the dry climate and it's a great place to run. At least you don't have to dodge bullets while you're cutting your way through the air– yet. One thing's for sure. It couldn't be less like Boston!"

He took her remark wrong. "Hmmm– Guess that's what you were looking for."

"That's not what I meant, Nick. You know I love it in Boston. But things change and you just adapt. If I didn't learn to like it down there, I wouldn't have lasted the first year. And I've been there for seven." He couldn't believe the time had gone so fast.

"Say, I was thinking we could go by and maybe visit Mom tomorrow. She'd be upset if she found out you were in town and didn't come to see her."

She burst out laughing. "Your mother thinks I'm Eva Braun, Nick. We never got along. Have you forgotten all the trouble we had?

"Yeah, yeah. But she's gotten a little older and wiser and she's probably can't remember who Eva Braun was anyway." Then he chuckled. "I take that back. Mom remembers everything. Anyway, she was a wounded person most of her life. First the war, then loosing Dad the way we did. You know the list. Some people just take longer to heal than others." Niklas realized he was talking about himself as well. "Besides, the kid doesn't get around to see her much and she could use the company." He often felt guilty about not visiting his mother more often. Every time he walked into the old house he was reminded of how much he missed his father, even after all these years.

"I'm sorry I never got to meet your father. He must have been quite a man– to father such a child." He appreciated her weak attempt at humor.

"Well, you know, a lot of times I thought maybe I was adopted or something," he said. "I mean, my father was so unlike me. Handsome, intelligent, funny. Hey, come to think of it, we do have a lot in common." They laughed, but then Niklas face darkened. "I just wish he had been truthful with me about his illness. I never expected him to die, and I never got the chance to say good-bye to him. I think I've held that against him all these years. He wasn't really himself for the last few months he was alive. He had these terrible seizures and then would just sink into a pathetic kind of depression."

"Why couldn't you tell how sick he was?" Anna asked. "It sounds like it must have pretty obvious he was dying."

"I was a kid. I thought my father was immortal. Besides, I think when somebody's dying like that, you get satisfied with less and less. You manage to find hope in the smallest, most insignificant things. Anything to deny what's really happening to the most important person in your life. So, when he died, it was like– Jesus– somebody killed him." Niklas felt a lot of uncomfortable emotions rising up inside of him that he didn't want to deal with now. He got up and went back into the kitchen to get a couple of more beers. The phone rang and he picked it up before the second ring.

"Hello– Yes, this is Dr. Koppernick– Uhhh,– Oh, yeah, sure. Who's calling?– Just a second." He raised an eyebrow as he brought the phone over to Anna. "It's for you. 'Commie'?

Sounds a little stressed out."

Anna sat up straight. "He wouldn't be calling unless something bad was going on."

As he handed her the phone, Niklas asked if he could put it on the speaker and she just nodded. When he pushed the speakerphone button they heard faint music and a room full of people who sounded like they were enjoying themselves. Sounded like a party.

"Commie, I'm here with Niklas. What's going on?"

"It's hitting the fan down here. Place is crawling with NSA agents. They've locked me out of the SEC and I know somebody has searched my room because the tapes are gone. I think you should get back here. Simms said something about Rand and your husband having a confrontation." Niklas grinned.

"Yes. I'll tell you about it later," Anna said. "A lot more important stuff has happened up here. We have visual confirmation."

"Huh? What do you mean, 'visual'? Of the line? You've seen it? Fan-fucking-tastic!"

"Where are you now?" she asked.

"In Socorro, at the Capitol Bar. They know I usually come here on weekends so it didn't attract much attention when I left. I got your husband's number through the University exchange."

"Good. Pick me up in Albuquerque tomorrow. Call the airport and find out when the flights are coming in." She looked at Niklas, who was shaking his head. "I'll be on the first morning flight out of Boston, okay?"

"I'll be there. Jesus, this is incredible! See you tomorrow!"

Anna hung up the phone and looked at Niklas. "The son-of-a-bitch is going to cover this up. He's going to keep the biggest discovery in history in box. Shit!"

"Why do you need to go back there tomorrow morning? It'll still be there Monday," he said.

"It's Commie. He's an emotional guy. A kid, really. Smarter than hell, but sometimes he has trouble knowing when to keep his mouth shut. I'm worried about him. Sounds like he needs some moral support." She came back to the phone and called the airport, booking the first flight out the next morning, which took off at 6:15 AM. As she put the receiver down she said, "God, this trip is going to kill me. You think I'm going to sleep a minute tonight?" She was frantically gathering up her things, and Niklas could see that she expected him to drive her back to the hotel immediately.

"Hey, what's this? Leaving so soon?" he said. "The sleep-over invite hasn't expired yet." He was looking for his car keys as he said it, because he knew that once Anna decided to go somewhere, she was as good as gone.

"Nick, I have to be at the airport at the crack of dawn. I have to pack, get cleaned up– check out. I just need to get back to the hotel. All right?" She all but dragged Niklas out to his BMW. As they were driving to the hotel, he did some fast thinking.

"You know, I assume you came up here this weekend for some help with what's going on down there. But I think what you have in mind is just going to make things more difficult for you."

"You're telling me. This clown Willoughby probably can't wait to interrogate me. You know, there's something about him— I can't quite put my finger on it. He reminds me of someone." All of a sudden she looked terribly tired.

"What are you talking about?" Niklas asked.

"Oh, never mind. When he sees MOLO's pictures and finds out a roomful of people at Harvard have been studying this thing for the last week, he's going to go critical mass. But he won't be able to do a damn thing about it."

"Listen, I don't think you should tell Willoughby we talked about any of this. You just had a nice visit with your husband. A dinner. Couple of beers. A little hanky-panky." He got one of those little grins.

"I don't know if he'd buy that. Just because he works for the NSA doesn't mean he's a total imbecile."

"Very funny. Let me worry about it. I'll think of something. It wouldn't be smart for you to put a guy like this Whiggleby into a corner. The best way to deal with him is to make a pre-emptive strike. Hit him with all you've got from an unexpected angle, when he's least expecting it."

"So, what do I do in the meantime?"

"In the meantime, you lie through your teeth. And let me get in touch with you. No sense in running up your own phone bill." Niklas liked playing games with bullies. He liked being able to push them around. And he would really enjoy yanking the NSA agent's chain.

"Don't wait too long." They got to the hotel a few minutes later and, before she slid out of the BMW, she leaned over and kissed him on the lips. He could smell the beer and spicy food on her sweet warm breath. And he could smell her smell. The familiar, clean, soapy scent that used to drive him nuts. At that moment, he knew he would do whatever it took to help her. As she slid out of the car, all he could do was stare at her, completely speechless. Something was changing.

iv

Early the next day, Anna boarded an airliner bound for Albuquerque. Even if her closest friends had seen her that morning, they might never have recognized her. With no pre-sunrise run, no time to put on any make-up and no sleep the night before, it was the closest she had ever come to looking her age.

The flight back to Albuquerque had been more pleasant than the one she had taken from there a couple of days earlier. Smooth all the way. And no pompous executive ordering the flight attendants around. She actually managed to eat and get a little sleep during the trip. Twenty minutes from arrival, she went into the lavatory and did a little primping. No sense in scaring Commie out of a year's growth. She tried not to worry about what was going on at the Array. Niklas would come up with some way to deal with Willoughby and they would be able to get some outside people involved.

The landing jarred her out of a light sleep. Anxious to see Commie and get back to the Array, she scrambled to be one of the first to de-plane. As she walked into the terminal, she kept looking for him, but couldn't spot him anywhere. Then, just as she was about to head for the ground transportation area, Angie Ryerson walked up.

"Dr. Marks couldn't make it. I told him I wouldn't mind picking you up. I had to be in town this morning anyway." Despite the friction existing between them, Angie was being friendly, even helpful, and it was a pleasant surprise.

"Oh, well, uh,– sure. Thanks for meeting me. Is Commie, er– Dr. Marks all right?"

"Things are awfully tense out at the Array, Doctor. That Willoughby has kind of taken over and he treats everybody like shit– uh, I mean, he's very rude– to everybody. Even Dr. Simms. I don't know who he thinks he is. I thought he was just supposed to be some kind of government liaison. He acts like they're bankrolling the whole project." It sounded like Angie had had a run in with Willoughby. Or Simms had. In either case, she seemed to have decided it would be better to have Anna as an ally than to continue with her attitude.

"What's Roderick have to say about all of this? He talks to you about it, doesn't he?" Anna didn't think there was any point in playing stupid about the special relationship Simms and Angie shared.

"Roderick– I mean, Dr. Simms is furious! I think he's really sorry he cooperated in the beginning. Now Willoughby just orders him around and has done everything but move into his office."

When they reached Angie's car, a small two-seat convertible, she opened the trunk and put Anna's carry-on into it. There would have been room for nothing else.

The seventy-five mile drive back to the VLA started with Angie raving about how terrible Willoughby had been treating Simms. She seemed to be completely oblivious to what had been going on in the SEC over the last couple of weeks, or at least she hadn't mentioned anything about the message. Eventually, their conversation came around to more personal subjects.

"You know, Angie, I really don't know anything about you. How did you come to work in Socorro?"

"Oh, I used to work for Dr. Simms at the NRAO. When he came to SETI, he offered me the job as his executive assistant. I really hated living in Washington, so I jumped at the job. Of course, I really like working for him. You probably guessed that a long time ago." Angie looked over at Anna with a sheepish smile. "He's just so intelligent and handsome. Don't you think?" Anna could see that Angie was watching her closely, looking for some tell-tale sign of interest.

"Oh, yes, but Dr. Simms really isn't my type. I like short, bearded guys, you know. They say they have bigger telescopes." Anna smiled and watched Angie laugh until she contracted a terrible case of the hiccups.

After a couple of miles and a minute or so of holding her breath, Angie had cured them and turned to Anna. "I hate those damn things. I get them every time I laugh too much. And they hurt, too." Angie paused for a moment and then turned back to Anna. "You know, since I came here, I've watched the men look at you, Doctor, and I've heard them talk about you. I've never seen or heard anything disrespectful. I mean, they never treat you like a–you know–"

"Like a woman?" Anna offered with a sarcastic grin.

"You know what I mean. You're here because you've got

brains and experience. I'm here because I have Roderick. I think that always pissed me off about you. And it wasn't right. I probably haven't been very nice."

"Don't beat yourself up about it, Angie," Anna said. "And don't discount how much you help Dr. Simms. He thinks the world of you and if you didn't do a great job, he would never have brought you down here to begin with."

"I know, I know. He's very demanding– About work, I mean." Angie blushed and then changed the subject. "What about you, Dr. Koppernick?"

"Please, call me Anna."

"Okay– Anna. Where'd you come from? And what's with all the running? I could never jog. It hurts too much." Angie grimaced as she put an arm across her ample bosom. "But I'd kill for your legs."

Anna chuckled. "I ran track at Berkeley, where I went to grad school. Did a little high jumping and long jumping, but I loved the eight-eighty. My favorite thing. I just love running. I guess I've been hooked on endorphins since I was a kid. Anyway, I actually went out for track to meet guys. But it didn't work out. I think a lot of them thought I was gay or something. You know, tall, jock girl who never wore make-up, from the Bay area. The guys just ignored me. I ended up spending most of my time in the library or the observatory. I think I had about two dates the whole time I was in college."

"They were just afraid of you," Angie said. "They didn't want to get rejected by someone who was so beautiful, so they stayed away. Always happens to the prettiest girls. Men can be such pussies." Both women laughed as the sports car entered the small mountain range just outside the Plains of Saint Augustine. By the time they reached the Array, Anna felt she had defused whatever tension there had been between her and Angie. As they pulled into the Administration Building parking lot, she thanked her for the lift and gave her a hug, then asked her for one more favor.

"Angie, could you keep your ears open for me? I mean, if you hear anything about what Willoughby is up to, could you please let me or Dr. Marks know? It's very important. Especially the things he says to Dr. Simms. There's a lot going on and the only way we're going to get on top of the situation is to stick together."

On the way back to her room, Anna dropped by Commie's room. She had to knock several times before he finally came to the door.

"God, am I glad you're back. Sorry I couldn't pick you up, but I'm under some kind of damn house arrest, if you can believe that shit!" He looked extremely agitated. He grabbed her bag and started to walk her to her quarters.

"That's preposterous! What happened?" Anna was as angry as she had ever been.

"It was about a nanosecond after I hung up the phone with you. Two of Willoughby's Klingons yanked me out of the Capitol and brought me back here. Willoughby started interrogating me about who I was calling and what I had said to my friends. I kept waiting for a big bald guy with no neck to come in and pull out my fingernails."

"Jesus, Commie. What did you–."

"I didn't tell him shit! So he got pissed and told me I

couldn't leave the Array until he spoke with Washington tomorrow. Guess they don't work weekends." They entered her room and he put her bag on the bed. "Okay. What happened in Boston." He walked over to the window and peered out between the curtains. "Did you bring anything back with you?"

"Something really strange is happening." She walked over the couch and plopped down, exhausted from her two-day trip.

"Yeah, the LAPD has taken over the VLA!"

"No. That's not what I'm talking about. Something strange is happening out there." She pointed up as she got up and walked over to her purse. She removed a large manila envelop from it and took out a stack of what looked like color laser prints, held together with a rubberband. Then she whispered. "You want to know what the line is, take a look at these babies." She spread the pictures out on her bed. "The line is a celestial object that has appeared well beyond our Horizon line, beyond the edge of the observable universe. It's been all but invisible to terrestrial observatories because of its distance and the fact that it's not emitting anything in the infrared, or ultraviolet range. Not even any x-ray emissions."

Commie was staring at the pictures. "This is– incredible! he said, struggling to keep his voice low. "Look at this thing! It must be– huge. Wait a minute. What do you mean, it's way beyond our horizon? If that was true we wouldn't be looking at these pictures. Even MOLO wouldn't be able to see it."

"That's what I said."

"Well, what's your husband think it is?"

"He hasn't got a clue. And that's got him rattled. Me, too."
She went back to the chair and sagged into it. "It doesn't
seem to be behaving like anything we've ever seen. And it
appears to be getting wider." Was her fear showing?

"The voice," Commie said. "I always thought it sounded a
little scared. They could be a lot closer to this thing than we
are." Anna could see the look of excitement on Commie's face
transform into an expression of deep concern. "So what do
we do now? The place is locked down tight. Willoughby has
no intention of sharing this information with anybody. My
guess is he's got his people leaning on every other station in
the VLBA network."

"A classic paranoid." Anna's voice was filled with disgust.

"Hey, that makes two of us!" Anna was aware Commie
had never even gotten a traffic ticket, much less been taken
into custody by federal agents. He gathered up the prints,
wrapped them back up with the rubberband and waved
them. "We need to get these to CNN my pronto. Or the UN.
Or Larry King!"

"The pictures, by themselves, won't do anything. They're
too easily faked. We need everything to come out together
and make sure it's presented in a calm, scientific manner.
That's the only way something this strange is going to be
taken seriously. If we handle it wrong, it'll just end up on the
Discovery Channel, sandwiched between those erectile
dysfunction commercials. Niklas asked me to keep quiet until
I heard from him. Based on what's gone on here, I don't see
we have any other choice."

A forceful knock at her door startled them both. Anna

dropped the laser prints into the wastepaper basket and then opened the door.

"Ah! Welcome back, Dr. Koppernick. How was Boston?" Willoughby somehow managed to walk into her room without appearing to barge in. Anna knew he had probably perfected this skill only after years of practice. He didn't even look at Commie.

"Boston was quite nice, thank you. I wish I could have stayed longer." She was very cool, determined not to let the agent rattle her cage. As he glided across her room like some apparition, she finally realized what had seemed so oddly familiar about him and the thought helped sustain her phony smile. He reminded her of the old actor who had played Dracula. Pale, thin, with black, slicked-back hair and the effervescent personality of the Undead. When the image of a wooden stake crossed her mind, she almost laughed, but then decided there was nothing that funny about this particular bloodsucker.

"And how is the other Dr. Koppernick? I understand he managed to find some time for you after all."

"Yes, I was shocked. I called him when I got into town and he insisted on seeing me. I think he's a little lonely. Hasn't been nearly as exciting up at Harvard as it has been here, don't you think?" She smiled the most empty smile she could manage. "We did bump into your Mr. Rand at a nice little Italian place we used to frequent. Imagine my surprise. Small world." She could see that her attitude was getting to him.

He stalked over to the door and as he was leaving, he said, "Dr. Koppernick, before you leave the Array again, please see me first. I'm sure Dr. Marks can fill you in on everything else that's required. Welcome back."

As he closed the door behind him, Anna thought, "Buy garlic!"

"You know, this is going to sound really stupid, but does that guy sort of remind you of that old monster movie actor, Bela Lugosi?" Commie asked.

v

On that Sunday morning, Niklas made the ten minute drive to his mother's house to check in on her. She was eighty-seven years old and, despite having a lot of physical problems, her mind had been completely lucid. However, he was starting to see that her surprisingly clear recollection of events in her distant past was not always a good thing. Her fond memories of Warszawa, and walking through the Rynek Starego Miasta, the Old Town Square, holding her mother's hand, were as clear as ever, and she often talked about them with her son. But she had also told him how frightened she was when her family had barely escaped the invasion by the Nazis. ZOB, the Jewish combat organization, had been instrumental in getting many refugees out of Poland. She could describe in the great detail the fear in her mother's eyes. And she would clutch her stomach as she recalled how sick she had gotten during the long voyage to America.

His maternal grandfather had been a auto mechanic in Warsaw and his grandmother worked part-time in a bakery. They had left Poland with several other families, among them, the Koppernicks. Like most Varsovians, they became clannish, and, despite the disparity in their educational backgrounds, they stuck together and provided each other with a valuable support system. Aaron's father had been a college professor and spoke English quite well, and this had given his family a distinct advantage in the New World. So in 1953, when Desta Weiss became engaged to the Koppernick's son, her family was over-joyed. And greatly relieved.

It had all happened long ago, but she still wept sometimes when she spoke to him about them. Too frequently, she said it was like yesterday that they had all celebrated her wedding to his father, her "handsome Aaron".

Niklas pulled into the empty driveway of the old house at around 10 AM. His mother hadn't driven for years and had no need for an automobile. Inside, she had coffee and hot biscuits waiting for him, as well as a freshly made supply of his favorite raspberry jam.

"Anna was in town yesterday," he started. The subtle approach had always eluded him.

"Oh—, I didn't see her. She was here and didn't even call? Strange she didn't mention it when I spoke to her last week on the telephone." It was an act he had seen before. His mother was pretending to be angry about Anna not calling on her. But she hadn't had the energy to hate for many years.

"Well, you haven't seen each other in a long time, and you haven't exactly made an effort to keep in touch with her, either. She was going to come by today, but she ended up having to rush back to New Mexico unexpectedly. I think they got a message from some Martians or something." Niklas grinned.

Desta chuckled. "And they said what? Take me to your leader, I suppose." She began to laugh at her own joke, but a coughing fit stifled her. Congestive heart failure does that, Niklas thought, as he got her a glass of water.

"You know, Mom, I think my feelings about Anna have never really changed. Maybe that's why I never pushed her to sign the divorce papers. I think we just made things too tough on each other. She's quite a girl." Niklas laughed to himself when he realized that the term "girl" still worked for Anna.

"What do you mean, 'we'? You make things tough on everybody, Nikki." Desta said. "She couldn't take it, so she left."

"I think things were a little more complicated than that, Mother." He still didn't like it when his mother wagged her finger in his face.

"So, now you want to recon– reco–uh–what's that word? It's–"

"Reconcile, Mom. The word is reconcile. I don't know. When she was here, it was just like old times. I guess I never realized how, uh–"

"Odludny, Nikki. Lonely, to you. Don't talk to me about lonely. It's been more than forty years since your father passed. You want to talk 'old times'? There's only three people left from the old Wailing Wall. Only three left out of all those dear friends. Everyone else gone." Tears were welling up in her eyes, and Niklas got up and handed her a napkin. While she dabbed her cheeks, he poured her another cup of coffee. "Nikki, I love you. You've always been a bright boy. But you've made a paskudztwo where your heart is concerned. A mess. If you're lonely, you have time to do something about it. Your Universe and her Martians shouldn't hold it against you."

"The Beast holds everything against me." He smiled, realizing his cynicism was stubborn as ever.

"Well, don't let your Beast make you into a beast. It shouldn't get the satisfaction." She sipped her coffee. She was doing what she liked best. She was being a mother and her words rang true.

There was a time when Niklas had assumed that learning the secrets of the Beast would give his life meaning and substance. When he was a child, looking at the heavens through his five dollar toy telescope, he saw a divine order and beauty that appeared close enough to touch. But as he grew older, the opposite had proved to be the case. As a scientist, he saw only chaos and cataclysm.

Lately, though, he was beginning to realize that he might have had things backwards. He had been depending on the Universe to bring meaning and value to his existence. Now it was dawning on him that his life should be giving the Universe meaning. Perhaps, once he could accept that in his heart and not just his cerebrum, the Beast could be tamed and he would be freed from his emotional straight-jacket. But it hadn't happened yet. Something was blocking it and Niklas didn't have a clue what that something might be.

He laughed and sat back in the uncomfortable kitchen chair. He tried to remember what his parents had been like together all those years ago. His mother had changed so much. What would his father have been like now? Would they be friends? Questions he had never gotten the opportunity to ask. So now, he thought, was as good as time as any to ask her a question she had never really answered to his satisfaction.

"Why didn't you ever tell me how sick Dad was? I mean, I was a pretty tough kid. Mentally, anyway. Why not just tell me? I never even had a chance to say good-bye to him." Niklas accompanied the question with a faint smile, trying to soften the effect of what he knew would open an old and deep wound.

Desta turned slowly to Niklas and frowned. "He made me promise things, Nikki. He wanted things a certain way, and he didn't want you to know. He didn't want you to have to look at him every day, knowing he was dying. If you found out how sick he was, he wouldn't have been able to explain things to you."

"What 'things'?" Niklas leaned forward in his chair.

"That he refused treatment," Desta said. "He wouldn't even explain it to me. It was like he was punishing himself for some terrible sin. I'm sorry. I should have found a way to tell you, but I promised him. I promised too much." She started to weep softly and Niklas thought there was something else bothering her. Something she was holding back.

"What is it, Mom? What else did you promise?" Niklas instantly regretted asking her the question. He wondered what good it could possibly do to open these old wounds. Both he and his mother were damaged people, hurt by his father's short-sighted decisions so many years before.

"Aaron— your father— he insisted on being cremated." She stopped weeping and looked up at Niklas. "He didn't even want a Shiva. I told him it was wrong— a disrespect for the living, but he was a stubborn man. He said someday you would understand, but I could never bring myself to tell you."

"You mean we buried a coffin filled with ashes?" Niklas stood up, stunned by the revelation.

Desta looked across the room with a vacant expression. "No. It's my greatest shame. His ashes weren't even there."

"What?" Niklas fought to control his emotions.

"I had to beg the Rabbi." She began weeping again. "He would only do the service if I agreed not to put your father's ashes inside the coffin. He said cremation was against the kevod hamet— a disrespect for the dead. I told him I wanted you to say the Kaddish, but with no service, that couldn't happen and your father's soul would be lost." She cried harder and Niklas sat down, taking her by the hand.

"Where's Dad, Mom? Where are his ashes now?"

"In the basement— a cedar box. You wouldn't go down there again after he died, so I thought it would be a good place to keep them." She stood slowly, touched his cheek and went to the basement door. Niklas got up and helped her down the stairway he hadn't used for thirty-seven years. At the bottom of the steps he paused and looked around. The room was much smaller than he remembered.

Images of his father's smiling face flashed in his mind as he recognized the musty smells that still lingered there. Most of the old junk had been taken away and the clutter was missing. It was a barren and lifeless place now. A fitting Mausoleum, he thought. Desta walked across the room to one of the old filing cabinets and opened the top drawer. When she started to reach inside, he gently took her arm.

"Don't disturb him, Mother. Not now." Niklas went around to the opposite side of the drawer and looked down on the plain, undistinguished wooden box containing the worldly remains of his father. "Goddamnit, Dad." Tears began to stream down his cheeks. Desta reached over and touched her hand to his face again.

"I am so sorry, Nikki. I broke my promise to your father by having the service, and then I never told you the truth. I couldn't do anything right. Please forgive me. I just didn't know what else to do. I felt so guilty. So ashamed. And I took it out on the people I loved– you and, I think– I know, Anna." Niklas looked up from the dust-covered box to his mother's pleading face and he began to understand many things that had happened between them.

"You did everything you could." He slowly pushed the file cabinet drawer closed. "He had no right to put you in that position, Mom. It wasn't fair." He walked his mother up the basement stairs and switched the light off as he closed the door behind them. They sat down at the kitchen table and he poured he another cup of coffee. After sitting in silence for a couple of minutes, he heard her sigh deeply.

"How is your lovely Anna doing?"

The sudden shift in the conversation could have been a symptom of her advancing age. Or maybe, deep in her memories, she had discovered some subtle link between his relationship with his father and the troubles with Anna. And maybe getting all the painful secrets out had removed a great burden from her heart. He looked up at her and smiled. She seemed calmer now. Even relaxed. Niklas decided he would keep things that way.

"She's got some excitement going on down in New Mexico."

"Oh, yes, the Martians." She took another biscuit.

"Actually, we're pretty sure it's not the Martians. Somebody a lot further away. She needs some help. I think I may head down there in the next few days."

Desta smiled. "Ahhhh! And while you're down there, you'll tell her she lives too far away."

He had decided not to tell her what it was all about. He didn't understand it himself, so how could he expect her to. Her biggest concerns were her friends and her son. And he figured those things gave her all the worries she needed. The revelations of the day had been cathartic for him and seemed to jar loose old emotions. Perhaps, he thought, this was the beginning of a healing process he and his mother had never been able to go through. And maybe now, the timing was better for other things as well.

                              vi

After guiding their talk to less stressful subjects and another hour or so of visiting, Niklas got up, cleared the coffee table and then helped her clean up the small kitchen. He asked her if she needed him to go to the market for her or anything like that, and she castigated him for implying she couldn't manage things herself. Smiling, he kissed her on the forehead and in less than a minute, he was back on the road.

On the way home he decided to stop by his office. He was interested in checking out the status of the line and he needed Dirk Anders to do some things. When he arrived, the image of the small cedar box was still haunting him, until the news Dirk had pushed it from his thoughts.

"You're sure about this?" Niklas was incredulous.

"As sure as I can be about anything. It's definitely generating some kind of thermal emission." Niklas could tell by Dirk's subtle accent that he was alarmed.

"Hmmm— How fast?" Niklas sat down in his chair without taking his eyes off Dirk.

'That's the other thing. It looks to be moving faster than three hundred thousand kilometers per second. A lot faster. And accelerating. I know it sounds crazy, but–"

"No. Not crazy. Just impossible. Faster than light?"

"I think it's all the line's thermal and particle energy catching up with its own image. Like a sonic boom trailing after the jet creating it. Except this boom is accelerating, so the jet gets caught this time. Breaks just about every law of physics, but it does have a certain elegant logic to it. I think–"

"So, eventually, everybody who can see the line is going to be hit by this wave of energy?" Niklas grimaced. "Jesus, just when I thought I could have a few laughs about this thing it steals my fire. Okay– Good work, Doctor Anders."

"Thought I was President?" Dirk managed a brief smile.

"You've been promoted. Now, the Jeopardy Bonus question is whether or not, over the next few hundred million light years, this thing's energy is going to be absorbed by the interstellar plasma,– decay on its own–or–"

"Or flood us out?" Dirk's face was slack and expressionless. Niklas knew it wasn't because he didn't realize what he had just said, but exactly because he did. He had used a benign analogy to describe an indescribably catastrophic event. Nearly a minute passed before either of them spoke again.

"Okay. We have some work to do." Niklas put his hand on Anders' shoulder, which, on the six foot tall Dane, was just about even with his eyes. "I think, as far as the line is concerned, we stick with the MOLO program. But I want to try something else with this wave of yours. It's still too far out to know the relative distances between bodies, so let's use Local Group density as a benchmark and just take a wild guess at its rate of acceleration. I think it would be a good idea to start putting it on DVT."

He squeezed Dirk's shoulder and led him down to the Bridge. Not many people knew MOLO had this capability because real-time digitized video of celestial events was normally considered a waste of time. On that scale, things moved so slowly that suns could be born and die in the span of the most subtle galactic movement. Even so, Digital Video Tape could give them high-quality, high-speed playback capability that might reveal some clue about the light wave's properties, in the same way sped up film of a clock revealed the movement of its hands. Anders said it was a great idea and went to pick up the phone.

As he was about to leave the Bridge, Niklas turned to

Dirk. "Oh, and Dr. Anders? What's your week like?"

Dirk seemed confused by the question. "Uhh—"

"Keep it open." Niklas smiled and returned to his office. Sure that Dirk had all the help he needed, he had some important phone calls to make. Time to call in some big favors.

Chapter 6
The Plains of Socorro

i

Anna was already more than half-way around the Array as the Sun neared the horizon early Wednesday morning. She had run every day since her return from Boston and was just starting to get her legs back. She couldn't believe that a three-day lay-off could get her so out of condition, and thought it might have been the stress of the trip and the situation at the VLA wearing her down. She hadn't been sleeping well either, and spent a lot of time reading and catching up on letter writing. Every time she sealed an envelope, she wondered if some jerk at the National Security Agency would be steaming it open and redacting portions he felt were a threat to national security.

She also had spent a lot of time thinking about Niklas. He had changed. Sure, he was still a shark-toothed curmudgeon, but he seemed less bitter– even less self-absorbed, if that was possible. She had been surprised at the way he opened up so easily during their brief, but sentimental conversation about his father. What a shame the two of them had never been able to share a glass of the dark red wine he liked so well and discuss the exciting work they were both doing.

As her long stride carried her past another of the big parabolic dishes, she thought of Niklas and said out loud,

"Where the hell is he?" She had almost called him three times since Sunday night and it had taken all her will power not to call Desta and try to set up another motel connection like she had the week before. "He said he was going to call, and he's going to call." She said it sucking wind between each word. She had to take Niklas at his word, but her nerves were wearing thin and she was seriously considering taking action on her own. After all, she wasn't totally unconnected. But she sure as hell wasn't bosom buddies with the Attorney General of the United States.

The brilliant orange sun had popped above the horizon and she could feel its heat warming the backs of her legs. She still had a mile to go when she heard a heavy thumping noise behind her. When she turned around to see what it was, she was temporarily blinded by the sun's glare. She could feel the deep basso-profundo thump-thump-thump deep in her chest. As she wiped the perspiration from her eyes, a large, dark form began to take shape just above the mountains, about three miles away.

"What the hell is that?" she thought aloud. And then, when it was almost upon her, she realized what it was. The Marine Corps' new Assault Turbo-Chopter. It looked like a giant black locust. She had read about it in a science periodical. The military had made its development public just a few months before, with great fanfare. These things were high-tech hunter-killers designed for duty in Mideast. They had Smart Anti-Tank Missile capability, could carry the new EBB's— Extra-Brilliant Bombs— and, if they had to engage in ground support, they had ELF, the nasty Extremely Low

Frequency Laser mounted in the nose. Heavily armored, it was impervious to small arms fire and RPGs. Very fast. Lethal. U. S. tax dollars doing what they do best. When it occurred to Anna that the money it took to build just one of these killing machines could fund her entire program for nearly a decade, she turned around, running backwards, and flipped it a double bird.

The Chopter flew directly over her and headed toward the VLA complex, about a half mile away. All sorts of ugly scenarios raced through her mind as she continued her run at as fast a pace as she could manage. In all likelihood, this was something Willoughby had cooked up to intimidate the VLA staff. A show of military force. If somebody tried to drive off the site without his authorization, they would have to hide from this bad boy.

The Chopter came in gracefully toward the asphalt parking lot and slowly descended, kicking up a huge whirlwind of sand and dust. The pilot must not have been running his noise dampeners, because the thing was making enough racket to wake the dead. As Anna rounded the last dish and headed toward the parking lot, she could see people pouring out of the buildings, among them Simms, Willoughby and several of his agents. Strange, she thought. Maybe he wasn't expecting its arrival. But if this wasn't Willoughby's doing, whose was it?

The Chopter cut its rotor engine and the turbo-jet which gave it such great speed. Then it just sat there for a few moments while the rotor wound itself down and the noise abated. A group of about twenty early risers had gathered in front of it, keeping more than a safe distance from the slowing double-edged props.

Suddenly, the side door of the Chopter lifted up and two figures jumped down onto the now dust-free asphalt surface. One of them reached back into the craft and grabbed two briefcases, a dufflebag and a black suitcase with wheels. Anna recognized the passengers. It was Niklas and Dirk. They both crouched down needlessly as they ran out from under the double props. Anna could see Niklas' grin from a hundred yards away and it gave her goose bumps.

Just about everybody there knew who Niklas was, and Anna saw Simms jogging forward with his hand extended. Willoughby wasn't moving. The Chopter had had a powerful effect. Anna hoped it was sending a message directly to Willoughby's limbic brain that these visitors had friends in very high places. Not only that, they had also just used one of the Army's most expensive and, up until quite recently, most secret weapons of war as a private taxi service. She thought it was one of the greatest entrances she had ever seen.

The two scientists stopped short of the group and Niklas set down his things when he spotted Anna. She ran up and gave him a long hug.

"So, who do you want me to kick the shit out of first?" Niklas said. "Just point 'em out!" The others hadn't been able to hear his words, but they definitely heard his laugh.

Anna was grinning broadly. "What did you do? Where did you get that thing?"

"You ain't seen nuthin yet, kid." They both approached the group. Dr. Simms shook Niklas' hand and picked up his suitcase and briefcase, which he insisted on carrying. Nobody had offered to carry Dirk's dufflebag.

"Nice to see you again, Mr. President." Anna gave Dirk a warm smile.

He shook her hand and laughed shyly. "It's 'Doctor' now. I got promoted."

Leading both men around by the arms, Anna made the introductions, saving Willoughby for last.

"And this is our NSA advisor, Mr. Willoughby." She looked Willoughby right in the eye. Her cavalry had arrived.

Willoughby stepped forward and extended his hand. "How do you do, Dr. Anders." After shaking hands with Dirk, he turned and offered his hand to Niklas. "And Dr. Koppernick. A pleasure to finally meet you. Did you enjoy your flight?" Willoughby came across as smooth as ever, but Anna could see the suspicion etched on his face.

"Oh yes," Niklas said, giving Willoughby a dead-fish handshake. "I especially liked the part where we strafed the tour bus. A real E-ticket. Say, haven't we met before. You look really familiar." They all started towards the administration building.

"It's possible. I was on the security staff during a couple of your MOLO shuttle missions. Got to spend some time in Boston. It's been a long time. I'm flattered you remember. So, what brings you to the Plains of Socorro, Doctor?" Willoughby's expression was emotionless.

"Hey, where can a guy get a toasted bagel and some hot coffee around here?" Everybody laughed, except Willoughby, who remained stoic. Anna was trying to figure out what was going on inside him. He probably didn't like having his questions ignored, but he was being surprisingly patient. The group made its way to the commissary. Commie showed up just as they reached the door. Anna intercepted him and, again, handled the introductions. He shook hands with Dirk first and then turned to Niklas.

"Nick, this is Dr. Carl Marks, one of our hotshot radio-astronomers. Dr. Marks, Niklas Koppernick."

"Call me Commie, Dr. Koppernick." He smiled and reached for Niklas' hand.

"Commie? I would have preferred Groucho or Harpo, but, then again, I'm short and Jewish. Come to think of it, so was Karl Marx." More laughs as they crowded into the commissary. Anna thought, considering the tension they had been experiencing at the VLA for the last several weeks, the scene was amazingly cheerful.

Everybody dispersed inside the commissary, getting their own versions of breakfast and sitting in their usual small groups. Anna, Commie, Dirk and Niklas took the largest table and, in few moments, were joined by Simms and Willoughby.

"So, Dr. Koppernick, you never answered my question. What brings you to the VLA?" Still as smooth as ever.

Abruptly turning to Willoughby, Niklas said, "Dr. Anders and I are here to share some interesting astronomical data with Dr. Simms and Dr. Koppernick. It's sort of technical, sciency stuff. Not really your field, Mr. Quilby." Niklas had sounded phony before, but Anna couldn't recall just when he had been quite so transparent about it.

Anna stood up and asked if anybody wanted more coffee

and Niklas and Dirk both said yes. She didn't even look at Willoughby or Simms as she turned away from the table.

—ᴡᴡ—

"I may not be a scientist, Doctor," Willoughby said, smiling again. "But the government seems to think I can be of some use down here."

"The government's thinking again? Well, this is unexpected news." Niklas was ready to pounce. The agent was just as creepy as Anna had said and Niklas was anxious to put him in his place. But then he realized something about Willoughby. A large grin grew on his face when it suddenly dawned on him that his subconscious had made some kind of a connection. He now knew what was so familiar about Willoughby, and was about to make his observation known to everybody at the table when Anna set his coffee down in front of him.

"Um—why don't we get you guys situated in the visitor's quarters and then we can meet later over in the large conference room? Commie, could you show Dirk to his room? We'll come over and get you around 9 AM." Everybody nodded and, as they all stood up to leave the commissary, Simms stalked over to Anna and spoke quietly, but not so quietly Niklas couldn't pick up on what was being said. He guessed Simms wanted him to hear the admonition, but didn't have the nerve to say it to him directly.

"What's going on here?" Simms said. "You know Willoughby isn't going to stand for being locked out of this. You're putting me into a very difficult position here."

"What are you talking about? Willoughby isn't being shut out of anything. Nobody is. That's the whole point of this meeting." Shaking her head, she stepped out the door with Niklas.

On the short walk to his room, she squeezed his arm and began to explain what had been going on at the Array since her return from Boston.

"You know, I love watching Willoughby squirm like this, but are you sure alienating him right off the bat isn't just going to piss him off? Jesus, even Simms is upset."

Trying to sound serious, Niklas cut her off. "Do you guys have an overhead projector and a Blu-Ray player in your conference room? I rented some really hot porno flicks."

As usual, she ignored his remark. "Uhhh– we've got the player and I'm sure we've got an overhead somewhere around here. What do you have?"

"The only way you're going to get someone like Willoughby off your back is to make it real obvious he's no longer in control of the situation. So we're going to put on a little presentation, and the more people who see it, the better. A lot's happened since Saturday, Anna. That's why I just decided to just show up without calling. A little shock value."

"Hmmm– and shocking it was. How'd you manage to hitch that ride? Scared the shit out of me."

"Hey, I don't mess around. Cost me about two million frequent flyer miles. Worth it, don't you think? I could have rented a Hyundai, but it just wouldn't have been the same. By the way, I saw your two-fisted salute. For a second I thought you'd found out I was coming."

"Nick." She groaned his name, and he decided it was time to cut back on the relentless sarcasm.

"The outfit that built the ATC also manufactured some of the lunar observatory components, so I got to know a lot of the corporate bigshots. Did the trip from Albuquerque in about fifteen minutes."

"Jesus, is there anybody you don't know?" She managed a sarcastic grin of her own as they reached the door of the guest quarters. She followed him into the room and showed him where the towels and other motel-like amenities were located. "So, how long are you staying?"

"They're sending the ATC back for us tomorrow, which should give us plenty of time. Got some wild stuff here. Not sure how it's all going to play." He knew "wild" was the wrong word. "Scary" would have been much more accurate. The thought made him turn serious for the first time that morning. "You been all right?"

"Yeah. Tired. It's amazing how draining doing nothing can be. Thanks for asking. I'm glad you're here." To Niklas' surprise, she came over and kissed him on the lips, then turned to walk out. "See you in forty-five."

As she closed the door behind her, Niklas thought, "Damn. The timing could have been a little better for that. Damn." He sat down on the bed with his briefcase in his lap and took out the small disk and the envelope with the film cells. He knew what he had to tell these people would ruin their day.

ii

The Main Conference Room was standing room only. Almost all of the scientific staff was there, in addition to the National Security Agency people Willoughby had brought in the week before. Niklas and Anna were the last to walk in and Dirk was already setting up the DVR and the overhead projector. Willoughby was sitting at the head of the long conference table with his arms folded across his chest. As soon as he saw Koppernick, he called for people to take a seat, if they could find one. Once people had settled down, he stood up and addressed the group.

"Ladies and gentlemen, as you know, we have a distinguished guest. Dr. Niklas Koppernick, from the Harvard Smithsonian Observatory and Director of the Mobile Lunar Observatory project, has paid us an unexpected visit and he would like to share some important 'astronomical data' with us. I would like to remind everybody that certain security restrictions are still in place." Willoughby nodded to Niklas who had made his way to the front of the room. Before Willoughby could re-take his seat, Niklas laid his briefcase down right in front of his chair.

"Excuse me, Mr. Quilby. If you don't mind–" Niklas had all but pushed Willoughby off center stage and, again, had refused to show him any respect. Willoughby hesitated, then stepped aside and went fuming to the opposite end of the conference room. There wasn't a chair left for him to sit in until one of his agents finally offered him his seat. Willoughby took it without showing any appreciation for the gesture.

"I'm Niklas Koppernick. Sorry about all the noise this morning, but I don't do rental cars." Everybody, except Willoughby and his agents, chuckled. Niklas surveyed the room and saw Rand sitting just to his right. "Ah, Mr. Rand. Good to see you again. The kids were asking about you." Niklas took momentary delight in watching the veins in Rand's temples and neck distend, then he addressed the entire gathering. "My associate, Dr. Anders, and I are here to share an interesting discovery. Three weeks ago, the Lunar Observatory detected an unusual phenomenon at the extreme boundary of the visible Universe, in the general direction of the Fornax System. At first, we thought this phenomenon was a video glitch or a transmission anomaly, but all indications are that it was neither. The reason we'd like to share this with you today is to alert SETI of the sighting and to request that you target your search in that area, which, as you will see, is damned big." Niklas nodded to Dirk.

Dirk stood up, cleared his throat and took over the presentation from the back of the room, where the overhead projector was located.

"On March 10th, MOLO was focused on a White Dwarf in the Fornax System. During a photographic survey of the object, we inadvertently captured another image." Dirk clicked on the overhead light and an image appeared on the large screen behind where Niklas sat. The room went dead silent. It was a beautiful color slide of the Fornax System and the White Dwarf star. But it was also a picture of the line. Using a laser penlight, Dirk pointed out the areas he was talking about on the projected image. "As you can see in the deep background, there is a thin arc which traverses the entire photograph." He put a new cell on the overhead. "This is a closer shot. As you can readily see, it passes behind the star field and has varying brilliance, with its brightest point right here." He pointed to the center of the arc. "There is a dark area, right here, either in front of or within the phenomenon itself. It may be a very dense nebula or an extremely large cloud of Dark Matter. We're not sure, yet. But, whatever it is, it's ultra massive."

Everybody in the room appeared dumfounded. Except Willoughby. For the first time, he looked visibly upset. Niklas noticed the shift in attitude and assumed the agent was angry because his little secret was a secret no more, and he would never be able to contain the event now.

"Did you contact any other observatories to verify this?" Simms asked. Niklas could see he was holding onto his skepticism like a drowning man to life vest.

"Not right away, Dr. Simms," Dirk answered. "But they-"

"Ah, well then, how can you be so sure you don't just have some kind of technical glitch here?" Simms asked the question but didn't seem interested in an answer.

Niklas stepped in. "As Dr. Anders said, the phenomenon is behind the star field. So, if it's a glitch, it's a damn clever one. Pay attention, kids."

The usually animated group of scientists now sat very still, their eyes fixed on Dirk as he proceeded.

"We've found that this phenomenon does not emit anything in the infrared or ultraviolet ranges of the spectrum. There is no measurable gamma-ray emission, either. So, it would be invisible to inframetrics. The line was only barely visible to MOLO." Turning to Simms, Dirk emphasized his next point, "So we're confident no terrestrial observatories have been able to see it."

Commie asked, "How far out is it?"

"We're not exactly sure, but it's on the order of fifteen or sixteen billion light years," Dirk replied. The group of scientists seemed to blink in unison and Niklas wondered if it could have been a flinch.

Simms' demeanor turned somber, as he closed his eyes and rubbed his forehead.

Niklas thought, "Right now, Simmsy boy, you're thinking maybe your voice from space wasn't a hoax after all." He could tell Simms had finally made the connection between the pictures and the voice, and he wondered how Simms would deal with it.

"All right," Simms said. "What the hell is it then? Some kind of fracture in space-time?"

"That's as good a guess as any." Niklas said. "It could be some kind of an elongated rift. It's not a conventional celestial object. Not a galaxy or giant nebula being observed edge-on. And it's not a comet or anything else that has ever been observed." He nodded to Dirk, who put up another cell on the projector. "This is a side-by-side comparison of two shots taken of the line, two weeks apart. Based on this and a series of photographic programs done to verify it, we've concluded that the line is widening. The increase is pretty obvious in this comparison. By our calculations, it's doing it at a rate of five hundredths of a percent per day. Roughly speaking." He turned and winked at Anna. "It's too early to tell if this is an accelerative process."

People in the room started talking among themselves, momentarily bringing the presentation to a halt. Niklas nodded at Dirk and another cell was put on the projector. Niklas next comment regained their attention.

"That's the good news, folks. In photographing this phenomenon at different focal lengths and for different exposure periods, we have also observed what we believe is a related event." He interrupted himself. "Dr. Anders?" As every head turned toward Dirk, Niklas felt like the two of them were playing in a tennis match.

"The image MOLO photographed is what we are calling, for want of a better term, a precursor image– a reflection which we believe travelled to us at a speed greater than three hundred thousand kilometers per second." Niklas had expected the snickers he could now hear all around him. In theory, only a few flaky subatomic particles could surpass the speed of light. Niklas nodded at Dirk, encouraging him to press on. "This, we believe, accounts for the absence of any spectral data. The line itself is not red shifting or blue shifting, and as far as we know, it's absolutely stationary. At least, it's not moving in relationship to anything else in the observable Universe." There was an even more pronounced reaction to this statement. Nothing in the Universe was truly stationary. There wasn't a soul in the room who didn't know that even the Milky Way Galaxy was moving at a half million miles per hour through space. Niklas saw Dirk swallow hard and clear his throat. Now he spoke a little louder to be heard over the grumbling audience. "However, we have observed an energy wave which appears to be trailing the precursor. We believe the thermal or particle energy generated by the line is now catching up with it."

"Let me make sure I've got this right," Commie said, leaning forward. "You're saying that the line, unlike everything else in the Universe, is standing boneyard still. Right so far?" Dirk nodded. "Then you say the light from this line, your 'precursor', travelled to us faster than– the speed of light?" Dirk nodded again. "And, finally, you say this light has an energy– 'wave' you call it, following it?" Dirk nodded a third time and Commie slumped back in his seat. "Say what!" The rest of group let out a nervous laugh.

"All you have to do is look at this thing to see that it hasn't been covered on any Discovery Channel specials," Niklas said. "This is an extra-universal event, folks, and it's ignoring all of our rules." He paused for a moment, then walked the length of the room. "I'll make it simple for you. Anybody here still dumb enough to smoke?" One of Willoughby's agents who was sitting on the far side of the conference room sheepishly raised his hand. "Okay, got a match?" The agent reached into his pocket and produced a cheap plastic lighter. "Light it up." The agent flicked the lighter and a two inch flame leapt from it. "Good. Now keep it going." Niklas looked around the room, making eye contact with each person. "Okay. After the lighter lit up, it took a fraction of a nanosecond for the image of the flame to reach my retina. And that amount of time is governed by our basic laws of physics. Now, if we had a hyper-sensitive thermometer, we could tell precisely when the heat from the flame reached me. But I don't, so I can only guess that it had a measurable effect in just a few seconds. The heat's travel time would be dependent on temperature and atmospheric factors in the room. Less oxygen, lower temperature means greater resistance, and so on, again obeying all our silly rules. With me so far?" Everybody nodded and the agent holding the lighter used the pause as an opportunity to switch hands. "Now, imagine this flame is our line. The first thing it does is fly through the wall at several hundred million miles per hour. Or, at least, it looks that way because, unlike it, everything around it is in chaotic motion. The Earth is rotating at about eleven hundred miles per hour and revolving around the sun at over seventy thousand miles per hour. The solar system is orbiting around the center of Milky Way at about five hundred and forty thousand miles per hour. The Milky Way is orbiting the Virgo Cluster, inside the Local Group, at nearly nine hundred thousand miles per hour. The Local Group is headed towards the Virgo Supercluster at over a million miles per hour. And, as every seventh grade science class knows, the Virgo Supercluster is headed towards the Great Attractor even faster." Then Niklas turned and pointed back to the lighter. "But the goddamn line isn't moving. Scratch rule number one. Now, let's say our friend here was sitting about sixteen billion light years away when he decided to light up. When he flicked his Bic, everybody in the Universe saw it at the same time. The only problem is, the Universe is less than fifteen billion years old. So, how'd the image of the flame get to everybody so fast? Scratch rule number two. After he lit up, the heat from the flame moved slowly, appearing to follow the rules. After all, heat is just an excited molecular state, and all that stuff has mass and can't move faster than light. Right? Sorry, not this time. As the thermal energy emitted by the line is moving through the interstellar medium, it seems to be accelerating, as if it's being propelled by some external, pushing force. Scratch rule number three."

Willoughby tried to commandeer the floor. "Very intriguing, Dr. Koppernick, but it sounds to me as though you just have a lot of wild theories about this– wave. How do you know for sure these pictures aren't some kind of system malfunction? I'm sure you can understand how difficult this is for some of us." Willoughby sat back with a smug expression on his face.

Now Niklas got the big sarcastic smile on his face. It was the one he got right before he squashed somebody like a cockroach.

"I appreciate your skepticism, Mr. Quigby. Perhaps you could notify all the folks who invested the twenty-six billion dollars to build MOLO that their little tinker-toy is seeing things, and that the staff at the Harvard Smithsonian Observatory is on crack. And, while you're at it, you can call Karl Mant at KECK and Dr. Keinz at Mt. Parnal to inform them they should get out the Windex, because yesterday they both called me and said they were starting to see this line, too." Now Niklas' smile vanished. "And then, in a few days, you can inform the President of the United States that he should just ignore the big line up in the sky that will soon have the whole planet in a blind panic!" Niklas heard somebody clearing their throat on the other side of the room. It was the agent, still holding up the burning lighter. Niklas grinned and told him he could put it away.

He turned to Dirk and nodded again. The television came on and he could hear the electronic whir of the DVD disk sliding into the player.

"This is a sped-up recording of the line, made over a seven day period," Niklas said. "I want you to pay particular attention to these very small blips of light appearing across the width of the picture. These– the ones that are further above and below the line are easier to pick out. They look like very tiny plumes. You see– Right there. Hit pause, please, Dirk." After Dirk froze the picture, he put a new cell on the overhead projector. It was a close-up photograph of what they had just viewed on the TV monitor. "You can see the small groups of flash points here– and over here." He turned and looked at the room waiting for someone else to say what he knew he would eventually have to tell them.

"What are they?" Anna asked.

"They can only be one thing– celestial objects which are being struck by the energy wave Dr. Anders and I have just described to you."

"But, what could they be? The distance is so– How could they...." Anna's voice trailed off as she began to realize what she had to be looking at.

Niklas pointed at one of the pinpoint flares. "We think this was a spiral galaxy."

The room was still. Not even the sound of rustling clothing was heard. Each person was studying the projected image of the line. Some were trying to count the small pale blips. Most had worked at Project Phoenix and the Array for several years. They all believed in its mission and had hoped that one day they would make contact with some distant alien intelligence. Deep in their hearts they believed the Universe was teeming with life of all kinds. So they all knew what they were seeing represented a catastrophe of unimaginable proportions.

"Wait a minute!" Commie said. "Your hypothesis is that this energy wave is catching up with the precursor image. But how do you explain these so-called vaporizing galaxies becoming visible so quickly? If these are what you say they are, shouldn't their images be traveling at normal– light speed?"

Niklas could see the hopeful looks spread around the room. Everybody hoped Commie had hit on something which hadn't occurred to he and Dirk already.

"Yes," Anna said. "It should have taken billions of years for the light from these images to reach us."

"Yes, you're correct. In fact, under normal circumstances, with the expansion of the Universe, we would never be able to see these objects at all." Dirk moved closer to the screen. "Any photonic or gamma ray emissions from these events won't reach this part of the Universe for more than ten billion years. But that's not what we're seeing. This is a simple refraction created by the precursor."

"What do you mean 'simple refraction'?" Simms asked.

"The line is projecting a continual stream of its own version of light toward us, and you can't see that light until it strikes a surface. Light in empty space is invisible. All these galactic events are giving it some massive deflecting surfaces to bounce off. And these create refractions moving as fast as the precursor light. So we're not observing the actual events in their true space-time. Just their refractive pre-images." Niklas could see everybody in the room sag back in their seats as they absorbed the logic of his explanation.

Niklas stood up and walked slowly around the room, heading in Willoughby's direction. "Okay. I've shown you mine. Now it's your turn to show me yours. Quid pro quo. I can't imagine that the shit isn't hitting the celestial fan out there. Surely you guys have picked up something." He turned and looked directly at Simms. "And, if you have, there's really not much point in keeping it under wraps now, is there?" He turned to Willoughby, who was glancing nervously around the room at his operatives.

"We have a recording of a WOW." The look on Simms face was half embarrassed and half scared.

Commie jumped up. "You damn right, we do!" He scowled at Willoughby. "At least, we used to." The room came back to life. Willoughby slammed his fist down on the table and stalked out of the conference room. His agents looked around at each other for a moment and then followed.

Niklas went over to Anna and crouched down next to her.

"Do ya think it was something I said?" The humor didn't work this time. She couldn't laugh. She just stared at Niklas a moment and then put her face in her hands.

Simms stood up and went to the head of the table and got the room back under control. "Folks, listen up, please! I want to break up this meeting. Some of us still have jobs to do. Let's get the SEC re-opened and turn up the hearing aid. Anything comes in, I want it immediately posted on unsecured e-mail to everyone. From now on, nobody is kept in the dark. I would only ask that you continue to refrain from discussing this with anybody outside the project. Something like this shouldn't end up being announced on some slimey tabloid talk show. Everybody got that?" The room seemed to be in agreement with him and they began to file out the door in small groups, talking quietly amongst themselves. Simms turned to Anna, Niklas, Dirk and Commie. "Let's go over to my office? Try to figure out what the hell we're going to do now."

Niklas followed Simms out the door and grabbed him by the arm. "Congratulations. That took cajones. Willoughby and the NSA have no business taking over your operation. Besides, I thought we got over all of that government intervention bullshit in the last century."

Simms only frowned. Niklas could see he was probably wondering if he had done the right thing, but it was too late to turn back now. They would deal with Willoughby, if they had to, later.

—⚊—

Willoughby summoned all of his agents to his room. He was trying to maintain his professional detachment, but the verbal whipping he had just taken didn't aid him in the effort. Once all the men had settled down, he made it short and sweet.

"We're redeploying. I want everybody back at the station by tomorrow afternoon. If you must, take different flights. Nobody– I mean nobody– discusses this with anyone. I'll take care of the notifications. Copy that? Okay, move!" He turned to Rand, who was slowly shaking his head in frustration. "Agent Rand, please stay a moment. Let's have a chat."

—⁓—

As they all sat down around Simms' large black slate desk, he called out to Angie, "Ms. Ryerson, could you please bring us some glasses? Thanks, honey." Niklas noticed this momentary lapse in decorum and assumed Simms was still in a mild form of shock from the meeting in the conference room. Simms looked around and gave the group a less than half-hearted smile. "I don't know about you folks, but after your little presentation, I could use a drink." He reached into the bottom drawer of his credenza and pulled out an unopened bottle of brandy. By the time he got it open, Angie was walking in with a tray of glasses and he poured a generous portion for each person in the room. When everybody had picked up their glass, he raised his to the center of the table. Everyone else did the same, touching glasses, and Simms said, "Lord, what the hell do we do now?" Then they all took long swallows.

Commie was the only one to empty his glass. "Okay. If nobody else is going to ask it, I will." He tried to get one more swallow out of his glass. "Is this thing going to hit us?

Dirk and Niklas looked at each other, then Niklas said, "The problem is, we can't really be sure what the exact rate of acceleration is, or even if it will be sustained."

"And it's still so far out, it's impossible to measure relative distances," Dirk added.

Anna leaned forward. "Come on, Nick. Your best guess."

Niklas sat back in his chair and took another long swallow of the brandy. At first it burned his throat, then he felt its warmth in his stomach. Good anesthetic, he thought. He hoped there would be enough of it for everyone. "Anything we said would just be wild speculation, Anna. It's an unprecedented phenomenon. If the current rate of acceleration continues, it might get here in a matter of months. Maybe weeks."

Simms grimaced. "God, the speed must be unbelievable!"

"Yes, many many thousands of times the speed of light," Dirk said quietly. "And getting faster all the time."

"Is there any hope it will decay before it reaches us?" Anna looked desperate for some good news.

"Yeah, that's a lot of galactic material and plasma to move through," said Commie. "Maybe it'll just degrade."

Niklas shook his head. "This thing isn't acting like the kinds of particle energy we normally see. Its speed is just one indication of that. It may simply move through matter like a neutrino, like an anti-cosmic ray. Or it could be some kind of infinitely low frequency laser emission. No, I don't think we can count on any attrition or decrease in velocity. Believe me, I wish I had better news for you. For all of us."

Simms slumped in his chair. "You realize what you're saying." Niklas looked over at Anna and just nodded.

"So, what do we do now?" Commie stared at the floor.

Simms stood up and grabbed the bottle. "Have another." Everybody shifted in their seats. Commie got up and paced the room, occasionally stopping to drink. Angie Ryerson, who had overheard the conversation, was standing in the doorway, looking at Simms. Each of them was wrestling with a new scale of mortality, imagining what those final, terrible moments would be like.

Simms, without taking his eyes off Angie, broke the silence. "Something like this... we should probably just keep to ourselves?"

Commie managed a cynical laugh. "Hey, if these guys are right, the whole world's going to be seeing that thing up there pretty soon!"

"Yes, but nobody'll know about the energy wave unless we tell them," Simms said. "Right, Dr. Koppernick?"

Niklas nodded and looked around the room. The predicament sounded vaguely familiar to him, but at the moment he couldn't pinpoint why.

"God, think what might happen if this got out," Anna said, closing her eyes.

Niklas leaned forward in his seat. "Yeah, it wouldn't be pretty. But it would give people a chance to–"

"A chance to what?" Commie was becoming visibly upset. "Get their affairs in order? In order for what?"

Again, Niklas looked at everybody. He realized the world might react much as this room was reacting. He was looking at a sort of miniature of the planet. Everybody would handle the news in their own way.

"Listen, I can only speak for myself. Would I want to

know? Yes." he said. Then he looked over at Commie. "It would give people a chance to... to say their good-byes." He looked up and frowned. "Do we make the decision here, in this room, to take that away from people just because we're afraid some of them won't handle it well?"

Niklas reminded himself of the stages dying people often went through when they found out they were terminally ill. Some went through the process very quickly and others got stuck in different phases. And some people, like his own father, had gone straight to the final phase. Simms seemed like that– to have accepted things. Anna was in denial, looking for holes in the evidence. Not believing. Commie was angry about the prognosis, but Dirk had been very quiet, perhaps bargaining with his own emotions. Niklas guessed Dirk had already come to grips with the grim prospects, since he was the first to identify the wave and see its destructive power.

Niklas examined his own reaction and it surprised even him. He felt more concerned about Anna and his mother than himself, which shocked him. He had always seen himself as totally self-absorbed, a dedicated megalomaniac without a single selfless bone in his meager body. But what he was feeling right now flew in the face of all that. Maybe he wasn't such an awful person after all. He might even be worthy of someone's love. That this realization should come at such a time, perhaps too late for him, should have made him even more angry with the Beast, but it didn't. His comprehension of this fundamental change sent a shiver through him.

He got up and paced around the room, stopping by the

large window looking out onto the Array. After staring through the tinted glass for a minute or so, he turned back to the group.

"Whatever we do, this is a decision we should probably all agree on, right? It's been a bitch of a day, and we've all got plenty to think about. Why don't we sleep on this–"

"Sleep?" Commie said. "I'll never sleep again!"

Niklas smiled. "Okay, then, whatever. I'm just suggesting we call it a day and meet back here in the morning. We'll make our tough decisions then. Make sense to you, Dr. Simms?"

Simms stood up and rubbed the back of his neck. "Fine. Nine o'clock, then."

—⟋⟍—

As the scientists filed out of the room, Angie rushed into Simms' office. He had collapsed back into his chair. He could see she was very upset and he motioned her over to his side of the desk. When she leaned forward and hugged him hard around the neck, he winced. The tension of the day had taken its toll. But he leaned back from her and wiped a tear from her cheek.

"Would you like a drink?" She kissed him and went to close the door. Everybody dealt with fear in their own way.

iii

That evening, Anna and Niklas drove in to Socorro for Dinner. They didn't do a lot of talking. She asked if he had told his mother about her visit and he told her about their conversation, without getting into the part that concerned the two of them. On the way back, Niklas couldn't help but notice how many stars were visible, and when they pulled into the parking lot, he suggested they sit and star watch for a while.

"After all, we are astronomers." He shut the engine off and settled back into the seat. "You know, I actually feel sympathy for the Beast." He was looking up and shaking his head.

"That's a new one." She smiled.

"Well, the old boy's getting the shit kicked out of him pretty good right now. Guess he's learning what I always knew. No matter how big and bad you are, somewhere there's somebody bigger and badder. Is that what people mean when they say size doesn't count?"

"For some people, size doesn't mean a damn thing— Nikki." For the first time since the meeting in the conference room, she laughed.

"What's that supposed to mean?" He stifled a laugh and looked out the windshield just in time to see a meteor burning up in the atmosphere. For a moment they were silent and then he turned to her. "Did you ever consider coming back to Boston? No." He corrected himself. "What I really mean is, do you ever think about getting back together? Us." The question took courage.

"For God's sake, Nick, why ask me something like that now?" She had a sad expression.

"I can't imagine a better time for it than now. Things seem okay between us lately, don't you think?" As he talked he was tapping nervously on the steering wheel.

"You're still an incredible pain in the ass."

"Yeah, but really. You could come home to Boston. Get your professorship back. We could play house. Maybe try to have some papoosi–"

"Aren't you forgetting?"

"What? You're in great shape and, besides, women a lot older than you are having babies now days."

"That's not what I'm talking about, Nick." She looked out the window, up at the sky and then looked back at him, on the verge of tears.

"Hey, I let the Beast run my life for the last thirty-five years. I'm not gonna let some new asshole just pick up where it left off. The way I look at it, we've got time. Maybe not much, but I refuse to just roll over and die." He was watching her face intently, looking for some hint of how she felt. "I've sort of had things backwards all these years, and I want to re-program the coordinates. You know, re-task my life."

She started to weep softly. "Oh, you goddamn jerk. You wait until the end of the world to go human on me."

He took her chin in his hand. "What do you say?"

She scooted across the seat and threw her arms around his neck and kissed him fully for the first time in more than eight years. The kiss seemed to go on for hours. In the nearly freezing night air of New Mexico, their warm breath condensed on the cold windshield. As the vista of stars began to disappear behind the fogged glass, the cold slowly seeped into the car. Despite the heat their bodies were generating, the inside of the car grew frigid and they could see their breath. Finally, they pulled back from each other, panting.

"Sounded like a big 'Yes' to me." Niklas laughed and

hugged her. "Come on. Let's get out of this refrigerator."

They went straight to his room, dead-bolted the door, and, on that particular night, for Niklas and Anna Koppernick, size really didn't count.

iv

The group began to straggle into Simms' office around 9:30 the next morning. Commie and Dirk were both rubbing their temples and tossing antacids down their throats, obviously sporting tremendous hangovers. Commie's skin had taken on the gray cast some people of color get when suffering from the effects of too much alcohol. Simms himself didn't feel much better, having slept for only a couple of hours. But when Anna and Niklas walked into the outer-office where Angie's desk was, only two minutes apart, Simms thought they both looked surprisingly well rested. Christ, even rosy-cheeked, he thought. Just looking at them reminded him that things could be worse. After all, the Sun had come up, as it always had. And it was a beautiful morning in the desert. They were each fully alive in the moment. Although he knew Commie and Dirk couldn't share that precise view with him right now.

—⁓—

Angie touched Anna's arm lightly, stopping her at the door. "Dr. Koppernick?"

"Good morning, Angie." Anna returned her smile. "How are you holding up?"

"I'm okay, thanks. Not much sleep. You asked me to keep

my ears open about Mr. Willoughby. Well, I think he and the rest of them left early this morning. I saw them all getting into a van when I was pulling up. Lots of suitcases and stuff."

"Oh? And he didn't even bother to say good-bye." Now Anna had two things to smile about as she thanked Angie for the information and went into Simms' office. As she sat down and looked around Simms' office, she realized her look of contentment was totally out of place. Niklas had told her the night before that he thought she was in denial about the situation. Maybe he was right.

They reconvened and Angie brought in a pitcher of hot black coffee and some freshly toasted bagels. She winked at Niklas as she set them down on the desk. The group chatted as they got their coffees and then Simms opened the discussion.

"I want to let you all know that Mr. Willoughby and his crew have left the Array. So at least we won't have to be dealing with him."

Niklas muttered, "Somebody must have told him Dr. Von Helsing was in town." Anna and Commie seemed to be the only ones who knew what Niklas was referring to, and they both had to bite their lips to keep from laughing outloud.

Simms grinned curiously and then went on. "Dr. Koppernick, I got a call this morning that your transportation will be here at 11 AM, so we have about an hour to go through this and come to some kind of consensus."

Anna saw Dirk wince. He didn't look like he was in any shape to be climbing on board a luxury liner, much less the low-flying giant insect he had arrived on the day before. God, just the thought of the damn thing must have made his stomach do a slow somersault. She felt sorry for him.

"We've all had some time to let this sink in. So the question before us is, what do we do now? Why don't we just go around the room. Dr. Anders?" This was a new style for Simms and Anna liked it. He seemed genuinely concerned about everybody's point of view.

"Do we tell the world?" Dirk popped another TUMS in his mouth, took a big swig of hot coffee and cleared his throat. "Isn't that something the government should decide?" He waved his hand at the group, indicating he didn't want to talk anymore, then closed his eyes and looked as though he was fighting back a wave of nausea.

Anna didn't know if it was physiologically possible, but Commie looked even more gray now than when she came in.

"If there is a right way to handle this," he said, "I sure don't expect the government to do it. But I don't wanna be the one who decides this, either, so maybe that's the only way..." Commie's voice trailed off to a whisper no one could hear.

"Regardless of what we decide here this morning," Simms said, "we won't have much to say about things once the government gets involved."

"If it's what we really want to do, we could always force the government to make some sort of announcement," Anna said. "Personally, I'd rather not risk spending my last few days on Earth locked up in a padded cell."

"Did you go to Berkeley or what?" Niklas had always given her a hard time about her Berkeley upbringing. "I think this

Whigby has really soured you folks on Washington. I haven't had that kind of experience with them at all."

"But you've never dealt with bureaucrats in this kind of situation either," Simms said. "You can't use your own experience to predict what they might do. None of us can."

Niklas paused a moment, then walked over to the window and looked out at the multi-billion dollar network of giant dishes cluttering the flat expanse of the valley. "Okay, maybe you're right. Maybe we can't trust the Great White Father to make the right decision." He turned around and looked around the room. "So who's going to Washington?"

"Washington?" Simms seemed surprised by the suggestion. "You think a trip is necessary for this?"

"You're not suggesting we deliver this kind of news over the phone or in an email?" Niklas said. "Somebody needs to go there and make sure those clowns understand what's happening." Anna figured Niklas already knew who should make the trip. As was his usual style, he was letting them briefly think they were playing a role in the decision, before informing them what was really going to happen.

"I'd like to suggest, if you don't mind, Dr. Simms, that you, Anna and I go to Washington. I need Dirk back at Harvard to continue monitoring this thing. Perhaps Dr. Marks should stay here and keep the headphones on. More messages might come in and they could be helpful. You never know."

Commie didn't appear disappointed about not going. With the way he must be feeling right now, Anna thought, the walk up to the SEC was probably all he would be good for over the next twenty-four hours.

Simms looked around and saw everybody nodding. "Okay, we're all agreed. So, who are we talking to?" Everybody in the room looked at Niklas. He was the one with the connections.

"Not much point in talking to anybody but the President," Niklas said. "I just hope we can get an audience with him before people start pointing up at the damned sky. I'll make some calls as soon as I get back to Boston."

"Okay, then we'll get all our tapes together and be ready to go whenever you give the word." With that, Anna's opinion of Simms completed its one hundred eighty degree turn.

"Uh, there's one minor problem," Commie said. "Willoughby had all the tapes confiscated from my room. We don't have any copies and he took the original DAT, remember?" Commie seemed about to retch just talking about the NSA agent.

"That's all right," Anna said. "I've still got the dubs you gave me. Those, and everything Nick and Dirk have should be more than enough." Anna actually had more faith in Niklas' persuasive skills than she had in all the photographic and recorded evidence.

Simms stood. "This went faster than I thought it would." Turning to Dirk and Niklas, he said, "This gives you a little more time to prepare for your trip back. I'll meet you outside when the helo arrives."

—⁓—

After the meeting, Anna accompanied Niklas back to his

room. As soon as they stepped through the door, Niklas looked at his watch and turned to Anna. "Hey, We've still got thirty minutes." He glanced lasciviously at the unmade bed.

"Do you think people realize middle-aged astronomers are just as horny as long-haired construction workers?" She stepped forward and wrapped herself around him.

"Hmmm," Niklas said between passionate kisses. "We sure never had any problem making out standing up, did we. All you have to do is bend your knees a little and all I have to do is stand up nice and straight."

She laughed into his mouth and was pushing her knee between his legs. "And you are definitely standing up straight," she said.

He laughed. "Boy, did I walk right into that one."

Moaning more than talking, Anna said, "I think I'm the one who walked into something."

Then, as they were falling onto the bed, he heard a deep thump-thump-thump-thump sound.

"Be still my beating heart." Even though he was making a joke, Niklas was disappointed that the Chopter had shown up early. Anna laughed and got up to help him get his things together, but he grabbed her and pulled her back down on the bed. "Why don't I tell the pilot to go strafe some off-roaders and come back for me in half an hour?"

"A half hour?" She said it with mocked disappointment.

He laughed. "Oh, you are cruel."

"Don't worry. They'll be other times. I promise." He could tell the kiss she gave him was carefully calculated to be long enough to show she meant what she had just said, but short enough not to encourage him to do anything about it.

Niklas pulled back from her and his expression grew serious. "You know, this is exactly why people should be told what's happening, Anna."

"What do you mean?"

"Do you think you and I would even be in the same room together right now if we didn't know what we know?" Niklas stood up, gathered up his things, and turned to see Anna wiping a tear from her cheek.

—∿—

Ten minutes later, everybody was standing in front of the Chopter, as its huge props maintained a steady rotation. Niklas and Dirk shook hands with everybody and Anna gave each of them a hug. She made eye contact with Niklas and mouthed the words 'I love you.' He smiled broadly back at her and the two men ran to the aircraft, again crouching needlessly. In less than two minutes, it was out of sight.

Chapter 7
Resolution

i

"The United States Attorney General's Office. How may I direct your call?" Niklas thought the operator's voice was warm, friendly and completely devoid of humanity.

"General Sokolsky, please. Doctor Niklas Koppernick calling." He used the title, hoping the indifferent voice on the other end of the line would be impressed sufficiently to at least put his call through to the right assistant. Just in case, Niklas prepared himself for the phalanx of receptionists, secretaries and aides he would have to wade through before he finally reached the right office. A week had passed and he had been unable to connect with his friend, Arthur Sokolsky. He felt Sokolsky was his best bet for arranging the meeting with the President, but he had been unreachable for days and Niklas did not want to leave a message that went into too much detail about the nature of the call. That he could only do in person. All he had said in the messages he had left was that it was very important that they talk. Nothing too extreme-sounding.

"I'm sorry, Dr. Koppernick, but the Attorney General is unavailable at this time. Would you like his assistant's voice-mail?" Another humanoid. Niklas frowned.

"Yes, thank you." Niklas left a brief but urgent message,

making sure the assistant knew it was not a personal matter. He tried to hide the frustration in his voice. The last thing he needed was to have some pissed-off administrative assistant deleting his message.

He had spoken with Anna and Simms several times on the phone, and they were becoming even more anxious about the situation. Word had gotten out something strange had been going on at the VLA. Simms had managed to keep the details out of the press, but Niklas knew it was only a matter of time before some TV reporter with a fat checkbook would get to one of the staff. He was also worried about what the big optical observatories would do. Several were now able to see the line and were frantically trying to determine what it was, but their pictures were too distorted by the atmosphere to give them a clear image. Fortunately, they knew nothing about the energy wave. To Niklas' relief, the Hubble Satellite Telescope had been down again, awaiting yet another shuttle repair mission. The HST's higher resolution photos might have been more difficult for him to explain away. He had been under a great deal of pressure from KECK, and Karl Mant had been quite upset with him for being so circumspect. Niklas would only tell him the Lunar Observatory was still surveying the phenomenon and that they had nothing conclusive to report on it. Which, in a way, was true. They still didn't know what it was. In the meantime, they were going to stall until they were able to turn their notes over to the government.

Niklas was about to call Anna and update her when Dirk Anders knocked on the door of his office. This was a highly unusual change in behavior for Dirk. Normally, he would just barge in and begin talking, so Niklas immediately knew Dirk was up to something. He had been maintaining his vigil of the line with MOLO and, until now, keeping Niklas apprised of its status by e-mail. In his usual fashion, Niklas decided to make a pre-emptive strike.

"The answer is no!" Niklas tried to look as stern as he could.

"Dr. Koppernick, I'd like to get some pictures of that strange dark area. The more the line widens, the less it looks like a foreground object. And it seems to be getting more prominent." Dirk seemed more distracted than usual, staring at the photographs he was carrying and speaking barely loud enough to be heard.

"If you can tell me anything about this situation that isn't strange, I'm real open to hearing it."

"It's not irregular enough to be a nebula or a cloud of dark matter. And it's too diffuse to be a foreground object. I would like to get a better look at it– take a couple of days, then we can widen right back out." He finally looked up at Niklas for his ruling.

"Yeah, all right. Go ahead. We could probably use some tighter shots of the thing anyway. Let me know what you see." Dirk nodded, looking back down at the photos as he walked out the door without closing it behind him. Niklas picked up the phone and put the call in to Anna.

"Anna Koppernick." She sounded relaxed enough.

"Good morning." Niklas couldn't help smiling when he talked to her.

"Hi. How are we doing?" Her calm tone disappeared and

Niklas figured just hearing his voice must have done it. He knew she had been stressed about his inability to connect with Sokolsky.

"Hey, I miss you, too." He couldn't really blame her for the antagonistic attitude. He had hoped they would be in Washington by now himself.

"Sorry. This waiting around is killing me. Simms, too. We're ready to jump out of our skins down here."

"Hey, keep the skin on. I like it fine where it is." His tone grew more serious. "I don't know what's going on. Sokolsky's usually pretty good about getting back to me. Maybe something's going on down there."

"You don't think Willoughby got to him, do you?" Anna asked.

"The Transylvanian? It's possible. I suppose he could have sabotaged us somehow when he got back to Washington. But then it would be his word against mine. My reputation's gotta be in better shape than that, for Christ's sakes. Maybe what we need to do now is just show up. Come through the saloon doors, guns blazing. Otherwise, we could be sitting on our asses like this for weeks." Niklas realized if she was right, and Willoughby was behind the non-response, his calls to Sokolsky might never get through. Maybe he really didn't know Sokolsky as well as he thought he did.

"We've gotta do something," Anna said. "What happens when this thing becomes visible to the naked eye? We'll get crucified for keeping it to ourselves for so long!"

"Whoa! Hold it. I'm with you. When can you and Simms meet me in Washington?"

"We're ready to go. Any time. Shouldn't have any trouble getting a flight out of Albuquerque." Anna sounded relieved.

"Okay. I'll meet you both in the lobby of the Mayflower tomorrow afternoon, around 5 PM. That'll give you plenty of time to get there. Oh. I almost forgot the most important thing." He sounded very serious.

"What?" she asked.

"Are we sharing a room, or what?" He braced for her answer.

"No,"

Niklas tried not to feel rejected.

"I think Dr. Simms would like his own room." She laughed. "Just make sure it's a king-size."

"The thought of anything smaller never occurred to me. See you tomorrow." Niklas hung up with a smile on his face and realized how strange it was that he could find any personal happiness during such an uncertain time. He immediately arranged for the hotel rooms and his airline tickets. Then he went down to the Bridge to let Dirk know what they were planning to do.

—ɯ—

Anna headed for Simms' office to fill him in. She was surprised by her ambivalent emotions. On the one hand, she was feeling overwhelming despair over what might lie ahead. On the other, she couldn't deny the anticipation she felt, knowing she would soon be with Niklas. It was an odd mix of feelings. After explaining the change in plans to Simms, she thought he seemed relieved they were finally taking the initiative. He asked Angie to arrange their travel itinerary.

Anna jogged over to the SEC to find Commie. She wanted him to know what was happening and where he could reach her in Washington, if he needed to do so.

"It's about time!" Commie said, with more than a little edge in his voice. He was obviously not coping too well with things. He had spent some time with his friends in Socorro, but told her that not being able to tell them what might be ahead had been very difficult. Now he couldn't even bring himself to go back into Socorro. "Is there a back up plan, in case– if I never hear from you guys again?"

"Very funny." It wasn't funny at all, Anna thought, but he was right. "Yes, we're all set," Anna said. "If they threaten to lock us up and throw away the key, Niklas says he has some sort of insurance policy. But it'll never go that far. We'll be okay."

"Yeah, well, I'd hate to have the last voice I ever hear be some scared shitless bug-eyed alien from Alpha Centauri."

"Commie, you need to get away from this for a while. Go back into Socorro tonight. Visit with your friends. Get laid, for God's sake. Forget all this shit for a day or so." She squeezed his shoulder. "Angie knows how to get hold of us if you need to. Okay? We're at the Mayflower."

Commie's shoulders sagged. "I'll think about it. Have a safe trip, Anna. And if you see that cracker Willoughby, tell him– tell him he needs to work on his tan." He sounded too emotionally exhausted to beat up on anyone else. Even Willoughby.

She left the SEC and went back to her room to get ready

for the trip. If the situation weren't so terribly desperate, it would have been something to look forward to. They would be meeting the Attorney General and the President of the United States. She hadn't voted for the man, but he was still the President. And she would be with Niklas. She thought, again, how strange it was, in the midst of this, that she could be feeling the way she was. Maybe her feelings for him had never really changed. Maybe they just needed time apart to grow back together. Whatever it was, she was grateful it had happened.

ii

Simms and Anna didn't get into Washington National Airport until 4:30 that afternoon. It was raining, and the three-mile-drive to the Stouffer Mayflower Hotel on Connecticut Avenue took more than an hour. The traffic was terrible. They had thought by flying to WNA rather than Dulles they could get to the hotel more quickly, but it ended up taking about the same amount of time. The good news was the hotel was only four blocks from the White House. When they walked into the lobby of the Mayflower, Niklas was waiting for them. They decided to freshen up from the flight and meet back in the lobby in half an hour.

Anna and Niklas went to their room and almost didn't make the scheduled lobby meeting. He had his favorite cabernet and a beautiful bouquet of flowers delivered to the room, and both were there waiting for them. The old colonial-style architecture and decor of the room felt like a different world to Anna, after the trendy southwestern motifs she had grown accustomed to over the last half dozen years. They had only taken two sips of wine before they started necking.

After a few minutes, the two managed to regain control of themselves. They cleaned up and took the elevator down to the lobby where they found Simms waiting. Because the weather was so awful, they decided to eat in the hotel's Town & Country Lounge: a good restaurant with a mediterranean menu. Once they were seated, Niklas filled them in on what had happened in the last twenty-four hours.

"I finally got a call from Sokolsky' office this morning. He's agreed to meet with us first thing tomorrow, but he can't guarantee we'll be able to meet with the President. I think it's a safe bet, once he hears what we have to say, he'll find a way to get us in." The waiter approached and asked if they wanted to order something to drink. Simms had been looking at the wine list and looked as though he was about to suggest a vintage when Niklas asked, "You guys mind if I order the wine?" Simms and Anna nodded, then Niklas ordered the Opus One. Anna noticed Simms' raised eyebrows and thought he must have known that the wine Niklas had selected was, with the exception of a few of the champagnes, the most expensive beverage on the list.

"Why'd you have to order this stuff? Used to be anything red was good enough." Anna laughed. "You a connoisseur now?"

"Sort of. I never thought I'd be a snob about wine. Mom and Dad just drank whatever was on sale, as long as you couldn't see through it. Dad let me have a sip once and I remember it took an hour for the pucker to go away." The waiter came, opened the bottle of wine, handed the cork to Niklas and began pouring the wine.

Anna held her glass up, enjoying the rich color playing off the lights in the restaurant, and guessed it was what Niklas liked most about this wine. The deep red hue must have reminded him of what his parents always drank. She brought the wine to her lips and smiled as she remembered the tart, harsh reds they once had to buy at a local discount market. In his early years, Niklas found them adequate. Then, like Desta and Aaron before him, he was willing to settle for less. But that had all changed long ago and, smelling the wine's complex bouquet, Anna decided it was okay. As she was about to take her first swallow, someone gently grabbed her by the arm.

"Whoa! I'd like to propose a toast." Niklas raised his glass. "Here's to the Beast. May he give as good as he gets." The atmosphere of levity at their table evaporated with the reminder of why they were in Washington, and they each took long swallows of the wine.

"So, how did Sokolsky sound?" Simms asked. "You think he's heard anything about what's going on?"

"Hard to tell. Artie's a cagey guy. Hard core Harvard Law. Never lets you know what's going on inside his noodle. But, I'm not going to worry about it. Whatever he's been told, he can't ignore what we have. "

During dinner, they each complained about not having any suitable clothing or umbrellas for the inclement weather. Anna hoped it would clear by morning so they could at least walk to their meeting. She wondered if she would ever get the chance to enjoy a run again. They agreed to meet for breakfast in the Hotel coffee shop at 8 AM and then went to their rooms.

iii

Early the next morning, Dirk Anders was starting to view MOLO's real-time images of the Line. He was concerned about how much it had widened and that it would soon become visible to amateur astronomers. Most optical observatories around the world could see it now, and it had been terribly difficult for Dr. Koppernick to organize their silence until after he had spoken with the President.

Now Dirk was getting obsessed with the dark area in the line. Even though it was amorphous, it appeared to abruptly cut off at the bottom and top boundaries of the Line itself. He was absolutely certain it was not a foreground object, but the resolution of the image was still unsatisfactory. He decided to do some timed exposures of the area and also some low-speed video at MOLO's maximum focal length range. The prolonged time exposures might reveal some extra detail in the darkest part of the image and the recording might show any movement which had been undetectable in the real-time playback.

Then he got an idea. Dirk had a close friend at MIT who was a professor in the Computer Sciences Lab, and while the timed exposures were being programmed, he made a phone call. He thought there might be a way to get more information out of the recording, in the same way the government often used computers to enhance their satellite imaging systems. At the least, he could learn whether or not the dark area was inside or in front of the line, and he might even be able to see what the damn thing was. What he wanted to do would require jumping onto their huge computer, ahead of a lot of other paying customers and faculty research projects. He realized he might have to come clean about the situation, in order to get the computer time, but he had no choice. He would need the most powerful computer imaging system available, with petabytes of memory, and MIT was the place that had it.

—␣␣—

He met with his friend for lunch that afternoon at a small cafe situated mid-way between the two campuses, on Massachusetts Avenue. Usually there were people seated outside at the cafe's small curbside tables, but it had been raining off and on, so the tables had been covered. Dirk arrived first and was already seated when Nori Fukuda came in the door. Dirk stood and greeted him with a handshake.

"Nori, good to see you again, my friend. How's things?"

"Good– Great, really," Nori said. "Having a blast in the lab. A lot of work, but the government is giving us pretty much carte blanch for research. How about you?"

"Never a dull moment with Dr. Koppernick," Dirk said.

"So I've heard. Is he as big a jerk as people say?" Nori had laughed when he asked it, but Dirk knew about Niklas' reputation for being difficult.

"Actually, he's not very big at all." They both laughed and then Dirk decided he shouldn't leave it at that. "Koppernick can be difficult, yes, but he's an amazing person. What is the word– unpretentious? I guess I've gotten used to his personality. It took some doing. But I must tell you he's the most brilliant man I have ever known. An original thinker. Exciting to work with someone like that." Dirk took a long gulp of his iced tea and watched his friend's reaction.

"I suppose you're right," Nori said. "Shouldn't judge him from all the gossip. There's lots of jealousy in the academic community and I suppose he's just gotten more than his share of attention. Probably got some people pissed. Anyway, enough about your boss. What's the occasion for the lunch? I haven't seen you in weeks. You getting married or something?"

"Oh, my God, no." At first, Dirk laughed, but then he shrugged at the realization he had no life. "I haven't even had a date in months. Too much going on." That was as good a lead in as any. "Actually, I called you because I need your help. Your computer's help."

Nori's demeanor turned suspicious. "My computer's help? What's that supposed to mean?"

"We– I mean, MOLO has observed something we're having trouble identifying. I thought, if we could run it through your enhancing software, we might be able to get something definitive." Dirk was prepared for Nori's response.

"Dirk, people– corporations– wait months to get on this thing for just a few minutes. You can't just drop by with a disk and boot up. Come on, you know better than that." Nori seemed more than a little put off by the request and Dirk could only hope the materials he had brought would change his friend's attitude.

"I know. I know. But this is different." He watched his friend roll his eyes. "MOLO has detected a phenomenon on the far side of the Universe– a line. We can't see where it starts or where it ends." Dirk saw Nori's smile transform into a look of bewilderment. "And this line is widening. Slowly, but measurably." Dirk now brought out his large stack of laser prints. The MIT professor went through the stack slowly, studying each image, occasionally glancing up at Dirk. With each glance his eyes grew wider.

"What the hell is this?" Fukuda finished looking at the pictures and laid them out on the table in front of him.

"As Dr. Koppernick says, that's the Jeopardy Bonus Round question. We don't know. It's completely outside of our scientific understanding of extra-galactic phenomena." Dirk thought about going into more detail about the line and the energy wave, but he decided he didn't want to risk throwing his friend into a panic unless it became absolutely necessary. He quickly went through the prints and pulled one out of the stack. "Here. Look at this shot. See this area right here?" Dirk pointed to what looked like a dark smudge on the print, which was clouding a portion of the line. Nori nodded and then looked back up at Dirk. "This is what I need your computer for, Nori. This dark area inside the line. If we can identify what it is, it might give us a clue about–"

"Jesus. This is the biggest thing since– since, shit, I don't know what. Why haven't I heard about this? It should be all over the news." The pictures had done the trick. Dirk had always known Nori to be a calm, taciturn guy, but right now he seemed almost frantic to help him out.

"Dr. Koppernick's in Washington right now, talking to the President. There should be some sort of official announcement pretty soon. The big observatories are cooperating. At least for now. So, what's it going to be? Am I getting in?"

"Be in my office at 7 AM." Nori was staring at the print as he talked and Dirk couldn't tell if he was alarmed or just impressed by what he was looking at. "I'll pull everything. But if I start taking a lot of heat about the computer being tied up, you may have to share this with some people. Will you agree to that?"

"Whatever it takes." Dirk took a deep breath. He and Nori both ordered salads and ate quickly. Nori insisted on paying for the meal and when they got up to leave the cafe, Dirk thanked him for agreeing to help out. After a perfunctory handshake, the two headed in opposite directions. Dirk was relieved that he might finally be able to resolve the mystery of the dark area. After he got that chore out of the way, he could get back to the more important tasks of monitoring the line's changing status and the progress of the approaching energy wave. Perhaps, by the time Dr. Koppernick returned from Washington, he would have something specific to report. And Dr. Koppernick liked nothing better than specifics.

—⚏—

Late that evening, during a break in the weather, Dirk was out walking his dog, a Jack Russell whom he had, oddly enough, named Jack. The cloud cover had temporarily opened up and he could see stars twinkling in the patches of blackness. He also thought he could see something else and the hair on the back of his neck stood up.

iv

It was like waiting on line to see the goddamn Godfather, Niklas thought, as they sat in the long hallway of the Department of Justice. They had been sitting in the anteroom for over forty-five minutes when Arthur Sokolsky finally came out and personally led them into his office. He apologized for the delay and said that some drug case appeal was being brought before the Supreme Court and he was trying to work out which DOJ attorneys would handle it. It would be a real career boost to successfully argue before the Court, so everybody was lobbying Sokolsky for the job. He was getting quite irritated with all of the politicking and was seriously considering just handling the case himself. But then he would have had an insurrection on his hands, so he would, in the end, pick the most qualified– and most persistent deputy to represent the government.

Niklas introduced everyone as Sokolsky served coffee to whomever wanted it. While the Attorney General had never met Anna Koppernick, he seemed to know all about her. Even so, Niklas could tell his friend was not prepared for her beauty and that, at first, he seemed quite nervous around her. Niklas was curious if Anna was flattered by the attention and wondered if he might even be a little jealous. Finally, Sokolsky sat down behind his large walnut desk and dropped his bombshell.

"You know, Nick, everybody in Washington knows about this line you people have been looking at," Sokolsky said, grinning.

Niklas felt his reaction being gauged by Sokolsky. He glanced over at Simms and Anna and saw they were as stunned as he was. The three scientists looked back and forth at each other until Niklas finally spoke.

"Okay, Mr. Attorney General, what exactly has your agent, Mr. What's-his-name, told you?" He usually called him Artie, but he wanted to know how thin the ice was before he presumed too heavily on their friendship.

"Oh, well yes. Uh, I have spoken to agent Willoughby." Sokolsky cleared his throat. "His report indicated that you've observed a 'line' across the Universe, several billion light years away, and that there's some kind of shock wave. He also said you think this shock wave is headed this way, but all your evidence is theoretical. Oh–" He looked at Simms and Anna "–and he said you've gotten some unusual signals at the Array, too. That's about it."

"Signals?" Anna was incredulous.

"He didn't give you any details about this little 'shock' wave?" Niklas asked.

"No, just that you thought it was moving faster than the speed of light. That's not possible, is it?" He leaned forward in his chair. "I thought it was a... uh... an absolute."

"Nothing about this is 'absolute'. Look, I don't think giving you a lecture on astrophysics would be helpful right now. You're an educated guy, Artie. You know those Ultra Short Wave Lasers the government was fiddling with during the old

Star Wars project?" Sokolsky nodded. "Well, this makes one of those look like a Hoppalong Cassidy cap gun. And its speed isn't consistent with any of our particle energy theory. There are some theoretical particles, like tachyons, that we think travel faster than light. Maybe this is something similar. We just don't know."

"Still, I'm not sure I can take this to the President, with so little information about it. A lot of what you're saying seems to be wild speculation." Sokolsky seemed terribly worried about his credibility. Niklas realized even intelligent people could be dumbed-down and turned into bureaucrats.

"Mr. Sokolsky," Anna said, unable to hide the frustration in her voice. "The kind of hard evidence you're talking about might not be available until just a few hours before the thing is on top of us."

Simms added, "We can't prove this to you any more than we can prove the sun's going to rise tomorrow morning." Then he looked out at the dark gray sky. "Believe us. It's coming."

Sokolsky looked at each of the intense scientists sitting before him, and Niklas hoped he was beginning to get the idea Willoughby had not told him the whole story. Sokolsky got up and walked around his desk and sat on its edge, right in front of them.

"So, if it does make it this far, what will it do? I mean, are we talking natural disaster here?" Niklas could see from his friend's body language and tone of voice that he was trying to make the question as benign as possible.

"Disaster? Yes. Natural? No," Niklas said.

"Give me the unsanitized version, Nick." Sokolsky frowned.

Niklas spoke slowly and quietly. "Barring a change in the wave's intensity, there won't be a second term, Artie."

"Jesus Christ." The Attorney General glanced over at the small photographs of his family sitting on his desk.

"It's not exactly a routine phenomenon." Niklas continued. "We don't know what it is or what caused the son of a bitch, but we have a pretty good idea of what it's doing. It's not slowing down. It's accelerating. We can't predict when it's going to get here, but we're probably talking days instead of weeks. And we can't count on it weakening."

"We would have gotten this news to you sooner, but your Mr. Willoughby did everything but lock us in our rooms," Simms said. "Scared the hell out of the staff down at the Array."

Sokolsky went behind his desk and stood with his back to the group, staring out the window.

"Why,...uh, what do you expect me... the President to do with this information? This isn't something you just hold a press conference about. My God,... I just–"

"Not all of us are sure this should be made public," Anna said, then she looked over at Niklas. "But some of us think people have a right to know what's coming." She closed her eyes. "I'm still not sure I would."

Sokolsky turned and slumped into his chair, rubbing his eyes. "Neither am I. It's going to... to frighten the hell out of everyone. If what you're saying is true, wouldn't it be better to just die ignorant, in your sleep?" Niklas noticed Sokolsky was taking short, shallow breaths, and realized the man was experiencing a mild form of shock. He'll get over it, he thought. Amazing how quickly human beings can adapt, even to news like this.

"No, it wouldn't," Niklas leaned forward slowly and clasped his hands in front of his chest, as if to pray. "Artie, you know what's going to happen now. And, because you know, you'll do things differently than if you were 'ignorant.' You'll get to make your peace with God... and maybe tell your son you love him a few more times than usual." Niklas sat back in his chair and lowered his hands. "How would you feel about someone else deciding whether or not you could do that?" Anna reached over and took Niklas' hand.

The Attorney General looked at Niklas, not saying anything for a few moments. Then he took a long, slow breath and reached for one of the phones on his desk. Niklas surmised it was the direct line to the Oval Office.

"Hello, Mrs. Pearson, Arthur Sokolsky. Is he available? When? I understand– Please tell him it is highly urgent I speak with him, face-to-face, immediately– Those words– Thank you very much, Ethel– You, too." He hung up the phone and said the President would get the message within the next five minutes. Then they sat quietly and waited for the callback. It came half an hour later.

v

Dirk met Nori in front of the MIT Computer Sciences building at seven that morning. Dirk brought two DVD/RAM disks with him, which he had made the day before. He also brought a low resolution dub of the DVDs that he and Fukuda could review in his office, before going into the lab. They would not have a lot of time on the computer and they had to be ready to get to work as soon as they got on line.

Fukuda viewed the DVD at least two dozen times without speaking. He just sat and stared, open mouthed. Dirk pointed out the area he wanted to enhance and asked Fukuda how long the process would take.

"I don't think it'll be too long. The area we're focusing on doesn't appear to be a complex image. Once we get it downloaded into the system, it could just take a couple of hours. Depends on how much information is on the disk and how much resolution you want. I've seen NASA downloads take days to enhance. But they're a bunch of maniacs." Fukuda managed a pathetic laugh.

Dirk remained serious and turned to face Fukuda. "I don't know if you've ever met Dr. Koppernick, but 'maniac' would be an understatement. I can't show this to him if it's inconclusive. If there's something on this disk, the resolution's got to be high enough to identify what it is– or what it isn't."

Fukuda nodded. "All right, then. But like I said, if anybody else in the department starts screaming, you have to let them in on this. Okay?"

"Like I said. Whatever it takes, Nori." They both turned their attention back to the screen and Fukuda explained how the process worked.

vi

"Yes, thank you. Put her through, please." The President

looked up from his desk at his visitors, waving his hand with his fingers spread apart, indicating he would be off the phone in a minute. "Hi. How's the trip, sweetheart?– Good.– How much longer are you there?– You're flying out of Orly, right?– Hey, I'm just trying to keep track of you guys. You do more traveling than I do.– Okay. See you Friday. Love to the kids.– Bye."

He hung up the phone and came out from behind his desk with a surprised look on his face, and Niklas guessed he hadn't expected a group. The Attorney General stepped forward and shook hands with him as if they were meeting for the first time, then turned to introduce the three scientists. The President shook their hands enthusiastically and led them to the sitting area across the room. The first thing Niklas noticed when he walked into the Oval Office was how much smaller it was than what he expected. Then he reminded himself that all of the film he had seen of it had probably been taken with wide angle lenses.

Though they had never met, the Chief Executive apparently recognized Niklas' face right away and congratulated him on the success of the MOLO project. As they sat down, a uniformed officer stepped into the room from behind a door that none of them had seen, carrying a serving tray with coffee and small cookies. The President declined a cup, but everybody else was served.

"So, Arthur, what's so urgent?" The President looked at his watch. "You've got ten minutes. Sorry. Best I can do."

"Mr. President, these people represent our top experts in the field of astronomy. As you know, Dr. Koppernick is a

Nobelist and Dr. Roderick Simms is the Director of the VLBA project for SETI, headquartered in New Mexico. Dr. Anna Koppernick is a radio-astronomer at the Very Large Array in New Mexico, and before that was a professor at Boston University. I'm telling you all of this only because what they are about to tell you will require your complete appreciation of their credentials." Sokolsky turned and nodded to Niklas.

"Mr. President, the reason we're here is pretty simple," Niklas said, looking around the room. "This is where the buck stops. The world should know what we know, and we think it should come from you." Niklas' voice began to crack and he asked for a glass of water, which was put into his hand no more than twenty seconds later by the same officer who had brought the coffee and cookies.

As Niklas gulped the cool liquid, the President held his hands out, palms up, and asked, "So, Dr. Koppernick, what exactly is this buck you're passing me?" He punctuated his question with what Niklas thought was an inappropriate chuckle.

"Very soon now, our solar system is going to be struck by a massive thermal energy wave." As he spoke, Niklas felt his throat muscles tighten, and the blood drain from his face.

The President's casual smile vanished. He abruptly stood up and stepped back from the group. For a few seconds, he acted as though he thought they were kidding, then he gave Sokolsky an angry look.

Simms said, "Sir, this wave has been moving towards us from the other side of the Universe for at least three weeks now."

Still saying nothing, the President walked around behind his desk and started to shuffle through some papers. That's what I would do, Niklas thought. Try to collect myself and stay calm. Then the President looked directly at him.

"Okay, what's it going to do? When it gets here." He seemed cooler now. Maybe too cool.

The three scientists looked at Sokolsky, who could only look at the floor and shake his head, making it clear he would not be the one to clarify the situation for the President. That would be going out on a limb too far, even for a cabinet member. Niklas turned back to the President.

"Excuse me, sir. I want to make sure you understand what we're dealing with here. MOLO has been observing this phenomenon for some time, and there's very convincing evidence that this wave is disintegrating everything it encounters." Niklas decided to quit hedging and cleared his still painfully dry throat. "After it passes through a system, nothing... everything will be gone."

The President took this with a blank expression, then he began to walk slowly around the room. He stopped to straighten a large framed photograph hanging on the wall next to the Rose Garden French doors, then went over to one of the chairs sitting in front of his desk and moved it about six inches. Christ, he's rearranging the goddamn furniture, Niklas thought.

Anna broke the silence. "We're not the only ones who've observed this, sir. There are... others." She glanced over at Niklas, and he nodded back to her. "We have audio messages received at the Very Large Array indicating that other—

extraterrestrial– lifeforms can see it, too."

"You have alien messages?" The President went behind his desk and when he turned around to face the group, Niklas hoped he had just imagined the faint smirk. "I want to hear them. I want to see whatever you have. And I should have my science advisor here, too." He picked up his phone and asked his assistant to find out if Dr. Frederick James was in the building. "I need Freddy here now. Send a car for him, if you have to." Niklas wondered how Dr. James liked being called "Freddy." Sounds as bad as Nikki, he thought.

After hanging up and returning to the group, the President asked, "How soon?" His words conveyed none of the urgency Niklas thought such a question warranted. The man appeared to be thoroughly distracted or, worse, disinterested.

Niklas leaned forward and looked the President directly in the eye, trying to summon all of the persuasiveness he had.

"Sir, within the next 48 hours the source of this energy wave will probably become visible in the night sky. It will be unlike anything anybody has ever seen before. And when that happens, the whole world is going to start asking questions. We think waiting would be–"

"I agree with Dr. Koppernick on this, Mr. President." Sokolsky was finally jumping in, in an awkward attempt to redeem himself. "Of course, we can't eliminate panic entirely, but people's reaction might not be as disruptive to this news if you issued a statement while things still looked... normal."

The black phone on the President's desk rang and he walked over to answer it. Before picking up the receiver, he rubbed his eyes, and said, "After seeing the latest polls, I'm the one who should be panicked." When the President chuckled after making the remark, Niklas knew the cause was lost. The man is in total denial, he thought.

"Yes– Good, send him right in." He turned to the group. "Freddy's here."

Dr. Frederick James, reported to be seventy-eight years old, was a world-renowned biophysicist. Also a Nobel Prize winner, he had received just about every other scientific accolade the world had to offer as well. His research on proteins had lead to important breakthroughs in the treatment of multiple sclerosis and muscular dystrophy. Niklas had seen him in numerous television interviews, and knew he was barely five feet tall. So, when the white-haired Dr. James walked spryly into the Oval Office wearing his trademark black-rimmed glasses, for the first time in recent memory, Niklas Koppernick was not the shortest man in the room. Niklas liked him immediately.

Following the introductions, they positioned extra chairs in front of the video console built into the Oval Office wall. There were seven monitors, one for each network, including CNN, and one for C-SPAN, which the President had frequently referred to in public as the Lie-Fi Channel. The seventh was a free monitor, connected to a DVD player, and this was the one all eyes focused on for the next half hour. The three scientists went through the chronology of events, beginning with the first message, four weeks before.

While Simms carried on about Mr. Willoughby's activities at the VLA, Niklas thought about pressing the President harder to go public, but he knew it would just be a waste of breath. For whatever reason, halfway through their meeting the man had begun to act like a politician, rather than the leader of the Free World. Briefly, Niklas considered informing the room of his little insurance policy, to force the President's hand. A dozen of his associates, world-famous astronomers, were standing by to hold a news conference in two days, should the President decide to withhold the information from the public. All Niklas had to do was make a phone call. But, faced with that extreme option, he began to re-examine his own feelings. How would he have felt if he had known the truth about his father's illness? Would it have brought them any closer together during that final horrible year? No. Not possible. Would it have made his father's slow deterioration any less painful to watch? Again, the answer had to be no. He scratched his beard and grimaced. Could his father have been right to keep the truth from him? Maybe knowing, Niklas thought, is highly over-rated after all.

When his attention returned to the conversation, Niklas noticed that the President seemed to be studying the faces of everybody in the room.

"What do you think, Freddy?" Niklas could hear genuine respect and affection in the President's voice. Whatever James said, he thought, would carry a lot of weight.

"It will be– the most important speech any President has ever made." Everybody looked at Dr. James and then back to the President, who was looking out the window and shaking his head. "And, it would be immoral to remain silent."

Niklas looked at the man with great admiration. Good for

you, Freddie, he thought.

—⁓—

A little more than forty-five minutes after they had walked into the Oval Office, the President was ushering them out and asking his personal secretary to make sure she had all of their cellphone and pager numbers. He mentioned that he wanted to be able to reach any of them at a moment's notice.

Sokolsky couldn't get a read on what the President's decision would be. He had asked Dr. James to stay behind after the meeting and put a call out to his Chief of Staff. The Attorney General interpreted those actions as a sign the President intended to make an announcement of some kind. When they stepped into the outer hallway, Sokolsky took note of the White House staff's mood. After what he had just heard discussed only a few steps away, he thought the atmosphere seemed terribly– normal, with the security and administrative staff chatting and laughing as they went about their routines. None of them seemed to notice the grim expressions on the three visitors who had just come out of the Oval Office.

He walked Anna, Simms and Niklas downstairs to the side entrance of the White House, where a car was waiting to take them back to the Mayflower.

"What are you folks going to do now?" Sokolsky asked.

"What I always do after a meeting with the President," Niklas said. "Go home and get shit-faced." Then he stopped in the doorway, turned to Sokolsky and extended his hand. "You can do me one more little favor, Artie?"

"Name it, Niklas." Sokolsky said, shaking Niklas' hand.

"Say good-bye to Artie Jr. for me, will you?" Niklas let the Attorney General's hand drop, and walked from the building without waiting for a response.

Sokolsky's voice cracked as he called out to the departing scientists. "I appreciate what you all did here today. I-I- well, um- Just have a safe trip home. Okay?" He waved and managed a very weak smile as they all climbed into the limo and drove off. When he turned to go back up to the Oval Office, he was greeted by a familiar face.

"Mr. Willoughby," Sokolsky said, frowning. "Follow me."

—∧∧—

It had been a long day for all three of them. The trip, the meetings, going through everything all over again, had taken a physical toll. Anna fell asleep in the car during the five minute drive to the hotel. Nobody spoke.

Niklas tried to imagine what the world would be like in a couple of days. What would the President say? Would he offer false hope? Politicians hate delivering bad news. Would there be bedlam in the cities? Then, he wondered, what if they were wrong? What if they turned out to be Chicken Littles, and the beast never materialized? No, that wouldn't happen. He knew it was coming.

When they got back to the hotel, Simms paused at the lobby entrance and buttoned up his coat.

"Think I'll stretch my legs a little," he said.

"Uh, not a great idea, Doctor," Niklas said. "This area is notorious for brutal muggings. When I got here yesterday, the

Concierge told me they had just had one around the corner."

Simms nodded. "Oh, I'll be okay." He tipped his head back and headed down Connecticut Avenue. It was starting to get dark and looked like it might start raining again at any moment. Maybe, Niklas thought, the Washington sky wouldn't reveal any secrets tonight.

"Does he seem okay to you?" Anna asked, as they watched Simms walk down the sidewalk. "He's usually not this quiet."

"He'll be all right. If you weren't here, I'd be acting the same way he is." Niklas turned to her. "Say, I don't know about you, but I'm not very hungry. If you want to eat, how would you feel about just getting some room service?"

"The two most magical words in the English language." She kissed him on the cheek as they walked into the warm lobby of the hotel.

vii

"I strongly recommend against making any announcement, Mr. President." Willoughby paced the Oval Office nervously, trying to show the men who were watching him how dangerous he thought the situation was. "It is simply not warranted."

The President, Sokolsky and Freddy James were sitting in front of the fireplace. All three were visibly irritated by the agent's behavior. Dr. James' face reddened at the agent's less than subtle suggestion that they withhold the information from the public.

"Mr. Willoughby." The displeasure in Dr. James' voice was

evident to everybody in the room and Willoughby expected it. "You've heard the playback of the meeting with Dr. Koppernick and his associates, yet you still insist a public announcement is 'unwarranted'?"

Willoughby, realizing his performance was just upsetting his audience, walked over to the group and sat down. The question had given him time to transform his demeanor. Now calm, he confidently argued against the speech.

"Dr. James, I have great respect for you and for science. And I understand your desire to tell the world what you now believe to be true. However, there is simply no hard evidence this phenomenon is going to reach us. You heard Dr. Koppernick himself say that it's billions of light years from the Earth and that its behavior is inconsistent with the physics of the Universe. The obvious question, then, is how can he be so positive about the sequence of events? Without predictable cause and effect laws at work, how can anybody know what's going to happen?"

Willoughby paused and looked each man in the eye, and when he came to the President, he saw something in the man's face. What was it? Relief? Confirmation? Whatever it was, the President seemed an eager listener. Willoughby stood slowly and walked to the glass doors looking out onto the Rose Garden. Then, without turning to face the three men, he spoke.

"Mr. President, what if you made this public? What would happen? Some people might react constructively. You would. Dr. James would. Certainly Professor Sokolsky would go home to his family and spend the remaining hours he thought he had with his son. But what about the other seven billion or so people? Would they all be as responsible? As loving?" Willoughby turned around to face them. "Is anybody in this room naive enough to say 'yes' to that question?"

Willoughby returned to his seat, clasped his hands and leaned forward, resting his elbows on his knees. It was a relaxed and confident pose. The hints of concordance he had read earlier on the President's face were now less subtle and, seeing this, Willoughby wasted no time in closing his argument. "What if, after that terrible, destructive reaction, absolutely nothing happens?"

The President loosened his tie and shifted into the same body language as the NSA agent. After a few moments, he said, "Humpty-Dumpty." The President looked over at Sokolsky. "How long would it take to put the cities back together again after the smoke clears?" Turning to the agent, the President didn't intend to wait for an answer. "Your arguments are very reasonable, Mr. Willoughby. You've certainly given us a great deal to think about before we do anything foolish."

Dr. James moved to the edge of his chair, shaking his head. "You're ignoring all the evidence we've just seen, Mr. Willoughby. And what about the line? What will happen when it becomes visible to the naked eye?" Dr. James turned to the Chief Executive. "Mr. President, everything this man is saying is based on the assumption that these scientists are simply mistaken. I know about this fellow, Koppernick. Nobody in his field has his credentials." The President pressed his finger-tips together and nodded patronizingly.

"I've seen the evidence, too, Dr. James," Willoughby said. "What I have not done is draw the same conclusions as Dr. Koppernick. This is a man who loathes the very subject he has dedicated his life to studying. The 'Beast', he glibbly calls it. He expects it to devour us because that has been his personal philosophy for his entire life. For him, disaster is the only logical outcome, whether the facts warrant it or not. I know this fellow Koppernick, too. Almost as well as he knows himself. And his conclusions about this phenomenon are no surprise to me at all." Willoughby stood and went back to his position by the Rose Garden doors. "This line of his, if it ever does become visible to the public, isn't going to scare anybody. You've seen the pictures. What is it about this thing he thinks will frighten people so much? It's just a hair-thin streak across the sky. May arouse some curiosity. Nothing more." The agent looked at Sokolsky, who was furiously rubbing the bridge of his nose. "Professor Sokolsky, you have a son. Even if you believed what Dr. Koppernick was saying to be true, would you tell your son what he thinks is going to happen? And, if you did, how long do you think it would take him to recover from the trauma of hearing his irresponsible prediction after the Earth survives his 'light wave'?"

The question had its desired impact on the weary Attorney General. He turned to the President. "Who's going to tell Koppernick?" Sokolsky asked.

"What a minute!" Dr. James rose to his feet. "I don't recall hearing any such decision." He addressed the President. "Sir, you know my recommendation and I stand by it. Mr. Willoughby has said nothing here to convince me otherwise."

Willoughby looked for some sign that the President had arrived at a decision. Up until that day, the man had only been required to make routine governing decisions and Willoughby knew he had a reputation for being a "fence straddler".

The President stood and walked to his desk. He sat down in his chair and rocked nervously for moment before speaking.

"All right. Freddy, thank you for your thoughtful counsel on this. And my thanks to you and Agent Willoughby, Arthur."

Willoughby smiled inwardly at how obvious it was that the President was speaking for the benefit of his recorders. "I would like to consult with the Joint Chiefs on this. Get their thoughts. As you know, Arthur, there are lots of constitutional questions about preserving public order. In my judgment, seeing this line will not foment any immediate instability. I have to agree with Agent Willoughby on that." The fence has been built, Willoughby thought. "My decision is to wait and see how the situation develops. If things remain quiet, so do we. If not, we'll reassess as events dictate."

Dr. James seemed quite upset as he strode to the door. "I think you owe it to Dr. Koppernick and his colleagues to inform them of your decision, sir– if you choose to call it that. Excuse me, Mr. President. Gentlemen." He pushed the thick black frames of his glasses higher on the bridge of his nose, nodded to the men in the room and left, letting a nearby security officer close the door behind him.

Willoughby stood. "Let me handle the scientists, Mr.

President. I speak their language." It had been an eloquent performance, and, as he glided from the room, Willoughby took great satisfaction from the fact that he had done it all without ever resorting to the truth.

viii

Later on that evening, Niklas' appetite miraculously reappeared and he and Anna were enjoying the most expensive meals found on the room service menu. When Niklas finished eating, he got up and walked over to the hotel window.

"You know, you have an interesting habit of always walking over to the nearest window whenever you have something important to say. Ever notice that?" Anna said.

He turned and smiled. "Nope, never did. Maybe it's a subconscious conflict. I either say what I have on my mind or I jump. Good thing what I usually have to say is never that important, huh." He nodded toward the window and then stepped back over to the table.

"What's on your mind, Nick?"

"Do you have to go back to the Array? I mean, right away. Do you have to go back to work?" Anna was not used to seeing him struggle with words.

She sat down on the bed, next to Niklas' chair. He wouldn't look at her. She knew he was dealing with many things. The Line. The energy wave. And she wondered if, during the discussion back in Sokolsky's office, he had been thinking about the way his father's illness had been withheld from him. She leaned forward and put her forehead on his shoulder. "No, I can come to Boston. I can come home."

Niklas put his arm around her and stroked her hair.

"Thanks."

Anna realized the emotional stress was finally getting to them. She came over to his side of the bed and took his shoes off and started to undress him for bed. When he started to reach for her, she pushed him back. "Nope, not tonight, Dear. We both have a headache, and I think we could use a good night's sleep."

In fifteen minutes, they had both fallen sound asleep to the patter of rain against the hotel window.

ix

American Airlines flight number 147, inbound from Orly/Paris, was scheduled to land in Boston at 5:35 AM. The Boeing 777-300LR was filled with the usual businesspeople and families, in addition to a few college exchange students who were getting an early start on their spring vacations. Most of the passengers were sleeping as the jet flew smoothly, twenty thousand feet above the weather system now enveloping the eastern seaboard.

The aircraft was two hours out from Logan International, flying at its optimal cruising altitude of forty-three thousand feet, when the senior flight attendant came into the cockpit with a tray of coffees for the crew. As she stooped down to serve the pilot and co-pilot, she happened to glance out of the front windshield of the jet. At first she thought what she was seeing was a reflection from the instrument panel. Then she thought it must be the vapor trail of some extremely high-flying aircraft catching the rays of the early morning sun. When she realized that they were facing the wrong direction for that, she pointed without saying a word. The co-pilot tilted his head and squinted his eyes to see what had captured her attention. Reaching from horizon to horizon, the long pale thread of light ran a perfect arc across the ultramarine evening sky. Without taking his eyes off the sky, he reached over and tugged on the captain's sleeve. As he emptied a second bag of Equal into his steaming coffee, the captain looked to his right, then in the direction his co-pilot was staring. When the flight engineer sitting at the back of the cabin realized all the cockpit chatter had abruptly stopped, he looked up from his computer console to see his three crewmates leaning forward, staring silently out the window of the airliner.

x

By the time Anna and Niklas walked into his house, it was 1 PM and they were soaking wet from the rainstorm. On the way home, the cab driver had mentioned something about "strange goings on up in the sky". When they got inside, Niklas immediately turned on CNN to see if there were any news reports. There were.

Several airline pilots had reported seeing something highly unusual in the night sky. They described it as a very faint, hair-thin line stretching as far as they could see, and appeared to have no beginning or end. When interviewed on the air, the pilots had not seemed too alarmed and Niklas decided that was good. If they had been visibly shaken by the sighting, the public would have picked up on it. One of them commented during his interview that he thought it might be a comet and he gave a sigh of relief. They kept waiting for the President to get on the air with a statement. But, for the next couple of hours, no reports came from the White House at all.

Niklas put a call in to Sokolsky, but he was unavailable. He thought about trying to reach the President, but figured it wouldn't be worth the long distance charge. They both unpacked and got cleaned up. Still no announcement. A half hour later, Niklas tried for Sokolsky again. Still not available. Son of a bitch, he thought.

On the third try, Niklas slammed down the phone.

"Goddamn idiot! Okay, he doesn't believe us. Maybe the light wave was too complex for him. But he's not even going to say anything about the fucking line! What can he be thinking? If the weather clears tonight, he's going to have millions of scared shitless people on his hands."

Anna grabbed Niklas by the shoulders. "What's the difference, Niklas? You've done everything you could." He gritted his teeth and took a deep breath. "Listen," she said, more calmly. "I want to call Commie, just to see how things are down at the Array. I'm worried about him." Niklas gestured toward the phone and left the room, as angry as he'd been in a long time.

—∿∿—

"Commie, how's it going?" She tried to sound upbeat.

"Well, you tell me. What happened with your meeting?" His tone sounded as if he felt a little better.

Anna explained what had happened and how angry they were about the President's silence. She told him Simms was on his way back to the array and that he would fill everybody in on the details.

"I'm going to be here in Boston for a while. If anything comes up, you let me know. All right?" While she was giving him the number, there was a loud knock at the door. Niklas didn't come out to answer it, so she rushed Commie off the phone and went to see who it was. When she first opened the door, she didn't recognize the man standing there on the porch, wearing an old hat and yellow rain slicker. Dripping wet, the pale-skinned stranger wore an odd expression on his face and didn't speak. Then she realized who it was, and found it difficult to hide how shocked she was by Dirk's appearance.

"Dirk, come in," Anna said, forcing a smile. "Niklas is in the bedroom. I'll get him." She left him standing in the entryway in an expanding puddle of water. He still didn't bother to remove his hat and raincoat.

Anna walked back out, with Niklas dragging behind her. Even though he had been so angry a moment before, she was amazed to see Niklas' reaction to Dirk. His anger seemed to vanish and she was touched by the caring tone he took with his friend, who looked like half his blood supply had been drained from his body.

"What's the matter, buddy? Here, take your coat– and that hat– off. Where do you get these damn things? You want some coffee or something?" Anna helped Dirk remove his wet raincoat.

Dirk didn't answer, but Niklas nodded toward the kitchen to Anna and she understood. Dirk had a package under his arm which was wrapped in plastic. He was holding it so tightly that it had almost prevented them from removing his coat. He finally let Niklas hold it until the coat and hat were off. They walked into the living room and Niklas noticed Dirk was shivering even though his slicker had kept him dry. Niklas threw a couple of logs into the fireplace and lit a fire while Anna brought in a pot of hot coffee.

"Okay, Dr. Anders," Niklas said with faint smile. "You walk into my house, do a couple hundred dollars worth of water damage– this better be good."

Dirk looked back and forth at both of them and after a minute he spoke. "You won't believe what we got. But it's... it's there. And I don't even–"

"Whoa, big fella." Niklas came over and sat next to his shaken friend. "Take it easy. What are you talking about?"

"Remember we talked about taking a closer look at that dark area– in the line?"

"Yeah. What about it?"

Dirk swallowed a gulp of hot coffee. "Well, I got some maximum range closeups, but the resolution wasn't all that great. So, I made a high-speed DVD recording of it." Anna came over and sat next to him. "Then I called a friend of mine over at MIT, Nori Fukuda. They've got an image enhancement program over there the government and NASA use sometimes to develop more information from their satellite reconnaissance pictures. It's even faster than the DOD's 'Roadrunner' down at Los Alamos. Capable of 100,000 trillion operations per second and–"

"Yeah, I've heard of it. Analyzes the pixels, makes assumptions about missing details and then sort of fills in the blanks. Right?" Anna sensed Niklas had no idea what Dirk was getting at and she was surprised by his uncharacteristic patience.

Dirk said, "It's called High Resolution Pixel Extrapolation. 'Herpes' Nori calls it." Dirk gave a smileless chuckle. "Anyway, yesterday we downloaded the DVD and ran the software. It just finished running late this morning. Got Nori into some hot water. I had to tell some of his staff what was going on. I hope you're not pissed off about that." He was looking down at the floor, rubbing the back of his neck.

"Is that what you're stressed about? Christ, haven't you heard? The cat's totally out of the fuckin' bag." Niklas squeezed his shoulder and shot a smile over to Anna.

Dirk looked up at them and it was obvious that Niklas' reaction had not eased his mind. "No, no, it's not that, Dr. Koppernick." He trembled and nodded toward the package he had been carrying. "It's all there– on the disk."

Niklas picked up the package and peeled off the dripping plastic cover. He walked over to the 42" plasma television with a built-in player. Dirk watched as Niklas turned on the set and slid the disk onto the tray slot and walked back to the couch with the remote.

"Okay– What do we have here?" Niklas asked as he pushed the playback button. Dirk stared intently at the monitor.

A remarkably clear closeup of the line abruptly popped

up. Niklas and Anna could make out the large dark area immediately, but it was extremely pixilated image. Niklas looked over at Dirk for some kind of explanation but got none. Then a window came up at the bottom of the frame. It was a time code counter that had been added to help precisely identify individual frames. The counter started, ran for about ten seconds, and then froze. Dirk nodded toward the screen.

Slowly, as the computer program did its comparative analysis of each pixel, the squared off, geometric edges of each one softened and began to coalesce with the others around it. Niklas got up and walked closer to the set. The dark image inside of the line nearly filled the large high-definition screen, and it was gradually taking on a distinctive shape. Within thirty seconds, they began to make out what it was.

Anna stepped up alongside of Niklas. "What the...."

Niklas turned and gave Dirk an exasperated look. "Is this some kind of goddamn joke, Dirk?"

Dirk didn't respond, and just kept staring at the screen. His silence and his expression answered Niklas' question.

Niklas looked back at the television and dropped down to one knee. At first, he was unable to accept what his eyes were telling him, and the luminescent screen seemed to drift into a long tunnel of darkened fog. The image assaulted him on every level, emotionally, intellectually, and even spiritually. Feeling faint, he lowered his head and pinched the bridge of his nose for a moment, then finally managed to suck enough air back into his lungs to speak.

"What the fuc–." Niklas choked the obscenity off, for some

reason forbidding himself to complete it. The dark area on the screen was a human face, cropped just below the mouth and above the brow, surrounded by an intensely bright halo of light. As the picture's focus sharpened, Niklas moved forward, even closer to the screen, until he reached out and touched the bright glass surface.

Anna leaned forward, shoulder to shoulder with Niklas, studying the face. It had gaunt, semitic features, with hollow cheeks and dark skin. When she realized the wide shadow beneath the nose was a mustache, she whispered, "Is it God?"

"Yes," Niklas whispered. Leaving his hand on the screen, he turned slowly toward her. "Yes. And his name is Aaron Koppernick." He turned back to the screen. "It's my father."

Chapter 8
Secret Places

i

"Are you sure, Nick?" Anna was sitting next to him on the floor, as he sat staring at the television screen. Dirk stood up and moved behind them so he could watch over their shoulders.

"It's been more than 40 years, but you don't forget your own father's face. I can't... I mean, it's something I never thought I would ever see again." He finally took his hand off the screen and clenched his jaw. What's the beast up to now, he thought.

Dirk sat down next to Niklas and studied the picture.

"You're sure it's your father? A lot of the face is cropped off. You can't see the hairline or chin."

"Hey, I can even tell you when this was– or is. Christ, what are we talking about here!" His voice trailed off to an exhausted mutter and he rubbed his eyes again, hard.

"What's that mean, you know when this is?" Anna asked.

"You see this?" He pointed to the shadow in the middle of the image. "Dad never wore a mustache. Not until the Holy Land expedition. He came home with a full beard– then my mother made him shave it off." Niklas shrugged. "Thought it made him look like a hippy. Anyway, he decided he liked the mustache and kept it until the day he died." He looked back at the screen. "Pissed Mom off with that one, didn't you." A tear slid down his cheek. "Jesus, Dad. What the hell did you do?" He reached up and gently touched the picture one more time.

Dirk leaned forward and looked closely at the screen.

"Can you tell where he is? In the picture, I mean."

"Shit, how would I know? Heaven? Hell?" Niklas peered closer, trying to see more detail in the bright areas on either side of the face, finally throwing his head back and staring at the ceiling in frustration. He couldn't seem to keep his mind focused on one thought at a time.

Anna abruptly stood up. "Come on, Nick!" She jabbed her finger at the television screen. "This means something."

"What? What's the difference?" Niklas couldn't– didn't want to think. Everything seemed to be converging on him.

"I know this is a shock to you. But this is the image of something that happened a long time ago! It's not happening now. So, please, try to remember. It was an important time in your life. Your father had been gone for months. What was he working on?" Niklas could see she wanted him to set his emotions aside, but couldn't seem to control her own. "Damn it, you're letting your goddamn Beast win again!"

Niklas flinched and looked at her. After a moment he began to calm down. "Okay. Okay. You're right. Let me think. Shit– He came back from the trip– We had gotten this big wooden– Hey, wait a minute." Niklas stood up and walked across the room, searching his memory, and then, suddenly, it all came rushing back to him. "He had this crate shipped to the house. From Iraq."

"How big?" Anna asked.

"Bigger than a fucking breadbox! Christ, I was only eleven years old, Anna!"

"I'm sorry," she said. "Whatever you can recall."

He nodded to her and came back over to them. "It was big! As big as I was, anyway. Four or five feet tall. He stuck it down in the basement. You know, I haven't even thought about this in years, but I remember he was more excited about opening up that crate than he was about being home again."

"So, do you remember what was in it?" Anna asked.

"Oh yeah. Wasn't the kind of thing you forget. Looked like a big vase. An urn, I think he called it. Had these incredible black elephants at the base with a globe on top. Like the Earth. I remember it being sparkly and colorful. Looked brand new. Nothing like the stuff he usually brought home to photo...." His voice trailed off and he scratched his beard.

"What?" Anna asked.

Dirk stood up and ejected the disk from the player, watching Niklas the entire time.

"I was leaving for school the morning after he got home, and he was down in the basement getting ready to photograph the thing. He had this old floodlamp," Niklas said.

"A floodlamp?" Dirk asked, looking over to Anna.

"I remember how hot the basement got whenever he used it. Thing was really bright. It was one of those cheap studio floodlamps, with an adjustable stand. He hated it. It was always– over-heating." Niklas looked back at the blank television screen, and wondered if what he was thinking could possibly be true. "I was in the kitchen, standing at the top of the basement stairs, when I heard something. Then I saw this flash of light downstairs. At first I thought it was a flashbulb. Then I realized it must have been the floodlamp bulb burning out. I'll be goddamned. You don't suppose—"

"The light wave." Dirk said.

"The flash of light," Niklas said, staring the television screen. "It's the brightness on either side of the face in the line. Christ, I was only a few feet away when this happened!"

"Did you go downstairs to see if he was okay?" Anna asked.

"No! Why should I? He was always photographing stuff down there. A fucking bulb burned out, for Christ's sake!" Niklas had raised his voice and realized he was being too defensive. "Besides, I wasn't even supposed to be home. I had this annoying habit of always being late for school."

"Do you know where this urn is now?" Dirk asked.

"Dad had it taken away— the next day, I think. Never saw it again. Mom might know something, though. She was probably at home when it was picked up." Niklas went over to his phone.

"We need to find it," Anna said.

All Dirk could do was nod in agreement. Niklas noticed that his young associate had at least stopped shaking.

As his mother's phone was ringing, Niklas turned to Anna and Dirk. "I don't want her to know about any of this." He nodded toward the television. "All right? I'm not even sure she'll remember anything." He knew better.

Then, at the other end of the line, "Hello."

"Mom? It's Niklas. How are you doing?"

"Finally he calls." She sounded glad to hear from him.

"Feel like some company? I've got some friends I'd like to bring over." He kept it as cheerful as he could.

"You're asking my permission to visit? Such thoughtful behavior all of sudden!" She laughed.

Niklas smiled. "We'll be there in a bit. Bye, Mom." He hung up and they all grabbed their coats and piled into Niklas' BMW. As they drove away from his house, the heavy rain kept them from noticing the dark, unmarked sedan parked up the street pull away from the curb.

ii

After Niklas introduced his mother to Dirk, she walked up to Anna with a curious expression. "And who is this?" Then a broad smile formed on her face and she hugged Anna. "So, you could leave the Martians after all."

Anna threw Niklas a shocked look and turned to face her mother-in-law. "How have you been, Desta?" Despite the circumstances of the visit, Anna still felt a little gunshy.

"Polka dancing I'm not, but I'm fine. And, every once in a blue moon, my little Nikki comes to see me." She smiled at Anna and they both laughed at his expense. "I am so glad to see you again, Anna. You are still so beautiful."

Anna hadn't been with her for more than a few minutes and already sensed a fundamental change in Desta Koppernick. No. She could actually see it, just as she had seen the one in Niklas. As if by magic, they had both shed their hostility toward life and she felt only warmth and love coming from them. What could have caused such a change?

She wondered if Niklas had already told his mother what was going on in the world.

Desta insisted on serving them hot coffee. They all gathered in the living room and took their cups from the old serving tray. Niklas whispered to Anna and Dirk that he didn't want to rush things and risk alarming his mother, but he couldn't wait.

"Mom, do you remember when Dad came back from that big expedition in Iraq? Right before he got sick?"

Anna watched Desta's jovial mood shift and the veil of sadness came over her. "Yes, I remember," Desta said. "That was when your father changed." There was nothing wrong with her long term memory. She could recall things from forty and fifty years ago with remarkable clarity– it was just the present which seemed to give her trouble now and then.

"When he came home, he was very thin. I could see his ribs when he got out of the shower. At first, I thought he might have picked up one of those exotic foreign diseases. Then I got very superstitious. I thought it was some kind of curse. You know, like that King Tut mishegas. Sounds silly, I know. But I knew he had been digging around in all those old places and I just couldn't understand what was happening to him." She stopped for a moment and took a sip of her coffee.

Anna tried to imagine how terrible it must have been for this woman watching her husband dying before her eyes while he fought her every attempt to help him. She wondered what could have driven the man to such self-destructive behavior. It takes a special kind of guilt to do that.

"I finally got him to see a doctor," Desta said. "But he

wouldn't let them treat him for the cancer. It was like he was punishing himself for something." Desta and Niklas exchanged looks of understanding and Anna realized they must have spoken of this before. "I'll never understand it. So tragic. Such a beautiful young man, your father was. He should still be here– with me."

"With both of us," Niklas whispered. Desta's eyes began to tear and Anna sat down next to her and hugged her. Then Niklas said, "Mom, I'm sorry." Anna could hear Niklas taking a deep breath and she understood how he must have hated probing such deep wounds. "I need to ask you about something that happened back– before Dad got so sick."

"So ask." She sniffled and straightened herself. She was all right. "I remember everything."

"What happened to the big crate and the urn he had shipped to the house from Iraq? Do you remember it?" The three watched her look back over the years. Anna was shocked by the incredible detail in Desta's answer.

"Oh, yes. Such a day that was. These hippies came to the house." Desta rolled her eyes. "Hair down to their backs and one had a beard. Who knows what was living in it. I never liked beards, you know. Made your father shave his off, but he wouldn't get rid of the mustache." Anna looked at Niklas and Dirk and smiled weakly. "Anyway, your father asked them to come and take the crate away. He seemed very upset and wanted it out of the house."

"Do you know where they took it, Desta?" Anna asked.

"Well, no. But they must have taken it to the Museum. Isn't that where all those things went?" She looked at Niklas as if expecting him to know the answer.

"No. Nothing like that was ever in the Semitic Museum," Niklas said. "Do you ever hear from any of the old faculty Dad worked with?"

"Oh, of course, Marty and Rachel Yamashita." She smiled. "I get a postcard from them every now and then. They live out in California. Winters got too cold for them here, I guess."

"Do you know how to reach them? By phone?" Anna asked.

"Let me go get my book." She went upstairs to her bedroom and they could hear her walking back and forth across the creaky floor above them. A couple of minutes later she returned, but with two books. One was a small, brown, vinyl address book, but the other was large and ornate. She handed the larger book to Niklas. "When Aaron was ill, I saw him reading this all the time. Don't know why I bothered to keep it."

As Niklas opened the heavy book, Anna came over and looked over his shoulder. It was a fifty-year-old English translation of the Hymns of the Rig Veda, the ancient and very sacred Brahmanic writings. They could see by the soiled edges which pages had been read and re-read, and when Niklas opened to them, he saw his father's scribblings in the margins. He also saw several passages had been circled.

While Niklas continued to study the note-covered pages, Anna went over to Desta, who was still going through her address book. She was having trouble finding the Yamashita's phone number, but, after a few minutes, she remembered she had listed them under R, for Rachel. As she turned to that section of the book, she mentioned that Rachel had been one of her last surviving Wailing Wall chums. Anna spotted the number immediately and took Niklas' cell phone from his jacket. While she dialed the number, she noticed Niklas still poring over the pages of the old book. The phone rang a half dozen times before an elderly lady finally answered.

"Is this Dr. Martin Yamashita's residence?"

"Yes, it is."

"Is this Rachel speaking?"

"Yes, it is. Who's calling, please?" Rachel sounded as if she was getting a little irritated.

"Oh, hello, Mrs. Yamashita. My name is Anna Koppernick."

"Koppernick? Desta's daughter-in-law?" Rachel asked.

"Yes."

"Is Desta all right?" When Rachel asked the question, Anna could hear the concern in her voice and immediately understood how a call from the relative of an old friend could produce sudden alarm.

"Oh, she's fine," Anna answered quickly. "She's right here." Wanting to make sure Rachel knew everything was okay, Anna passed the phone to Desta.

"Hello, Rachel.– I'm fine.– And how are you and Marty?– That's wonderful.– Oh, it's very rainy here right now. Not too bad.– Oh?" She covered the phone and said. "She says it's ninety degrees there now. Can you imagine the air-conditioning bills?" Niklas had stopped reading and came over to sit down next to his mother. "Pardon me, Rachel, but is Marty there? My son would like to speak to him about something.– Would you mind?– Thank you. I'll speak with you later.– Yes, I promise." Desta passed the phone to her son.

—⁓—

"Hello, Dr. Yamashita? This is Niklas."

"Nikki?" Yamashita's greeting put a brief frown on Niklas' face. "My, it's been so long. Please, call me Marty."

'Thanks, Marty. Listen, I need to ask you about something that happened way back when you all came home from the expedition– back in '70. Can you tell me anything about a large urn my father had shipped home from Iraq?

Yamashita whistled dryly. "Did you find it? Where was–"

"No, but we're trying to," said Niklas. "Anything you can tell us. I know it's been a long time."

"Boy, that urn was something. You're talking about the one with the mammoths, right?"

"Yeah, the one with the elephants. Dad showed it to me the day after he got back." Niklas glanced at Anna with a confused expression. "Mammoths?–"

"Ray Allen and I dropped by your house not long after your father died to see if it was still there. Doesn't your mother remember?" Yamashita sounded disappointed.

"She never mentioned it," Niklas said. "We thought maybe you knew where it was. It obviously never made it to the Semitic Museum or the Peabody. Can you tell me about it?"

Niklas listened intently while Yamashita told him everything he recalled about the urn and how it had been found. He remembered Niklas' father worrying about the expedition's credibility and, if it got out that a counterfeit relic had turned up in the middle of their excavation, a shadow of suspicion might be cast over all their work. He explained why he and Raymond Allen had decided, with some hesitation, to let Niklas' father deal with it.

"Actually, Aaron— your father— was quite insistent on that," Yamashita said. "I had x-rayed the thing when we were still over there in Baghdad and could see it was empty. I also did a rough translation of the lid. Confusing, as I recall. Anyway, by the time we got home, Raymond and I figured Aaron had decided it was an import of some kind and that he had just tucked it away somewhere, keeping it under wraps. Boy, I'll never forget the first time I saw it. It was the most beautiful thing I'd ever seen. Still is."

"Do you know how to reach Dr. Allen?" Niklas asked.

There was a moment of silence on the other end of the phone.

"Didn't you hear?" Yamashita's tone of voice turned somber. "Raymond and his son died in a diving accident. I thought Desta knew."

"Oh, Christ. No, I don't think she knows. I'm really sorry to hear that." Niklas looked over to Anna and Dirk.

"Yeah. It was, let me see, back in '74, I think. It was pretty heavily reported in the press. They were apparently diving quite deep and both of them got nitrogen narcosis. Rapture of the Deep, it's called. A real tragedy. Strange, too. Raymond's son was a SEAL, you know. A first-rate diver. Such a shame. Please tell Desta for me. I'm not up to delivering news like that. Especially to her."

"Yes. I'll certainly tell her. Listen, Dr. Yamashita— Marty, I appreciate all your time here." Niklas looked over at his mother. She had been chatting off and on with Anna and he knew she hadn't been listening.

"Please. Let me know if you're able to dig that urn up. I'd love to see it again. And give our love to your mother. Tell her to call more often. Rachel misses her old Wailing Wall friends."

"You bet. And Mother sends her love to you both. Bye-bye, Marty." As Niklas hung up the phone, he smiled back at his mother. "Nice man," he said. She smiled and nodded.

"He doesn't know where it is, I take it," Dirk asked.

"Not a clue." Niklas re-opened the book. "He said Dad was afraid the urn was a phony— wanted to keep it 'under wraps' to protect the credibility of the damn expedition. But I don't buy that. Not after seeing this." He pointed at the book, which he had opened to its most worn page. It was Book X of the Rig Veda, the Vedic Creation Hymn. Written at the top of the page, in his father's elegant but shaky handwriting, were the words 'Purusha's Urn'. The whole section was dog-eared, with many notes and small drawings cluttering the margins. Niklas thought it looked just like a college professor's working text.

"Purusha's urn?" Dirk asked, peering over Niklas' shoulder.

"Yeah, you've heard of the Purusha Atom, right?" Niklas looked down at the scrawls. "The Universe began as an infinitely dense singularity no bigger than the size of an atom. Some call this seminal particle the Purusha Atom. Everything in this Universe came from it. This is where that comes from. It says here Purusha was the most ancient of the Vedic Gods— a cosmic giant." Niklas pointed to the circled phrase. "This Purusha sacrificed his body to create the Universe, and, according to Dad's notes, the urn contained his remains."

Niklas looked up and raised his eyebrows.

"You sure you're reading that right?" Anna asked. "If his body is the Universe, how can his remains be inside an urn?"

"Baby universes," Dirk muttered.

Niklas smiled. "Yes. Quantum realities. If this means what I think it means, I'm even smarter than I thought I was."

"Excuse me, but what are you children talking about?" Desta seemed tired and Niklas knew listening to their conversation wasn't doing much to help keep her awake. She got up to take the coffee tray into the kitchen.

"Do you need some help with that, Mom?" Anna asked.

"No, no, no. I know where everything goes. You children talk," Desta said, as she walked away with the full tray.

Niklas was surprised. He couldn't remember the last time he had heard Anna call his mother that, and he liked it. As Desta disappeared into the kitchen, he turned back to Anna and Dirk.

"Anyway, where were we? Oh yeah, baby universes. All the evidence we have about the Universe points to it being an open, expanding system. But what if it's not? What if it's finite and expanding? And what if there's more than one?"

"Are you suggesting that the urn contains one of these quantum realities?" Anna asked.

"Quantum realities. Meta-universes. Parallel worlds. Whatever. I call them bubbles." Niklas winked at Dirk, who had seen him practice the bubble trick too many times to count. "Each one of the bubbles is a closed system."

"So there's no causal influences between them," Dirk explained to Anna. "At least, there's not supposed to be."

"Right," Niklas said. "A cause in one Universe should not have an effect in another. Otherwise, you'd have chaos. Each one has to have its own set of physical laws, and they would be incompatible with one another. If two adjacent planes of reality interacted—

Anna finished the thought. "Annihilation?"

"Uh-huh." Niklas frowned. "It would be like normal matter meeting anti-matter. I think that's what is happening right now. It's a chain reaction within the cosm."

"Hold it, Nick." Anna groaned. "You're inventing words again. The cosm?"

"Well, the shorthand description is that it's a causally-linked sequence of Universes, all sharing identical realities. The configuration is easiest to describe as bubbles within bubbles. And what happens in one bubble, happens in all the bubbles of that cosm. Actually, it's a theory I've been talking about for a long time." Niklas smiled at the coincidence, and then wondered if it really wasn't.

"So, when your father opened the urn— in this Universe—"

Niklas nodded. "He also opened it in all the other Universes of our cosm. We've just learned something very important here. The smaller the bubble, the faster the sequence of events in that reality play out. As you go up the chain of realities, from the microcosmic toward the macrocosmic, there must be a delay. You know, like what happens when you toss a pebble into a lake. At first, the ripple moves quickly, expanding out from the point of the impact. Then, as its circumference increases, it appears to slow down. That's why we're just now experiencing the effects of what my old man did forty years ago. Him and his goddamned floodlamp."

Niklas' mother came back into the room with a big smile on her face. "I have good news." Everybody turned to her in unison. "It's stopped raining." She seemed quite confused when everyone in the room laughed.

Niklas stood up and stretched, then went to hug her.

"Mom, we have to get going. We've got something we need to find right away."

"Oh, so soon!" Her yawn betrayed her. Anna hugged her good-bye and Dirk shook her hand politely. Desta turned once more to Anna. "Please come back, my dear. I would like to talk with you about– some things." Her smile was so sweet and sorrowful, Anna actually hated to leave her.

—⚋—

On their way out to the car, Anna and Dirk both asked Niklas the same question. "Where are we going now?"

"You guys forget I spent a lot of time at the University with my father. I have a hunch about where he might put something he didn't want people to find. If I'm right, it's been right under my damn nose for the last fifteen years."

Dirk paused at the BMW's door. "Anybody looked up lately?"

The clouds were beginning to break up in the early evening sky and the hair-thin line was now clearly visible. They noticed some of the neighbors on their front lawns, looking up. They reminded Niklas of the curious onlookers at an accident scene. None of them were involved and, not knowing any of the victims, they were strangely aloof and unaffected by the reality of the mishap. Cosmic rubberneckers, he thought.

"It's wider than I thought it would be," Dirk said. "Could be accelerating. Opening faster."

As Anna was about to climb into the BMW she froze. "Do you hear something?" They all stopped moving and listened. The still wet street was quiet except for a distant rumbling.

"Thunder?" Dirk suggested. "Haven't seen any lightning. Must be pretty far away. Wind's coming up. Could be wind, couldn't it?"

Looking up at the line, Niklas said, "It's not thunder. And it sure as hell isn't the wind." Niklas knew what most people didn't: sound could travel through space. The interstellar medium was not an absolute void, and, given a large enough source, a wall of sound could be generated there. The energy wave was pushing a gigantic crest of hydrogen atoms, plasma and planetary debris ahead of itself. He looked at Anna. "It's happening faster than I thought it would."

"They all seem to be taking it pretty calmly," Anna said, pointing at the people standing in front of their homes. "Just look at them. They haven't got a clue. Probably just think it's a comet or something."

"It's not right. People should be told." Niklas thought of his father's deception about his illness and the impact of that decision. The only difference here was, if he was right about the energy wave, there wouldn't be anybody left to suffer the consequences of the President's lousy decision. Guess that lets him off the hook, Niklas thought. Anna and Dirk couldn't see the small sardonic grin on his face.

—∿—

As the cold, damp wind began to increase in strength, they got into the BMW and drove off. The unmarked sedan followed.

iii

After a very bumpy four-hour plane ride and the ninety minute drive from Albuquerque, Simms finally arrived back at the Array early that evening. Angie had been waiting for him at the airport and drove him back. New Mexico's moonless, ultramarine sky made the Line seem closer than it really was, and the quiet stillness of the high desert made the approaching roar all the more disturbing.

Angie was frightened. As soon as he had retrieved his luggage from the trunk of her car, Simms went to her.

"Why does it have to make that awful sound?" Her voice trembled and her breathing was shallow and rapid.

Simms looked up at the cut-in-half sky. She was right. The sound was terrible. Like having your head gripped in the tightening jaws of giant crocodile. Guttural and inexorable. He tried to calm her, but she was inconsolable.

"Angie, please. Let's try to keep it together." He decided to lie to her. "We really don't know what's going to happen for sure." Quickly, he changed the subject. "Do you know where Commie is?"

She sniffled and regained her composure a little. "Up in the SEC. He's been up there ever since you and Anna left."

He took her by the arm and they headed in the SEC's

direction. When they looked up at the top of the stairway, they could see Commie standing there. He was also looking up– at the glowing amber line in the sky. Simms didn't think Commie saw them until they were almost halfway up the stairs.

"I thought I heard thunder and came out here expecting to see a storm," Commie called down to them. "God. Sounds like– war." Commie was right, Simms thought. It could easily have been mistaken for far-off artillery bombardment. The sound seemed to come from everywhere.

As Simms and Angie neared the top of the stairs, they could see Commie better. He looked awful. Two days growth of beard and no food or sleep can do that, Simms thought. Commie turned and went back inside before they reached him. They followed him inside to find him leaning on the recording console, resting his head on in his forearms.

"You all right, Commie?" Simms knew how silly his question must have sounded. Nobody was all right. Anywhere.

Commie looked up with reddened eyes and smiled.

"Ahhh! At least my hangover's gone. How are you?"

"Met with the President. Thought he was going to make an announcement, but it looks like that's not going to happen. Goddamn politicians." Simms growled weakly. "Anna went back to Boston with Niklas. Don't know if she'll make it back."

Commie sighed. "Just as well. Looks like this is happening faster than we thought it would anyway." He looked up at the ceiling. "Sounds like it, too."

"Anything coming through here?" Simms sat down next to

him and put his hand on Commie's shoulder.

"No," Commie said, sighing deeply. "Nobody's talking." Commie shook his head. "It's kinda like that old movie, On The Beach. About those people in Australia who survived World War III. Gregory Peck, I think. And some famous actress. Anyway, every day there were fewer and fewer people on the streets. The ones who didn't die from radiation sickness, committed suicide. Then, everyone was gone. I guess, pretty soon, we're gonna be the last ones on the beach, huh."

"Why don't you go get some food and some sleep? I'll stay up here for a while. If anything comes in, I'll make sure it's recorded. Go on! You look like hell." Simms tried to laugh. He knew Commie didn't have the physical or emotional strength to argue with him.

Commie nodded, then got up and went slowly to the door. Simms and Angie followed him outside, onto the stairway landing, where they all paused for a moment to look up once again. The roar seemed a little louder now, and they thought they could see tiny stars flaring and winking out in the blackness of the night sky. Simms hoped it was just his imagination and that they had more time. As Commie shuffled down the stairs, Angie grabbed Simms' arm and squeezed it tight enough to make him wince. He reached back and put his arm around her.

"Can you stay up here with me, Honey?" Simms asked, not taking his eyes from the sky.

Angie didn't answer. She just held his arm even tighter.

As Commie stepped off the stairs below, Simms called

down to him.

Ava Gardner! It was Ava Gardner and Gregory Peck."

Commie laughed and kept walking, and Simms tried to remember how the film ended.

iv

As the three ran to the front entrance of the Science Center, they looked up at the widening amber frown in the sky, which was now really too wide to be called a line. The storm clouds and pollution over the city had been blown seaward by a growing easterly wind, which only added to the din of the advancing energy wave. The amorphous dark area within the Line was now becoming visible and, as he rifled through his wallet searching for his cardkey, Niklas wondered if the whole world would soon be able to make out the face of– Purusha.

—ɯ—

A few seconds after they entered the building, a black sedan parked next to Niklas' car. Despite the thundering sky above them, the two men inside sat and waited patiently.

—ɯ—

Niklas led Anna and Dirk down the stairs to the basement level of the Science Center. The lighting there was notoriously bad, which had contributed to its lack of visitors. The primary reason most people came down there was because it was where the restrooms were located. Even so, in its busiest times, the basement never buzzed with activity, and security was so lax that students had been known to live there while they were looking for apartments. Some of them had even had the audacity to complain about the chronic plumbing problems in the bathrooms. All in all, it was a dark and dank place, filled with esoteric scientific memorabilia nobody was interested in anymore. Niklas figured that was exactly what Aaron Koppernick had counted on so many years before.

They passed the unmanned security desk standing at the beginning of a long hallway which ran the length of the building. Niklas found some light switches on the wall and tried them. Only two lights came on in the long passageway, but the three proceeded anyway, trying every door they passed. Some were storage rooms, some were maintenance lockers and others were the cubbyholes of academics who hadn't been important enough to warrant a window office. The further they went, the dimmer it got, and Dirk commented on how good he had it up on the eighth floor. To his own surprise, in all his time at the University, Dirk had never been in this part of the building.

Exasperated, Anna asked, "Nick, do you have any idea what you're looking for? It's creepy as hell down here."

"Double doors. I remember coming down here with Dad and watching him push open some double doors. It was like his personal storeroom." Niklas tone became very serious. "He always said that, in some future millennium, the archaeologist who found this room would unlock the secrets of the Ages."

"What'd he mean by that?" Anna asked.

"He meant even an archaeologist wouldn't be able to find it." Dirk said it as though he thought the meaning was obvious.

Niklas laughed. "Until a few hours ago, I would have agreed with that."

"Well, good thing none of us are archaeologists, huh. Now I know where you got your sense of humor. Interesting. Never heard of sarcastic genes before." Anna was only half-joking.

As they were nearing the end of the hallway, they came to two large gray doors on their left. Rather than a cardkey slot, the doors still had their original deadbolt lock in place. Anna and Dirk groaned.

"You know, I've been in this building for a long time." He held up a keyring with at least a dozen keys on it. "Since before they upgraded the security lock system, as a matter of fact." He selected one of the keys and smiled. "Never bothered to turn in my master." He inserted the key in the old lock and took a deep breath. He had no idea whether or not they had ever changed the locks in the building. When he turned the key and heard the deadbolt sliding, he grinned in relief. "This must be the place."

They could barely see inside the room. Very little light spilled in from the hallway. As their eyes grew accustomed to the darkness, they found themselves in a large room filled with dusty file cabinets, cardboard boxes, old mailing tubes and outdated audio-visual equipment. Niklas noticed an old floodlight in the corner and, for a moment, thought it might be the one his father had kept in their basement. There were a few wooden crates that were too small to be the urn. In the back of the room was a large canvas tarp draped over something. Covered with dust and cobwebs, it looked quite ominous. They stared, and for a moment, it was perfectly quiet. Except for one thing.

"Jesus, you can even hear it down here," Anna said.

They all listened to the faint rumble. Dirk finally stepped forward and pulled the rotting tarp off the old, five-foot-tall shipping crate.

Dirk whispered, "Is this it?"

Niklas moved forward and almost reverently put his hand on it. "It looks about the right size, I think."

Anna stepped closer. "Okay. Now what?"

"Well, only one way to know for sure." Niklas was looking around the room for something he could use. Then, out of frustration, he yanked at one of the top slats. It came right off in his hand. "Hey, I guess all that time in the gym is finally paying off." What a time to joke, he thought.

"Why don't we take it up to the front, where the light's better," Anna said. "This place is beginning to give me the creeps and I'm not even claustrophobic."

"Okay." Niklas noticed Dirk was starting to shake again, but not because he was cold. Niklas could feel himself tremble as well. Every sphincter in his body was clenching tighter at the thought of what they might have sitting in front of them.

Niklas went to the opposite side of the crate. "Okay, I'll take this end. Dirk, you take that one. Anna, you kill whoever drops his end."

The three of them carried the crate up the hallway, back to where the security desk was located. The light was better there, but not by much. Once there, they set it down gingerly, after briefly arguing over which end was supposed to be up. Without pausing to think about what they were doing, they immediately began to pull at the remaining slats and panels of the crate. The humidity in the basement had always been kept very low, to protect the delicate scientific collection on display there. This had, to some extent, preserved the crate's wood, but nearly forty years had not been kind to the nails and dried-out slats.

First they removed the top of the crate, leaving the packing material in place. Then they pulled off the side slats and, one by one, removed the four side panels. The many years in storage had frozen the wood-shaving packing material into the shape of the crate, even after the side panels had been removed. Niklas started to pull it away, from the top down, and, in the process, found a mailing tube and several large envelopes packed inside. The top of a canvas blanket protruded from the shavings, and as he began to peel the rotted fabric back ever so carefully, he saw the urn.

As it was revealed, he was stunned by its pristine condition. It was just as Niklas remembered it from so many years before– brilliantly colored, with numerous tiny white gems glittering across its surface. As the last of the shavings and blanket were pulled away, he saw the incredibly detailed ebony elephants– 'mammoths', Yamashita had called them– with the pearled tusks. He remembered that he thought they looked as though they might actually move. He tried to imagine what it must have been like for his father, Marty Yamashita and Raymond Allen, as they stood around this incredible object, under a tent near ancient Babylon.

"Wow," Anna whispered.

"Looks fresh off the assembly line," Dirk said.

"Yamashita said they never figured out how old it was. It was found in the deepest chamber of the ziggurat, and Dad suspected it was at least as old as the ziggurat itself. More than five thousand years old." Niklas picked up one of the old envelopes and opened it. It was the x-rays Marty had told him about. The three film sheets were brittle and the corner of one broke off in his hand. He held them up to the light in the ceiling and identified the closeup shot of the lid. "Here. Look at this one. The lid. See these things? Dad made some notations about them in the book. Called them 'locking pins.' They fractured along the curve of the inner side for some reason." Niklas stepped over to the urn and studied the lid and then looked back at the x-ray. "Looks like a pretty complicated for an ancient relic. Wonder what could have caused the fractures."

Dirk hadn't been paying attention. "If there's a quantum bubble in this thing, and quantum realities follow the same causal pathways, we must be inside an urn just like this one." He glanced up at the ceiling, then looked at Niklas. "But why an urn?"

Niklas squatted down next to the urn. "You want fairy tales or facts? Cause I'm not sure which one my theory is."

"You already have a theory?" said Anna.

"Yep. But it's a little weird. Once upon a time, a long time ago, some very smart ETs stumbled onto a micro-universe– a bubble. Maybe it was drifting between galaxies, orbiting some dead star, or just hovering in a dark cave somewhere. Doesn't really matter. What does is that it managed for billions of years to escape contact with any of the matter or energy in this reality."

Dirk said, "Lucky for us. If it had, our pathway would have ended right there."

"I think so," Niklas replied. "Given an essentially infinite number of opportunities, interrupted pathways are probably not all that uncommon. But our good fortune didn't stop there. Whoever found this bubble was smart enough to know what they had on their hands, and they figured out a way to contain it without actually making contact with it. Maybe some kind of electro-magnetic buffer. Yamashita told me he had x-rayed the urn and that it looked totally empty. The gamma shower probably just followed the outside contour of the buffer, like light waves bending around a massive object. Once the ETs had it contained, they had to figure out where it would be safest."

"This is sounding a little like Chariots of the Gods, don't you think?" Anna laughed nervously.

"It's the only way I know how to explain this. If you knew anything that happened to this little bubble would eventually happen here, in our Universe, where would you put it for safe keeping? You'd find an environmentally-stable planet orbiting a young, main-sequence star, in a non-fluctuating ecosphere. Then you'd locate a place in that planet's temperate zone with minimal tectonic and volcanic activity. The most stable place on the most stable planet in the most stable solar system on the outer edge of a spiral galaxy. That's where you put something like this. And then you'd bury it deep." Niklas paused for a moment, then said, "But they had to deal with another problem."

"Homo Sapiens," Anna said.

"Right. And this is where the real beauty of the urn comes in. Maybe they saw all the tribes scattered throughout the area and knew that one day, no matter how well they buried it, one of those tribes might dig the thing up. They were smart enough to anticipate that."

"So, they put it inside something that would evoke a predictable response?" Anna sounded skeptical.

"Exactly," Niklas said. "If, by some chance, the urn is found, it gets treated like some sort of mystical object. The local shamans develop a mythology around it, and, over time, it becomes a sacred and inviolable relic. Literally, a gift from the gods. Anthropologically, a fairly predictable sequence of events, don't you think? We always seem to end up worshiping what we can't explain." Niklas looked at the top of the urn. "I'm sure this inscription was written to encourage certain beliefs about the urn, without giving any specific information. Dad's notes say it's a combination of Sanskrit and cuneiform. Nice touch."

"Pretty gutsy," Dirk said. "Using ambiguity to get a specific response."

"The more mysterious, the better. Probably one of the reasons it worked for six thousand years. At least until Aaron Koppernick opened it and exposed the contents to this Universe's physical forces." Niklas spoke in a whisper.

"More like the gift from Epimetheus," Anna muttered.

"Who?" Niklas asked.

"Just a story from Greek mythology I remember. Epimetheus gave his wife a present, but it was a trick. When she opened it, all the evils of the world were set loose."

"Sounds familiar," Dirk said.

"It should. His wife's name was Pandora." Anna smirked.

"This thing makes Pandora's Box look like my mother's needle-point kit. Dad never had a clue what he was opening."

Anna walked around to the other side of the urn and looked down at the lid. It wasn't perfectly flush with the top of the urn and was slightly raised. She started to touch the small crown-shaped handle and then pulled back, as if afraid she might disturb something lurking inside. She folded her arms and walked back around to where Niklas was.

"What you're saying doesn't make total sense, Nick," she said. "Why go to all the trouble of creating this urn? Surely beings smart enough to seal a quantum bubble inside an urn would have figured out a way to make it inviolable—unopenable. And why put it here, on this planet? Why not put it on an artificial asteroid or set it adrift in the void between galaxies? It would have been a lot safer out there than here, don't you think?"

"I wonder if you can really make something 'unopenable' without doing it from the inside," said Niklas. "Maybe the nature of their containment method required some sort of access. Or maybe they wanted to keep the option of being able to take it out and study it. If they sealed it off forever, they wouldn't have been able to do that. If you're an intellectual being, it would have been a huge temptation."

"And I thought you hated guessing." Anna chuckled.

"Hey, the only folks who really know this thing's story are the ones who put it here. God knows where they are now."

"Yeah, what about that? asked Anna. "Why not keep it wherever they are, where they could keep an eye on it themselves?"

"Well, leaving it here could have been a temporary arrangement, and they always intended to return for it. Or maybe they were passing the baton."

"Sorry, I don't get you."

"You know, if they felt the bubble was too important to leave in the hands of an indifferent Universe, setting it adrift in the intergalactic plasma might not have been too appealing to them." Niklas laughed and looked at the urn. "Maybe they didn't trust the Beast, either."

"I don't know," Anna said, shaking her head. "I realize we're standing here looking at this incredible thing. And I know we can't ignore what's going on in the sky, but what you're suggesting is just so– so out there."

"It's just a theory, Anna. Just a–"

"But a very interesting theory, Dr. Koppernick." The familiar voice startled them as it came out of the darkness like an unexpected gust of ice cold wind.

"Goddamn it, Willoughby!" Anna shouted.

The agent stepped from around the corner into the hallway and approached the three startled scientists, with Rand at his shoulder. Rand's threatening, white-toothed grin was visible even in the dimly lit hallway and Niklas quickly came to the conclusion it would be a bad time to remind him about the school bus incident.

"Listen, Whigby, or whatever your name is," Niklas said, moving in front of the urn. "If you've heard all of this, then you know what we could be dealing with here."

"Trust me, Dr. Koppernick. I've been listening to everything you've had to say for a long, long time. And I know a great deal more about the urn than you might think."

Dirk came forward and poked his finger into Willoughby's chest. "You, sir, are a fucking fascist!"

Rand gauged the distance, took the necessary half-step to get within range and threw his fist into Dirk's jaw, knocking him back, towards the urn. Only Niklas catching him at the last second prevented a collision. Niklas heard Anna emit some kind of feral grunt as she leapt forward and kicked Rand squarely in the testicles. The agent screamed, dropped to one knee, and then rolled onto his side, moaning and clutching his groin.

As Niklas knelt down to assist Dirk, he shouted at Willoughby. "You fucking idiot! The world's going to end any minute and you're acting like Himler!"

Willoughby stepped over his incapacitated associate and frowned as the moaning agent struggled to his feet. Then he turned to Niklas.

"That should not have happened. I must apologize for Agent Rand and his over-reaction."

"Over-reaction? Fuh!" Dirk's words were slurred. He flinched and jerked his hand up to the side of his face.

Willoughby was staring at the urn, and seemed to be losing a struggle to control his emotions.

"I have my instructions, and neither you, nor anybody else is going to keep me from following them." He looked up at the ceiling and let the roar overhead emphasize his point. Then he turned to Rand. "Take it."

Rand stumbled forward, pushing Niklas and Dirk aside as he picked up the urn. Anna made a move to block his path to the stairs, but she took one look at his expression and backed off. Willoughby turned to follow, then paused a moment and faced the three scientists. His mouth opened, as if he was about to say something, then he changed his mind and started up the stairs.

"Instructions? From whom?" Niklas called out, not really expecting an answer. "Where are you taking it?"

Without stopping, Willoughby said, "Good-bye, Doctors," before disappearing from view.

For the first time in his life, Niklas' verbal weaponry was jammed. He was now dealing with a man who was essentially invulnerable to his intellectual firepower. So now another part of his brain took over. He ran up the stairs and overtook Willoughby in the entryway. Spinning the agent around, Niklas grabbed him by the throat and cocked his other fist. Through gritted his teeth, he shouted, "Goddamn it—Willoughby!" It was a blurring rage Niklas had never experienced before. The most important thing in the world, at that instant, was to spill Willoughby's blood. A split second before letting his fist fly, the look on Willoughby's face flickered into Niklas' consciousness and managed to register. Niklas glimpsed an expression filled with the same fear and anxiety he was feeling. It wasn't the look of some soulless fanatic. It was just a man. Niklas took a deep breath and shut his eyes for a second. Then he relaxed his fist, let go of Willoughby's jacket and angrily pushed him away.

"The name isn't Willoughby, Doctor."

Chapter 9
White Night

i

Commie was carrying a large brown shopping bag over to the SEC. He had cleaned himself up a little and raided the commissary for some soft drinks and junk food. While he was in his quarters he thought about trying to get some sleep, but one look out his window at the ripped sky convinced him it would be impossible.

At its widest point, the line now filled a full five degree arc of the sky and had a scythe-like shape. Each end of the tapering crescent disappeared at the horizon. The distant rumble had grown to a ominous roar and Commie thought he could feel the floor of the Rio Grande Valley shake beneath his feet. As he walked back over to the SEC, he paused to look up at the line and thought he could see a faint dark area at its center resembling a human face. He shrugged it off as an optical illusion. Creatures in the clouds, he thought. When he was a kid, he had always been able to imagine the shapes of people and animals in the big cumulus clouds rolling in over Chicago.

As he was climbing the SEC stairs, he glanced up again and thought he might be experiencing some kind of regressive shock. Whatever it was, he really didn't care, one way or the other. When he got to the top he had the presence of mind to knock before going inside.

"Come on in," Simms called out.

Commie opened the door and saw Simms and Angie sitting closely together at the console. Her hair was a little messier than it had been when he left earlier that evening. She looked like she had been doing a lot of crying and didn't look up at him. Simms gave him a half-hearted smile. Commie stood in the doorway, not sure if he should stay or not. Maybe he should give them the time to be alone.

"No signals for the last half hour," Simms said. He had to raise his voice in order to be heard over the noise coming through the open door.

"Maybe there's no one left to send them." Commie tilted his head toward the ugly sky.

"Whaddya' got there?" Simms nodded curiously at the package Commie was carrying.

"Oh. Just some eats. Not that I could hold anything down. Thought you guys might be hungry, though." Commie managed to smile at Angie, but she didn't seem to have the energy to return it.

"Getting louder, isn't it," Simms said.

"Yeah," Commie said. "You can feel it in the ground, too. Not as strong up here."

"Come on. Let's close this damn door," Simms said, taking the bag off Commie's hands. "The insulation here is thick enough to keep most of noise out. Besides, I don't want to have to look at the thing." Commie stepped inside and watched the steel door swing shut. Simms was right, he thought. The heavily insulated walls and metal door managed to keep out most of the sound and all of the light. For a while.

ii

By the time Anna and Dirk reached him, Niklas was standing in the entryway and the two agents had already gone outside.

"Did I hear that right?" Anna asked. Niklas looked at her and grimaced. As he opened the door, the blast of the howling wind and the awful roar from above exploded into the first floor of the Science Center, pushing them a step backward. The campus street was deserted, not only because of the late hour, Anna thought, but also because people were probably huddled inside their homes— basements, if they had them— holding each other and praying. They caught up with the agents a few feet from their car and Niklas grabbed Willoughby by the arm once again. Anna got ahead of the agents, putting herself between them and the dark sedan.

"What the hell does that mean?" Niklas shouted. "Your name isn't Willoughby? So who the fuck are you?" To Anna's relief, Niklas let go of the agent's arm. Rand was standing right there and, even though he was holding the urn, she figured he could still be dangerous.

"My family name is Khafeer." He looked at Rand, motioning him toward the car, and then he turned to Niklas. "I am only returning the urn to its rightful owners."

"You bastards!" Anna shouted.

"Okay, let me guess— Mr. Khafeer." Niklas leveled a hateful stare at the man. "In the not-too-distant future, some lunatic jihadist who's had one too many at the Allahu Akbar is gonna show up with the urn wearing a semtex corsette. Right? Of course, he'll demand the death of all Jews! You son of a bitch."

Rand moved past Anna slowly, clutching the urn to his chest with one arm, glaring fiercely at her. She wanted to gouge his eyes out, but guessed he had intentionally kept one arm free in case she tried anything. Down in the basement she had caught the agent off guard. But she knew she wouldn't be so lucky this time. She turned around and watched him carefully place the urn in the sedan's trunk.

Suddenly, Dirk bolted past her and ran to the driver side window of the sedan. He looked up at Anna with a distorted half-grin, reached inside the car and pulled something out. The keys. The idiots, she thought, must have left them in the ignition. Rand was coming around the side of the car.

"Anna!" Dirk shouted, tossing them to her.

For a half second Anna didn't know what he expected her to do. Dirk's move had surprised her as much as it had the two agents. Then she heard Niklas.

"Run, Anna!" Niklas shouted.

Anna got all the incentive she needed when she saw Rand coming at her. She gripped the keys tightly in her fist and took off like a gazelle. Turning the corner of the Science Center, she looked up the Oxford Street straightaway and put her long legs into overdrive. Nobody was going to catch her. It felt good to run– to release the pent-up nervous energy. If she had to, she could run all night. But as she reached her stride, she wondered where she would go. Who could offer her sanctuary from everything that was happening? She looked ahead and saw no signs of life. Everybody, she thought, had gone underground. She began to realize the absurd futility of what she was doing and, slowing to a trot, she looked back over her shoulder. There was no one coming after her. She thought the street lighting might be playing tricks, hiding her pursuers in the shadows. She came to a stop and turned to look more carefully. No one. Fighting her panic, she worried what might be happening to Niklas and Dirk. She had to go back.

The line was growing brighter, and the landscape around her was bathed in its sickening amber glow. The pavement began to vibrate, subtly at first, then stronger. She ran back to Niklas as fast as she could.

—⟋⟍—

Niklas was relieved, but a little confused when neither Rand nor Willoughby took off after Anna. At first, he thought it was because they didn't want to leave the urn unguarded, even to retrieve the keys to their car. Or maybe they realized chasing after her on foot would be a waste of time. They wouldn't take his car because the urn was now locked up inside the sedan's trunk. Then he felt a strange rumbling in the ground and he looked up at the sky. The line was now so bright he had to squint in order to see the dark area within it.

"Goddamnit, Dad!" Niklas shouted. "What the hell did you do?" All of the anger and frustration bound up inside of him coalesced in that instant. He wondered how long they had before the sky fell on them and he decided it had been a mistake to tell Anna to run. He wanted her there with him. He looked down just in time to see the two agents getting into the sedan. A second later the engine started and the car lurched out of the parking place. Niklas could see Khafeer behind the wheel.

"Shit. Extra set of keys," Dirk cursed.

—⟋⟍—

Rounding the corner of the Science Center, Anna saw the headlights of the sedan come on. The two agents weren't anywhere to be seen. The night sky was now so bright she saw everything perfectly, as though it was high noon. She even noticed the sedan's color was actually a deep blue. Then it pulled away and she saw Niklas rushing toward her.

"Extra keys! Let's go!" Niklas seemed frantic. They dashed for his BMW and, as they pulled away from the Science Center, they watched the sedan turn onto Massachusetts Avenue. Niklas floored it. His car was only a couple of years old, and quicker than the Detroit V-8. He was less than a hundred yards behind when the sedan turned onto JFK Street and headed for the Anderson Bridge, which crossed over the Charles River. Niklas had closed the distance to a few car lengths when the BMW was nearly broadsided by two cars racing up Memorial Drive. At the last instant, Niklas slammed on the brakes, throwing the BMW into a brief four-wheel slide and the two cars flew in front of them.

"Jesus Christ, Nick!" Anna said. "You're going to get us killed." Niklas ignored her and put the accelerator back on the floorboard. Anna regained her composure and apologized. She hadn't seen them coming, either. But when they flew by, she did notice something else. "Did you see who was in those two cars?" she asked.

"AJ-fucking-Foyt and Mario-goddamn-Andretti!" Niklas

yelled. "Shit! How could I? They must have been doing a hundred." Anna knew Niklas hated to drive. He didn't exactly have the best temperament for it. But, as shaken as he obviously was, she could tell he was too intent on catching up to the sedan to slow down now. "Who gives a shit who was in them, anyway?" he yelled.

When she answered, Anna's voice was filled with alarm.

"Two carloads of bangers."

"Come on, Anna. You couldn't see any better than I could."

"Well enough to see the 'H' scratched on the door."

Niklas glanced over at her and grimaced. "No shit. The Howard Beach gang? In this part of town?" The small but ultra-violent gang's random killings had been highly publicized for years, with news of its atrocities even being reported in New Mexico. Its well-known symbol was always brazenly displayed by its members, scratched deep into the paint of their cars.

"Just be careful," Anna said. Even though they were in the heart of the Ivy League, her senses were on high alert. They were between Soldier's Field and Harvard University, only a few miles from the MIT campus. After crossing the Anderson Bridge, Niklas turned left onto Soldier's Field Road, which ran along the river. They could barely see the sedan's taillights.

—⟨⟨⟩—

"Hey, you see that muthafuckin' unmarked, man?" The big one in the passenger seat was called Rama. His huge muscular arms were covered by hundreds of obscene tattoos, which he had collected during an eleven-year stay at Rahway

State Penitentiary for armed robbery. He had gone in when he was eighteen, but nobody knew for sure how old he was. Since he had never had a birthday, even he wasn't sure when he had been born. His eyes, which were half-covered by thick, heavy lids, had the look of someone who didn't care if they lived to see another day. "You see those goddamn plates? The muthafuckin' Man." There were three others in the beat-up Caddie. They had been sitting at the corner of Western Avenue and Soldiers Field Road, passing a huge bottle of Chivas Regal between them. It was one of many items Rama had recently "liberated" from a nearby liquor store, where he had left the old Italian shopkeeper in a pool of blood. After the killing, he had walked slowly to the waiting getaway car, looking for a confrontation with a police department that never showed up.

"What the fuck you talking 'bout, Rama? How you see that shit? The dude was slicin'." The driver of the Cadillac was half the size of Rama. A skinny, fast-talker named Blade, it was his car, but he went wherever Rama told him. "Sides, we ain't seen no fuckin' pigs for hours." With that, one of the bangers in the back seat reached out the window with his Max-9 and fired a ten-round burst. Then he raised the bottle of scotch to his mouth and took three deep gulps.

"Yeah, see dat. No cops here. They punkin' shit." Rank was doing the talking but it had been his buddy, Jacks, who had fired the 9MM automatic. Both were twenty years old, strung out on drugs and booze, with nothing to lose. But what made them the most deadly was their mindless allegiance to Rama.

"Get the muthafucka!" Rama's voice boomed as if it had risen from a deep well filled with molten lava. "I seen the E on those plates. He know what the fuck is going down." Rama glanced out the window, at the orange glow in the sky and sneered. He didn't understand what was happening above him and he didn't really care. All he knew was that he hadn't seen a single cop all night and that had ruined his plans. "He the Man and I plan to be pillin' the muthafucka's ass." Blade burned rubber as the Cadillac pulled onto Soldiers Field Road, right in front of a speeding BMW. Rama raised his Tech-9 and checked the clip. It was the second one he would be using that night.

—⋙—

"Goddamn!" Niklas shouted, braking hard to avoid a collision with the Cadillac.

"This is what I was afraid of," Anna said. "No 'H', but I swear I saw a gun sticking out the back window."

"Oh great," Niklas said with contempt in his voice. "Must be a mess downtown. You can bet your ass there's no cops out this way." A moment later, even though he had dropped back nearly a quarter of a mile, he saw the sedan make the right turn onto Cambridge Street. And then he saw the Cadillac do the same. "Not good! I think these assholes are following Khafeer."

"Why would they do that?" Anna asked.

Then Dirk, who had been holding on for dear life in the back seat, leaned forward.

"Two white guys with short hair in business suits in a dark

four-door with government plates? Pretty obvious," Dirk said, falling back into the seat, holding the side of his face.

"Oh, no," Anna said, her voice dropping. "They think they're narcs. Willough– I mean, Khafeer– might as well be driving around with a bumpersticker that says 'Shoot me'."

"Jesus." Niklas gritted his teeth as his car made the sliding right turn onto Cambridge Street.

"Where are they going?" Anna asked.

"Looks like I-90. We'll know soon enough. The Turnpike isn't much further. If they get on that, no telling where they're going. I just hope these homeys in the Cadillac get bored and decide to go play somewhere else."

—∿∿—

"We have another car behind us," Rand said from the passenger seat, looking back through the rear windshield. "Looks like four adult males. Two front, two back." He looked over at Khafeer. "I thought I saw a weapon."

"Street gang," Khafeer said. "Get out the shotgun. I'll try to keep them from coming alongside. If they do, don't wait for their fire. They probably have automatic weapons. Take out the driver." Rand reached under the seat and lifted up a short barreled, pump-action shotgun. He reached into the glove compartment and took out a box of number-two shot, twelve gauge shells and loaded nine of them into the unplugged weapon. Then he climbed into the back seat. He removed the .45 caliber semi-automatic from his shoulder harness, checked the clip and laid it on the seat next to him. The Cadillac had moved to within four car lengths of them.

—ᕬ—

"Okay, fools. We got two," Rama said, coolly. "One muthafucka in the back seat. Shotgun. We pull up on the left. Jacks, you take out the fuckin' back window. That'll keep the pig in the hole. I'll do the sucka who's drivin'."

Jacks laughed, inserted a full clip and pulled back on the breach to load the old Woodsman .22 caliber LR semi-automatic. Then he took another long gulp of the liquor.

"They goin' up the damn Turnpike." Blade sounded disappointed. "See. They headin' towards the booths. Shit!"

"Who the fuck cares!" Rama said. "They be just as dead!" He reached into the back seat and yanked the bottle from Jacks' hand and took a long swallow.

"Aw shit, man." Blade was whining and sounded as if he was late for an important appointment. "We be goin' out in the damn woods. All the fuckin' fun's back in town, Rama." Then he felt the cold muzzle of Rama's Tech-9 touching the skin of his temple.

"The faster you catch the muthafucka, the faster you downtown." Rama said it with no emotion and his bass monotone made it clear he didn't care who he shot, as long as he got to shoot somebody.

When they got on the I-90 Turnpike, there were no attendants in the tollbooths, and all of the metal gates were raised. As Blade drove between two of the booths doing eighty-five, he looked in his rear view mirror and saw the BMW following them.

"Where the fuck is that dude going?" Blade said.

Rama looked back, through the rear windshield. "If they

following us, they goin' to the boneyard."

—⚍—

"Don't get too close," Anna said. "If these guys think we're following them, they may decide they like BMWs."

"Christ, how far are they willing to go just to shoot up some cops?" Dirk said.

"Khafeer could be driving all the way to Maine, for Christ's sakes," Niklas said, keeping back as far as he could without losing sight of the sedan. As they approached the I-95 junction, he saw the sedan get into the right lane and exit onto Route 128. Niklas heart sank when the Cadillac followed suit. There was no doubt now that the gang was out to kill cops, no matter how far from their turf it might take them. Niklas kept hoping their speed would attract the attention of a state trooper, but the Turnpike was deserted. He wondered if there were cops anywhere in the world right now.

When the sedan finally got onto I-95 and continued north, Niklas guessed what Khafeer was doing.

"I'm willing to bet he's going to Portland."

"Why there?" Anna asked.

"Easternmost port," Niklas said. "Not a major seaport, but big enough for most freighters. The only law enforcement is one over-worked Coast Guard cutter. Great place to smuggle out something. Homeland Security at its best."

"Great," Anna said. "So he's probably got a small army waiting for him at the dock."

"Doesn't seem to care about being followed," Dirk said.

"Oh, Christ," Niklas said. "He doesn't care because he's

probably got the Maine State Police waiting for us. We're following two NSA agents in a government car." He reached into coat pocket and took out his cellphone. "Here, see if this thing is working. If it is, try to get through to the Port Authority in Portland." Anna flipped the phone open, and pushed "zero" and "send". Nothing but static in the earpiece. She tried 9-1-1. Same thing.

"This is a goner," she said.

"That's what I was afraid of," Niklas said. "Atmospheric interference. God knows what kind of radiation is being generated by that thing."

"So?" Dirk asked. "What do we do now?"

"We follow," Niklas said. "What have we got to lose."

—ᴍ—

"You pissin' me off with this shit," Rama said. "Get the fuck up alongside these pigs. Now!" Blade pushed the accelerator into the matted carpet of the floorboard and maneuvered the Cadillac to the left of the sedan. When the Caddie was only a few feet away, the sedan's left rear window came down and something came out of it. Before Rama could tell Blade to brake, sparks and smoke shot out of the end of the shotgun, the blast hitting the right rear window of the Cadillac and catching Rank full in the face. Blood, tissue and shattered glass flew into the rear windshield and, just as a second blast came from the shotgun, Blade hit the brakes.

"Oh, muthafucka! Those fuckin' pigs!" Jacks was screaming. Blood and part of Rank's brain were dripping off the side of his head and shirt. Rama reached into the back seat, opened the door and threw Rank's body out of the car with one huge arm. Then he grabbed Jacks by the throat.

"Shut your muthafuckin' hole! Move your punk ass over to the window. We takin' these cocksuckers out! You got that, chump!" Rama turned to Blade. "Don't make me tell you again."

—⚛—

"Oh, God!" Niklas shouted as he swerved and barely missed the flailing body which had just been tossed from the car ahead of him. "That was too close. I'm backing off."

"Good," Anna said. Dirk just nodded his approval.

—⚛—

"Why didn't you take out the driver like I told you?" Khafeer was upset but not angry. He knew his partner had never had to shoot to kill before. Even though he had been trained for such an eventuality, actually pulling the trigger was a different matter. "What happened?"

"The passenger window was open. I thought I saw a muzzle flash. I missed and hit the back window." Rand's voice was quivering. Khafeer began to worry whether or not they would make it to the rendezvous site alive. He looked ahead and saw the sign indicating the I-495 Junction was only a mile ahead. Without slowing, he shifted quickly into the far right lane, got onto the 495 and headed east, toward Salem. He stayed in the far right lane and, after traveling only a couple of miles, he entered an offramp.

"You're getting off the Turnpike?" For the first time, there was fear in Rand's voice. "Where are we going? We don't stand a chance off the highway!"

"This is where is I've been instructed to go." Khafeer said. On the frontage road, they would have to reduce their speed considerably to avoid losing control of the car. With their cargo, they simply could not risk a crash. "Be ready."

He was beginning to question the wisdom of the orders he had received earlier in the day. The voice on the phone had delivered them in the proper dialect and he could not question them. But he knew now that they might lead to something far worse than his own death.

—m—

"Get on this chump's ass!" Rama said, and Blade pulled the Cadillac onto the off ramp.

—m—

"This guy's nuts," Niklas said. "They'll catch him on a frontage road for sure." He got into the off ramp lane and exited the Turnpike. "Maybe he's leading them into a trap."

"Or he's leading all of us into a trap," Anna said. "Are you sure you want to be doing this?"

"Fuck no," he answered.

—m—

The frontage road went straight for a quarter mile, then made a sharp turn under the Turnpike and into a densely forested area west of the highway. It was a remote and infrequently travelled area, halfway to Salem. There were no other vehicles in sight. The narrow, two-lane road became extremely serpentine and Khafeer was forced to cut his speed by more than half to safely negotiate the curves.

"Get on the right side of the car," Khafeer said. "When they try to pull up, I'll veer into the left lane and force them to come up on the right. Take out the driver this time."

"Don't worry." Rand sounded scared but determined as he pumped the spent shell out of the shotgun.

—ɯ—

"Pig's drivin' like yo' raggedy-ass momma," Rama roared. "Do it here." With the tires on the Cadillac screeching on the fast curving road, Blade closed the distance between them.

—ɯ—

Niklas had to slow down more than he wanted. If the bangers did catch the sedan, it might be sitting in the middle of the road and he wouldn't see it until the last second.

"If it wasn't so damned light out, I could tell where they were by their headlights," Niklas said. "Now I can't tell shit!" As they came around a very sharp curve, Niklas noticed a side road cutting into the forest. He could see dust still swirling where the two cars had just entered. "Oh, Christ. This just gets uglier and uglier. If you guys don't want me to go in there, I won't." He looked at Anna and Dirk and, after a few moments, they nodded towards the small dirt road. "You guys are crazy," he said. Niklas had to slow the BMW to a crawl as he drove down the winding narrow dirt road.

And then the engine died.

"Christ!" Anna said. "Not here. Please." The BMW coasted on the slightly downhill grade and Niklas gripped the steering wheel, trying to maneuver it through the next turn without the use of his power-steering. As the car rounded a curve and rolled to a slow stop, they looked up and saw they were parked directly behind the Cadillac and the sedan. Niklas came to the horrifying realization that the bangers were now trapped between his car and Khafeer's and he could only imagine what would happen next.

Suddenly, a flash of light, incredibly brilliant, filled the sky and Niklas raised his arms reflexively to shield his eyes. Dimly, he realized everyone else must be doing the same. The whiteness filled the car and every shadow around them, eliminating any sense of color or shape. The roar overhead grew even louder and he could feel the car vibrate from the low, rumbling sound. Niklas had imagined this was how the end would start. First the light and then the absolute heat. A millisecond of indescribable agony, then oblivion. He reached for Anna, whom he could barely hear sobbing next to him. She pushed her face into his chest and he covered her with his arms. He would have spoken to her, telling her how much he regretted their time apart and that he loved her, but the words would have been crushed by the horrendous thunder of the light wave. Realizing he would be denied the chance to say good-bye to her, his anger boiled.

"I love you!" He shouted the words into her ear as loud as he could, but having been unable to hear them himself, he wasn't sure if she had. He tried to raise up her face, to look at her once more, but she resisted. Perhaps, he thought, she was afraid she would look up and see the slavering fangs of his Beast, waiting to gaze into her eyes before devouring her. He finally was able to bring her face in front of his and he cupped his hands above her tightly shut eyes, trying to shade them from the blinding whiteness. He moved in even closer to her, and she brought her hands up to help him block out the light. Now, the only thing either of them could see was each other's eyes, and the tears streaming from them.

iii

As the flash of brilliant light came through the open door of the SEC, Angie whimpered and ran toward Simms, who was helping Commie back inside. The young scientist had made the mistake of covering his ears rather than his eyes and was experiencing what Simms hoped was temporary blindness from the burst of light. Not that it mattered much. They would probably all be dead long before he could see anything again anyway.

In the last few hours, Commie had become obsessed with the large dark shape in the line. He had told Simms he no longer believed the face he saw there was just an illusion or figment of his imagination. Simms had glanced up at it, then quickly looked away, shaking his head. He also had thought it looked like a face. For a moment he even considered it might be God, coming to end the world. But that fantasy soon passed and Simms decided that it would be a bad idea to say anything that might encourage Commie's fixation, so he kept it to himself. Even so, despite Simms' warnings that he could be damaging his eyesight, Commie persisted in going outside to observe it.

As they came inside, Simms pulled the door shut as hard as he could, slamming it and breaking the pneumatic locking system that would have automatically closed and locked it behind them anyway.

"Goddamnit!" Simms bellowed in the relative quiet of the SEC. They went to the far side of the room, sat on the floor and leaned up against one of the tall computer banks. As they huddled together in their dim, windowless sanctuary, waiting for the final maelstrom, Simms began to whisper a prayer. "Our Father, who art in Heaven...." And then he broke down.

iv

As suddenly as it came, the brightness began to dim and the noise seemed to recede. Niklas and Anna lowered their hands and looked around. The landscape around them took on shapes and subtle color again as the light abated.

"What the hell?" Niklas said. "Did it stop?"

"If it did, our troubles could just be beginning," Anna said as she nodded toward the cars in front of them. The bright light continued to fade and, in a few moments, their surroundings appeared to be totally normal. Then Niklas got a strange look on his face.

"Hold on just a minute here," he said.

Anna and Dirk sat up and began looking around. The appearance of everything around them was slowly changing. There was no piercing white light and no thunder in their ears, but neither was there any starlight or even the ambient glow from the nearby city.

"Look." Anna said, pointing at the floorboard of the BMW. "No shadows." Somehow, light was finding its way into every nook and cranny inside the car. They could see everything in perfect detail. Niklas looked out the front windshield, searching for a non-existent light source and looked up at the sky. It was pitch black.

"This is weird." he muttered. "No light, no shadows, but we can see everything!" The sky was absolutely empty. He rolled down his window and listened. "Hear that?"

"I don't hear anything," Dirk whispered.

"Ever go into the woods at night and not hear a billion bugs and animals humping in the dark? And I get no pine smell, either. We might as well be in the clean room at the computer lab. This is nuts."

"Niklas." Anna said, again nodding toward the Cadillac as both of its doors began to open. An enormous black man with a shaved head emerged cautiously from the passenger side, holding a small weapon. Or maybe, Niklas thought, it just looked small in his huge hand. Two considerably smaller men came out of the driver side, and, unlike the larger man, they seemed scared and jumpy.

"Jacks, watch the fuckin BMW. Blade, with me." Niklas watched the one called Jacks come toward his car. He could see blood all over the frightened man's face and shirt. As Jacks neared the BMW's side door, he looked inside and Niklas saw the thug's eyes widen when he saw Anna. Oh, Christ, Niklas thought.

"Get the fuck out of the car, muthafucka, or we kill your ass right now!" It was the big man's voice again, presumably shouting at the two men in the sedan. Niklas wondered why the agents hadn't fired again. Certainly they had had the opportunity. As Niklas watched the two predators standing on either side of the sedan, he thought he saw something out of the corner of his eye. A movement between the trees. A bear or deer, he thought.

The sedan's doors opened and Khafeer and Rand stepped out, their hands raised. Suddenly, Khafeer threw something deep into the woods and Niklas wondered if it had been the keys. The big man grabbed Rand by the neck and threw him towards the Cadillac. Blade pushed his pistol into the side of Khafeer's head and walked him in the same direction.

"Hey! Guess what the fuck we got us here." Jacks had a wide grin now and, with the drying blood and other tissue still caked on it, his face was nightmarish. The giant tattooed man, Rama, came to the front of the BMW, whipping Rand around by the collar like he was a recalcitrant child, and then he looked into the BMW through lifeless, half-closed eyes. It took a few seconds for the thin, frightening smile to grow on his mouth.

"Outta the fuckin' car!" He pointed his weapon right at Anna. Silently, they began to climb out of the BMW, too frightened to utter a word. Niklas motioned for Anna to slide out his side, hoping they wouldn't be separated. She stood next to him, squeezing his arm tightly. As Dirk was climbing out of the passenger side, Niklas again thought he glimpsed something moving in the trees. Then he saw Rama staring at Anna and heard him mumbling something under his heavy breathing. As the others moved closer to his car, Niklas shook his head.

"Why didn't you blow these assholes away when you had the chance?" Niklas asked the agents, not caring if he lived to see what he knew was about to happen. Before Rand could even think his answer, Rama whipped the muzzle of his pistol into Niklas' face, stopping it an inch short of his forehead. Anna screamed and tried to reach for the gun, but the brute's open hand slammed into her face, throwing her backward onto the hood of the BMW.

"Eat this, meat!" Rama shouted and Anna heard the firing pin of the pistol click. Nothing happened. "Shit!" Rama re-cocked the pistol and, again, the clicking sound. "Goddamnit! Give me your muthafuckin piece, Blade!" Anna looked away and, again, they all heard the click of a misfire.

"We are with you again." The unearthly voice seemed to come from all around them.

Anna flinched. While Rama and Jacks were spinning around, trying to figure out where the strange sound had come from, she slowly edged her way back over to Niklas.

"It's the same voice," Anna whispered to Niklas. "From the VLA message."

Niklas, shaken by his near-death experience, managed to nod. "Yeah, I recognize it from the tape." He remembered how Anna had described it– a dry-throated, synthetic sound– perhaps from lack of use, he thought. One thing was for sure. It wasn't human.

"What the fuck was that?" Rama bellowed, as he whipped his pistol around.

"Let's take the bitch and the Beemer and get the fuck outta here, Rama," Blade said.

"Don't you guys get it?" Niklas said. "Cars don't work. Guns don't work. Got no light but can see everything. Are you too fucking stupid to understand what's going on here? It's the end of the goddamn world."

"Jesus Christ," Anna whispered. "Will you shut up?" She sounded more frightened than angry. Rama strode over and put his hand around Niklas' throat and lifted him off the ground.

"I think I'll pull your fuckin' head off," Rama snarled.

—⚊⚊—

"Your weapons will not function within the dampening field," the creature said, as it stepped onto road, followed closely by two larger figures.

When Rama released him, Niklas fell back, clutching his throat and gasping for air. He had heard the words and assumed they had come from the small one. It had a vaguely humanoid appearance, with pale gray skin, immense slanted eyes and a disproportionately small nose and mouth. The head had a subtle, inverted triangle shape, almost flat on the top, with a tiny pointed chin. The classic "Gray" that had been written about in thousands of tabloid stories, Niklas thought. The one on the left was quite different and could have been a totally different species. Even though it was hunched over, it was the tallest of the three. It was darker in color and almost insectile, with exoskeletal plates forming a geometric pattern over what he could see of its body and small, externalized mandibles where lips should have been. Its eyes were even larger than the gray-skinned being's, and its elongated neck had a distinct ribbed texture. The third figure, however, was a mystery, because it was clad in a hooded robe which completely concealed its appearance. It was also bipedal and Niklas could see what he thought were arm-like appendages beneath the heavy fabric.

—∿∿—

Stunned and scared by the creatures standing before him, Rama's street instincts took over. He needed to get away from these things as fast as he could. He would find a way to survive this, as he had every other horror of his life. Moving very fast for a man of his size, he grabbed Anna by the hair and started backing down the road, toward the highway. His two friends jumped behind him.

"You take one fuckin' step toward me, she dead." Rama's voice had a higher pitch now, and was cracking from fear. "Just leave us the fuck alone." He was still pointing the useless gun in their direction.

"Hold," the small one said, flatly. Then the tall insect-like creature moved forward with remarkable speed. Rama put his huge arm around Anna's throat, pointed the gun at her temple, and began to squeeze her long, delicate neck.

"I'll snap the bitch's neck, you muthafuckin' bug!" The creature came to within a step of them and stopped. Rama was taller and tried to intimidate the creature by glaring back into its huge eyes. He had used this tactic quite effectively many times before, but this time the results were different. In a blur of speed and dexterity, the creature grabbed both of Rama's wrists simultaneously and held his arms rigidly out to the sides. Anna fell to the ground in a clump. Next to her head, Rama's feet were dangling in mid-air. Holding the big man absolutely still, six inches off the ground, the creature extended his ribbed neck to its full length and looked down on the relatively fragile human in his crushing grip. Rama felt as if his arms were coming out of their sockets and the bulky sinews in his shoulders and chest began to rupture.

"You tearing out my fuckin' arms!" screamed Rama. He turned his head as far as he could in the direction of his friends just in time to see Blade and Jacks take off in a dead run toward the highway. He tried to call out to them, but he couldn't seem to bring enough air into his lungs. He teetered on the edge of blacking out and caught glimpses of the monster's face and the woman crawling away. Then he heard someone rushing up behind him, screaming.

"Put him down, goddamnit!" It was Blade. "Let him go!" Blade came up alongside the creature, stepping under Rama's outstretched arm. "Stop it, you muthafucka!" Blade was crying and screaming at the same time. Rama's head lolled to the side and he looked down to see his small friend furiously swinging his weapon toward the exposed midsection of the monster. Out of the corner of his eye, Rama saw a quick movement from the hooded being standing a few feet away. In mid-swing, Blade dropped his weapon and crumpled like he had been shot through the head. Rama looked into the face of the creature who held him fully expecting to be torn in half at any moment.

After exchanging a glance with its small gray companion, the bug-like being gently lowered him to the ground. Rama's feet sunk into the pine needles, finally settling on solid ground, and the creature released his arms. In agony from the torn muscles in his chest, Rama looked down at his would-be rescuer and back up to the looming monster. Then he heard the voice of the small being.

"Leave us," the gray one said.

Rama bent over and, grunting, picked up Blade's limp body with the only arm he could move. He carefully put him over his shoulder and, as he backed slowly away from the group, wondered if he would have come back like his fallen friend had. No, he realized. He knew he wouldn't have and, for the first time in as long as he could remember, Rama felt shame. It took balls for the little man to do something like that for him, he thought. When Rama reached the curve in the road, he turned and headed for the main highway.

v

"His companion will recover. But it will make no difference if we do not act quickly," the gray said.

Every time the voice spoke, Niklas could see Anna flinch. The small being turned and spoke directly to Khafeer. "You are Oosra Cadima?"

Niklas saw Khafeer's head jerk, as if he had been slapped across the face. He watched the wary man come forward, his eyes wide and unblinking.

"Yes," Khafeer finally answered, speaking just above a whisper. "I am Haris Khafeer. Devoted of the Oosra Cadima, the ancient–"

"Yes. The ancient family. You know us as the Anunnaki, and we are the ones who instructed you to come to this place," the alien said. "You have been faithful to your charge, but we must now move without delay if we are to preserve the Kaun– and ourselves." Niklas could see the astonished expression on Khafeer's face. As if the Anunnaki's words had some strange power over him, Khafeer took a step backward and bowed his head in reverence. "This is Ki–" the alien gestured to the insect-like creature who had now resumed his position on his right "–and this is Ani." The hooded being bowed. "I am called Enlil. While we look different from one another, we are the same. We are the guardians of the Kaun."

—⚏—

Niklas felt a momentary light-headedness. Almost being choked to death will do that to you, he thought, as he was regaining his coherence. With his renewed focus, thousands of questions poured into his mind.

"We cannot answer your questions now, Niklas." As Enlil stepped forward, looking directly at him, Niklas realized the being was reading his thoughts as fast as he could formulate them. "First, we must stop the approaching energy. The dampening field we are standing in will only allow us to work for a brief period."

"You mean, it hasn't stopped?" Anna asked.

"No. This field is only a temporary barrier to the sound and light," Enlil said.

"But you can stop it? The light wave?" Niklas asked.

"It is possible, but certain data is required. When we saw the human face within the line, we deduced what had happened. We must know where and when the Karura was opened. Without that information, we can do nothing. Can you help us?" Even the strange alien quality of the being's voice could not mask the subtle hint of desperation.

"The face in the line— it's my father," Niklas said. "He opened the urn—" Niklas glanced at Khafeer. "—the Karura, in the basement of our home in Boston." He bowed his head, as if in shame. "But it was many years ago."

"You must be more precise, Niklas. Where did this happen? Show us." As Enlil spoke, his cloaked companion held out a surprisingly human-looking hand, which held a globular object the size of a tennis ball. The object had a number of small protrusions of various shapes and lengths extending from it, and the being used the fingers of the same hand to push one of them. Instantaneously, a large holographic image of the city appeared in mid-air directly in front of Niklas. It wasn't just a topographic map. It was a brightly-lit, three-dimensional reproduction of the entire Boston area, with grid lines of latitude and longitude superimposed over it. Niklas, momentarily stunned by its luminescence, moved closer to it and was astonished by the detail. Then he noticed something else about the image's incredible resolution. He could see small fires everywhere and automobiles moving on the otherwise empty streets. My God. It's as if we're flying over the city right now, he thought. He looked up, expecting to see a giant hovering alien craft, but saw only the blackness.

"Please hurry, Niklas." Enlil's voice now had a fearful urgency to it. Niklas quickly located his old neighborhood and then traced his finger to his mother's house. When he tried to touch the image of its roof, he felt the tingle of static electricity in his finger tip. The map suddenly shrank to a point of light and disappeared. Niklas noticed the hooded figure close its hand around the object and lower its arm. "Now, when did this happen? Please be as exact as possible."

Niklas closed his eyes and thought back. He was finding it terribly difficult to concentrate, but willed himself to remain calm and recall whatever he could.

"1969, I think." Niklas said, then he shook his head. "No, it was '70, right after an archaeological expedition my father had been on in the Mideast. March?" He closed his eyes, straining to remember. "March,...March 15th, if I... Christ, it was so long ago."

Again, the cloaked figure held up the globular object and touched another of its protrusions. This time, in the same location as the previous image, a circular star-field appeared before them. Niklas began to study it, trying to find a recognizable pattern, but before he could identify anything familiar, the points of light elongated and formed moving streaks. Niklas assumed the brilliant, elegant pattern before him represented the paths of stars as they were being tracked in reverse. After a minute or so, the ends of the streaks began catching up with themselves and soon the star-field was again a myriad of points of light.

"The date is incorrect," Khafeer said. "It was the eighteenth of March." Then he smiled at Niklas. "A Tuesday. The day before the Karura was removed from your home." Once again, the image adjusted, but this time for only a fraction of a second before resolving back into the star-field. Niklas now noticed one star was blinking at regular intervals.

"The time? Can you remember the time, Niklas?" Enlil now sounded more hopeful.

Concentrate! Niklas told himself. It was morning. He was late for school. He saw the flash of light down in the basement and then he was out the door, barely making it to school on time. He remembered the campus was about a fifteen minute walk from his house, but, on that particular morning, he was sure he had run most of the way. Classes started at 8 AM sharp, so, if the flash of light he saw that morning was what he thought it was, he could make a reasonable guess about the time when his father had opened the urn. But it would still only be a guess.

"It had to be somewhere between 7:45 and 7:50 AM," Niklas said. "Probably closer to 7:50. I'm sorry. That's the best I can do." Enlil looked at Ani and the hooded figure selected another protruding stem. The star-field zoomed in on the blinking star. The three astronomers moved closer to the image and saw the first human view of the solar system from an angle perpendicular to the plane of planetary orbits. Again, an area of the image enlarged until the third planet filled the entire holographic image. The view was from high above the northern pole, looking down on the Earth. The resolution and detail was spectacular and what they were looking at appeared fantastically solid. A bright yellow dot was blinking on its circumference, slowly rotating towards the area of the globe that was in sunlight. Boston moving towards morning, Niklas thought. The rotation of the Earth seemed to speed up, quickly bringing the blinking dot to a position Niklas assumed was somewhere around 7:50 AM, on the morning of March 18, 1970. The blinking light brightened and the image of the Earth shrank to that point and disappeared.

"We can proceed to construct our message," Enlil said.

"You can send a message– back in time?" Niklas said, disbelief in his voice.

"A quantum system construct. Quantum particles do not travel through time and space, like your conventional radio or microwave signals. A construct requires manipulating a present-time quantum system in such a way that it will have a non-local, recognizable effect on a past system. You must speak now, Niklas."

"What do I say?" Niklas asked, not understanding the alien's explanation. "How will he–"

"That must be your choice, Niklas," the being said. "He is your father. Who better than you to know what the message should be? Speak to him as if you knew he was listening right now. And you must hurry."

Niklas hesitated for a moment, as it suddenly dawned on him he was about to speak to a man who had been dead for more than four decades. And not just any man. His father, whom he had loved and missed more than anything else in the world. He was being given an opportunity people only dream about, and his mind began to fill with things he wanted to say. For an instant, he was paralyzed by an onrush of conflicting emotions.

"Niklas!" Enlil's commanding tone jarred Niklas. "You must stop your father from–"

"Close the fucking urn." Niklas spoke the command without really thinking, delivering it in a flat, colorless tone, as though each word had been mechanically selected. Then he looked skyward, imagining the gigantic, fiery vision of his father's eyes gazing down upon him. Goddamnit, he thought. There was no time to say the things he wanted to say. Then, a lifetime of sadness and anger, feelings that had haunted him since childhood, exploded from his gut in a scream. "Close the fucking urn. You're killing everything,"

Shocked by the power of his own voice, he sensed the words had come from some place deep within himself. A place that knew exactly what needed to be said and how.

The hooded figure manipulated the object in his hand once more and a new pattern appeared in front of them. This time, it was an abstract image composed of several clusters of tiny points of light that would disappear and then reappear, in slightly altered states each time. At first, Niklas thought it was chaotic but then he saw the patterns had symmetry and, at times, seemed almost crystalline in structure. And then, one more time, the image collapsed to small point of brilliant light and disappeared.

"The message has been constructed," Enlil said.

"Constructed?" Niklas already knew the answer.

"Your words, your voice," Enlil said, and Niklas closed his eyes, trying to recall exactly what he had said. "Now we can only wait."

After a few moments, the three beings looked at one

another as the protective field surrounding the area began to erode. The sound of the energy wave reappeared, amplifying steadily, and the brilliant white light started pouring in on them once more. In a less than a minute, the intensity reached the same level it had been at before the dampening field first fell around them.

"Oh, God. It's still coming," Anna shouted, covering her eyes with her hands.

Even though Niklas had not been able to hear her, he guessed what she had said. He threw his arms around her and looked up, cursing the white sky until its brightness forced him to turn away. Only seconds now, he thought.

Chapter 10
Revelations

i

Despite the deafening sound more than thirty stories above it, the only noise in the Executive Operations Complex was the constant drone of the climate control and air filtration system. Designed for the Executive Branch and located three hundred meters beneath the White House, it was connected to the Pentagon by a light-rail shuttle. Coincidentally, the shuttle's maximum capacity was just enough to ferry the Joint Chiefs and their assistants between the two locations in a single trip. A similar conduit was currently under construction that would give the Congress access to what the White House staffs had referred to as the "Bunker."

The EOC was an elaborate command communication center. It included living quarters for more than one hundred, and, of that number, roughly half were the critical operating staff. The remainder were chosen at the discretion of the President and only the most influential people made it onto that list. And those people didn't even know they were on it until that afternoon.

Prior to 4 PM that day, the Bunker had been relatively empty, with only the routine security and maintenance teams present. The Secret Service had received instructions to check all the food stores and the drinking water supply.

By 6 PM, crucial staff was already on station and the FOPs, the so-called friends of the President, were arriving with their families. By 8:30 PM, the White House was as deserted as it had once been during the Civil War.

An hour and a half later, thanks to reports concerning the deteriorating conditions on the surface, the atmosphere throughout the EOC had become somber. But when Dr. Frederick James arrived and demanded to speak with the President, the quietude ended.

"You ignorant son of a bitch! I told you!" Dr. James was shouting and his rage made his whole body quake. "Koppernick tried to tell you. But you couldn't handle it– so you took the coward's way out and did nothing. Now you sit down here, in your goddamn Bunker, waiting for the end like a rat!" His high-pitched voice echoed down the hallway of the complex.

"Freddy, please." The President was in a highly emotional state. The First Lady and his two children had been on Air Force One, returning from Paris, when the flash of brilliant light had occurred. As had happened with hundreds of other aircraft, the pilots had been blinded and the jet was being flown the rest of the way to Washington by its onboard computer. But the terrific vibration being generated by the strange phenomenon in the sky was now causing problems for those fragile systems. Airports up and down the east coast were making preparations for emergency landings. In the meantime, all the President could do was wait for telephonic reports of their status. "I know you don't agree with the way I chose to handle things, but it was the only prudent decision I could make. We just didn't have enough–"

"You knew all you needed to know," Dr. James snapped. "It was on disk, for God's sake!" The President got up from the communications console he was seated at and approached his old friend with a sad expression.

"Freddy–" Just as he was about to say something, Phil Crawford, a senior White House aide, came through the open door with an armed Marine and a Secret Service agent. In extreme national emergencies, protocol governing access to the President was much more relaxed.

"Oh, excuse me, Mr. President," Crawford said.

"That's all right, Phil. What've you got?"

"The latest UCC reports are in." The Urban Crisis Center was a new information gathering network the Executive Branch used to monitor civil unrest in the large cities. Its primary purpose was to help the government allocate law enforcement resources in severe cases which the local municipalities could not manage. "This information is only a few minutes old, sir." Crawford handed the President a manila envelope and, as he went through its contents, the aide gave him a brief description of what was happening. "The criminal elements are responding in predictable fashion. Widespread looting and vandalism. Several metropolitan police departments are reporting organized gangs making raids into the suburban areas, Mr. President."

"What about the Guard?" the President asked, struggling to keep his focus on the growing national emergency. "And the state and local police? What's their status?"

"As you know, sir, most of the Guard is currently deployed

to Iraq, Afghanistan, Pakistan and Sudan. Only thirty percent of the active Guard state-side has responded to the alert. Even the transport pools are having trouble getting personnel in. And the police are out-manned and out-gunned. To be honest, sir, I think the cops are staying home for this one, too. The press won't even go into the streets." Crawford paused and looked around the room. Then he swallowed hard. "We're projecting similar problems on the west coast as it moves into darkness, Mr. President. We've grounded all non-essential flights, and curfews are already in place."

"Thanks, Phil. Make sure the Joint Chiefs get a copy of this." The President closed his eyes and lowered his head, as if saying a prayer. Then he noticed someone else had walked into the room. It was Arthur Sokolsky. "Arthur, you're here. Did your family make it down here all right?"

"Yes," the Attorney General said, his voice raised. "But I'm afraid there won't be room for the other three hundred fifty million people up there. Have you seen what's happening?"
The President collapsed in his chair and sat staring at the floor.

Then the SatPhone beeped. With the Geo-Stat satellite communications system, the call could have been coming in from anywhere in the world. The President spun around in the chair and grabbed the receiver.

"Yes," the President answered. "Yes. Please speak up. I can barely hear you.– Yes, I'm aware of that.– What do you mean, computer failure?" The President stood abruptly and began looking around the room, as if there was someone there who might help him. "Get to the point!– No. Oh no.– Where?– How close?" His voice became somber. "Survivors?– Oh God, no." The President's face went blank and he let the phone drop to the floor. Arthur Sokolsky stepped forward and picked it up.

"This is Arthur Sokolsky. With whom am I speaking?– Yes.– Would you repeat that.– Yes. Thank you." Sokolsky put his hand on the shoulder of the President of the United States, who was now sobbing. Sokolsky looked around the room and shook his head. "Air Force One has crashed one mile short of Dulles. Preliminary reports indicate no survivors." The Attorney General pushed the zero button on the SatPhone. "This is the Attorney General. Get me the Vice President, please." The other men began to walk slowly from the room.

Dr. James paused at the door and looked back at the President. "I am very sorry, Mr. President." When the Chief Executive didn't respond, he left.

"If I had said something," the President sobbed. "If I'd just warned people, my kids– they'd still be...." He couldn't finish the terrible thought.

"I know, sir," Sokolsky said. He squeezed the President's shoulder and shook his head sadly. Then he noticed something strange. He thought he had felt a subtle vibration in the room. He called in a security officer and asked him to have the system's powerful air-movers checked.

vii

The group of humans huddled closer together, and the three alien beings remained still as the ground shook beneath them. Niklas pulled Anna closer. Then he reached over and put his hand on Dirk's shoulder, squeezing it hard. Khafeer and Rand drew in close to them as well, and they all hid their faces from the furious white storm coming down on them.

Niklas was holding his breath and had his eyes squeezed tightly shut. He could feel the blood pounding through his temples. He was holding Anna so tightly that she could only manage shallow breaths– when she took them at all. He tried to smell her hair one more time and feel the familiar contour of her body against him, but his senses were overloaded. Nothing could cut through. The fury of the energy wave would even deny him his last few tactile human experiences.

Then he noticed something odd. He turned his head slightly to the left, away from Anna, and listened. Something was happening. Anna, sobbing, pulled him back, burying her face in his shoulder. He leaned away from her again and tried to concentrate on what his senses were telling him. He was sure he had felt the rumbling beneath him lessen. He looked at the others and saw Khafeer doing the same. Then he was sure.

"It worked!" he shouted in Anna's ear. She lifted her face and looked at him with a confused expression. "It worked!" he shouted again, taking her shoulders in his hands. "Can't you feel it? The ground? It's stopping!" She looked down at her feet and then looked back at Niklas.

"God! It is!" she said. She looked around them and pointed at something to her left. "Look! Shadows! Between the trees!" She threw one arm around Niklas' neck and hugged Dirk in with the other. Niklas saw a smiling Khafeer hugging Rand, patting him furiously on the back.

viii

Simms had been right. Commie's eyesight was slowly beginning to return. He would undoubtedly be seeing spots until the scorched areas on his retinas healed– if he lived that long– but the actual blindness caused by the flash had been temporary. Angie was weeping, her face in Simms' chest, and Simms was staring at the door, as if waiting for the heavy metal barrier to explode in on them.

Commie abruptly raised his head. He rubbed his eyes, and stood up.

"Hey, you feel anything?" he asked Simms.

"I'm totally numb." His attention on Angie, Simms hadn't really heard Commie's question.

"The floor. Do you feel anything through the floor?" Commie pointed at his feet. Simms looked at him, stood up and walked towards the door. "The vibration. The rumbling. It's... it's not there." Commie's voice was filled with hope.

Simms looked confused. "Hey, yeah. What the hell's happening?" He reached for the door.

"Don't open it!" Angie cried. "I don't want to see it." Simms looked at her and shook his head.

"Something's happening. Hide your eyes if you have to, but I'm opening this door." Simms leaned against the door; with the locking mechanism broken, it swung open easily. As the fading rumble of the wave filled the room, Simms stood in the doorway, silhouetted against the night sky. Commie came over and stood beside him. Angie watched from where she sat for a moment, then stood up.

"It's not as loud." She moved cautiously towards the door.

"What's happening?"

Simms turned an smiled. "Come here and look at this, Honey." He raised his arm and she stepped under it.

It took her a moment to realize what was different. Then it hit her.

"It's gone?" she cried. "The line. It's gone!" The three of them crowded the doorway, staring up at the starlit sky. The rumble was fading in the distance, receding like a murderous tide. Simms kissed and hugged Angie, and Commie clapped his hands and whistled loudly.

"What happened?" Commie asked. "How could it just stop like that?"

"Who knows? And who the hell cares?" Simms held Angie tightly. "Why don't you try to reach Niklas and Anna in Boston. I'll get on the horn with Kitt and Greenbank and find out what they see." As Commie went back inside to make the call to Boston, Simms propped the door wide open. "Don't mind the view so much now."

ix

It had been impossible to tell when the sound peaked and then started to fade. It happened so slowly that the change was nearly imperceptible. The diminishing intensity of the light took a little longer to notice. But, after a minute or so, it was clear the light wave was fading. They no longer had to cover their eyes or shout to be heard. Tears flowed down their faces as they smiled at the strange creatures that stood before them. Niklas looked up and saw the faint glimmer of stars returning to night sky, and spoke softly.

"We did it, Dad."

An odd, dark shape scuttled past him. It was Ki, the powerful insect-like being, taking short, rapid steps towards the rear of the sedan. Before Khafeer could stop him, Rand moved toward the trunk, in what Niklas thought must have been a reflexive action to guard the urn. Ki stopped, turned to face the agent and stood erect, again stretching his ribbed-neck to its full length. This frightening change in Ki's appearance gave him the look of a black mantis nearly a foot taller than the agent. Rand froze in his tracks, apparently realizing that, even if he could, it was unnecessary to protect the urn from the aliens. Ki then resumed his less aggressive posture, moved to the trunk and proceeded to pull it open with his shiny, clawed hands. Niklas watched Khafeer and his partner shrink back as the creature removed the urn from the trunk and returned to his position next to Enlil.

—⚘—

Anna was shivering from the rush of cold night air and was experiencing a mild case of shock as well. Niklas put his coat over her shoulders and pulled her closer to his side.

"We're gonna be okay," he said, cautiously.

Her head tilted, Anna appeared to be listening for signs of life around them but the only sound was the fading rumble over their heads. There was still a subtle glow in the evening sky. Looking over at the three aliens, she asked Niklas, "Who...what are they?"

"Beats the hell out of me," Niklas said. "Came through like the Three Musketeers though, didn't they."

"Athos, Porthos and Aramis, at your service." The sound of Enlil's voice caused Niklas to do a double-take, then he grinned at the thought of how fantastic it would be if these incredible beings turned out to have a sense of humor.

"And how dull we would be without one." This time, Enlil's voice had a definite smile attached to it, and Niklas felt a tremendous sense of relief. He now knew they were dealing with beings who were not so completely advanced that they had evolved beyond the complex range of emotions humans took for granted. There was common ground.

"More common ground than you know." Enlil looked at Ki and Ani, as if exchanging thoughts, and then turned back to Niklas. "We must leave soon. But before we go—"

"Yes, before you go, just one thing? Maybe you could explain why your ancestors left that thing here?" Niklas' disrespectful tone shocked the others and they looked at him with alarmed expressions, but he knew he had asked the supremely relevant question.

"Not our ancestors. It was us," Enlil said.

"You? What are you? Immortal?" Dirk asked.

"No. We have been on a long voyage, traveling faster than light. From Earth's perspective, more than five thousand years have passed since we were last here. But for us, time was significantly slowed. You call the effect time dilation."

Without any visible direction from Enlil, Ani raised the device in his hand and produced another image in front of them. It was a galaxy which, at first, none of the astronomers recognized. As Niklas stepped forward to get a closer look, the rest of group followed closely behind.

"Our home was in the galaxy you call Andromeda." The image shifted to a new angle and the configuration suddenly took on a familiar shape. The astronomers realized they had previously been looking at the galaxy from an angle no human had ever seen.

"Was?" Dirk asked.

"Andromeda was consumed by the light force. We were unable to stop it in time."

Anna raised her hands to her cheeks.

"Your kind sympathy is appreciated, Anna," Enlil said. "But our world's time was short anyway, and many of us had already left." The image of Andromeda enlarged and zoomed in on a tiny speck of light at the galaxy's outer rim. Soon, they were looking at a brilliant red giant star. "Ten thousand years ago, our star unexpectedly went into its red giant phase and began emitting intense bursts of gamma rays. Before we could shield ourselves, our DNA suffered irreversible damage, and our species became infertile. Since that time, we have been attempting to repair our genetic structure. This research has taken us throughout the Local Group of galaxies and beyond, in search of beings with a genome compatible with our own. By grafting compatible DNA sequences to our own, we had hoped to restore our reproductive capability and save a portion of our genetic heritage. Unfortunately, our efforts have done little more than enable us to alter our physical appearance. There are things about the structure of organic matter which we are unable to control. Things that we believe are influenced by what you call quantum particle behavior. We found that when you look at life too closely, it appears to have no substance at all. No materiality. We could not manipulate what was, in effect, not there."

"Your race is dying," Anna said.

"In a manner of speaking, yes. And when our quest brought us to the outer fringe of your galaxy, we encountered the Kaun, the microcosmic Universe, drifting in the void. Fortunately, we were able to identify what it was before interacting with it, and encased it in a protective containment orb. We would have ended our mission then and returned home with it, but we could not risk neutralizing the Kaun's mass while accelerating to light speed. And we could not consider a subluminal intra-galactic crossing because it would have taken thousands of years. We would have returned home to a long since dead planet. So, we set about finding a suitable planet for the Kaun. A planet that could provide it with a stable environment and assure its continued security, regardless of the outcome of our own predicament. Everything about the Earth and its inhabitants filled those needs. We constructed the Karura and hid it in such a way that would ensure its discovery. By its design, we ensured that whoever found it would devote themselves to the guardianship of the Karura. What has happened here has been, as you say, a predictable sequence of events."

Anna bumped Niklas with her elbow, and gave him a nod of congratulations. He seemed to have figured out the mystery after all.

"So, you used the Cadima– my family, for your purposes." Khafeer, the man once known and despised as the self-assured Willoughby, seemed distraught now, and Niklas thought he understood how the man must feel. The higher purpose of his family's ancient mission had just been relegated to an act of genetic manipulation. Like Dorothy peeking around the curtain, Khafeer had just seen the Wizard and learned his five-thousand-year-old family legacy had been little more than an extraterrestrial parlor trick.

"The urn gave your people a sense of purpose, Haris. By its own free will, the Oosra Cadima chose the most vital and honorable of all missions. You should be proud of your family."

"Okay, I can understand why you left it here," Niklas said. "But why in God's name would you put this 'Kaun' into something that could be so easily opened? My father wasn't a physicist. All he had were some simple tools."

"Our greatest miscalculation. The locking mechanism should have made the urn impenetrable, even to a highly advanced technology. But the micro-universe inside the Karura was expanding, just as this Universe is, and the force of that expansion was powerful enough to fracture the mechanism. But understand this: If your father had not opened the Karura when he did, we might never have realized our oversight until it was too late. The entire containment orb could have ruptured. Then the entire–"

"...Universe would have been destroyed," Niklas said.

"An entire chain of Universes, your Cosm, would have ceased to exist. Your father's curiosity prevented that."

"So, what happens now?" Niklas asked.

"No place is more suitable for the Kaun than Earth. We will return to our ship, place the Kaun in a new containment orb–

one capable of compensating for its continued expansion. Then Ani, and others like him, will return with it to the Oosra Cadima."

A new voice came from behind the scientists. It was Rand.

"I am Iban, cousin of Haris Khafeer and devoted of the Oosra Cadima. You say this Ani will join our family. Why? To rule us?"

Khafeer put his hand on Iban's shoulder. "Iban is part of the new generation to take its place in the Cadima." Khafeer's tone was still saturnine. "He has prepared all his life to fulfill a very old destiny, so you must forgive him for having difficulty accepting that his future will simply not unfold as he has been raised to believe. The idea of extraterrestrial beings ruling the Oosra Cadima– this will never work." Khafeer shook his head sadly. "Our family will be torn apart. Your Ani, and his like, will have to watch over the Kaun without us."

—ᔕᔕ—

At that instant, Enlil took a step backward and the hooded figure, Ani, stepped into his place. Khafeer noted the symbolic nature of the shift. He had seen it before in the cellar of the old house in Iraq. He came slowly forward, moving past Niklas, with Iban at his side, and stood before the mysterious being.

"I am not here to rule." When Ani spoke, the sound had none of the alien qualities of Enlil's voice, and Khafeer immediately recognized it as the one which had given him the instructions over the phone to come to this place. Ani bowed his head forward, raised his hands to the hood of the robe and, after a brief pause, pushed it back. The first thing Khafeer saw was a mane of long, shiny black hair. Then Ani looked up at the two men standing before him and, for the second time that night, Khafeer felt as though the wind had been knocked out of him. He tried to speak but could only stare open-mouthed at Ani's face. He had seen old photographs of his grandfather, Ejan, taken when he was a young man with all of his teeth and hair, and when his skin was smooth and dark. The being standing before him could easily have been the man in those faded old photos; young, vital and, most important of all, human. Khafeer wondered if he could be looking at the first Jeda of the Oosra Cadima.

"Yes, I am," Ani answered Khafeer's thought. "But I am no more than you. And I will not rule as your Jeda. I would not show such disrespect for your old ones. I will join you, and together we will fulfill the destiny of the Oosra Cadima. You'll do no less or more than I." Ani bowed, and after a brief hesitation, Khafeer and Iban returned the show of respect.

"One of you will accompany us to our ship." Ani turned to the young man, smiling. "Iban?. Will you come with us?"

Iban was surprised by the request. Then he looked at Khafeer, his eyes filled with uncertainty, but also with excitement. Khafeer smiled and nodded his approval. The serious young man turned back to Ani.

"Yes. I'll go." Iban came forward and stood next to Ki. The strange-looking being reached over, took his hand and placed it on the Karura. It was the most frightening, yet exhilarating moment in the young man's life.

—⟋⟍—

"This road intersects the highway one mile ahead. Now, please step back," Enlil warned them. "We will always remember this day of friendship and understanding, and hope we will meet again." A narrow shaft of light came down from above them, enveloping the four in a greenish glow. Within seconds, their bodies had lifted into the air inside the beam and then disappeared in a cloud high overhead.

A few seconds later, the engine of the BMW and the Cadillac started up, their headlights flashing on at the same time. Niklas jumped.

"Christ, my nerves are shot." When he finally calmed down, Niklas heard sirens in the distance. The roar in the sky was now almost completely inaudible and the wind had turned into a gentle breeze. The cool night air had a freshly washed taste that was so clean they could smell the wet pine. The serenity of the moment was palpable and, for the first time in more than a month, things seemed truly peaceful.

"So, Mr. Khafeer," Niklas said. "What's all this about an ancient family?" The three scientists now faced their former nemesis with curiosity. Khafeer, freed from his role as a government agent, seemed ebullient.

"You've already heard most of it," Khafeer said. "My father came to this country as a young man, long before your father's expedition to Iraq. He married a beautiful American girl. I was born a year later. Seeing that I had inherited my mother's fair complexion, my father arranged for the birth record to show I received her last name, Willoughby. I suppose he felt it would help me assimilate more easily."

"Jesus. So how long have you been tailing us?" Niklas laughed.

"Longer than you can imagine." Khafeer said, smiling. "The first time I saw you was many years ago, in Boston." His expression saddened. "I attended your father's funeral."

Niklas' mind travelled back to that hellish day– a day he would never forget, and he pictured the small group of mourners. When the image of the dark-skinned man and the pale little boy flashed into his consciousness, Niklas said, "I'll be damned. I remember."

Khafeer's smile broadened. "My grandfather was Ejan Khafeer, your father's Master Digger at the excavation in Iraq. They became close friends, and this friendship interfered with my grandfather's mission, which was to prevent the discovery of the urn at all cost. When your father brought it to this country, it became my father's responsibility to track its location and, if possible, take possession of it. But your father hid it from us and, when he died, we could only hope one day you would lead us to it. That's why I have had to follow you both for the last twenty years."

"You've been watching us for twenty years?" Anna laughed weakly. "You must be bored out of your mind."

"Actually, things became quite difficult after the two of you separated, especially when you took the position in New Mexico." Then Khafeer looked at Niklas. "By the way, you owe me a dinner, Niklas."

"I know things are different now, Khafeer," Niklas laughed. "But let's not get cocky. If anybody–"

"I have it in writing." Khafeer reached inside his coat and

took out an envelope. He opened it delicately and removed a worn piece of yellowed paper.

Niklas took the paper from Khafeer with a sarcastic grin on his face, and unfolded it in the glow of his car's headlights. Then, for the second time that evening, he saw his father's elegant handwriting. The note read:

"My dear Ejan, I regret that I was unable to say good-bye to you and your wonderful family. I shall always treasure the warmth and hospitality you showed to my unruly band of intruders. If any of you ever come to America, please do not hesitate to call upon me, so my family may return your many kindnesses. I wish you a long and healthy life, my sadiq, with many more grandchildren to keep you young. Aaron."

Niklas looked up, tears filling his eyes. Reading the short note had been like hearing his father's voice again, and any remnant of the demons that had once held a firm grip on Niklas' heart were brushed away by the small piece of paper.

"Okay. I owe you a dinner. I know this great little Italian place. Maybe Rand– Iban– told you about it. Delicious cannolis." Niklas laughed through the sting of his tears.

Khafeer turned to Dirk. "Dr. Anders. Before Mr. Willoughby disappears from this part of the world, I'll see that the government compensates you adequately for your pain and suffering. My cousin is young and strident. I'm sure he regrets his actions. Especially after the painful lesson he received from Dr. Koppernick's wife."

"I hope I didn't damage the future growth of your family with that kick," Anna laughed. "I sort of lost it when I saw Dirk go down." She smiled over at Dirk and then shuddered when she saw how the swelling and discoloration had worsened.

Niklas was perplexed. "I don't get something. If you guys have been around all this time, why didn't you just come to our home and confront my father about the urn? He was so ill, he probably would have just led you right to it."

"My grandfather forbade it." Khafeer bowed his head as he said it. "The Jeda's word is our law. When Ejan learned of your father's illness, he instructed the family not to interfere. Even though we weren't sure where it was, as long as the Karura was safely hidden and its existence kept secret from the world, we were to respect your father's house. Of course, we did not know he had attempted to open it."

"So, you didn't know anything about the—" Niklas glanced upward, where only clouds drifted soundlessly through the night sky.

"We only knew what our ancestors had passed on to us. We knew the Karura contained the Kaun— a Universe. But, until today, we didn't fully appreciate what that meant. We were bound by three hundred generations of unquestioning devotion." Khafeer's eyes saddened for a moment and Niklas assumed he was still feeling the impact of the night's revelations. "I'm sorry," Khafeer said. "I should get going. It's getting late and Washington will be expecting me to report in. And I have to come up with a plausible explanation for Agent Rand's sudden disappearance. At least till I'm ready to join him."

"I'd like to keep this note. If it's okay." Niklas knew the piece of paper must have had some value to Khafeer as well.

"I'm sure my Jeda would have it no other way." Khafeer

grinned. "It's yours to keep. Just don't forget the dinner. I'll be collecting on that debt some day." He started towards the sedan and then turned once more. "By the way, don't blame your friend, Professor Sokolsky, for the President's inaction. I'm the one who convinced him not to make the announcement." Khafeer looked up at the star-filled night sky and, hearing the sounds of sirens in the city, he said, "From what happened here tonight, I imagine it wouldn't have made much difference, either way."

As Khafeer walked to the sedan, he picked up the weapons that the bangers had left behind. He tossed them into the back seat, climbed behind the wheel and nodded a final good-bye. Then he reached for the ignition.

"Oh, no," Khafeer laughed, slapping his forehead. "The keys! I threw them into the woods so the gang wouldn't be able to get into the trunk." He climbed out of the sedan with a flashlight in his hand and headed into the woods.

"Hey, wait a minute!" Anna called after him.

When Khafeer turned around and shined the light on her, he saw his original set of keys dangling from her hand.

X

Commie, Simms and Angie worked their way down the long stairway. None of them took their eyes off the sky during the entire descent and, as they reached the bottom, Commie was the first to hop off onto solid ground.

"I wish I could've reached Anna and Niklas," Commie said. "I'm worried about Willoughby."

"Yeah." Simms elated expression turned serious. "The cities

are probably no picnic right now, either. Hell, you'd think we'd be able to pick up at least one decent news report with one of these damned electric umbrellas."

"I don't think we should be too worried about them," Angie chimed in. "Those are two of the smartest people in the world. Besides, Anna could out-run just about anybody." Simms looked at Commie, raised his eyebrows and then smiled at Angie.

"You're probably right," Simms said. "But we'll keep trying to get through to them every hour or so, anyway."

"Hey, Dr. Simms and Ms. Ryerson, I propose that we take a little drive. To the Capitol Bar. I called over there and things are pretty cool in town. Got some friends I'd like you to meet and I'm sure they're on their way there right now. What do you say?"

"Oh crap, Roderick. I'm a disaster," Angie groaned. "I'll probably scare your friends to death, Commie."

Simms hugged her and laughed. "Sounds like a great idea, Commie. Nothing's going to happen here until everybody else is on line anyway. But there is just one condition."

"What's that?" Commie asked.

"No more alien messages for a while. Okay?" Simms chuckled. "I'm getting a little bored with them." The relief in their laughter echoed across the Array. Then Simms said, "Oh, by the way, Dr. Marks. I'm buying."

"You bet your sweet ass you are!" Commie laughed.

On the way to the parking lot, Angie ran into Simms' office to retrieve her purse. Then she spent the entire drive into town, putting herself together. By the time the trio arrived at the Capitol Bar, the party was just getting started. Commie walked through the double doors, ahead of Simms and Angie, and several of his friends shouted their greetings.

"You guys will just not believe the shit I have to tell you," Commie said.

As they watched Khafeer's tail-lights disappear around the curve, Anna said, "Well, hasn't this been a fun evening." When Niklas nodded in agreement, they both laughed. But when Dirk tried to join in, he groaned loudly and held his jaw.

"Jesus, Dirk!" Niklas said. "How are you doing?"

"I, uh, think it's broken. Hurts to move." Dirk winced as he tried to manipulate his jaw with his hand.

Anna looked at the swelling. "Come on, you need to have that looked at. We'll get you to a hospital." When they stopped talking and headed over to Niklas' car, the din of far away sirens became more evident. "Damn," Anna said. "I'll bet you the hospitals in town are standing-room-only. Probably take hours just to get a doctor to check him out."

"Yeah. I'd rather not drive through town right now. It's going to be a while before they get all the crazies under control." Niklas got to the side of his car and slapped himself on the forehead. "Hey, I got it. Harvard!" Dirk and Anna gave him a quizzical look. "Harvard, as in Oak Ridge, for Christ's sakes. They've got an infirmary at the observatory and a retired surgeon who lives right around the corner. A small town perk for visiting eggheads." They climbed into the car and began the forty-five minute drive over to Oak Ridge.

For a short time, they all remained quiet, and seemed to

be enjoying the silence in Niklas' car. Anna was stretched out as much as the passenger seat would let her.

"Where do you think the Oosra Cadima will put it? The urn." she asked.

"To be honest, I don't want to know," Niklas said. "I don't really feel like spending the rest of my life worrying about the damn thing? As far as I'm concerned, they should bury it right next to Jimmy Hoffa. I'd just like to get back to work. I'm a little worried about how all this shit may have affected my goodies up on the moon."

"You're worried about your telescope?" Anna laughed and shook her head.

"Hey, me and my MOLO. We're inseparable." Niklas chuckled but he could see Anna wasn't buying it.

"Bullshit, Nick. When the smoke clears, we're taking a vacation. Let Dirk deal with your goodies for a while. Right, Dirk?" She turned around to look at Dirk just in time to see his brief smile convert to another wince. Niklas put his arm around Anna and nodded towards the crystal clear sky, filled with twinkling stars.

"One thing's for sure," he said, looking up. "Our workload has been drastically reduced."

Anna looked up and frowned. "We're the only ones who'll know." Niklas understood what she was saying. Only astronomers, looking into deep space, would be able to see the real devastation. The ordinary person on the street would see a perfectly normal night sky because the objects they could see were all located close by, in the Milky Way. But then he realized that wasn't exactly correct, and he began searching a portion of the sky. After a few seconds, he seemed to find what he was looking for, and Anna watched a sentimental expression come over his face. "What is it, Nick?"

"Andromeda. You can still see her. She's gone, but— but there she is. Strange. I remember the first time I saw her and realized how far away she was. Thought she might not be there at all. Like some sort of galactic mirage. Funny feeling— knowing that's all she really is now. Just a light wave remnant. Sad. Some day people are going to look up at that part of the sky and she'll be... gone."

They watched a formation of low-flying military helicopters pass overhead and Niklas snickered. "You know, all my life I thought the Beast was out there, hiding in all that stuff. But it's really in here." He tapped on the side of his head. "I guess he had me fooled for a while, huh." Then Niklas looked at Anna with a sly grin. "Say, after we get Dirk fixed up, what say we go make sure Mom's okay?"

"You know, for the first time in twenty-five years, I'm kind of looking forward to seeing her." Anna smiled, rested her head on his shoulder and closed her eyes.

Niklas kissed the top of her head. As he drove along the winding, forest-lined highway, he said quietly to himself, "The Beast is dead. Long live the Beast."

Epilogue:
Ashes to Ashes

i

After the night of mayhem, the Boston Globe had estimated it would take at least six weeks for the city to clean up and make repairs to its infrastructure. LaManna's had been looted and partially burned, but the LaManna family had worked together day and night, and, to the delight of its regular customers, managed to re-open in just a week.

"Be serious, Nick," Anna said, taking another bite out of the stale breadstick. "I'm too old to have a baby."

"You're not that old. What are you? Forty-two?" Niklas said it with a straight face. "You're just a kid, for Christ's sakes."

Anna abruptly reached across the table, grabbed the half-empty bottle of Chianti and sat it in her lap.

"That's it. You've obviously had way too much vino," she said. Niklas pointed to his empty glass with one hand and motioned for the return of the wine with the other. "Having a kid at 52 is just too risky."

"Right," Niklas said with more than a hint of sarcasm. "Fifty-two going on thirty-two. Look at you. You're—"

"We've been through all this. It's not how old I am. It's how old my eggs are." She took a bite of the steaming hot lasagna and then cooled her mouth with a swallow of the Chianti.

"Yadda, yadda, yadda. I know all that crap." He rolled his

eyes at the familiar sound of their conversation, but then his expression grew serious. "I... uh...I talked to Dr. James a couple of days ago." He took a long gulp of his wine.

She gave him a confused look, then snickered. "Oh, 'Freddy'? Why'd you talk to him?"

Niklas started pushing the fettuccine around on his plate with his fork like Tony Soprano.

"Boy, he's pissed at El Presidente," he said. "Sent him a letter of resignation, but the President hasn't responded, yet."

"Figures."

"You know, he's a biochemist. Sharp guy," Niklas said.

"Yeah, well, I think that's a requirement for Nobel Prize winners. At least, most of them, anyway."

Niklas, wanting to keep the conversation headed in a more constructive direction, decided to ignore her jab.

"I, uh– talked to him about our little fertility thing." He had delivered the news as delicately as he could, knowing she did not like him talking about their sex life with anyone else, be it for clinical purposes or not.

"You did what?" She dropped her fork in her plate.

"Now don't get pissed," he said, holding his hands up in front of his face, as if to ward off a blow. "I just asked him about this new thing he's working on. For women with... uh, you know, uh, with old–"

Anna squinted her eyes and sneered. "You talked to Freddy about... my eggs?"

"Well, yeah. He's got this treatment–"

"I can't believe you'd do something like that without discussing it with me first!" She planted both elbows on the table and tapped her fingers together. "How dare you–"

"Please, sweetheart. I'm really sorry, but..." Niklas stopped himself when he noticed the corner of Anna's mouth turn up ever so slightly. Had he just detected a smirk? He leaned back in his chair and tapped his fingers on the red and white checkered table cloth. Then he cocked one eyebrow and narrowed his eyes.

"Okay, what the hell gives?" he asked.

Anna slowly picked up her napkin, dabbed her lips and looked up at Niklas, struggling to maintain a straight face. Suddenly, she burst out laughing, and Niklas looked around the restaurant to make sure nobody was watching them.

"Freddy called me yesterday, while you were at the observatory." She finally regained control of herself. "He told me all about his phone call with you and this new fertility treatment of his. Ovum Chromosomal Screening and Protein Rejuvenation, I think he called it."

"Very funny," Niklas said. "You really like making me squirm, don't you."

"Nope. I don't like it at all." She took another sip of her wine. "I love it."

"Okay, you got me. So what do you think?" He watched her take another bite of lasagna and refused to let her see how much anxiety she had just caused him. She finally swallowed, but then prepared to take another bite. When Niklas didn't go for the bait, she smiled.

"Well, Freddy gave me the name of a specialist in Boston, and we have an appointment next Tuesday. At 11 AM. He also warned me that there could be potentially dangerous side effects."

"Side effects? He never..."

"He told me there was a high probability that a successful procedure could result in an unusually short, pathologically cynical offspring." She laughed.

Niklas smirked, then leaned forward, waving his hand.

"Very funny. What do you mean 'we' have an appointment, Kimo Sabe? You're the one with the old eggs."

"Nick!" She raised her voice. "It takes two to pull this off, you know." He acted embarrassed and motioned for her to lower her voice. "Jesus," she groaned. "You're the one who's been pushing for this. You and your obsession to produce a miniature 'Aaron Koppernick'."

As the tiny, self-satisfied grin formed slowly on Niklas' face, Anna slumped back in her chair and rolled her eyes.

"Turn about's fair play." Now it was his turn to laugh.

"Dork," she muttered.

"Hey, I invented that word, you know."

"Yeah, well, I'm sure it came naturally," Anna snorted.

"Oh, come on.." He leaned forward and took her hand.

"You know I'll be there, babe. Whatever it takes."

—∞—

When they got home from dinner, Niklas left the car parked in the driveway and, as they were walking toward the front door, he looked up and took a deep breath. A cool, early summer evening, there was a pleasant breeze moving across the city. It was a clear night, except for a small cloud drifting over head and about to cover the bright half moon.

As they came through the door, the peg and groove hardwood floor creaked where Dirk Anders had stood dripping only a week before, leaving a small lake in the entryway. The water damage would probably require some repairs to the sub-floor. Anna removed her coat and Niklas flipped the living room light switch on as he closed the door behind them.

"You know, this'll mean no running for a while," he said.

"I know," She groaned. "Guess I'll have to get my exercise some other way." When she turned around and saw the stunned look on his face, her salacious smile quickly disappeared. He was staring past her, at something in the living room.

"What in the hell is that doing here?" he said.

Anna turned slowly and, when she saw what was sitting in the middle of living room floor, she gasped. The Urn. They stood in the entryway, not moving for a moment, and then Niklas moved past her. He approached the object as if it was a sleeping predator he didn't want to awaken. Anna followed close behind, peering over his shoulder.

"It is good to see you again, Niklas and Anna." It was Enlil. Startled, Anna grabbed Niklas' arm and squeezed hard. When they looked in the direction the voice had come from, the small being emerged from the shadows of the adjoining dining room. This time he was alone.

Niklas cleared his throat. "Good to see you, too, Enlil."

Anna could only nod.

"You may open the urn," Enlil said.

"Open it?" Niklas was confused by the request.

"Yes. Open the Karura. It is safe to do so." Enlil moved closer to the Urn, which was only slightly shorter than he was, and he caressed the tusk of an ebony elephant with his long, delicate fingers.

Niklas gazed down at the small, crown-shaped handle on the Urn's lid. He looked at Anna and back at Enlil. Then he gently grasped the handle, using his thumb and forefinger, and lifted. The lid rose smoothly and, as the opening appeared beneath it, Niklas paused once more to look at Enlil.

"I assure you, Niklas. It is empty."

Niklas lifted the lid free of the Urn and leaned forward to look inside. He saw the faint nacre color of the inner surface and motioned Anna to look inside.

"I don't understand," Niklas said. "Why are you showing this to us?"

"It is yours." Enlil's voice had the smile again.

Anna's head jerked up, and Niklas opened his mouth to speak but no words came out.

"Ani has spoken with the Jeda of the Oosra Cadima," the alien said. "They have agreed."

Niklas took a step back from the Urn and scratched his beard. "No, I-I can't. I can't accept responsibility for this," Niklas stammered. "It's the most valuable object on the planet. Jesus, maybe on any planet. What if someone breaks in here and steals it? No, this is–"

"If the Karura is ever taken from you, Ani will know how to find it," Enlil explained.

"I don't know." Niklas was still worried. "Something like this belongs in the Smithsonian... or the Louvre."

"Call it a souvenir. A gift from some very old friends of your father. The image of our home planet will be your remembrance of us."

"This was your home?" Anna asked.

"Yes," Enlil said, moving his pale-gray fingers tenderly across the globe's surface. "Long ago, before the change in our star, it was the most beautiful planet in Andromeda."

Anna went to Niklas' side and took his hand. Then they both began shaking their heads and smiling.

"What are we going to do with it?" Anna asked. As Niklas walk slowly around the Urn, she could see him admiring its beauty, but worried it would only remind him of his father and that morning so many years before.

Niklas stopped, looked over at Enlil, and a thoughtful smile appeared on his lips.

"Ashes to ashes," he said, speaking in a whisper.

"A most worthy resting place, my friend," Enlil answered, understanding.

"What?" Anna said. "Did I miss something here?" She looked from Niklas to Enlil, then back to Niklas. "What ashes?"

"Something I just found out from Mother. I'll explain later." Niklas smiled and gently replaced the lid.

"Now, I must leave you again." Enlil nodded and turned to go out the rear door, which led to the small backyard.

"Wait a minute," Niklas said. "Just one more question before you– beam up. About the message– your construct– backward in time."

Enlil took a step closer to them and whispered, as if sharing a special secret. "Really just a small trick of physics.

You are very close to achieving this yourselves."

"Yeah, some trick," Niklas' laugh was forced.

"While the message was actually constructed inside your father's brain, on a subatomic level, he perceived it as an auditory experience." Observing their slightly mystified expressions, Enlil made it as simple as he could. "In other words, your father heard a voice. Your voice, Niklas. And, if you were standing close by, you would have heard it as well."

"So this message actually formed inside his brain?" Niklas looked over at Anna and his expression turned more serious as a dark thought crossed his mind. "So... Could something like that... I mean, could it have—"

Enlil realized what was driving Niklas' curiosity.

"Quantum systems impact neurotransmitters. Nothing more. They do not disfigure chromosomal structures or cause genetic mutations. No, Niklas. The message did not trigger your father's disease. Trust us, we know your biology better than you."

Niklas blinked his eyes and nodded, relieved that he hadn't played some bizarre role in his own father's death. He felt Anna hug him and he kissed her on the cheek.

"Where will you go?" Anna asked.

"Now that Ani has returned to the Oosra Cadima with the Kaun, the Anunnaki have a new task to perform. We have been conducting ecogenetic surveys in a number of star systems, and had collected the DNA sequences of many promising species before they were destroyed by the paracosmic event. These will soon be reborn in your galaxy. In time, your 'Milky Way' will become a much more crowded and exciting place, indeed."

Listening to Enlil, Anna wondered if, faced with its own extinction, the human race would have responded as nobly as the Anunnaki.

"What a wonderful thing," she said, a tear trickling down her cheek. "We should call you Noah."

Enlil smiled. "Ah, yes. The analogy is appropriate." He turned and stepped outside, glancing upward, while Niklas and Anna watched from the doorway. "Thank you. We could not have succeeded without your help. And Niklas' father's as well. Together, we have preserved the future of this Universe—the Cosm. That is all that matters. Good-bye."

Suddenly, the small being was bathed in the brilliant green glow and lifted into the air. Anna and Niklas moved quickly into the backyard, looking up in time to see the light disappear inside the small cloud drifting above the house. As they watched, the cloud grew smaller and smaller, finally disappearing in the star-filled sky.

Anna wiped the tears from her eyes as she looked up at the stars. Sniffling, she turned to Niklas.

"What ashes?"

Niklas laughed and held her tightly.

End